# The Half-Life

# The Half-Life

a novel

## Jonathan Raymond

BLOOMSBURY

Author's note: The events, characters, cultures, and geographies depicted in this novel are fiction. Many, many liberties have been taken with historical accuracy.

The poem that appears in the final chapter is drawn largely from the artwork *When I Put My Hands on Your Body* (1990), by David Wojnarowicz. Reprinted with the permission of Donadio & Olson.

Published by Bloomsbury, New York and London
Distributed to the trade by Holtzbrinck Publishers

All papers used by Bloomsbury are natural, recyclable products made from wood grown in well-managed forests.
The manufacturing processes conform to the environmental regulations of the country of origin.

Library of Congress Cataloging-in-Publication Data

Raymond, Jonathan.
The half-life: a novel / Jonathan Raymond.
p. cm.
ISBN 1-58234-448-5 (hc)
1. Northwest, Pacific—Fiction. 2. Communal living—Fiction.
3. Motion pictures—Fiction. 4. Teenage girls—Fiction.
5. Friendship—Fiction. 6. Trappers—Fiction. I. Title.

PS3618.A985H35 2004
813'.6—dc22
2003022602

First U.S. Edition 2004

1 3 5 7 9 10 8 6 4 2

Typeset by Palimpsest Book Production Limited,
Polmont, Stirlingshire, Scotland

Printed in the United States of America by
R R Donnelley & Sons, Harrisonburg, Virginia

For Mom and Dad

The bird a nest, the spider a web, man friendship.

William Blake, *Proverbs of Hell*

B ETWEEN TWO RIDGES *carved by a silver creek, in a forest of black fir trees, there was a place where the hills came to a shallow bowl and the earth went soft. The mountain heather and sword fern thinned at the edge of an open meadow, and a field of smooth cordgrass began, which led to the banks of a stagnant marsh.*

*In the summer, dragonflies flickered over the marsh's mirrored plane and frogs croaked from its damp shadows, while many-headed pussy willow bobbed in the wind. In the autumn, arrows of geese landed there, and during the spring mosquitoes rose to the surface at dusk, where hordes of bats would descend to pluck them from the air. When it was hot, the water lay still and reflected the clouds; when it rained, its skin came alive with dilating rings of energy.*

*At the bottom of the marsh's black water, hidden from view, lay two bodies, one with a crack in its skull and the other with a shattered chest.*

*Over time, the seasons cut through the marsh like a knife, changing the shape of its banks and the texture of its silt. The plants on the shoreline grew and died and decomposed, which nourished the algae, whose cells divided and fed the mayflies and waterskippers.*

*Sacs of eggs burst into tadpoles, which became frogs and laid sacs of eggs.*

*And all the while, beneath the surface, the two bodies settled deeper into their soft beds. Their ribs gradually emerged from their dissolving skin, and their eyes became empty sockets. Their muscle and fat disappeared, and their skulls emerged, fastened to long chains of vertebrae.*

*Soon enough, only white bone remained, fixed in the velvet mud. Two skeletons at the bottom of a pond, side by side, their long fingers wrapped in a delicate grip.*

# Part One

# 1

FOOTSTEPS ON THE forest floor made a noise like paper crumpling in a child's fist. One after another the sounds disturbed the still air, settling in dry explosions of snapping, and fracturing, and the fine shattering of small branches and twigs.

High above, the boughs of the fir trees shifted in the wind, revealing white fragments of twilight sky, and the trunks made melancholy aisles into the gloom. The only thing moving near the ground was a single gray moth, batting its way over the mossy earth, bobbing and looping, until finally disappearing into black shadows.

Cookie Figowitz, the youngest partner in the Wild Panthers fur-trapping party, five weeks out from Colter's Hell, Sioux Country, knelt in a bed of ghost fern in the massive rain forests of the Oregon Territory staring into the surrounding trees. His hands were quaking, and a cold, trickling dampness was creeping into the knees of his pants.

Steadily the footsteps seemed to be coming closer, never moving more than three or four strides before pausing to wait. At which point the air would go still. And the life of the forest would stop. And then the footsteps would begin again. Somewhere else. Grinding the dead leaves and dry seed husks under their ominous weight.

More often than not, Cookie realized, mysterious sounds in the woods were nothing to worry about, just falling pinecones or a mischievous crow. But for some reason these particular sounds had gotten him more spooked than usual. The way they stopped and started, and seemed to exhibit some kind of intelligence, made him wonder if perhaps they belonged to something more purposeful than a swaying pine tree or a bird. He shaped each sound to the gait and heft of some terrible danger—cougars, ocelots, brown bears, and black pumas—testing his fears against each other like a set of bright marbles, until finally, after careful consideration, he settled on the image of a painted Indian, creeping toward him with a sharpened stone spear in hand, and the entire forest seemed to thrum with new dread.

The footsteps came to a stop near a white birch tree just a few yards from Cookie's hiding place. The trunk rose high into the air, splitting into a maze of branches, themselves splitting into smaller and smaller segments. Cookie watched the white birch through the limp fronds of the ghost fern, listening to his own breath whistling in his nose. His heartbeat echoed on his narrow wrist, blood rushing through the shoals of his body in tides.

Deep in the forest a branch snapped, a sudden and distant crack, and somewhere closer a bird cooed softly, then stopped.

The wind pushed hard against the treetops and the whole forest shook with a long sighing whoosh, which receded quickly into the distance.

"Whoo . . . Whoo," Cookie called out—the company whistle, off pitch but still recognizable—but there was no reply. The white, papery bark of the birch tree continued to soften in the darkness.

Gradually, as the forest became silent again, Cookie's mind began to crawl out from its blind ditch and start functioning better. The footsteps were probably just settling branches, he told himself, or a foraging deer, or a squirrel moving a cache of nuts from one knothole to another. They could come from any number of creatures, all of which were more frightened of him than he was of them, and most of which were much smaller, too. Cookie muttered into the club moss, "Nothing out there. Nothing to worry about. Everything's fine," his dry lips catching on his teeth.

He took a deep breath, and in a burst of resignation rose to his feet. The denim of his pants rasped loudly and an acorn snapped underfoot, making his heart jump. "Yessir," he said for no reason, and cleared his throat. Cookie brushed off his pants and glanced over his shoulder. The men would be missing him by now, he figured, even if

6

his mission into the woods to find supper had been something of a failure.

Cookie lifted his boot and took a tentative step toward the camp, scanning the ground carefully for good footholds. He planted his heel on a patch of fir needles, when suddenly the whole forest seemed to shatter. He heard wood breaking, leaves ripping, the huff of air releasing from between layers of moss. A shock of fear ran down his spine and back up again. The stalker had returned, he realized, closer than ever this time, his footsteps fitted precisely into the sound of Cookie's own gingerly motions.

Cookie swallowed hard and felt his skin ringing with panic. Without a word he lurched forward into the trees, a din of breaking leaves and twigs raging around him like a fire.

Cookie raced down a deer run and leapt over a snag, nettles and switches slapping him across the face, then tripped over a hard root and almost fell into a prickly mooseberry bush. He dashed through a thin stream of water and flew past a mossy stump, at which point a strange thought came to him. The noises chasing after him were possibly not a bloodthirsty Indian at all, but rather his very own footsteps banging on the ground underneath him, which made Cookie, in a funny way, the invisible stalker of himself. With this, the recognition that his senses had betrayed him so badly, Cookie's panic flared up even hotter than before, and he fled faster, chased by his own roaring footsteps into the quiet landscape of the woods.

As suddenly as the chase began, it was over. Cookie stumbled from the underbrush into a small clearing in the trees, where a black stew pot simmered over a campfire and wood smoke pulsed blue in the twilight, obscuring the faces of eight ugly men lounging about on stumps and rocks, whittling and polishing their guns. The ground was littered with packs and boxes and bundles of beaver pelts and other half-finished, partly opened things. The air smelled of steeping broth heavy with oil and chicken fat. Hanging on the branch of a sapling chestnut was Cookie's silver triangle, bending the limb under its metallic weight.

"Ahem," Cookie said, gasping for air, and when his breath had returned, "Fellows."

The men around the fire looked toward him evenly, mildly surprised by his sudden arrival, but not enough to show it, and without a word they returned to their business, staring into the trees, or scratching their armpits, or looking at the fire lost in their own mulling thoughts. They were a grizzled bunch, with creased, weathered faces and fat bumps of chewing tobacco wedged between their cheeks and what remained of their teeth. Most of them wore layers of buckskins and colorful beads, along with gaudy rings and pendants on top of soiled bandannas, each with a peculiar hat or contorted posture of smoking to set him off from the rest. One of them unsheathed a long dagger from his boot and began stabbing at a log over and over again; another one ripped a leaf into smaller and smaller pieces.

On the far side of the fire, a jug of corn whisky was making the rounds from one thick-fingered claw to the next, pausing at each man's mouth to tilt and gurgle. Cookie watched as the jug came toward him unhurriedly, rosy at its rounded parts from the throw of the firelight, and felt the warm prick of anticipation.

"Cookie," drawled one of the men from across the fire. He wore a shapeless leather hat and a sheepskin vest. "How 'bout some of that buffalo steak for breakfast tomorrow? With them fried cakes you make? In the beef fat. That stuff's good."

"Soda bread," the man beside him grunted.

"Dried apple pie," another one added.

"Yessir," Cookie said, keeping his eye on the whiskey. "I'll try my best." Three men down from him, one of the trappers had taken ahold of the jug long enough to gulp down two mouthfuls, and the man beside him was getting visibly impatient.

"Hold up, there, mister," the waiting trapper said to his neighbor, and grabbed the bottle from the man's puckering mouth, causing a large gulp of whiskey to shoot out onto the ground.

"Hey there, that's a waste," one of the other men said.

"He's drinkin more'n his share," the trapper holding the jug said.

"Well now no one's got it," someone else piped in.

As if on cue the men began rising to their feet, pulling their knives and clubs from their belts and squaring off for some mutual satisfaction.

After four months on the trail together, the trappers in Cookie's hunting party had come to hate each other. The way someone picked his teeth, the way the saddlebags were packed, anything was a good enough reason to come to blows. They hated each other simply for being alive, for breathing too loudly or not loudly enough, depending on what would allow them to hate each other more. To make matters worse, they were already two weeks late in reaching Fort Vancouver, the lone trading post in Oregon where they could change their pelts into silver, and their daily hikes did not seem to be bringing them any closer. The rivers they were looking for did not seem to exist, and the stars that might guide them were buried every night inside a thick layer of rain clouds. The one thing the men could agree on was the map they had was practically worthless.

So every morning they packed up their load and every night they strapped it back down, letting beavers and mink and muskrats scurry past them in plain view, unable to drag any more along if they wanted to.

"Get over here," one trapper murmured, shifting his weight from one boot to the other.

"You first," another one said, sliding his blade over his thigh.

Cookie backed away quietly, moving toward the gravy train, where he generally hid out during the men's free-for-alls. He was not one for fighting, being too small to do much damage, and the thrill of the spectacle had worn out for him long ago. He climbed up the wooden spokes of the wagon wheel into the canvas tent, where the smell of dry wood mixed with oregano and wool blankets came over him, the reassuring sensation of a clean, well-ordered space. Along the walls, Cookie's kettles and skillets hung in tidy rows, and a heavy Dutch oven sat neatly in the corner. His knives were tucked into the shelves, and the matches and flint were sealed in waterproof containers fitted into the side flaps.

As the men began their yelling and swearing, Cookie made himself a little bed of cornhusks, with a pillow of folded gunneysacks, and lay down for a moment of rest. He heard the loud rip of a shirt, never a good sign, and the thump of a few punches landing in someone's abdomen, followed by the crash of a body onto a pile of chains. He clasped his fingers behind his neck and closed his eyes, letting the sounds fade from his mind, concentrating on the simple enclosure of the canvas walls all around him.

Soon enough the sounds of the fighting began to die down, and the men seemed to be resuming their positions around the fire. The forest became almost quiet again when the silence was broken by the twang of a Jew's harp.

"None of that tonight, bub," someone said gruffly. "Had about enough of that for one life." Then the cracking sound of someone punching someone in the jaw.

Outside, the horizon pinched off the last fragment of the sun. The darkness poured in more swiftly now, the half-light halved again, and the surrounding landscape was slowly erased from view. Soon there were voices and footsteps nearby. Cookie's quiet contemplation was ended.

Two men approached the wagon out of the darkness and handed Cookie a stack of dented tin plates and utensils beaded with creek water, which he took and stowed in the back. The forks still had grit on them, and the plates' faces clung to each other on thin panes of grease, but Cookie was too tired to wash them over again. When everything had clattered into place, he emerged from the wagon and went to find the officers for his nightly report.

Cookie located the commander and second in command seated beside a fire deep in the woods, talking and filing their corns. The commander was rumpled and fat and the second in command was clean and thin and they had a certain symbiotic relationship that resembled a friendship, but was not quite so simple as that. Or perhaps it was a friendship, but one that would only be recognized when it was long over and done with.

"Pardon me," Cookie said, but the commander and second in command ignored him and continued working on their corns. Cookie stood in place, his hands wandering up and down his wooden shirt buttons and under his suspenders, until finally he put them in his pockets to keep them still. The second in command seemed to sneer, though perhaps it was only a trick of the light.

"Well?" the second in command said. "Did you find anything? The men are still hungry."

"Yes," Cookie said. "Some wild leeks and a digger squirrel." He paused and looked at the fire. "I had the squirrel but it got away," he added.

"And what's in the larder?" the second in command asked.

"Seven eggs and ten dry biscuits," Cookie said. "Plus a stick of jerky and plenty of salt. Enough for about a morning's eating."

The captain raised his whiskered face, his nose greasy in the light of the fire. "And what will we do after that, Mr. Cookie?"

"I . . . I don't know, sir. Find more food, I hope."

For the past five days Cookie had been stretching the supplies as far as he could, thinning the cornmeal, shaving the gristle from the salted horsemeat and combining it with the beef gravy, hoping that some new food source would turn up, but so far none had arrived. Since crossing the Cascades, the game had been scarce, and even if it had been plentiful, there was no way to catch it. The men had already used all the gunpowder and ammunition shooting at buffalo and snakes in the plains, then at moose and longhorn, then at owls and bears, whatever the landscape provided to aim at, most of which they had left to rot. Every day it was getting harder to make ends meet. The tubers and berries Cookie found were getting progressively stranger, and the mushrooms likely poisonous to the touch.

The second in command got up and departed into the darkness, shaking his head.

"It's the Cookie's job to improvise," he said. "Don't forget that, boy."

"Yes, sir," Cookie whispered.

The fire hissed and wheezed and Cookie and his commanding officer sat there watching it a while longer. The commander stared into the flames with glassy, exhausted eyes, and finally lifted himself up as well, and shambled into the trees.

Cookie remained by the fire. A log crumbled and fell to the red cinders, sending sparks toward the sky in a crackling plume. He rubbed the stubble of his neck and cheek and jawline in a slow, languorous pattern. He had drawn first-patrol duty that night, which meant he would soon be circling the camp, protecting the men from whatever harm might come their way. Perhaps, he hoped, he might turn up some more food on the watch. Something small, like radishes or carrots, or a nest of quail eggs. Perhaps a well-baked brisket.

Cookie sighed and tightened his bootstraps. Out in the darkness, he heard a rustling of leaves, which he hoped was only a muskrat, or some wayward, nocturnal bird.

An hour later, after cleaning the stew pot and pitching the tents and avoiding an argument about the proper way to tie a Cincinnati bowtie using a length of rope no longer than a foot, Cookie crept toward the edge of the camp to begin his watch. The rows of tents glowed in the moonlight like a range of tiny, box-shaped mountains, the shadows of the men folding along the planes of the canvas as they moved about, illuminated by kerosene lamps and wax candles.

Cookie carried a wicker basket over his shoulder and wandered the forest, lifting the skirts of spreading ferns and scraping the white shingles of meringue-like fungus from the trunks of trees. He found a cluster of wide mushroom caps fanned with gills in the root system of a massive cedar, and a writhing crowd of potato bugs under a rotten log, their armored bodies curling into tight balls when they were touched by the air.

Some dogs remained among the company, but to eat them would certainly panic the men.

On his way from one side of the camp to the other he walked along-side the edge of a cliff, where a panoramic view of the forest stretched out in a patchwork of black masses. The clouds had parted to let down the milky light of a full moon, revealing rows of mountains receding in lighter and lighter waves, pressing against the distant skyline like a saw blade. At the base of the cliff was a creek, which passed by a marshy expanse full of tall grass and pussy willow, softened under the nacreous lamplight of the stars.

As Cookie stood there awhile, and time moved a little, the severity of his thoughts bundled into a kind of majestic doom, and oddly enough he began to feel a bit better than before. His longing for safety and acceptance transformed into a vague resolution, and his thoughts gradually fell into a new, more optimistic order. For no particular reason the men began to seem just fine to Cookie, quite fine, and small in comparison to the grandeur of things like the mountains and the moon. The secret language they spoke did not bother him. The waterfalls, and snowy ridges, and Indian populations ceased to pose a threat. He trusted the men and himself to move through each day's tests with stern resolve. They were his men, after all. They had embarked on this journey together.

Cookie lingered on the edge of the cliff, taking heart in the reasonable thought that Oregon, like any other country, was created to bear the fruits and meat of man's nourishment. Soon there would be settlers and farmers and women and children here, who in turn would need schools and churches and stores to shop in, and thus more men and women and children to come join them. Among those people he would surely find a place. He imagined, as he sometimes did, that history emanated from some central spot, Paris perhaps, or London, and arrived to distant regions in ever weaker pulsations, and that perhaps he had beaten it here, and could prepare for it this time.

Cookie pulled a cigar from his pocket to savor the picture he had constructed for himself. After some effort he got the cigar burning and continued stepping through the foliage, feeling the emptiness and ferocity of the forest on his one side and the dignity of the camp on the other, as the tip of his ash glowed and dimmed with his breath.

He passed to the opposite side of the camp, stepping over a patch of sticky currant, when suddenly a gentle scraping sound caught his ear. He paused and peered into the trees but there was nothing to be seen: only the remains of an evening meal left out on a fallen log where a man had apparently taken his supper and then forgotten to return his plate.

Cookie was bothered by this—the forgotten plate invited predatory animals and more generally violated the higher discipline of the corps—until it occurred to him that he had not yet located any main dish for the following day's supper, and furthermore that the company's flour and cornmeal and drippings of fat were entirely depleted. He was a miserable failure in his duties as a cook, he realized, and there was no one at all to share the blame with. All at once, Cookie was at odds with himself again.

Mechanically, Cookie proceeded over to the tin plate, reaching downward to grasp its lip between his thumb and fingers. He pulled it toward himself, and was surprised to find the plate recoil from his tug. He pulled again and it recoiled again, as if held in place by a powerful magnet. Cookie stood there, staring at the plate, while icy fear ran through him.

Curled around the rim of the plate from the opposite side of the log was a human finger, latching it in place like a buttonhook.

Cookie inhaled on his cigar sharply, illuminating the darkness with a feeble red light. Behind the fallen log hung a pair of hollowed-out eyes, and beneath them a chapped mouth hanging partially agape. Below that was a wide, stubbled chin, and a man's naked collarbone forming a distinct strut across a hairy, well-formed chest. On either side of the chest were arms that tapered to strong wrists, and up top again was a fuzzy bundle of knotted blond hair, pulled back in a messy ponytail, filled with burrs and twigs. Cookie assembled all these elements into an image: a naked man, with matted hair and stunned blue eyes, crouching behind a log in a rain forest in the middle of the night.

Cookie's cigar dropped from his mouth and hissed out on the moist forest floor.

"Hello?" he asked in his regular voice. "Are you all right?"

"Hungry," the naked man replied, and then quickly, "No need to call anyone."

The man stood a head or so taller than Cookie, clasping his hands over his naked body, clearly disoriented by the sudden meeting. He picked uncertainly at a nearby mulberry leaf. He merely wanted to know the time, he said, and Cookie told him. Then the man sat down on the stump, legs crossed at the knee, and eventually spoke again: "I guess your Cookie has retired for the evening."

"I doubt it," Cookie replied.

The stranger seemed to struggle with himself then, muttering doubtfully, "Don't suppose you could call him out here a minute? Quietly?"

Cookie felt the time had arrived to identify himself: "I am the Cookie."

The man coughed and whispered to himself some more, staring out into the forest. His profile was limned in moonlight, his nose turned up at the end, his chin strong, and his brow open. Although the resemblance was slight, something in its melding of features oddly reminded Cookie of himself. Cookie had small eyes and a beak-like nose, a nest of black curls exploding from his head, and a physique like an old scarecrow, but something in the man's face, the purse of the lips, perhaps, or the way their color rose from the chalky whiteness of his skin, seemed to reflect him nonetheless, and Cookie interpreted it as the mark of some latent nobility.

"I'm Henry," the man said. "Been walkin in this durn forest all night. Reckon I might just stay here awhile."

Cookie could almost hear the thick foliage growing around them, tiny clicks and gasps amplified by the towering trees.

"Wait here," he said, and without another word he went to find Henry a shirt and pants, and perhaps a scrap of food as well. At the drape of the gravy train canvas he paused. The tents were dark, and the moon cast a bluish light on their peaked roofs. A snore emanated from the commander's flap, and stony silence from the others. Cookie ducked inside and seized a flannel shirt and a pair of woolen pants from his own rucksack, and located a cold biscuit and the last dried stick of jerky from a tin box.

When he got back Henry was sitting just as before, glowing softly in the moonlight. He devoured the jerky, gnashing at it with his jaws and violently drawing it downward with the corded muscles of his neck, and then turned to the biscuit, barely softening its dry grain before forcing it into his stomach to join the meat. When that was done, he wiped the back of his hand over his mouth and slipped his legs into Cookie's pants, which were a little tight, but which Cookie admired on him nonetheless. Seeing his own clothes on someone else made them seem better than before.

"Strange business," Henry said as he buttoned the shirt, but then he trailed off without finishing his sentence. He slouched his shoulders and weakly shook his head in an effort to gather his strength to explain.

"Later," Cookie said, and led Henry stealthily from the woods to the covered wagon, where he cleared away a small space deep in the rear, behind a shallow wall of wooden boxes containing the crumbs of oats and the scraps of wood shavings that had once protected the shells of eggs. It only took a moment. The boxes were nearly weightless and easily rearranged. Behind the makeshift wall he laid out a bed of empty gunnysacks and cornhusks.

Almost before lying down, Henry was asleep.

Cookie watched him for a moment. Henry's nostrils widening and closing, his eyelids fluttering with visions. Henry's hair was a yellow nest and his face was blotched with scratches. His lips were cracked and pale. But the features of his face seemed golden somehow, lit from inside, and when his mouth opened to let out a breath, his teeth flashed small and straight in the darkness. Something in Henry's sudden arrival had raced past Cookie's normal defenses, and he hoped the odd man would stay awhile.

Cookie went to awaken the second in command for his round of sentinel duty and finally made his way to his own tent. He pulled the woolen blankets around himself and pressed his head to his pillow. Nervous imaginings boiled inside him. He had plenty to worry about.

The stock of food was gone, hardly a biscuit remained, and although he had not told anyone yet, their one chicken had been killed days ago by a bobcat or a lynx. Unless some food source was discovered soon, or the walls of Fort Vancouver suddenly opened before them, the fur party was marching straight into the jaws of hunger and despair. In addition, he now had a stowaway sleeping in the bed of the food wagon, without the permission of the other men. Cookie's thoughts crowded in one on top of the other and canceled each other out, until finally, after much tossing, he fell asleep, his final vague impression before drifting off being something about the company's trust, and that now one more stranger was trusting him as well.

# 2

THE FIRST TIME Tina Plank heard the name Trixie Volterra, she was sitting in the passenger seat of a U-Haul trailer, driving north on I-5 from San Jose to Portland. She and her mother had been driving for over eight hours now, and the road had long ago become a treadmill of dull, repeating, white lines. They had passed the Nut Tree sign outside Vacaville around noon, and hit the hot spit of road between Red Bluff and Redding not long after that. Mount Shasta and the Siskiyous had come next, where the radio signal had crumbled in the dead airwaves, and then came the gentle countryside between Ashland and Eugene, where the strange, opaque syllables of Oregon began: Umpqua, Klamath, like cold stones in the earth. And the walls of Douglas fir, three hours so far, and counting.

Tina sat patiently with the hot wind blowing through her hair, surrounded by the hum of the engine and the rattle of the window in the door, waiting for her mother to answer a question that she had asked her almost two minutes before. The blasting air was hot and clean, and smelled like Scotch broom baking in the sun.

"Trixie Volterra," her mother finally said. "That's her name." She yelled over the sound of the beating air. Tina's mother was a handsome woman, with blue eyes and raspy blond hair frayed with split ends.

"Huh," Tina said, and returned to watching the trees streak past the gray shoulder of the road. "And she's the only one?"

"I think so," her mother said, and glanced toward her daughter with a worried look.

"Huh," Tina said again.

"But you'll like her. She's very smart. She had a tough time for a while, but I hear she's starting to really get it together."

"Oh yeah?" Tina said. "'Tough time' how?"

"Well." Her mother glanced in the rearview mirror and Tina waited silently for her to remember what she was saying. "She was expelled from school last year, I think, down in L.A., and then her mom and dad kicked her out of the house. And she's been living with Beth since then, figuring things out. But she's very sweet. Very good kid. She just made some bad judgments is all."

"What'd she do?" Tina asked.

"I don't know," her mother said. "But I'm sure you'll find out."

"Yeah," Tina said, and cupped some rushing air in her palm. "Eventually."

As the afternoon wore on, the U-Haul rolled past pulp mills and shacks armored in thin, stained siding, acres of shuffling lettuce and hops, until eventually the miles to Portland narrowed down to single digits. The gray concrete widened, and then split into multiple arteries, bending into bridges and underpasses, and the clean, modest downtown of the city appeared. After twelve hours of nothing, it was a little less than Tina had expected, but it was civilization at least, better than the mind-numbing trees. She counted a handful of gleaming buildings, gray, pink, black, surrounded by a smattering of lower brick structures, before the city disappeared behind a smooth retaining wall and the sound of the laboring engine pressed in against them.

The U-Haul continued north along Highway 30, through an industrial neighborhood smelling of burning tar and fresh bread, until the buildings ended and the river appeared. After a few tries they turned up into the dank hills toward the coast. The road became gravel, and the blackberries crept closer in, and after a few long loping bends they found themselves deposited in a shapeless parking lot spotted with patches of meadow grass and Queen Anne's lace.

Tina's mother guided the U-Haul into a spot between a Volkswagon Squareback and a beat-up Capri, and finally they stopped. The emergency brake squealed, and the engine shut down, and the silence rushed in around them.

"OK," Tina's mother said. "We're here."

Tina rolled out of the cab and stretched and shook out her legs. Her right arm was bright red from hanging out the window all day, and her knee took a few painful readjustments to begin working again. On either side of the gravel lot, walls of forest rose along parallel ridges, fir trees mixed with elm and maple and alder, and the sound of a nearby creek seemed to hush everything down to a whisper. Even now, in the middle of August, the forest held an invisible chill, a cold current locked inside the heat, which Tina could smell in the fungal scent of the fir trees and the leaf litter mulching the ground in a damp tissue.

"Peggy?" someone said from the trees. A deep, croaking, male voice. "Peggy Plank? That you?"

"Peter!" Tina's mother said sprightly.

Tina turned around to find a man emerging from the thick under-brush. He was a gaunt but healthy-looking man, arms tanned and well-muscled, veins ropy, wearing faded burgundy corduroys and a misshapen T-shirt advertising a resort called Kah-Nee-Tah. His eyes were deeply recessed and his nose jutted out between high, ruddy cheek-bones, framed by long, greasy, brown hair. As the man came closer, Tina noticed something else in his leathery features as well, a dark confusion of some kind, as if something bright had been extinguished there long ago. His irises were the color of bleached cornflower, surrounding pupils the size of needlepoints.

"You remember Peter Sessions," Tina's mother said, and Tina nodded politely, though she did not. The webs at the corners of Peter's eyes creased, and with some effort his mouth grinned to reveal a beveled, blackened front tooth.

"You've sure grown up," he said, staring into Tina's eyes as if there was some deep subtext to his comment, and then, after an awkward pause, "Welp. Come on. I'll show you ladies around."

Peter Sessions turned abruptly and walked to the edge of the parking

21

lot, into a patch of yellow cattails. The golden filaments chafed in the summer heat. Tina and her mother followed him to the other side of the short meadow, where a powdered dirt pathway appeared, running alongside a shoulder-high bamboo fence. They turned left and Tina fell a few steps behind.

Peter began scratching his arm vigorously. "So what brings you ladies up here?" he asked. "Heard you all were coming."

"Ronald fucking Reagan," Tina's mother said, smiling. "Cut all the funding for solar research in the country. I haven't been able to find a job down in California for six months."

"I hear you," Peter said, staring straight ahead. "I hear you."

They passed a weathered gate marked by a ceramic Buddha figurine holding the ashes of incense, where the eggy smell of sulfur wafted in the air.

"Hot springs," Peter said, nodding, at which point the fence ended and the creek appeared, a smooth, silver blur over the rocks.

Soon the dirt path crested and a collection of cabins came into view, cupped in a valley of descending basins. They were ancient, clapboard shacks and a few newer-looking A-frames, about fifteen in all, bordering a large garden filled with cabbage and corn and tangles of butternut squash. The tarpaper rooftops made a simple geometry of black planes, mended in places with discarded lengths of wood and rusted wire, shingled with flattened tin cans that shone whitely when the sun hit them from above.

Tina and the two adults paused for a moment as a dog barked somewhere in the distance and a woman in a batik skirt rose from the strawberry patch to fan herself with a floppy straw hat.

It had never occurred to Tina that she might have been happy before, living her old life in her old house with her old friends, but in retrospect she now realized that she had been, perhaps even wildly so. Looking over the mangy cabins, the empty dust pathways, the sprawling, unknown geography spreading in every direction, a sense of immeasurable self-pity rose up in her like a wave. She felt like she had arrived on the farthest edge of the known universe.

"It's beautiful," Tina's mother said, and Peter said yep, though it had obviously ceased to register for him, and then the three of them trudged their way down toward the cabins.

Tina's new house was very small, just two rooms and a kitchenette, with a small porch in front littered with a collection of agate left by the last inhabitant, the son of a banker on his way to the canneries in Alaska. The walls were covered in splintery wooden shingles streaked with some kind of black scum, like a dirty beard, and a camellia bush pressed up next to the front window. A broken wind chime dangled from the eves, and one of the windows had a transparent sticker of a moon on it.

The screen door was propped open with a sanded river rock, and with a light push the front room slid into view. The walls inside were raw wood, the floor a puzzle of warping planks and seams, the overall light yellowed and diffuse. The smell of mildew seeped from the moldings. Tina and her mother walked from corner to corner, crossing each other's paths, testing the different trajectories they could make.

"It's cozy," her mother said three times, to which Tina replied three times that it smelled like a health food store. "It smells brown," she said, but her mother had begun to ignore her.

"Have you heard from Barry lately?" Tina's mother asked Peter.

"Yep," he said. "Still with Maria," and then more adult names followed. Cynthia, Ralf, Todd, a different world of adult subjects and adult interests and adult lives.

Tina stepped into the back room, which overlooked the garden, its berms of rich earth held in place by creosote-covered railroad ties and cylinders of chicken wire filled with moldering orange rinds and coffee grounds and banana peels. Above the plateau of the parking lot, the hills framed a crisp block of sky over an empty field of lamb's ear and heather. Tina shifted her head a little and made a wobble of glass move over a fence post, up and down like a shimmer of heat. The window-pane was so pebbled it looked like someone had doused it with a bucket of water.

From the other room Tina's mother called out, "You can take the back room, honey. What do you think? And I'll take the front."

Tina was about yell back, "Fine," but she was cut off by a sudden thunder of footsteps and voices rushing in the front door, shaking the floorboards and knocking loose crumbs from the planks in the ceiling. The windows rattled in their mullions and for a brief moment she felt a sharp pang of longing for California's earthquakes.

"Hey! There you are!"

"Fucking shit!"

"About time, you slowpoke!"

Tina stepped back into the front room to find a whole gallery of adults streaming in the door, hugging her mother and making themselves at home. "Oh my God!" a woman shrieked. "You're here!" Heather Murphy and Margaret Thomas appeared, thick-waisted dykes from her mother's anti-nuke days, and Bob Grossberger, whom Tina had known, he liked to say, since before she was born. "Hi, gorgeous," he drawled toward her mother. Coming in behind them were a few frazzled women in Guatemalan huipils, bright orange and purple flashes on their chests, holding plates of sushi stuffed with clumping brown rice, and behind them a man with cutoffs so short Tina could see the furry pouches of his genitals when he sat down on the floor and crossed his legs. Tina's mother greeted them all with her most blissful smile, the one meant to dissolve any conversational tension before it began and to set a mood of healthy, open, nurturing communication.

Tina's first reaction to the sudden invasion was to flee, but she decided against it. She should make an effort to appear amiable, she thought, if only to buy credit for the future. She should meet everyone and make a decent impression, and then leverage that good impression into a kind of benign neglect that she could exploit for the use of greater unsupervised freedom. One thing she had learned at school: The first impression was extremely important in securing a bit of privacy for oneself.

"Tina," Bob Grossberger said gravely, and before she knew it he was upon her, wrapping her in a long, full-body hug. When he pulled away, he placed his hands on her shoulders and stared into her face with an expression of such heartfelt sensitivity that it looked like he had been punched in the nose. Tina tried her best to avoid meeting his eyes. She looked down his long upper lip, glistening with after-shave, to his necklace of ceramic beads, and then to the tufts of black hair poking from his turquoise, collarless shirt, as all the while more adults came gathering in around her, chatting and jostling each other for position, peppering her with little questions.

"What grade are you in?" said a man with a gnarled wooden pipe.

"Tenth," Tina said.

"What a great shirt!" said a woman in worn, leather sandals.

"Thanks."

Someone hugged Tina from behind and she turned to find Beth Bowler, their old neighbor in Santa Cruz, wearing the same scoop-neck peasant blouse she had been wearing for the past four years at least, the one embroidered with roses that showed the rangy definition of her clavicles, and the contours of her tiny nipples underneath. She still parted her long, raven-black hair down the middle, Tina noted, to reveal the same stark white line down the center of her scalp.

"Tina," Beth whispered, smiling, "so good to see you again."

Before they could say anything else, Neil Rust loped over, the land-lord of the property, though no one would call him that, his lanky body moving like something held together with old rubber bands. Tina noticed that Neil had developed a slight potbelly since she had seen him last, and the wolfish look of his eyes had been replaced by some-thing softer and more vague. His brown hair fell down over his ears like flattened wings.

"Howdy, Tina," he said. The stubble on his face sparkled with tiny pinpricks of silver.

"Hi," Tina said.

"Drive all right?"

"Yep. Great." Everyone waited for some response from Neil, but it was slow in coming. Tina had forgotten his molasses-like pace. One day she had seen him spend four hours eating his lunch. "Hot," she finally added.

"Hmmm," Neil nodded, as if her words took him a long time to digest. Across the room Tina heard the zip of corduroy pants and two children with bowl cuts flew past, their bangs flopping over their eyes.

"You're really going to like Trixie," Beth was murmuring beside her. "She lives with me now. She's very creative."

"Very cool girl," Neil echoed gradually.

"I look forward to meeting her," Tina said.

"Tina," Bob Grossberger said abruptly, "I just have to say it. What a beautiful young woman you've become!"

"Oh Jesus, Bob," Tina said, and for a brief moment she worried that she had somehow hurt his feelings, which was ridiculous, she knew, but such was the passive-aggressive power of Bob Grossberger, who was born to forgive. And then, suddenly, all the adults were talking at once.

"So what are your interests?"

"What grade are you in?"

"How are you liking it so far? Up here, I mean?"

Tina could feel them closing in around her, pressing tighter with each question. The time had come to make a quick bid for freedom.

"Boy," Tina said to all of them at once, "Portland's really getting bigger these days, isn't it? So different since I was here last. I barely recognized it."

"No shit," said a man with leather bracelets. "Like fuckin' L.A."

"Everywhere is becoming exactly the same," Beth said sagely.

And with that the adults were off on the subject of local gentrification, expressing their timeworn indignation over all the new growth, and the new people, and their general distress over the wave of conservatism washing over the country, as if all of it was part of the same grand conspiracy. The best times were over, they agreed, the landscape had been ruined by condominiums and parking lots, the music had lost its soul. The world would never stop ending, it seemed.

"That's progress," Neil said, regarding the fate of a charming old bank that had been destroyed for a new Taco Bell on Union Avenue, but by that time Tina was gone.

From the garden Tina watched everyone leave the cabin, and take a group trip to the U-Haul and grab whatever they could, and then return to the cabin before repairing to the creek for a barbecue of fresh corn and coho salmon. When the coast was clear, she slunk back to the porch and went inside, eager to complete her unpacking and define some discrete space as her own.

Tina located her television set in the front room, lodged between a box of books and a blue packing blanket, and hefted it to her hip. The dials were almost as large as doorknobs, and the flap that covered the control panel popped open at the slightest touch, but its idiosyncrasies were easily gotten used to, and in some ways contributed to its hulking and dog-eared personality. Tina carried it into her room and shut the door behind herself with a swing of her foot.

"Ahh," she said out loud, and took a deep breath of dry wood and wool.

Tina set the television on a milk crate at the base of her bed and sprawled herself out on the naked mattress, where she buried her face in a pillow, and immediately succumbed to the sweet, enveloping sensation of utter boredom.

Tina was a great connoisseur of boredom. Living in San Jose one had to be. During her years there she had developed a whole taxonomy of stasis and inactivity, of dead zones and liminal periods, of ways to continue waiting for whatever was about to arrive. There was the boredom of going to a circus, the boredom of a long and boring film. The boredom of waiting to fall asleep, the boredom of talking to one's grandmother in anticipation of receiving one's birthday check. There was the boredom of doing one's homework, and the boredom of waiting for one's friend to finish her homework so you could go outside together and endure the boredom of figuring out what to do next. Most everything was a gradation of boredom, she had found, a holding tank for something yet to come, and among its many types, its many varieties and categories, the boredom that she currently indulged in was among the most delightful and nourishing of them all, the boredom of being alone in one's own room, with nothing to do but stare at the walls and gaze at dust motes floating in a shaft of sun.

Tina pressed her face into the folds of her pillow, and pushed her arm into a cool crevice underneath, until all the coolness had been exhausted and she began pleasantly to suffocate.

Someday, Tina told herself, she would not be bored anymore, after some things had happened to her. Until then she would just have to wait.

Eventually, Tina got up and plugged in her TV, and a moment later its reassuring whine was filling the room. She flipped through the channels and found only three stations that came in. The reception was snowy, but with some finessing of the antennae they became acceptable to watch. The ghosts returned to their bodies, the specks of gray and white receded from view.

"Welcome home, to NewsCenter 8," the anchorman said.

Tina slit open a cardboard box with the teeth of a key and pulled out her shoes, then unwrapped her camera from a woolen sweater and hung it from a nail. She plugged in her clock and arranged her lipstick and nail polish and eye makeup on the bureau top, glancing at the screen sometimes to register the names and faces of the local reporters. The faces were different from those in California, but not that different, a little mealier, and their backdrops were oddly colored and poorly proportioned in comparison. It made her feel far away from something in a way, exiled from her own life. It seemed there had been no fires or murders or hijackings that day. In other words, nothing of interest. More than usual she noticed how the newscasters pretended to like each other, and how obvious it was that they did not.

"Well, Tracy, we know what you did last night."

"You got me, Jim," Tracy said, and turned toward the camera.

"President Reagan addressed a group of World War II veterans in Washington today," the anchorwoman said, at which point Ronald Reagan appeared on the screen, speaking with the congressional dome behind him, and some men gathered on the stage to either side. He frowned with a cold glint in his eye and then smiled with a warm glint in his eye, and then Tina watched him watching a parade through the imperial avenues of the capital. History, she was coming to suspect, was something that happened very far away.

Tina continued unpacking while the sky outside her window turned hot pink. The square of her flickering television set appeared on her window pane, along with the reflection of a balloon of light from her reading lamp on the opposite wall. Tina's own reflection added to the mess, and the pane of glass became a teeming mass of images.

Tina approached the window and stared out into the gloaming, the grids of string throughout the garden disappearing from view, a cloud of bats flapping from the hills against the dimming sky.

Her eyes traveled up to the horizon line, a black curve bounded by two wooded inclines, seething with a soft carpet of long grass. On the far edge of the field a small figure had appeared from the reddening sunset and was beginning to make its way down toward the cabins through the dry pasture.

"History has unambiguous lessons to teach on the outcome of appeasement," the male anchor said.

As the figure came closer, it began to resolve into focus. A girl, about Tina's age, carrying what appeared to be a large, aluminum frame backpack on her shoulders, which shifted uncomfortably back and forth. She wore a white skirt and matching smock, like a nurse, complete with the square hat and thickly soled orthopedic shoes. Tina's heart suddenly throbbed in her chest.

Trixie Volterra, she thought. The only girl for five miles in any direction.

The TV played a snippet of ominous organ music, which matched the scene perfectly, but then switched to a candy-bar jingle, which ruined it.

"Bad news for the Blazers today," the sportscaster said.

Trixie Volterra approached the garden gate, where she glanced briskly around, as if some watchtower in the hills was tracking her every gesture, and slipped inside the fence. She wound through the pathways behind stalks of corn and cabbage leaves, her feet crunching on the gravel, keeping her eyes fixed steadily on the path just ahead. Her lack of expression was impressive, Tina thought. She knew how to deflect a gaze.

Trixie made her way to a cabin on the adjacent edge of the garden, a variation on Tina's own cabin, with brown shingles and tarpaper roof. She opened the back door and went quickly inside. Tina waited for a moment but nothing occurred. All the windows remained dark.

"And now we go live to Edna Highcastle," a man's voice said behind her, "in the Columbia gorge, with an update on the situation near Hood River."

"Thank you, Jim," a woman said, fixing her expression. "The Columbia River is home to many hydroelectric dams, which provide power to homes and businesses throughout the region. And while we depend on these dams for our everyday needs, they make it extremely difficult for returning salmon to travel upstream on their annual spawning runs."

Tina watched the screen reversed on the windowpane, stock footage of a flatbed trailer parked on a riverbank, a heavy box being lowered from a hydraulic arm.

"In recent years," the reporter continued, "the Army Corps of Engineers has begun pumping fish directly from the river into large trucks, which drive the salmon around the dams and deposit them on the opposite side."

Now the reporter returned to the screen, looking slightly stricken on the shoulder of a road. The wind blew at her hair and a blond lock slipped over her eyes.

"Earlier today, Jim, a truck full of salmon jackknifed on Interstate 84 near the Bonneville Dam, and the highway is now literally filled with stranded, dying fish."

The television cut to a helicopter view of the wet highway, the truck flipped sideways across the lanes, the fish like tiny apostrophes scattered on the tarmac. A close-up showed a fish gasping on the thin sheen of water, baking in the sun. A member of a local Indian tribe appeared saying it was disgraceful.

"No shit," Tina agreed.

Tina filled a few more drawers with clothing and returned to the window to find a light had flicked on in the cabin across the way, a golden rectangle against the darkened wood wall. Tina could see a large swath of the room quite clearly now, the foot of a bed with peppermint striped sheets, the edge of an orange couch, the corner of a drafting table with a reading lamp attached. Suddenly Trixie Volterra stepped into the frame.

"Oh," Tina said out loud. "Finally."

Tina took up a position at the edge of the window to keep her angle of watching oblique enough to guard against the other girl feeling her eyes, and picked at the mottled sill as the action began.

"Thank you, Edna," the anchorman said. "Truly a tragic accident. We'll have more later as the clean-up continues. And now to Oregon City, where one local woman keeps a very special pet. Not a dog, or a cat, but a two-hundred-pound Vietnamese pig."

"This I've got to see," the woman anchor rejoined.

Trixie Volterra unstrapped the backpack from her shoulders and dropped it onto the bed, where it bounced once and lay still. She looked at the scuffed green canvas on the red-and-white quilt for a moment, and then leaned over and unzipped the main pocket. Out came a sheaf of newspapers, which she carefully unfolded in a wide swath over her floor, as if lining an enormous birdcage. She returned to the backpack and pulled out a plastic bag filled with silver Christmas balls, probably twenty of them, which she dumped onto the unfolded newspaper and spaced out evenly across the floor. Tina lost sight of Trixie at times, but it was clear from the movement of her back, her arms, her backbones moving like little levers, that she was spacing the silver orbs with some care. She had blond hair, a pencil-thin neck, and what appeared to be a cute nose.

Trixie returned to her backpack once more and this time removed a can of spray paint, which she began shaking violently back and forth.

She stepped toward the window, yanking it open so the ticktack sound of the rattling can brightened in the air, and Tina realized how close they actually were, only about fifteen yards apart. Trixie had almond eyes and thin ruby lips, and her nursing hat was connected to her hair with a lattice of bobby pins. She pulled down the shade and her body became a shadow on the blind. Tina could hear the gasp of the aerosol can as it began to spray.

Just then there was a gentle knock on Tina's door and she heard her name called out softly through the wall.

"Yeah?" she called back, and her mother inserted her head into the room. Her face was torqued into a strange expression, her lips a little puckered and her eyebrows knitted, meant to suggest openness and concern. She stood there, offering her facial expression as some invitation to speak.

"The pig is much cleaner than the dog," an old woman said on TV. "And so much better with discipline."

Tina did not say anything and her mother kept gazing at her, with her face screwed into a pose of sympathy before the fact.

"What?" Tina finally said.

"Nothing," her mother said, and withdrew into the other room without saying a word. The door clicked quietly behind her.

Tina returned to her unpacking, putting her books on a shelf, and her socks in a drawer, and tacking some things up on the walls. She could hear her mother in the other room unpacking as well. Various clicks and rumbles and shiftings emanated through the wall. She heard a window sliding open and a cupboard slamming shut, the sound of a sheet snapping in the air and ruffling to conform to its surface. Tina moved randomly from wall to wall, drawer to drawer, emptying boxes and putting things away as they appeared in her hands, touching all the surfaces of the room until they began to feel like her own, wondering all the while if perhaps the other girl, Trixie Volterra, was watching her this evening, too.

# 3

**N**EIL RUST THWACKED his way through a woody rhododendron bush and came out on a trail leading through a stand of tall cedars, which filled the air with their sweet, hypnotic scent. He took a deep breath and got his bearings before angling through a bed of prehistoric ghost fern toward the marsh, where he liked to skip a rock or two and think about the larger shape of his day's progress before heading home for dinner.

"Hey, man," he said as a deer scampered out of sight.

Neil emerged from the shade of the forest into a tawny meadow, where a gnarled plum tree stood, its limbs sagging with the weight of its own clustered fruit. He plucked a few plums and continued on to the water, where black shadows of pussy willow jiggled on the surface and a quilt of pink duckweed clung to the rough edges. Neil stood there and watched the cattail and arrow arum and maidencane shiver in the breeze, polishing the plum on his pants. The low sun whitened the edges of his vision, and distant yelping voices rolled down the hill to his ears. Somewhere, someone was nailing, and the sound arrived doubled, a solid, tinking thunk followed by a solid, tinking echo.

At times like this, late in the afternoon on a warm summer day, Neil nursed in himself a sense of genuine well-being. He told himself that everything was all right in the world, that he was simply living his life, and that he was okay with it. He felt resigned to the fact that the pattern of his days had already gone full circle, and that everything ahead of him was likely just a variation on what had come before. The same problems in different forms, the same loves in different bodies, the same dreams on different nights. At times like this he actually believed he had achieved some wisdom in this knowledge, and that some strength was to be found in his abiding passivity. He raised his plum slowly to his mouth.

"Neil!" someone called out from across the marsh.

Neil squinted to find Peggy Plank waving strenuously at him in the distance, her hair a huge backlit mane, her smile enormous even from so far away.

"Hey, Peggy," he called back. "Everything going all right?"

"So far so good," she said, "just glad to be here," and a moment later she had disappeared into the trees, leaving an empty stand of bright yellow Scotch broom to ponder. Perhaps there was some future with Peggy Plank, he thought.

Neil bit into his plum and got to thinking about how light worked. How it traveled all the way through space only to die on the ground, or bounce off a yellow bush into the cones and rods of someone's eye. It was a thought that occurred to him pretty often, in fact, but which never went further than a dim speculation on his part. The way of light was a mystery that he doubted he would ever understand, that he doubted anyone would ever understand, even those who tried all their lives.

Neil poked around the edge of the marsh, keeping a lookout for lizards, or trash, or good rocks to throw, until he came upon the longest centipede he had ever seen, probably five inches, with black, wiggling lashes running down either side of its armored body. He saw a guppy scooting in the water, and a salamander scurrying under a leaf.

Near a shady bush he stopped and ran his hands through his hair, as a wave of prickling anxiety came over him about the problem of money in his life, and how he might go about getting some of it without doing anything he did not feel like doing already. He needed some cash pretty soon, he realized, and hated the thought of asking anyone to help him. Quickly, Neil marshaled his thoughts for quelling the anxiety, of which there were three.

One idea Neil had for getting more money was to grow flowers in his garden and sell them at the grocery stores around town. Lilies and orchids and sunflowers and such. He knew people who did that, and he figured if they could do it, then so could he. But the season was off, and he needed to get going on something soon.

Another idea was to log a bit of the forest with his horse and sell kindling, but that seemed a little rapacious to the land.

Neil's favorite idea for getting money, which he often thought about, even if it would not work, was that of turning his marsh into a terraced garden of goldenrod, and selling his crops to alternative medicine companies for their horse pills and nutrient drops. This idea seemed ingenious to him. The industry was getting bigger all the time, he believed, and he loved the look of a terraced field, like they built on hillsides in Southeast Asia.

He stood at the edge of his marsh thinking about the goldenrod project for about the four-hundredth time, mulling over the pros and cons and letting its implications brighten and fade in his mind before never coming to any real resolution. It was a kind of entertainment for him. He contemplated the wetland, and in his mind cubic forms became visible in the morass of paludified earth. Corrugated aluminum pressed against braces of wood, holding back the fetid water, the drainage system winding in forks and tridents of trench and pipe. He felt like Pharaoh, spreading his identity out over the trees and rocks and sky.

The geometry would be gorgeous, he thought, stepped planes shimmering with yellow goldenrod. But the integrity of the bog was beautiful as well. Its utter undoing of form amazed him, its collapse of beginnings and endings. To impose a shape on it was in a sense to destroy something, a whorl of disorder, a model of chaos. Once again, he could not decide.

Neil stepped through the thicket and came to the other side of the marsh, where the pooling water petered out into a dry, cracked bed. He had never seen the marsh so empty before, so webbed and parched from a summer's drought.

Neil stepped out into the exposed basin, moist beneath its crust, and felt the egg-carton dirt crackling under his weight. A few steps in he ran across an old, three-pronged fork on the ground, and some barbed wire encoated in orange crud, which he slipped into his pocket. He had a collection of old arrowheads and bullet casings and things like that that he kept at home.

He kept poking around, and found an old Fresca can full of mud, and a corroded hinge, which he put in his pocket as well.

Just as Neil was getting ready to call it a day and head back up to his cabin for a twilight drink, he came upon a white rock on the ground, the shape of a cantaloupe, half buried in the muddy, flaky muck. He dislodged it with his toe and tipped it up on its side. As the flatter part rolled toward him, he noticed that the stone had teeth. It was a human skull.

"Hello," Neil said.

It took awhile for Neil to accept the discovery as a fact. He looked at the skull from a few feet away, as if it might suddenly waver and disappear, and then took a step closer. The skull's eye sockets stared at him blankly, pools of brown water, and strands of dried grass stuck from its teeth. A centipede crawled out. He knelt down and dug at the skull with his fingers until he had uncovered a neck and clavicle, then found a dry stick for better scraping. He was just crouching down to continue his work when someone called out his name from the trees.

"Hey, Neil!" someone yelled.

Neil stopped his scraping and looked around to find Peter Sessions standing at the base of the pathway, cupping his hands to his mouth. The trees shifted over his head in the wind.

"Where's the shovel?" Peter yelled.

"Check the shed!" Neil yelled back.

"I did!"

"Well then, I don't know. That's where I keep it!"

Peter lowered his hands and wandered off as if he had some clear intention in mind. Neil watched him disappear, then turned back to his work.

Neil carefully scraped the dirt off the skull, and dug a shallow trench along its edges where it met with the caked earth. He followed the outline down to the shoulder, and along the arm, carefully piling the extra dirt a few feet away, until suddenly a shadow appeared on his hands.

"Hey, what's going on?" Peter Sessions asked.

"Found something." Neil said, without looking up. He had been hoping to surprise everyone with his discovery.

"Wow," Peter managed to say, and then he yelled over to Margaret, who was standing near a break of bulrushes, trying to catch a frog.

"Margaret!" Peter yelled. "Check this out. Neil found a dead body!"

"Geez," Margaret said, when she had made it over.

Neil kept scraping away. Off in the distance the ridge of trees went golden in the final throw of the day's sunlight.

Within twenty minutes a whole crowd had gathered around Neil to watch his excavation unfold, and once they were there he was fine with their company. In fact, an audience made the whole thing more exciting in a way.

He kept working steadily, and within an hour or so he had unearthed the whole thing, cranium to toe. The skeleton had a big crack in its head and an amber ring dangling on one of its fingers, and furthermore, right beside it there was another skeleton, a bigger one, with broken ribs and a damaged sternum. The two bodies lay there side by side, their arms reaching toward each other and their fingers interlocking like a little cage.

"Jesus," Neil said, when he finally stood up.

Neil and his friends stood around quietly in the dusky light looking at the skeletons, wondering what to do. The crickets breathed in the heat and the wind whispered in the leaves. For a while they were somewhat humbled by the sanctity of the gravesite, but soon enough that feeling wore away and they got to talking again.

"We should probably call the cops," Beth Bowler offered.

"I don't know," Peter said. "I say not unless we have to." A few of the other guys agreed with him.

"These bones are obviously long forgotten," someone concluded. "Got here way before any of us were born."

"Oh, come on," Margaret said. "You can't tell that. And the longer we wait to tell someone, the worse it'll be. Don't you watch TV?"

"No one's gonna find out," Peter said cryptically.

But Neil did not see how they could avoid informing the cops. As much as the thought of inviting police onto his property galled him, there were times when it was almost a relief to pass the responsibility on to someone else.

"No hurry though," he said. "I'll call them in the morning, after everyone has a chance clean up their cabins. Stash whatever you want to stash."

As the moon rose they drank some beers and made guesses as to who the skeletons might be.

"An Indian and his squaw," Bob Grossberger said.

"Jimmy Hoffa and D. B. Cooper," Margaret said.

"The career of John Anderson," Neil added, and people laughed.

After agreeing they had no idea how the skeletons had gotten there, or when, or what it all meant, the crowd finally went to bed one by one. Neil walked back up to the cabins with Beth, and said good-bye to her at the garden gate, then took a shower and changed into his sweatpants. After watching a little TV, he went to bed.

Neil lay on his mattress for over an hour, unable to sleep for a kind of nervousness and tension he had not experienced in years. He stared at the darkened walls, a bar of moonlight streaking the wood, and came to convince himself that the skeletons were a good sign somehow, a signal of some door opening onto a new and exciting phase of his existence. Whenever something strange happened, whenever anything got made that did not have to be made, it was like a victory retrieved from the inexorable white-out of time. He had felt that way since he was a child. Neil tossed and turned, thinking about his future and how things might actually work out someday if he really put his mind to it.

He thought about recording a new album, and renting out some of his sound equipment for spare money, even about leaving the ranch for a while to do some traveling, the freedom he could still have if he really wanted it. For the first time in ages he felt like things were coming into some kind of alignment again, like some pinhole was opening and he was starting to see light. He was almost giddy with optimism, like everything might float away at once, and converge somewhere high in the air, and everyone he had ever known would meet each other and fall in love. But then he always felt like that around this time of year. The late summer was his time of great optimism. He just never remembered it one season to the next.

# 4

E VER SINCE JOINING with the fur party at Fort Hall, after a meandering journey from the East going from job to job and camp to camp, Cookie had been amassing a sketchbook filled with clumsy pictures of the things he had seen along the way. There were sketches of saguaro cacti, weeping willows, hedgehogs and bison, fir trees, and furry brown stalks rising from the tufts of sword fern, drooping back down on themselves like melted question marks. There were vistas of rolling prairie grass, with tipis and wigwams, and even an attempt to capture a moonlight dust storm in the desert, which had looked like a procession of ghostly elephants moving across the plains in slow, underwater motion.

Cookie sat on a stump turning the oatmeal-colored pages, with a charcoal pencil clamped in his teeth. At the beginning he found a newspaper clipping ripped from the *Boston Herald,* a full-page advertisement for the enticements of the Oregon Territory. "Second Eden," it said in blocky letters, and went on to describe a land of infinite promise, full of fresh water and fertile soil crying out for men to come claim it. He remembered vividly the day he had torn it out, the throng of men all around him, the rattle of the carriages sweeping by. The last four coins in his pocket and the ripped seam on his shoe. The door that had just closed, and the words of the thin waiter still hanging in the air: no work, fella.

Cookie looked over the pictures he had drawn since crossing the Cascades. Heavy clouds grinding over the trees, stumps melting into the earth, wet shadows hiding slick toadstools and rotting plants. Oregon was not the land he had imagined it to be at all, he now realized. Oregon was not new, in fact, but incredibly old, and full of eerie gloom. It was rough-hewn and arctic, as if some glacier had only just receded and left the earth thawing from the ice. Oregon was a scene of patient, unceasing violence to itself, Cookie thought, and the idea of carving something from it seemed almost insane; a world of mold and lichens and mildew stood waiting to drag anything down before it was even begun.

Cookie had never thought he would miss the city before, all the people that had somehow added up to no one at all. But now, having spent some time on the road, he was not so sure. Rumor had it that Lewis and Clark had named their final campsite Cape Disappointment.

Cookie lifted his eyes from his book to map the layout of the camp, hoping that no one was approaching. He had been sitting outside all morning, reviewing his pictures, and listening to Henry snore loudly through the canvas bonnet of the gravy train. Whenever someone walked nearby, he whistled innocently to cover up the sawing noise, but it was only a matter of time before someone figured him out, at which point there would be questions to answer, and actions to explain, and suspicion heaped on abuse heaped on disrespect.

Across the clearing, near the remains of the fire, the commander was talking to an officer from a different company whom Cookie had never seen before. He could not hear what the men were saying, but the exchange appeared formal, inasmuch as a meeting between two trappers in the woods could be. The other officer wore a tricornered hat, and epaulets on his fringed leather jacket to mark his position in a line of command that was otherwise fairly indistinct.

Cookie's commander, wearing a dirty cravat the color of an apricot that was half buried in the folds of his unshaven neck, leaned on a rusting fencing sword, which bent a little beneath his weight. He shook his head and said something, and the visiting officer nodded with his hand on his waist. Then the roles reversed, and Cookie's commander stood still while the officer spoke. This went on, back and forth, until finally the visiting officer saluted and turned on his heel, mounting his horse and disappearing into the leafy scrim of trees.

The second in command approached the commander and they stood beside each other, nodding sporadically and gazing at the pocked surfaces of a damp rock. Cookie pretended to stare into the white plane of the sky above them, and pretty soon he actually was. What little light got through the clouds was caught by the boughs of the fir trees, leaving just a few feeble rays to disperse in the misty air. It was as if light came here to die.

Suddenly Cookie heard a snort inside the wagon, and a thump, and the regular in-and-out of the snoring stopped. He heard a wet cough, followed by a tense silence that seemed to call out his name to come look.

Cookie put his sketchbook aside and went unhurriedly to the rear of the gravy train, climbing up the spokes and into the bonnet, past the ladles and knives hanging from tacks and the empty baskets clinging to the wall. His feet clomped over the wagon floor, and when he stretched his head over the makeshift wall of boxes, there was Henry, blinking his eyes and picking a crust of dried sleep from the corner of his lashes.

The two men looked at each other calmly. The air was dank with the smell of sleep, all the oils and gasses expelled from a man's body at rest. Cookie let his stowaway piece together his situation for another moment before breaking the silence.

"A captain is here," Cookie said. "Talking to the commander."

"With a long mustache? Kinda like a dousing rod?"

"Yes."

"He's searchin for me," Henry said, and for a moment, in the quiet of the hidden place, separated from the world by a thin canvas draped over an armature of wood, the two men were all alive to each other. Cookie gazed straight into his stowaway's eyes, blue flecked with splinters of gray, and his stowaway stared back into his own.

Cookie sat down on an empty pickle barrel, and passed Henry a handful of berries, which he had scavenged from a bush that morning, and after drinking two mugs of water poured from a calfskin bladder, Henry seemed to relax. He looked over the clothes he was wearing,

43

examined the canvas rooftop above him, and stretched his arms and legs to get the blood to the far ends of his body. He seemed uncertain at first, but slowly he settled in to talking, and once he got going, it was hard to get him to stop.

"I suppose I got some explaining to do," he said, propping himself up on his elbow and popping a berry onto his tongue, which he squashed on the roof of his mouth. "Reason I snuck up on you like that in the woods. Wish't I knew where to begin, though. I don't even know where the story starts anymore."

"Start anywhere," Cookie urged. "The beginning."

"Well, I can start with my name, I suppose," Henry mumbled, his mouth full of berries. "It's Henry Brown, from the state of Ohio." He reached out and clasped Cookie's hand and gave it a hard squeeze.

"What's today?" he asked.

Cookie shrugged. It could be Monday, or Wednesday, of late September or early October, he had lost track.

"Well, doesn't matter much. I've been living out here in the Far Corner for about seven years now, in close neighborhood to these parts. I guess you'd say the Oregon country's my home, although it's changed plenty since I got here. More and more of you trappers and traders coming in, setting up camp. Won't be the same place much longer."

"Is that so," Cookie said.

"I'll say. But that's a whole other issue." He rolled a berry on his tongue and crushed it. "Few nights ago—excuse me for chewin here—I was on my way to a potlatch hosted by my old buddy Long Neck. He's a Chinook. Greatest fella you ever met. Got a lodge on the banks of the Columbia, a couple wives, a slave or two, but he treats them more like family. When he throws a party everyone goes. I'll tell you what. He sets out all his food and belongings and we come eat and drink him out of house and home, all his salmon and roots and hazelnuts. He gives it all away, because next year he figures other people will do the same, and he'll get most everything back.

To me it's a crazy way to live, but that's how they do it out here.

"Anyhow, I was all dressed up, wearing my best moccasins, my cedar-bark hat," he gestured around his head in circles. "I got there to Long Neck's and the table was loaded down with smoked fish, venison. The best viands an Indian can make. It was a big to-do. People dancin, and talkin, and drinkin a pipe of wine. Some elbow relations had come down from Nootka Bay up north and we watched a play they put on—actors in wooden masks with big nostrils and almond eyes, and hollow kelp stems to throw their voices with. It was something else."

Footsteps passed outside the wagon and the men hushed. Henry did not seem afraid of getting caught anymore, though, and took the opportunity to swallow some more berries.

"When the play was over," he went on, "we all just sat there, watching the flames, the sparks rising up in the air, and after awhile I stepped into the forest to relieve myself. I remember I slapped my pal Long Neck on the shoulders and caught his eye, but he was pretty well over the bay. I went on into the woods, and I was standing there against a tree when lickety-split everything went wild. All around me there was crashes and cries. Heavy footsteps and exploding sounds. Men yelling.

"I looked out from the leaves and the potlatch was overrun with white men, stamping through the fire and waving their guns. They came through there hammer and tongs, bayonets thicker'n hatchel teeth, wearing fur robes and tow shirts, black boots on their feet. They were firing their pistols, slashing with their bayonets, pushing everyone onto the ground and making them lie still. I watched it all from my covert. Judging from the habiliments I thought they was Russians, and the way they talked confirmed it. They went straight for Long Neck and grabbed him by the hair. Yankin him over this way, yankin him that way. They were saying he stole a horse, and they wanted to make a big impression. They stood there with the fire underneath 'em, holding Long Neck, yelling and screaming about this horse they lost, and how no one messed with their property, not Chinooks, not Flatheads, not

45

no one. And let me tell you, no way he stole a horse. He might gull you sometimes, play a little trick, but he's no thief. And even if he was, too bad. Then they gutted him from neck to loin, just like that, and there's no good reason for that."

Henry ran his hands through his hair. He was shaking with emotion.

"The Chinook are the purest blood Indians on the river, on any river for hundreds of miles from here. There's just no reason to do something like that.

"Well," he went on, "I had a flintlock pistol in my belt and when these fellas started retreating into the bush, I just couldn't take it. I fired right at 'em. Eye for an eye, I'm sayin. I saw the lead clip one of 'em on the neck and then I took off. I took off as fast as I could. They came chasing after me and I kept running. I ran down a gully, over a creek. I don't remember how long I ran, but when I stopped, I was all by myself again. I'd lost them but my mind was still racing like crazy, slipping from one thing to the next. The killing just kept coming back to me. I saw it every time I blinked my eyes. Long Neck standin there and then the knife cutting down his belly. I was lost, and I'll tell you, I started to lose my grip. The forest turned all strange on me, like it was chafing against my skin, the rubber of the maple leaf, the silk of the cedar bark. All of it was pressing in. I didn't know where to turn. You felt like that before? Well it's not a pretty feeling, is it? I felt like everything was falling apart. I took my clothes off piece by piece and stuffed them in hollow trees, trying to put it all behind me. And pretty soon after that I ran into you."

Footsteps again walked near the wagon and the men quieted. Henry stared at the ceiling and Cookie stared at Henry, whose eyes were dark and glistening.

"I don't think I ever got to tell old Long Neck how much I liked him, Cookie. I hope he knew it somehow. I hope old Long Neck got me."

Cookie found himself nodding slowly. "He did, Henry. I'm sure."

Henry choked something down. "Thanks, Cookie. That's the right thing to say."

"You stay here," Cookie finally said, and rose to his feet. It was time to locate the company's lunch. The berries were gone now, and the men would be getting hungry soon. He had plenty to think about in the meantime.

Before he left, Henry spoke up in a whisper once more, "I know you're risking your skin to keep me here, friend. I meant to thank you for that. It's really something. I mean it."

The men gathered around the fire with their plates in hand, jostling each other and pushing from the rear. They reached toward Cookie, making excited noises, their leathery faces gleaming with sweat. Today each man received a small portion of quail eggs, which had been stolen from a nest inside a pile of wood, then cooked with gray mushrooms picked from the basin of a fir tree, and seasoned with rosemary and salt. Although they grumbled at the size of their helpings, they all agreed that the omelette was delicious.

After cleaning the dishes, Cookie spoke to the commander about the company's course of travel that day. Having talked it over with Henry, who knew the land as well as anyone, he made the case that the best path to follow would be alongside the creek at the base of the cliff. Their fur party, he reasoned, was aiming to reach Fort Vancouver, which was located at the axis of the Columbia and Willamette rivers; the creek below them, as modest as it appeared, likely served as a tributary to one of those rivers; thus, to follow its course would eventually bring them to Fort Vancouver. The commander slowly came around to this course of logic, though clearly he had never considered it before, which spoke volumes to Cookie on the meandering progress of the wagon train so far.

The day's journey took them only a matter of yards closer to their goal. Instead of cutting their trail by the lay of the land, they took the most direct route, right down a hillside toward the water, and the steep terrain proved difficult to navigate. At various points they were forced to break out the winches and levers to make their way down without cracking everything apart, and during a particularly steep grade, they had to reverse the pack animals from in front of their loads to behind them. When a wheel broke, it delayed them for almost two hours.

They reached the creek with a few hours of daylight remaining, and started downstream. Their progress somewhat increased, but remained slow due to the men's hunger and the smooth, clattering surface of the river rocks underfoot. Along the way, Cookie managed to capture a handful of crawdads using a butterfly net. Grilled with a bouquet of wild garlic presented to him by one of the men and served with a small garnish of miner's lettuce, they rendered another modest yet well-received meal at sunset.

Feeding an extra man was a hardship, but Cookie made sure to keep a plateful of supper for Henry, who gratefully devoured it in his private cell. They kept quiet while he ate, and when he was finished, he told Cookie that he would get out of his hair as quickly as possible. He was still afraid of running across the company of Russians, but he promised that as soon as they reached the Columbia, he would swim across to British territory, where whatever crime he had committed would have no legal ramification, and where it was doubtful the Russians would follow him anyway, as they generally kept to the realm of the Northwest Company, not the Hudson's Bay. Cookie urged him not to worry, told him that he was no burden at all, and more than that, he meant it. The secret of Henry's presence in the gravy train was actually helpful in some way. It gave him something to turn over in the back of his mind while the other men ignored him or told him to move out of the way, and generally led him through the day in better spirits. It took his mind off the hunger, too. But Henry was adamant. He would leave when they reached the river.

The next morning there was no meal at all. The last of the food was gone, and the men shuffled about the gravy train despondently. They blamed Cookie, although it was not his fault, and to make matters worse, the commander was beginning to doubt the idea of following the creek. Cookie could tell he was looking for other trails to blaze, the way he kept walking off into the trees to check for folds and pockets in the land.

By noon the daylight had dried away the dewy shadows and the hunger was working inside the men like a machine. By mid afternoon it was slowing the progress of the very sun itself, enlarging every gnawing moment under a magnifying lens. Cookie kept his eyes out for crawdads, or carrot shoots, or marionberry bushes, but nothing presented itself. The creek was empty of any edible life, and the plants that grew along its sides were just brambles. The men fought each other for milk grass when it appeared, plucking the shoots with their thick hands and gnawing the drop of pulpy nectar from the hairline barrel.

Conversation dwindled and ceased, and the dawning realization of their plight made silent, worried glances go around. Some men faced the hunger with stern resolve, some with glimmers of fear. Others were too young or too ignorant to recognize the dire situation at all. They saw only healthy men around them, plodding animals, wagons of valuable fur, and were unable to conceive the thin tissue that separated them from the cold vacuum of something worse. The second in command scowled at the surrounding landscape, and at one point strode purposefully for the food wagon, hoping to find something there that Cookie had overlooked. Cookie intercepted him at the wagon's bonnet while he worked to untie the strapping, and the two men shared a long, significant stare. Eventually, the second in command lowered his eyes and murmured something, then moved away.

As the day's end grew around them, the men began surveying the land for campsites. Soon enough, a suitable clearing came into view and the corps silently began moving toward it. It was a rocky meadow, tufted with dried long grass and riddled with medium-size rocks. They started to set up camp, clearing space for the tents, and watering down the horses off to the side. During breaks in the unpacking, Cookie could hear a soft, crackling hiss in the air, like the sound of a woman brushing her hair. He lifted his chin to get a better fix on it.

The second in command heard something as well. He whistled sharply and waved his hands for the men to stand still and be quiet, and then he walked up a slope, cupping his hand to his ear. The men followed behind, stepping lightly on the pebbles and weeds, as the light continued to thin around them. They crept forward until the sound was unmistakable—rushing water, lots of it, like a crowd cheering for them in the distance.

On the top of the hill the Columbia River appeared. It was too big to be anything else, its rolling current licked with frothy whitecaps, bobbing like a sheet stretched over the flexing bodies of a thousand wrestling men. From shore to shore it measured the length of a rifle shot, and on the opposite bank rose an implacable forest of stately evergreens, matching the one they had just emerged from. Below was a rocky beachfront, where massive boulders piled on top of each other, guarding a narrow strip of sand. The men began whooping and calling out, and Cookie joined them. As the whooping continued, he realized the full extent of the celebration. Just beneath the glazed surface, the river was clogged with salmon, struggling toward their spawning grounds in the freshwater creeks and streams of the Columbia's headwaters. They darted and flashed and slid against each other in their race to the source. A stream of silver, single-minded life. A continuous plane of edible flesh. The men hollered and embraced each other, and even the second in command allowed himself a wry smile.

Immediately, Cookie made his way down to the bank with his butterfly net and waded into the rushing water. He could feel fish bumping against his knees and shins and lowered the net until a silvery body entered its ring, bucking and twisting. He raised it into the air and flecks of water showered his face.

Cookie returned to the water again and again, until he had assembled a handsome pile of flopping salmon, their scales gleaming in the moonlight. They were old fish, beaten and bruised, a little reddish around the gills, but each one was meaty and heavy in Cookie's hands. He set about cleaning them with his knife, which slid easily into each body's tender flesh, and he felt the nick of their bones through its metal. As each fish split open it exuded a fresh scent and a deep pink flash of coloring. Cookie formed a circle of rocks up on the bluff and built a fire. Soon enough, the first of the meat was sizzling on the pan.

In moments it would begin to flake, and white rivulets of fatty fluid would begin dripping from its side.

Cookie looked out over the river. The roaring sound of the current was soothing and the smell of the water was cool and clean. Jumping salmon made tiny stitches of motion.

Toward the middle of the river Cookie caught sight of a lone figure, swimming hard for the opposite bank. Henry was slowly receding into the distance, moving forward and sideways on his path to freedom. Cookie watched him go, and for a moment felt some cold iron press in on his heart. He wished time could run backward for a moment, and change itself on the next roll around. He wished for Henry to return already.

"Good-bye, Henry," he said under his breath, and returned to the wagon for some utensils and plates, and most of all for his triangle, which he intended to clang as loudly as he could. He overturned boxes and shook empty bags, searched the drawers and the cooking pots, but he could not find it anywhere. Perhaps the triangle was hanging on a branch somewhere, he thought, or hidden in a shrub. He could not remember. He would have to get a new one at Fort Vancouver, where they had almost everything, he was told.

Cookie did, however, find a gift from Henry resting on the blade of the butcher knife, which glowed when he passed the candle nearby. It was his amber ring, a thick, imperfect hoop the color of maple syrup, carved from a single block of ancient sap. Cookie lifted it to the light and turned it between his thumb and forefinger. Tiny oxygen bubbles were trapped inside, and also the body of a miniscule firefly, perfectly preserved except for one of its legs, which was detached and floating nearby. The bubbles caught the light when Cookie held the ring up to the flame, and he slipped it on his finger, twisting it with his thumb until he found the proper fit.

He emerged from the wagon to find the men already beginning to gather around, lured by the smell of the frying fish. Cookie balanced himself on the jockey box and a horizontal spoke of the wheel, pulling a long wooden spoon from his back pocket, which he began banging against the walls of a cheese grater. The sound it made was nothing like the rich peal of the triangle, just a rattling, tinny clatter, but it was enough to get the men to pause a moment, and look up, and finally to roar loudly in response. Cookie raised the grater higher and banged the walls some more, and the men raised their hands and cheered in return, then pressed in to collect their forks and plates. Cookie leaped from the wagon and squeezed his way through the crowd, hands tousling his hair and pinching his arms. When he got to the frying pan he made the men line up in single file, first come, first served. There was plenty for everyone tonight, and for once they might as well be civilized about it.

# 5

**D**URING HER FIRST two weeks on Neil's property, Tina ran into Trixie Volterra a total of three times, each time speaking to her as briefly as possible before scurrying away to test the meeting for soft spots. The topics of their exchanges were utterly innocuous. On one occasion they commented on the smell of some stir-fry while passing each other on the path—"Smells good," Tina said—and on another they raised their eyebrows when a gear grinded loudly in the parking lot. The third exchange was about the weather. But the brevity of the conversations did not stop Tina from judging them, and parsing every bit of meaning from them that she could, and laying awake for long hours afterward, replaying every miniscule gesture in her mind, and marking off the comments she was proud of and those that she might regret.

Tina found immediate reasons to dislike Trixie. Her shoes were too trendy, her hair was too blond, she seemed overly excited by other people's attention. Tina kept track of Trixie's minor infractions, and felt the contours of Trixie's personality reshape themselves with every new tidbit of information. Trixie read books in public, she sang out loud while listening to her headphones, she wore the same clothes sometimes three days in a row, all of which were subtle marks against her. Tina grew to hate Trixie over the course of her first week in Oregon, and then forgave her entirely when she saw her petting a cat, and then started hating her again when she cheered stupidly during a footrace between Peter and Bob.

Within two weeks, the girls had arrived at a silent crossroads, one path leading into a policy of avoidance and disinterest, the other timidly into friendship. It appeared the latter course would be taken. On their fourth encounter they had made a formalized date to hang out, set to begin in exactly ten minutes.

Tina hurriedly took off her sweatshirt, and put on her black lacy dress with the stovepipe sleeves, this time with a pair of ripped stockings and a black headband. She slipped on her pointy-toed pumps, then traded them for her black ankle boots with the zippers along the side. As there was no full-length mirror in the cabin, she had to go into the bathroom and look at herself in the small one above the sink, where she had to stand on tiptoe and crane her neck to get a view of her whole body at once, and even then was unable to gauge how her hemline draped over the top part of her shoes.

Tina stepped back and looked straight into her face, which was never a great pleasure or surprise. She had large pores on her nose, and tiny hairs above her lips, thick eyebrows that reached toward each other over the bridge of her nose. Her puffy cheeks were the color of a pale cauliflower, tufted in blond fuzz, and her eyes were muddy brown, like her hair, which was entirely shapeless.

Tina kept moving her face around until she found the angle where she was a little bit pretty, and put on some dark purple lipstick. She drew tiny lines with a mascara pencil on her eyelids and shook her hair out into a frizzy mess and patted it back down. Sometimes, when she was getting dressed, she could not tell whether she was putting on a disguise or wrapping herself up like a birthday present.

If worse came to worst, she thought, she would simply bore the girl to death. She would become the most boring person imaginable simply to avoid her.

When the knock on the door finally came, a tiny gush of acid released in Tina's stomach. She was more nervous than she had thought. She walked into the front room to find Trixie standing behind the screen door, raising her open hand to the mesh and shading her eyes to peer inside. Tina paused near the couch a moment and watched her searching the room.

Trixie wore an oversized pink-and-white jail-stripe blouse, with a thin, white, studded belt wrapped twice around her waist, and pegged blue jeans neatly ripped at the knee. Innumerable plastic bracelets clattered on her lithe wrist, and on her feet were a pair of beat-up pink jellies, little molded baskets of plastic. Her hair was done up into a shellacked-looking hive sprinkled in glitter.

By now Tina had reverted to her normal jeans and black T-shirt, and felt a little underdressed.

"Hi," Trixie said through the screen, catching sight of Tina in the shadows.

"Hi," Tina said, and a second later, just like that, they were walking down the dirt path together, talking about movies they had both seen of late, *The Omega Man* and *The Boys from Brazil* primarily.

"*Omega Man* was good," Trixie said, "but the zombies were really fake."

"Corny," Tina agreed, "but the city was cool."

"You thought?"

"I don't know."

They walked past cabins with porches and sunroofs and breakfast nooks, customized from their basic shoebox format into slight variations on a theme, and past some benches made of carved cedar below a macramé fort spun inside the limbs of an oak tree. Tina worked to catch glimpses of Trixie from the corners of her eyes, when the moment allowed, but it was difficult without appearing too eager. She noted that Trixie's head bobbed a little bit like a chicken, and that she habitually kicked at rocks. Tina quickly came to realize that the affected stride was a kind of swagger.

"*Omega Man* was not as good as *Soylent Green*," Trixie declared with an air of knowing dismissal. She sounded like she was holding something back, or saving her better parts for something else. Her voice was deeper than Tina had expected, scratchy somewhere in the back of her throat.

"No," Tina agreed, happy to follow the subject of movies, and the weak deception of good manners it allowed. "So, what else have you liked?"

"Well." Trixie thought about it a moment. "*Nashville,* I guess, *All*

*About Eve,* anything with Robert Mitchum." The same list of art movies that had passed through San Francisco over the last year. Overall, it was a list that Tina could approve of.

"*Carnal Knowledge,*" Trixie added, "Garfunkel was fucking amazing." Tina hummed in agreement.

Just then Bob Grossberger emerged from his cabin and waved at them, wearing only a golden loincloth and holding a yoga mat under his arm. His shoulders were tufted with black hair and his chest hair formed the shape of a mushroom cloud.

"No way," Trixie moaned brightly, averting her eyes. A musical tone of sarcasm entered her voice. "No fucking way." Tina caught her liquid glance.

When Trixie spoke again there was something different in her voice, something deep and breathy and unfocused.

"Girls," she said into the air, "could you please rub my fifth chakra, please? Really aching badly today. I would deeply appreciate the compassionate attention."

Tina started laughing. Trixie had become Bob Grossberger perfectly.

"Be Here Now," Trixie said, rubbing on her groin.

"Oh my God," Tina said, "that's really good."

Trixie smelled faintly of baby powder.

The girls walked until the cabins ended and were replaced by mountain hemlock and black twinberry, and then down to the loamy edge of the marsh, where they found a pathway into the woods and walked up alongside a gully carpeted with moss covering lumps and masses like hidden toys. From an outcropping of rock they could see the marsh, sleepy and sweet with marigold, and the first pause came over their acquaintance, a chasm that seemed to take on a palpable heft. The silence held between them for a long countdown, as both of them shuttled through their minds for something new to say.

"Bog," Trixie finally said out loud, as if the word itself was something funny enough to share. A squirrel scampered in a tree nearby. Its body made a wavelike motion.

"Gob," Tina answered back, after a while.

"Cob," Trixie said.

"B'Gog."

And it went on, until they began to feel like boys. Trixie made her voice deepen, and turn stupid, and Tina followed, and they both recognized the first hurdle had been crossed, they were collaborating on something now. "Big Bog," "Bog Cob," "Bog Cobbler." They could not seem to stop.

They both found walking sticks. Trixie's was slim and canelike, and good for swiping at branches and tall grass, while Tina's was bigger, more warlock-ish, they agreed, and made for a statelier gait.

"So how are you liking it?" Trixie asked, as they headed up into the trees, by which she meant Oregon in general.

"OK," Tina said, waiting for Trixie to press her a little more. She wanted one more stroke of interest before revealing anything of much importance.

"So why'd you come up here?" Trixie asked, and Tina told her the story of her mother's career, and her recent bout of unemployment due to Ronald Reagan's energy policy, and how the rents in California had become so extreme.

"It was either come up to Oregon or move into my grandma's house," she said. "My dad's out of the picture."

"Huh." Trixie said. Tina waited for more questions, but none came, and she found herself turning the conversation back on Trixie, although she still had things to tell.

"How about you? Have you been up here a long time?"

"About a year, yeah. I was born down in California, too. In the desert between Palm Springs and Phoenix. We lived in this stucco shack where my dad was building a kiln, way out there in the desert. No electricity, no water. But it was funny, though. Our nearest neighbor was Bob Denver—you know him? The guy who played Gilligan? He was hilarious. He lived like this bedouin prince in a tent out in the desert, filled up with throw pillows and a nine-stemmed hookah. Swear to God. My dad used to hang out with him all the time."

They came to a point where they could see the neighboring hilltops, and Trixie explained that the land surrounding the property had once been dotted with communes like their own.

"Up there was Cool Ranch," she said, pointing to a hump of fir trees, "and over there was Cloudburst, and up on the ridge was Rainbowville. All of them broke up or lost their lease, though. Or just lost it in the seventies. 'What a long, strange trip,' or whatever." She kinked her fingers in the air.

Trixie explained how the people from Portland tended to stick to themselves, and the ones from elsewhere to theirs. The ones doing each other were Amy and Bill, Susan and Julie, James and Patty, and James and Gwyneth. Bob Grossberger was a closet case and Beth Bowler was frigid.

"Oh, man. I don't want to think about that," Tina said.

"Totally," Trixie said. "Too gross."

"Neil owns the land," Trixie moved on, "so he's technically in charge, but everyone kind of hates him for it on some level."

"Oh yeah?" Tina said.

"Yeah. I'd say so," she said, swiping at a patch of dry grass. "He's too lucky. He takes too good a care of himself. You know what I mean? They owe him something and he won't let them pay it back."

To be loved you have to show weakness sometimes, Tina extrapolated. It is the flaws that people love. She would have to think about that later.

The girls pushed on through a bramble of blackberries and skirted an old, mealy snag covered in termite holes, and then went back and rocked it back and forth until it snapped. The spongy wood broke apart into tiny crumbs, and they watched the termites scurry across the leafy ground. Trixie crouched close down and poked at the bugs with a stick and they got onto the topic of Latin America, and how desolate it was because of the United States' foreign policy. On this topic Tina had plenty of opinions, she read *The Nation,* and Trixie nodded along as if her knowledge were indisputable.

"That's true," Trixie said, "I hadn't thought of that before. Absolutely."

They pushed at the dirt and rerouted the nimble ants in one direction and then another, while Tina told Trixie about the time she and her mother had visited Guatemala, and how the Guatemalan bus drivers drove through pitch-black mountain roads without any headlights, in buses filled with chickens and hogs.

"Oh my God," Trixie said. "That's totally insane."

Tina decided to save her story about climbing an active volcano outside Guatemala City for later, though. She did not want to give everything away at one time. She felt like Trixie was a customer walking through the aisles of a store and she was the store.

"Have you been to the development yet?" Trixie asked abruptly, and when Tina shook her head, Trixie rose to her feet and said, "Let's go."

At the edge of the property the forest fell away and the hills turned into a barren landscape of empty cul-de-sacs and vacant lots, with half-built houses rising from the blighted ground, their blond wood shiny in the sunlight. The dust was covered in footprints and trampled weeds and the cursive script of tire tread. Trixie kicked a No Trespassing sign as she walked past it, and Tina followed her lead, throwing a dirt clod at a wooden sign that said "Windsor Terrace." They walked past an empty foundation with a ladder sticking out, and stepped along a series of boards laid out in a row like piano keys. A cube of stacked boards was hidden beneath a black tarp, which crinkled in the breeze; a green rubber hose lay coiled into knots.

They talked about movies some more while they picked things up and threw them back down. Trixie liked *The Big Sleep* and most things by Alan Pakula. They disagreed on Warren Oates, whom Tina would watch in anything and Trixie found indifferent, and then Trixie talked about *Husbands,* by John Cassavetes, and the dim failure it represented compared to his other movies. Tina halfheartedly pretended she had seen it before and was simply having trouble remembering certain of its crucial scenes, to the point where she almost began to believe she had seen it.

They walked into one of the framed-up houses, and went from room to room, watching each other through the unfinished walls. Trixie had green eyes, and pink skin, and her tall hairdo was beginning to unravel a bit, strokes of golden hair flashing around her neck and cheeks. "These fucking jellies are the worst," she complained, and daintily shook her foot to adjust the fit. They stepped over bands of copper and bundled tufts of insulation, and listened to echoes of different things hitting wood. Tina kicked a plastic bag filled with bolts and screws. Trixie pulled a ream of silver-skinned insulation from the wall.

The girls arrived in a kitchen, with brand new cabinets, and rolls of linoleum sitting on the floor. The sink was a dull gray color, with bits of sawdust coating the basin, and its pipes were not yet hooked up.

Trixie jumped up on the countertop and pressed her hands against the ceiling. "You know what would be a good movie?" she said.

"What?" Tina said, and slammed a cupboard, dampening down the critical part of her brain in advance.

"Just an idea," Trixie said, "but a movie about a woman in her house, just doing things that people normally do. Cleaning, and cooking, and watering plants. But like a science fiction movie. Really weird and slow."

"Cool," Tina said, although she did not think it was all that cool.

"The camera could just follow this woman around, you know, really slowly, and all the surfaces of the house could seem almost radioactive. Really dark shadows, and the woman doing really simple actions. It would be scary. I've seen art movies like that, where almost nothing happens."

"Yeah," Tina said, beginning to see it. "I want to do a movie, too. A prison movie." She had seen a documentary about prisons recently on PBS.

"Oh yeah?" Trixie asked.

"Yeah. It would just be women talking to each other, and eating, and exercising in the yard. But they would communicate with each other at night down the hallways using little shards of mirror," she said. "That's how they do it. That's how the prisoners communicate."

"God, that would be great," Trixie said jumping down from the counter. They both wanted prison scenes, that they could agree upon. As they talked longer, their movies became one movie.

They left the kitchen and walked upstairs, where a small, glass chandelier had been installed in the bedroom ceiling and tiny seeds of light glinted on its crystals. An empty window frame looked out onto the cul-de-sacs and vacant lots. From above, the streets looked like a child's maze, simple and serpentine. The girls stood side by side at the empty window and smoked a Camel Light from Trixie's pocket as a yellow pickup truck moved toward them through the streets, creeping slowly past the construction sites. It stopped sometimes, and waited for something, and then crept forward again. The girls watched it like a fly on a windowpane. Slowly, it was getting closer.

"That's Larry," Trixie said. "He guards the place. He's a total dick."

The truck edged forward and Trixie deepened her voice again.

"Uhh. Trixie?" Tina gathered it was Larry speaking. "Uhh. You know you shouldn't do that. Uhhh. Does your father know you smoke those things?"

"Yeah, Larry," Trixie answered as herself. "He gave them to me. He's a Parliament man. He likes it real smooth."

"Uhh. Uhh. Smooth, eh? Heh. How old are you, Trixie?" Trixie's eyes had gone glassy and her head had sunk toward her chest.

Suddenly Bob Grossberger chimed in: "Larry. Goodness gracious, Larry. Look at you. Your chakras need attention. You should never let them get so clogged up like that. They're just asking for a release. Let me take care of that for you right now. Come here, Larry. I visited the bushmen of the Amazon rain basin last year? And they taught me some wonderful ancient techniques on releasing the downtown chi." She half started to laugh, taking gulps of air.

"Uhh. Bobby?" Larry returned. "Uhh. My chakra down there is doing okay, I think. No need to knock yourself out. I'm, uh, uh. Hey

61

now, not so bad." She was laughing uncontrollably now, and Tina joined in. "Downtown chi," she gasped.

The truck was getting close enough that the girls could hear its engine rattling, and see the rust spots on its hood and roof. The man in the driver's seat had a mustache and a flannel shirt. He peered out the windshield at each unfinished house, like it might be on some kind of invisible fire.

Soon the yellow truck had stopped in front of their house, and the girls crouched down to hide. They heard a car door slam and they kept very still, listening to each other breathing until their knees began to cramp. Finally Trixie lifted herself to the window and glanced outside.

"He's coming," she whispered, and the girls walked briskly from the room. They stamped down the stairs and ran through the empty walls of the dining room. When they reached the back door they jumped into the dirt yard—there were no stairs yet—and ran for the woods.

"These shoes fucking suck!" Trixie said, but she kept going. The Scotch broom streaked behind her. As they ran they heard a man yell "Hey!" but they did not look back.

The girls ran down a deer run, through clumps of riburnum and saxifrage, until they emerged on a cliff with a huge chestnut tree gripping the ledge like a clenched fist. Tina caught her breath in its shade and realized that she was utterly lost, she had no idea what direction she was facing. She had followed Trixie blindly through the woods, and now she was floating in space.

"Here we are," Trixie said, and Tina shook her head while sucking in air.

When she looked up, however, everything became clear. She felt her mental map crystallize. All the little pieces she had been outlining since arriving in Oregon suddenly knit together, unfurling in a full, comprehensive grid of the property.

Directly below her, at the base of the cliff, was the creek, swirling and eddying and catching the sunlight in metallic glints. Green algae clung to the rocks, breathing in the current, and wide, white rocks formed islands in the middle. Low brush hung over the banks, and upstream a little way, the water became molten with sunlight, running past the crumbling brick chimney of an old foundry, its gaping mouth rimmed in rusted iron. Behind it, past some trees, rose the parking lot, lined with scalding cars.

Across the creek stood all the cabins and the garden, connected by the beige pathways, where various adults wandered about doing their chores. Tina could hear their voices, detached from their little bodies, and sometimes the distant crack of a slamming door. The sounds were indistinct, and seemingly unrelated to the movements of the colorful blobs.

Far in the distance, over a ridge of fir trees, the peak of Mount St. Helen's shimmered against the blue sky, accompanied by a huge, cathedral-sized white cloud.

"I saw it blow up," Trixie said. "Last year. It was incredible. It rained ash for weeks."

"Shit," Tina said.

"It used to look like an ice-cream cone," Trixie added, "but now it's all scooped out like that."

Trixie handed Tina another cigarette, then reached toward her with a lighter. Tina's cigarette glowed red, and Trixie lit her own.

"Come on," she said, "I'll show you something," and she began climbing the chestnut tree with her cigarette clamped in her teeth. Tina followed her, grasping the branches that Trixie grasped, and placing her feet in the footholds that Trixie did.

"It's good," Trixie said over her shoulder, regarding whatever they were climbing toward.

"I believe you," Tina said, but it got lost in the sounds of climbing. Flakes of lichen and dirt rained down on her head.

As they went higher a hump of hills came into view, covered in wild vetch and redtop and velvet grass, and on the far side a row of new corporate offices gleaming like shrink-wrapped boxes, and behind them the Gothic vaults of the St. John Bridge. The leaves framed a panoramic picture of the whole countryside, and Tina's eyes wandered over the scene, from the mountain to the corporate park to the bridge sparkling with indecipherable cars. Trixie climbed higher, until the marsh became a brownish, silvery expanse, filled with sticks of trees and plants, and in open patches the reflections of the sky overhead.

They kept going until they were hanging out over the creek, where the branches got smaller, and the way more treacherous, but Trixie seemed comfortable with every step. Tina refrained from looking down, feeling the pull of gravity when she moved her hand from one spot to another, forcing herself to stick her foot in each new fork of wood.

"Come on," Trixie said. "This is it."

Trixie moved out of the way and Tina pulled herself up beside her. Hanging on a branch above them was a metal triangle, its surface covered in orange rust. The chain that held it had long ago been absorbed into the tree's thickening flesh to make a pronounced cleft, like a wire cutting through clay. When Tina tapped it it spun in the air, and tiny shadows burrowed into its skin's smallest crevices.

"It grew all the way up here," Trixie said, "with the tree."

Tina stared at the triangle awhile. "Wow," she said. After sitting silently for a minute, they both began talking at once.

"You go," Tina said.

"No, you go," Trixie replied.

Both of them had ideas for more movies to make. Tina wanted a costume drama set in nineteenth-century Philadelphia, the weirdest place she could imagine, and Trixie wanted a movie about a love affair between a doctor and a patient.

While they talked, a flock of chirping swifts rose out of the foundry and collected against the sky. Their wings made a soft beating sound as they pivoted and flashed against the light. Tina released her grip on the branch to ignite another cigarette, then gripped it again quickly, as a smaller stream of birds broke off and curled into the air and returned to the larger mass.

"The swifts nest there every year," Trixie said. "It's cool."

Tina nodded, and the girls fell into a quiet trance, watching the flock of swifts spread out and come together, making nimble shapes in the air with every breath. After long flights over the cabins and marsh they would funnel back to the chimney in a furious rush, like bundles of black smoke billowing in reverse.

# 6

AFTER SELLING THE pelts to the good representative of the Hudson's
Bay Company, a pair of muttonchops in waistcoat and starched
collar, the men of the fur party divided up the profits and went their
separate ways, some north to the Yukon, others south to California,
and others on ships to Canton or Bombay. Since then, it had been
raining pitchforks at Fort Vancouver for three weeks straight, and
Cookie was almost broke again.

Sometimes, when the rain let up, he would take long walks in the
hills just west of the fort, following the gauze of clouds as it rose above
him. From some places he could see the lower planes of Mount Hood
in the distance, stabbing into the dirty lamb's wool of the sky, though
he was beginning to doubt he would ever see its peak.

On his way back down the hill, Fort Vancouver would return to
view, a cluster of log cabins surrounded by a wall of stripped tree
trunks coming to sharpened points. The administrative offices were
attached to the walls of the wooden fortress, creating an open-air
marketplace in the middle, where mountain men and hunting parties
and corps of exploration brought their beaver pelts to exchange for
the national currency of their choice. Some stables abutted the fort,
outside its walls, and also a tilled plot where some vegetables grew,
but which was fetid and decaying now, in the late autumn chill. Around
the fort walls was a hatchwork of rutted streets, with a general store
whose prices were no better than the company store inside, and a
haberdasher specializing in the production of beaverskin stovepipe hats.
Everything else was saloons, and above it all flapped the wide, wet
flag of the Hudson's Bay, a blue field with a golden beaver on it. They

called the settlement a town, but it barely qualified as that. It was just a few streets with flat façades and wooden promenades, and hardly a woman or a girl in sight.

As Cookie got closer he drew his coat tighter around his body and pulled his head in toward his chest. The air was cold and wet, and his hands and feet felt like they were stored in tin buckets full of ice. Long puddles of rainwater formed mirrors on the shoulder of the road. He passed by the store and a row of saloons, each one more tired and mean-looking than the last, and the corner where men loitered on the street, and always seemed to be hatching some bad plan. Today there were two rail-thin trappers, with dirty beards and satchels, and one Indian, with a dead, milky eye. Cookie continued on toward the opposite edge of town, about forty feet ahead, dutifully ignoring the mumbling that resumed the moment he was out of earshot. He had not spoken aloud in nine days straight, and the longer he went, the more difficult it became to start again.

The buildings ended, but the road continued on, right down to the river, a gray ribbon in the gray light, swirling with tan mud. Some ships were anchored at the pier, and their masts formed elegant silhouettes against the pearl-colored sky, like calligraphic letters in some foreign language. Cookie could see men loading them with wooden boxes, moving up an angled plank from the pier to the deck. From so far away, their labor looked effortless.

He stood there awhile, the wind poking inside his clothes and mud slurping at his feet, and wondered where to go next. Once again, he had reached the end of the line. He could either turn around and walk through the streets again, hoping that something would catch his eye this time, or he could return to the lean-to in the woods where he had been sleeping at night, and where he generally whiled away his evenings all by himself. He knew exactly where the latter path led, straight to silence and darkness, and maybe the occasional fright from a wandering deer or owl. And as for the former, he knew where that one went, too, another night on the edges of things, looking for something to look at without offending anyone or getting into trouble he could not get out of. Those were his options. He weighed them against each other until he decided to try his luck in town again. He would be back in the woods soon enough as it was, and at least in town he had some chance for a surprise.

So he turned around and retraced his steps, pretending he had some reason for going back. He walked past the men again and waited out of sight until he could emerge on the street without seeming too lost. He peeked in windows and examined the seams where walls came together. The sun was setting, and the town's shadows started to lean at sinister angles.

When groups of trappers drifted by, he scurried out of their way, and the things he overheard them saying seemed rife with double meanings. "No way to treat a fella," someone said, and Cookie imagined that he, himself, was being accused of treating someone poorly and that everyone knew why but him. He wandered past a team of horses feeding from a trough and could have sworn he heard someone whisper at him, but when he turned around, it was only the dun-colored gelding, with a stream of urine connecting its body to the black earth like a rod of glass.

Eventually, Cookie found a perch on an empty wall near a sputtering rain gutter, with a view of the north edge of town, all two corners of it. He entertained himself by surveying the ground beneath him as if it were someplace very far away, using his curled hand as a telescope. He moved his viewfinder from place to place, the ants near his feet and the tufts of grass where the muddy street began, and on his way up he caught sight of a dainty little foot stepping around the edges of a brown puddle. This foot was not the foot he was expecting to see, however. It was not a foot covered by a jackboot or moccasin, as all the men's feet were, but rather by a darling leather sandal with a brass buckle and flat soles. Cookie opened his hand and took a better look at the only little girl he had seen in days.

The girl was wearing a gingham dress and pigtails, and she swung an empty wooden bucket back and forth playfully. She was not the prettiest girl he had ever seen—she had swinish eyes and a jagged mouth—but he was excited by her sudden appearance nonetheless. Cookie watched her as she bent and brushed off her shoe, and then, out of boredom and despair, he began to follow her. It was a half-hearted chase, as the distance from the store to the tobacconist was only eighteen steps, but when she began down the street toward the fort he found himself pursuing her more doggedly. He did not know why, but he felt compelled to trail her. He figured that she might lead him to someplace a little more gentle, a little less depressed, and once he decided upon that, he became convinced of it and imagined that she was somehow his salvation. He became anxious when he lost her for a moment, passing behind the corner of the fort wall, and he was jubilant when he picked her up again on the other side, just as she disappeared into a tavern that seemed like it once had been a farmhouse.

Cookie watched the door close behind her, and the face of the building go blank, just two yellow windows glowing on the blood-colored wall. He approached the door slowly, and listened as the sounds from inside became louder, full of laughter and clanking glasses. Although the structure was something like a barn, he could see that the ground around it was not the farming kind; it was trampled and hard, and everywhere stones were sticking out, with hardy weeds poking from underneath. The fir trees rising behind it looked like they had been violently brushed the wrong way.

Cookie stared in the window, which was just a square cut into the building's clapboard front. Inside were about two dozen men, Hawaiians, Frenchmen, Indians, Russians, mixing together around card tables in a random arrangement. Lamplight spilled around the room and all the mens' shadows moved across the walls and ceiling like black butterflies. One man drew on a long pipe, and another two played at mah-jongg. Cookie leaned against the wall and listened to the muffled laughter inside. When he looked again, a man was yanking on his own throat with an imaginary rope, and sticking his tongue out until his head collapsed against his chest.

Suddenly the door of the saloon slammed open in a burst of noise and the little girl came back out, her wooden bucket now sloshing with beer. Its lip was greased in fat to keep the head down, and she needed both her arms to carry it. "'Scuze me, sir," she said, and Cookie made way, and a moment later she had disappeared into the darkness, avoiding the puddles and heaps of horse manure in the street as she strained against the weight of her load. The last thing he heard from her was a boyish belch, and then the street was empty again. He girded himself a moment, and stepped inside the saloon on the door's third or fourth swing.

Cookie was greeted by a gust of hot, smoke-filled air, suffused with the smell of stale beer and the stink of men who had worked and sweated and slept in their clothes. It was a long, dirty room, with a wood stove burning in the corner, beside a tattered blanket on the wall, where some of the Indians stood half undressed in the heat. Their broad chests were traced with welted tattoos in the shapes of killer whales, and owl eyes around their nipples, or so Cookie surmised from the stylized lines. The customers were mostly speaking a strange pidgin language that had evolved in a rough bartering of words and syntax, grounded in English but grown to include phrases and inflections from the Indian tribes' dialects, and from French, and from Polynesian as well. It was spoken all the way from here to China, the trappers said, but the rudimentary nature of the palaver kept the men on simple topics, and often relying on grimaces and sneers to get their meanings across, and most often of all to songs about drinking.

Cookie walked slowly toward the bar and felt his skin flush beneath his clothes, convinced that all the men were staring at him. He felt like he was stepping onto a stage without any direction or script. No one spoke to him, though, and so he girded himself and kept walking.

At the back of the bar waited a red-faced man, with a mustache and fogged-up spectacles, framed by a row of bottles and a cash register and a cracked mirror that stretched the length of the room, corroded in places with a yellowish soot. Cookie pressed up to the counter and set down a nickel for a glass of whiskey.

"Sure thing, kid."

The drink arrived in a thick tumbler, and when Cookie raised it to his lips, he caught sight of his own face in the looking glass behind the bar. It appeared white and pasty in the faint light of the saloon, and somehow undefined. The longer he looked at it, the more he came to think it did not look like his own face at all. It was the face of a woman, he thought, a girl's face, and a lonesome and scared girl at that. Cookie swallowed his whiskey and put down a nickel on the bar for another. He had better be careful, he thought. He was up against something new here.

In the corner a table of Flathead Indians were drinking rye and talking in their own bizarre, clacking tongue. A pinched-looking white man followed Cookie's gaze and spoke up. "Next they'll be letting in the horses," he said, and Cookie whispered unintelligibly in response. He felt working inside him a kind of contempt for all men, including himself, that he had never experienced so deeply before. He looked in the mirror again and took another drink. He supposed women were not so much to blame. They were not running the show. It was men who made the laws and enforced them, and thought the whole perform-ance was so wonderful.

The men in the bar began to laugh and again he thought they were laughing at him, but in fact no one was paying any attention to him at all. They were laughing at a man who had just come in, a huge man with red hair that stuck straight out in bristles, and who carried with him a red-haired child. The man was unnaturally large, his hands, his arms, his shoulders, his head, everything seemed too big for everything else. Only his eyes were small, and pressed deep in his face, utterly disconnected from the nose and mouth and ears around them. The child he held looked just like him, big, with the same small eyes.

The man sat down right beside Cookie, talking to himself under his breath. He set the child on the bar, and all the men in the room began to shout and laugh. Cookie realized soon enough the man was one of the simple kinds, the ones who mutter to themselves on the street and who men and boys will send on fool's errands, after a round square or a dozen post holes. They laughed at him whenever his head was turned, calling him "cracked" and singing songs like, "The crack is getting wider in the old tin pan." Someone sang the chorus and they all laughed some more.

The man had a drink, the cheap two-cent stuff, and then another, and Cookie started getting a feeling from him that perhaps he was not so mild after all. He glanced at the big man in the mirror, and around the room at the trappers, and the red-faced bartender. He looked back at the redheaded man again and his odd child.

"Sonsabitchs, sonsabitchs. Trappers all sonsabitches," the man muttered to himself and to his solemn-faced kid. Maybe he wasn't so cracked after all.

Two or three men in the room kept laughing, and one in particular was worse than the rest. He was the one who had started the song, and he could not seem to help showing off. Soon enough he was getting bolder. He stood up and began walking up and down the room, singing the song over and over again. He wore a fancy vest with brown tobacco spots, and glasses, and every time he made a joke he thought was funny, he winked at the others, who dutifully broke into guffaws. The bartender knew there was some danger in this behavior, and kept leaning over the bar and saying, "Shush, shush. Quit it now," but the man refused to stop. He went up behind the big man and put his hat on to one side and sang the song again.

Suddenly, without warning, the big man's hand flashed out and grabbed not the show-offy man but Cookie by the shirt, and yanked him against his body. Cookie's face came close to his, so he could smell the big man's breath and feel his heat, and the man said slowly, with his big lips moving open and closed, "Now you watch him, and if you let him fall, I'll kill you." His eye widened toward his child on the bar, who threw his arms around Cookie's neck, and the big man whirled around and grabbed the show-off's shoulder and began shaking him back and forth. Cookie closed his eyes. When he opened them again, the big man's fist was just coming down in the other man's face, whose eyes looked like he was about to be hit by a train. The show-off's hat

73

flew off, and he reeled backward holding his nose and stumbled into an empty chair.

Before Cookie knew what was happening, the whole room had risen to its feet and rushed him out the door, pouring out into the street and forming a loose circle around the newfound fighters. Cookie took a place among them, his hand tightly clamped on the clammy, dirty, wriggling fingers of the red-haired child.

"Pick it up!" someone yelled. "Kill his guts!"

"Eliminate his map!"

The glow from the bar window painted everything in a sallow light, and the two men began circling each other, fists in the air, shifting their weight from side to side. The crowd booed and cheered at random whenever one of them feinted or dodged. The big man seemed barely able to hold his hands up, they were so heavy and huge, and the little man bobbed like a bird, gulping sometimes in fear. Before anyone could lay another punch, however, a third man strode into the circle to break things up. He was a barrel-chested fellow with a bowler hat and suspenders, and an uptight gait, like he carried some small stone between his legs. He walked between the men with his arms raised. "All right, all right, let's break it up," he said, but the crowd yelled its dissent. The man in the bowler frowned and shook his head and kept on acting the adult, telling everyone what they did not want to hear, until finally someone else in the crowd, a rangy man with a mustache like a hand broom and a mournful set of eyes, walked over to him and slapped him in the face with an open palm.

The man's bowler slipped off his head and plopped into a puddle, and as he bent down to pick it up, the man with the long mustache raised his boot in the air and shoved him face-first into the mud.

The crowd cheered at that, and for a moment all four of the men inside the circle froze. The big man, the show-off, the peacemaker, and the mustache, all of them just stared out at the crowd, until, as if by some telepathic communication, the circle widened and the two fights proceeded side by side.

First, the big man closed his tremendous arms around the show-off, but came up empty-handed, and then swished his head around to see where his opponent might turn up next, while the peacemaker wrapped his arms around the mustache's waist and buried his face in his stomach. The mustache pounded on the peacemaker's back a few times and pretty soon they were both down writhing in the mud. Soon the big man got the show-off on the ground as well, and the two wrestling pairs were bumping into each other and bouncing off each other's elbows and knees.

Cookie looked down at the child to see how he was responding to his father's efforts, but the boy was focused on a jawbreaker he had pulled from his pocket, peeling off the lint with his mouth hanging slightly agape.

Eventually the show-off and the big man were split apart, each sitting in a puddle trying to get his bearings. The show-off had blood running down his face, and the big man looked a little sad and confused, like he had forgotten how he had gotten into this thing in the first place. He stared into the darkness and screwed his eyes into a wet twist, until he seemed to remember something and a look of murder came over his face; his eyes glinted and his skin turned purple, and suddenly his whole weight was crushing toward the show-off again, and pinning him to the ground. The show-off was helpless beneath him now, and took a rain of blows that sounded like wet sponges hitting the earth. The big man's elbows poked into the air over and over again, and Cookie was glad that the other man was obstructed from view. The pummeling was finally stopped by the other two men crashing into the big man and knocking him off his perch.

A sheet of muddy water splashed up onto the crowd opposite Cookie, flecking them with brown spots and tear-shaped streaks, which only inflamed them further. Cookie watched the assembly of men bellow from their diaphragms, clenching their fists, and slapping each other on the backs. They were like a single organism, he thought, attached by folds of flesh to each other's hips. Some of them held mugs of beer, which sloshed and foamed, and their faces flashed and receded in shadow.

It was unclear where or when it began—likely with some pushing and shoving from the rear for better position—but at a certain point the crowd began to turn on itself, and the fighting began to spread out in every direction like a brushfire. It erupted in different segments at almost exactly the same time, and soon enough, the street had become a kaleidoscope of swinging arms and thrusting knees, and miniature dramas playing out between two or three protagonists at a time. There were men pushing each other onto the ground and grinding their heads in the dirt, men bending their knees and straightening their spines, and holding their fists in the air like professional knucklefighters. There were men choking each other, and men frozen in place waiting for an attacker from any direction. The sound of ripping shirts, and gargling throats, and clattering change dropping from upturned pockets formed a kind of musical din, underscored by the percussive beat of bone pounding on bone.

Cookie was a small man, and he did not favor the impact of some drunken trapper landing on top of him, so he ducked down and crept toward a wooden banister fronting the promenade, where he planned to hang on for dear life. He hauled the child along with him, tiptoeing over the bodies that already lay on the ground, and avoiding the ones that tumbled around him. Everywhere men were falling and bouncing up for more, ganging up on each other and then changing sides. One man with a scar running from his forehead to his cheek stumbled into Cookie's path and made a gesture as if to wring his neck, before suddenly dropping to his knees and pitching face-first onto the muck, a lump rising on the back of his head from a blackjack meant for someone beside him. Another man grabbed Cookie's sleeve and cried for help before getting dragged away by a couple of young toughs who looked like brothers. At the edges of the fight a few constables from the corporation leaned on their blunderbusses, making sure the crowd did not get any political notions.

When Cookie finally reached the railing, he settled down and made himself as small as he could, staring through the slats to watch the show. He became fixated on a pair of thick, middle-aged men grappling in a motionless bear hug. Each of them was straining to gain some leverage, but they were unable to pry themselves loose, and so they satisfied themselves by speaking softly into each other's ears. "You've always been a girl," one of them said. "I'm never going there with you again," the other replied. They grunted and shook, and remained glued together as they waddled slowly about the crowd, and eventually disappeared from view.

Just about then a body came sailing toward Cookie, crashed into the railing beside him, shaking the whole armature, and slumped over the banister in a pile. The man's hair fell over his face and a corncob pipe dropped from his mouth, which he must have been smoking in the midst of the brawl. He wore a tan buckskin with brocade accents and fringe dripping from the seams, and matching knee-high moccasins. The man moaned, and started to push himself back up on his feet, at which point Cookie got a closer look at him and felt his grip on the child's hand tighten like a vise.

"Henry?" he asked. "Is that you?"

When the man turned his face toward him he saw that it was Henry, but he was not yet entirely awake. His face was clean shaven, and his hair had been washed, and there was a bruise coming in on his forehead like a wine stain on a cotton shirt. He stared ahead uncomprehendingly and tried to stagger to his feet. Gradually the mist cleared from his eyes, and the world seemed to return to him in degrees, at which point he finally raised an eyebrow and pushed a wide, half smile across his face.

"Cookie? You don't say!" he exclaimed, just as a bottle sailed between them and exploded against the wall. Henry ducked down and scrambled toward the saloon and Cookie unclasped his hand from the grubby child, placing his arms around a hitching post. "Don't move," he said, and a moment later he was embracing his friend. They thumped each other roundly on the back and Henry stepped back with his hands on Cookie's shoulders, and looked him up and down. They laughed at each other, and at their luck.

"I thought I might find you around here," Henry said, slapping

Cookie on the shoulder with his hat. "Let's get ourselves a drink."

Cookie made a move toward the child at the hitching post, but Henry grabbed him by the sleeve before he could make it. "Leave him be," Henry said. "Or you'll never get rid of him."

The bar was deserted now, and the bartender was clutching a long-neck shotgun in case the fight decided to come inside. While the two men waited for their drinks to arrive, Henry pulled out a sack of tobacco from his pocket and rolled two cigarettes in brown licorice paper. He handed one to Cookie, and lit them both off the same match, and as the hot smoke expanded in his lungs, Cookie looked around the room peaceably, at the empty tables and burning embers in the woodstove, the corks nailed to the ceiling and the peeling wallpaper of scarabs and jellyfish. Everything seemed a little bit brighter than before, and the chill he had been carrying around seemed to back away from his skin and bones. He looked at Henry and they both laughed again.

Soon enough the men began returning from outside, singly and in pairs, and taking their seats where they had left them. Some were grinning and some were bruised and manhandled, dabbing the blood from their lips and temples, but no one seemed to be in the mood for fighting anymore. Near the back a pair of young men struck up with a banjo and a fiddle, and launched into a song about a tragic murder in a copse of pine trees. They played quick and fast and slapped their feet on the floor to keep the beat, but there was something mournful in the song all the same, and Cookie felt something sweet from it, as did everyone else in the room, it seemed, for they kept still and talked under their breath, and when it was done, they all burst into applause and showered the boys with pennies and nickels, which spun and flashed in the air.

Henry, it turned out, had been living the past month in a stone hut just a few hollers from the walls of Fort Vancouver, probably a mile from Cookie's own lean-to in the woods, ever since returning to his lodge on the banks of the Columbia and finding it burned to the ground. Most likely, he had deduced, it was the Russians who were responsible, the ones who had chased him to Cookie in the first place, and although the thought of doing some vengeance against them had crossed his mind, he had decided in the end to refrain from pursuing it. The odds were stacked against him and furthermore no one would benefit from his actions anyway, even if he pulled off something grand and bloody. According to rumor, the marauders had since left the region, striking out for warmer hunting grounds down south, and he was able to console himself with the notion that he had perhaps played some small part in driving them away. For the last month he had been picking up odd jobs around Fort Vancouver, right back at square one, alone in the damp wilderness of Oregon with no one to watch him or listen to him or help him out with his prospects.

He invited Cookie to bunk down with him, and Cookie accepted, locating his shack the very next day, nestled in a grove of poplar trees at the edge of an open meadow. It had a puncheon floor, and oiled paper for glass, and a stone oven made from river rocks, with a flat iron for cooking on. Cookie took the corner near the stove for his rucksack and bedding, and before anything else, swept the floor of the grit and trash that Henry had allowed to collect over the past month of living alone.

"Well!" Henry said. "This place looks better already!"

They lived well together, it turned out, and settled into an immediate pattern, as if they had known each other for many years. Cookie took up the domestic chores, the sweeping and tending of the fire, and Henry chopped wood and foraged about for food. He had a Kentucky rifle, made of smooth steel and sugar wood, which he used to hunt rabbits and quail, which Cookie in turn dressed and baked with johnnycakes or cornbread. For fun they got to calling each other grandpa, and said things like "Grandpa, I'd like some of your salt pork," or "Grandpa, my pie is cold," which they thought was hilarious. During lazy after- noons they would take a pile of old apples from a nearby arbor, and while away their time playing skeets, one of them lofting fruits in the air in wide arcs and the other trying to bean them from an angle.

"Not so bad," Henry might say.

"Thank you, Grandpa. Now toss one higher."

During the daylight hours Henry toured Cookie around the countryside, showing him the lay of the land. All the swimming holes, and monkey trees, and other local places that only time spent in a region would reveal. They made a funny pair, the two of them, Henry rugged and blond and a little thick sometimes, Cookie scrawny and anxious and prone to overthinking. But while they stomped around the landscape together, Henry leading the charge through burning nettles and brier patches, Cookie tagging at his heels, they came to an understanding of sorts. Cookie relinquished a part of himself happily, and allowed the stronger man to control him in a way, while Henry blossomed under the weaker man's constant attention.

"Well, I say I'm from Ohio," Henry reported over his shoulder, while Cookie struggled to keep pace, "but that's not exactly true. Haven't been back there in ten years at least. No one there would know me from Adam. But I grew up there, on my daddy's farm, bailing hay and tossin watermelons with my brothers and sisters. It was a fine enough time. Husking corn, swimming in the creek. Have you ever been?" he asked abruptly.

"No," Cookie said, panting a little.

"It's pretty," Henry said, "but not much opportunity. Farming and family life is about as far as it goes. When I was about twelve, my daddy indentured me to a shipping company, and by the time I was fourteen, I'd circled the world a good four times. I've seen the northern lights, and the Southern Cross, the pyramids in Egypt. I'll tell you all about it some time.

"I was about fifteen when I ended up out here, looking for the Northwest Passage with a crew of Englishmen. Never found it, you could guess that, but we were a good four months up and down the coast, mapping all the bays and inlets and trading with the local Indian tribes. Metal buckets for whalebone trinkets and sheep-horn throwing sticks and the like. Captain collected plenty of rocks and plants for the geographical museum in London. There's even a peninsula to the south named after me, Henry's Finger. We all got something. There were more nameless things back then than you could shake an eel at."

Cookie and Henry had arrived at an outcropping of rock, where the gorge spread before them in a massive arrangement of water and rock and cloud-spotted sky. Across the river there was a waterfall spouting from a high cliff, like a trailing ribbon of lace, disintegrating as it fell to the earth.

"Gift from the Great Mystery," Henry said, pointing at the mist. "Coyote made it by twisting young lenzel shoots into a rope, and stretching it across the creek, and then he turned the rope into rocks." They sat down and he pulled out a flask from his pocket, which he handed to Cookie.

"Yep, those were some good times," Henry went on, his eyes softening, his voice growing a little wistful. "Few years at sea, going from one port to another, city to city, you get a little jaded about things. Maybe you know what I mean. Seeing something so unexplored brings out something bigger in you. It's a rare thing in the world these days. Pretty much everywhere's been touched by now."

"That's true," Cookie said.

"Anyway, the ship ran aground that winter," Henry went on briskly. "Hull shattered on the rocks. Whole crew was lost but me. I washed up on shore not so far from here, covered in bullwhip kelp and a mouth full of sand. Chinook Indians took me in, and I woke up in one of their lodges, the smell of smoking fish and wet dogs all around. I remember the men staring down at me, dressed in their cedar bark armor and the women in their domed, spruce-root hats. Babies with planks strapped to their heads, to stretch out their skulls while they were still soft. It's a mark of distinction among the Indians here, you know. The badge of the slave-owning class." Henry always liked to add in a little lesson here and there.

"Anyway, that was seven years ago," Henry said. "A man could really spread out back then. You could wander the woods for months on end without ever running across another soul. These woods were so crowded with deer and fish and birds you'd think it was the Garden of Eden. And the beavers. They lived in big dams like brownstones or Tudors in Boston or New York. Whole cities of them, gathering up twigs, mixing mortar, patting it down with their tails, all split up into little groups of labor. Smart animals, the beavers. Some of them grew to five feet tall, but they've all been killed off already, the first to go when the white hunters arrived. Well I'm partly to blame for that I suppose. I sold some of the first pelts to the Hudson's Bay Company when their fort opened three summers ago.

"I have to admit, though," Henry said, getting up to piss against a tree, "the coming of the white man ain't all bad. I like the Chinooks and all, the Flatheads, too, but there's something about talking in your native tongue that just lets the friendship flow better. You know what I mean? You can tell a white man things that you just couldn't get across to an Indian." He winked over his shoulder. "Devilish things, like what you would do with a pile of money if you had it, and how fur gets traded from place to place. The Flatheads can't understand that so well. They never want more than what they got, and they don't find too much interest in the idea of traveling or owning things. I'm gettin older, though, Cookie. I'm almost twenty-three now. I need to start thinking about getting a little money saved. That doesn't go over so good out here. It's against their nature."

On the way home Cookie and Henry passed a few neighbors, men Henry knew from poker games and barn raisings, or simply from wandering around. He prided himself on his good relations with everyone in the Columbia Basin, the French, the English, the squatters, the bushwackers, the jayhawkers and half-breeds.

They passed a Clatsop on his way to visit the Old Lady in the Pile of Wood, and the Scotsman who sharpened knives in town, out collecting kindling for his fire at home. Henry introduced Cookie to each of them, and to a fat, half-blind, ripe-smelling man who he claimed was the chief of the Klickitat.

"There's no clear nations out here," Henry explained as the old man continued into the woods. "No real magistrate or governor. Just the corporation, which is pretty much anyone that wanders in. And I'll tell you what, once a man arrives, there's no telling what direction he'll go. Some'll go native, dress up in the cedar pants and the whale bone, others'll get more like what they were to begin with, keep up the teatimes or siesta hours of wherever they came from. New characters gettin born every day here, and old ones gettin sloughed off like snake skin.

"It is good to be shifty in a new country," Henry added. "You never know who might end up writing the rules come sundown."

Soon they came to a drop-off, where the packed dirt became cinders and slanted toward a field of red paintbrush, glowing in the afternoon sunlight. Henry went running ahead, plunging down the embankment, and Cookie watched his body cut back and forth, his hair flying around his shoulders, his arms pinwheeling to either side. The fringe of his jacket beat up and down and his blond hair caught the light. The momentum of the run shot him out into the field, where he carved a path in the crimson flowers and finally flopped over and rolled back and forth. When he got back on his feet he yelled up at Cookie, "Come on, buddy! That's a good ride!"

In Henry's years in Oregon, it seemed, something had been forgotten, and something new had emerged. The normal withholdings and veiled menace that got in the way of most men knowing each other had drifted away. The strictures of class, creed, religion meant almost nothing to him, except as explanations of certain men's peculiarities of taste and disposition. He gazed straight into men's eyes, a little stupidly perhaps, but also with absolute faith that his gaze would be returned with respect. He made plans based purely on the stated goal and resources at hand. He took what parts of ideas made sense to him from whatever system of belief came his way. A little Indian land worship, some Protestant manifest destiny, a halo of Taoist animism. No matter what he did, however mean or ill-tempered, there was something innocent about it, as if he could never be held accountable for anything but good intentions.

He was an American, all right, Cookie admired, and launched himself down the hillside of ashes.

Being an American, Henry was obsessed with money. Sometimes, to make a few dollars, he and Cookie sold beaver and muskrat pelts to the corporation, but that was no way to get ahead, they found. The land around the fort was already picked clean, and the prices at the company store were so high that anything they made got taken back immediately. Henry traded labor with a few neighbors here and there, flatboating, hog driving, rail making, and made up modes of exchange with them involving strings of dentalia shells. They could get jobs down at the wharves, they realized, but that was even worse—then they would be giving up their freedom. Sometimes they thought about making a claim on some land, but that seemed pointless too, unless they intended to farm it, and they were much too restless for that just yet.

Many nights Cookie and Henry sat in their cabin and talked about capital, and how they might get some if they tried hard enough. Henry had many plots, involving whatever he had read about in the paper that week. One day it was hazelnuts and the next it was ambergris.

"This is a land to be big in," Henry said. "Could really be something out here. I been most everywhere in the world at this point, and there's no place with the natural resources of Oregon. The wood, the animals, the who knows what buried in the ground. There's ocean on the one side and mountains on the other, and deep rivers to link them in arteries of trade. And the people here are exceptional. Doc Bridges writes poetry and reads the latest literary magazines from Philadelphia and St. Louis. And Boggs Co. is known all over the world for its tricorner beaver silk hats. And the Indians we got are a source of mystery and admiration to men everywhere, even to other Indians. There's a chance to build something here, Cookie, from the ground up. I'm tired of having nothing, seeing these other fellers who just made it makin out better than me after seven years' time.

"If I could just milk it somehow," he said, "I might come out on the other end all right, set up for life. And you too."

The problem Henry always ran into, however, was in the getting started. He could not for the life of him figure out how to worm into the game without any funds to back him up.

"No way for a poor man to make a start," he said. "Just ain't possible. Can't grow a batch of nuts and then harvest them up, crate them, ship em to market, balance a payroll, all without receiving payment on em till afterwards. Can't get a project rolling without any leverage."

Cookie shrugged. The problems of the entrepreneur had never occurred to him before. As long as Henry was around, he was happy enough. He would be willing to get a job on the wharves, even, watching the boats go in and out, at least until some families arrived that needed cooks or waiters. But he was always happy to talk about how money was a cage.

Henry could not stop dreaming, though. He planned his hazelnut farm down to the seeds and compost, with radially planted trees and the latest in irrigation systems.

"Got a spot in mind," he said. "Just a few miles from the fort, out in the valley of the Willamette. More loose land out there'n anyone knows what to do with."

"Could do strawberry fields, too," he said. "Or corn."

Cookie embroidered Henry's dream with a few additions of his own. He could build a simple bakery somewhere nearby, he said, out of native wood and stone, and he would educate the workers on the making of hearty rye loaves and flaky croissants. Henry listened attentively, curious that men had lived out here without such stuff for so long as it was. Cookie would build a house, too, a Victorian with curling eaves and shuttered dormers, and an iron lightning rod in the shape of a crowing rooster. He wanted an English garden with flagstone pathways leading through azaleas and a reflecting pool with a fountain.

"Sure," Henry said, "why not. Let's think big," and he would pour another cup of bourbon and they would begin their cycle of conversations all over again.

\* \* \*

Two months into their living together, just as the first clues of spring were beginning to be revealed, the knobs of camellia blossoms and such, Henry came home with an extraordinary idea.

Cookie was fixing some bacon and eggs after a night of long drinking when suddenly his bunkmate burst through the door in a huff. Henry pulled off his coat and draped it on a chair, went back outside to take off his boots, and came back in and began packing his bag. Cookie could tell that something was different than usual.

Cookie watched his friend for a while without asking any questions, and eventually Henry walked over and pulled a vial of amber fluid from his pocket, which he uncorked and pushed up toward Cookie's nose.

"This is it," he said. His eyes were gleaming. "This is the thing."

"Is it?" Cookie asked, pulling his head away. The vial exuded a sweetish, musky smell. "And what is that?"

"Castoreum oil," Henry answered, and when Cookie failed to cry out in recognition, he continued, "It's a medical wonder, Cookie. Cure for earache, deafness, dropsical abscesses, not to mention gout, headache, and colic." He bent his fingers back one after another as he counted the many uses: "Also stops hiccoughs, induces sleep, prevents sleepiness, strengthens sight, and when you snort it, it causes sneezing to clear the brain. Helpful in madness, too, particularly if the victim is taken to a quiet pond for recuperation." Henry was on a real selling streak. He was so excited, he was stumbling over his words, and pacing back and forth to stare at the oil-paper windows as if he could see something outdoors.

"No one in America believes in it much," he admitted, "but there's a market for it in China, where they don't worship modern science the way we do here. I'm not lying, Cookie. I've been there. They know the power of plants and animals and minerals and herbs. They got whole traditions there that no one in the West ever heard of before, older than the cathedrals in Rome. In China, men pay good silver for this stuff," he said, shaking the vial up and down, "cause in China silver is abundant and castoreum is rare, which is the whole trick of international finance, after all, Cookie, don't forget that. Scarcity and abundance. It's like water passing from glass to glass." This did not seem a particularly apt metaphor, but Cookie knew more or less what he meant.

"The beauty," Henry went on, "is where the castoreum comes from. Guess, Cookie."

"Guess?"

"Come on, just guess."

"I can't."

"All right." Henry rubbed his palms together. "It's the beaver. The beaver, Cookie! It's excreted from the anal glands of the beaver! There's more skinned beavers on the edges of Fort Vancouver than anyone knows what to do with, all waiting to get tapped. And there's more comin in every day." He turned to Cookie and looked at him sternly. "There is a window of opportunity here," he said. "Ships traveling back and forth to China, beavers filled up with castoreum oil, and no one else even knows that the market exists. But it won't last forever." Henry became doubly stern. "I've seen the beaver population starting to wither away," he said. "Now's the time. Now's the time to move on this thing."

He returned to his satchel and threw in a shirt and pants.

"I signed on with a ship to China this morning," he said over his shoulder, "taking a cargo of pelts to Canton in a week from now. I aim to carry as much castoreum with me as I can, and when I get to China, I'll do some dealings and maybe even set up something more permanent-like."

Cookie stirred the eggs and scraped the dry crust off the bottom of the pan. He had yet to see where he fit into this plan.

"The ship could use a cook," Henry said, and although Cookie could not tell exactly what he meant by it, he took it as an invitation. Though it seemed like Henry was going regardless of what Cookie decided to do.

Cookie stirred the eggs and flipped the bacon and let the whole situation take shape in his mind. The sound of the sizzling grease filled the room, the pan seething with viscous fat, brown at its edges where the frothy parts pooled and swam. It was like some light had flashed on in a strange, dark room, and then flashed off again, and it was taking him a moment to map the arrangement of the furniture. He had just been growing accustomed to Oregon, the distance to the store, the length of the days, and now all of a sudden the ground was getting swept from beneath his feet. He had just come to the point where he could walk through the town like a regular citizen for once, greet a few people by name. He had a tab at one of the taverns and a regular partner to go drinking with.

On the one hand, he reasoned, he could go to China and return with enough money to found a bakery, build a small house perhaps, settle down in a safe, respectable way. On the other hand he could stay where he was, all alone and poor as a pauper. It did not take long for a new pathway to unfurl ahead of him, leading across the ocean to the Empire of China. He waited for a moment and said, "All right, Henry. That sounds fine. I'll be the cook."

"Great," Henry said, "that's just great," and kept tossing socks and belts and knives into his knapsack. Cookie eyed his roommate with a mixture of irritation and affection. He was so eager to get going that he was packing a week in advance.

Cookie scooped the bacon and eggs onto two plates and walked outside the cabin to eat his breakfast on the steps, where the yellow grass of the orchard sloped down to a break of alder and sycamore trees, and in the distance the mountains rose in a purple, white-capped ledge. Henry continued rattling around inside, mumbling to himself and occasionally laughing under his breath. Cookie blew on his eggs and began eating.

Perhaps America was not a country at all, Cookie thought, but simply a place in one's mind, a place with one's friends. It was a place he never wanted to leave again, he knew that, even if it meant never coming back.

# 7

THE DAY AFTER the skeletons appeared, Neil pruned the laurel hedge outside his cabin, and took the clippings down to the compost pile, and made some phone calls to a guy with a pair of speakers to sell, until eventually he could not put it off any longer, and got out the phone book and found the nearest police station and called the authorities for the first time in his life.

First he spoke to a police operator, and tried to explain to her that he had found some human remains on his property, but that the remains were not new remains, and that he had found them in a dried-up marsh where he hoped someday to plant terraces of goldenrod. The police operator quickly transferred him to someone else, to whom he explained things again, this time a little more clearly, and who decided that the person he must speak to was located in another office entirely. Neil called that person, Sheriff Bill Youngbar, and explained again the events of the day before, how he had found two skeletons in the marsh on his property, how they were probably old remains, and how they were holding hands in a sad and brittle old grip. He described the fracture on the smaller one's skull and how the marsh had never gotten this dry before, not in the seven years he had been living there, as far as he could remember.

"I assume the remains are pretty old," Neil repeated. "But I really have no idea." He did not want to call too much attention to his own theories, as that might make him look somehow suspicious.

Sheriff Youngbar took down the information and told him he would come investigate the scene later in the day, after four o'clock most likely, and not to touch anything please.

Neil spent the rest of the morning cleaning his cabin, and hiding all the incriminating paraphernalia that he found there. He dusted his crystal collection, all the agates and thunder eggs, and straightened his bookshelf; he pushed his eight-track recorder off to the side of the room and coiled the patch cords into spirals of red and blue, which he twisted off with plastic bands. Every now and then he worried that he had made the wrong decision, that inviting the police onto his property had been a mistake, tantamount to inviting vampires into one's house, but he realized also that the decision was largely out of his hands. To be sure, society presented false choices sometimes: a job or happiness, friends or family, and one could often slip out of these yokes without ever taking one path or the other. But when it came to finding human remains on one's property, you were really obligated to notify the authorities; it was just common sense. And as long as he could reassure himself of this fact, he felt a little better.

Neil got into a cleaning jag. He vacuumed the Persian carpet and brushed off the taxidermied deer head that hung over his stereo, and stood there pondering for a moment its weird reminder of death and death's disguise. It was so strange, he thought, how people killed things and then tried to make it look like they had not. Finally he watered the succulents and stashed his pot in the back of the freezer.

By the time the sheriff pulled up, the house was clean, and Neil met him at the door with a respectable handshake.

"Howdy," Neil said.

"Mr. Rust," the sheriff replied. The sheriff was a narrow guy with a brushy mustache and wet-looking lips, and with him was a forensic anthropologist named Mr. Grimsrud, who taught seventh grade science class and sometimes did freelance work for police investigations. He was a stooped, potbellied man, and his hair fell in long plastered fingers over his head, like seaweed on a smooth rock. He wore a turtleneck sweater with big gobs of dandruff on the shoulders, and olive polyester pants that buttoned like old wrestling shorts.

"Nice to meet you," Neil said.

"Mmm-yes," Mr. Grimsrud replied. Something about Mr. Grimsrud looked familiar, and Neil found himself shuffling through his mental archive for some match. Perhaps it was the man's big teeth, he thought, or the way his gaze came out of his eyes somewhat crookedly, as if he was staring at your belt or your hand. He felt along those synapses—big teeth, wall eyes—and sensed he was being placed as well. The two men looked at each other quizzically for a minute until finally they put it together:

"Tacoma High School. Class of 1964," Neil said, and the forensic anthropologist blanched a little and nodded. When he smiled, his eyes seemed to cross.

"Wow," Neil said, and could not think of where to go from there.

"Long time ago," Mr. Grimsrud said, a little cagily, and Neil nodded soberly in return. There must be some reason they had never been friends, but they needed some time to remember it.

Everyone watched closely as the three men walked down the path. A couple of the women stood up from the strawberry beds; the girls, Trixie and Tina, tracked them closely from the roof of Tina's cabin and whispered as they edged nearby. Next to the garden, Neil noted, a cord of wood had arrived, which needed chopping and stacking.

Neil looked at the cabins through the sheriff's eyes and for a moment he felt vaguely suspicious of himself, imagining the collection of buildings as the scene of some hideous crime, a grisly murder or organ-farming scheme. For a moment the cabins seemed full of portent and hidden clues. It all looked a little dirty and seedy, the tie-dyed curtains and homemade ceramic bowls sitting out, open windows and sandal tracks. He found hidden threat in some dried flowers in a peanut butter jar, a peach pit covered in ants. But the sheriff seemed to take it all in stride, and Neil tried to put his worries out of his mind. Up ahead the fir trees and escarpments of rock were illuminated in the aging light of the afternoon sun, and their three shadows stretched ahead of them in long pillars, flashing and mingling on the pebbly ground.

When the skeletons finally came into view, revealed in the divot of earth scooped out from the dried swamp, Mr. Grimsrud murmured excitedly and rushed forward for a closer look. "Very interesting," he said under his breath. First he walked around the dug-out pit a few times, simply looking at the bones from different angles and bending over to see something near to the ground. They were half-buried in hardened mud, and it caked to their surfaces. The smell of arrow arum rose with the breeze, and lingered over the soft stasis of the marshy earth. Up above, the sky was traced with high cirrus clouds like fading breath on a windowpane.

"You performed the excavation yourself?" Grimsrud asked, and Neil promptly said that yes, he had, just the day before.

Mr. Grimsrud continued circling the remains gingerly as dried cattails seethed behind him. He got down on his knees and bent over as far as he could go until his ass was wagging in the air and it appeared he might topple into the pit. He craned his neck like an old turtle to look at the braincase of the taller skeleton, squeezing one eye shut and then the other. His face was alive with little tics and grimaces, registering each passing insight. The hairs on the back of his neck needed shaving, Neil observed, and his burly forearms held much more strength than he imagined the man ever had cause to use. Finally Mr. Grimsrud rose from the ground and brushed the dust off of his pants and crossed his arms over his chest.

"Strange," Mr. Grimsrud said. "Two complete skeletons like this, side by side. Normally they would get scrambled together over time." Neil took this as a vague indictment of his digging work. "I'd say they are at least fifty years old, possibly more, judging from the decay along the edges of the tibulas."

"Great," the sheriff said happily. That meant he now had no recent homicide to investigate, or paperwork to fill out, and Neil nodded in agreement because it meant he was off the hook as a suspect of any kind, and there would be no cops rifling through the property. It was good news all around, and Neil took the opportunity to ask Mr. Grimsrud politely, "So who do you think they are?"

"Well," Mr. Grimsrud warmed up, "the major clues we have in a case like this are the skeletons' height, sex, age, and facial structure. With those things in place you can start piecing together the identity of any remains." Mr. Grimsrud pointed to the braincase of the tall one. "The big one there is most likely Caucasian. You see the long, narrow shape of the skull there, and the constriction of the forehead behind the brow. You see how high it is."

Neil nodded, yes, he could see those things.

"That's a characteristic generally common to Europeans. He lived to a pretty old age. I know that because of how the skull looks. There are many, many bones in the cranium, which all grow separately into adulthood, and allow the face and head to change shape as we mature. But once skull-growth is complete, the contacts begin to knit together, and by middle age the bones of the face are pretty much fused. Eventually, the sutures are so thoroughly interconnected they can't be seen anymore, which is a state we call 'obliteration.' This skull is pretty well obliterated, which means this was an old guy."

"As for the smaller one," he said, "look at the small, worn-down teeth. And the flattened facial structure. The smaller chin, the face less protruding. He's Mongoloid or Indian, I'd say, but don't quote me on that. The fracture along the upper lobe there was probably the cause of death, you can see it didn't heal before he ended up in this pit. Probably he was bludgeoned to death. Or fell down. Got hit by a rock."

"Mongoloid or Indian?" It seemed like a pretty wide berth.

"Yup. Native American and Japanese cranial characteristics are quite similar. It's well accepted at this point that North American Indians are directly descended from nomadic peoples entering the continent from northern Asia, over the Bering Strait. Maybe even coming in boats across the Pacific as well. So we won't know for sure where this fellow came from until I run some tests."

"Some Indian princess, maybe," Neil joked.

"Princess?" the anthropologist repeated. "I don't think so. No. A woman would have lower, broader pelvis bones than that. No, these are both men." And sure enough, looking at them Neil could see they were both fairly narrow down there after all.

"Huh," Neil said.

93

The three men stood silently for a moment, staring into the pit at the two skeletons, as shadows collected in the craters of their eyes.

"Butch Cassidy and the Sundance Kid," Neil said, and the sheriff forced a little guffaw.

On the way back up to the parking lot Neil and Mr. Grimsrud talked about Tacoma a little bit, an old hamburger stand that had burned down twenty years before, a football player they had known who went on to the NFL, but reminiscing did not seem to excite the portly science teacher much, and so Neil let the subject drop. Neil tried a different tack, mentioning the various artifacts he had found on his property over the years, some horse shoes, bits of ceramic, stone pestles.

"I've got some pieces of chipped rock that look like spear heads," Neil said. "It's all in a few cigar boxes at home. Might be something to look at."

"Ohh, yes," Mr. Grimsrud made a groaning sound of interest. "That could be quite helpful in fact." They agreed that he would return the following day, to take measurements and photographs, at which time Neil would show him the collection. When they reached the car, the three men shook hands again.

"So tomorrow is all right?" Grimsrud clarified. Neil looked over at the police officer for some kind of permission, but the sheriff just shrugged his shoulders; he had no interest in the case anymore.

"Sure," Neil said. "Whenever you want, make yourself at home."

"Wonderful. This is really a much better find than I had expected," the anthropologist added, and his eyes crossed again as he smiled.

Neil's pal Sarah Thompson became the first of Neil's friends outside the commune to hear the epic story of his discovery of human remains. She worked at a diner on Interstate Avenue, a thoroughfare full of old split-level hotels and roadside restaurants from the days before I-5 was built, and he told her all about his adventures while she filed her nails at his booth. He described the moment he recognized the skull in the dirt, how the crowd had gathered around him, and about the forensic anthropologist's terrible dandruff, which was her favorite part.

"That's a pretty good story, Neil," she said. "You should tell my brother about it."

Neil hedged, "I don't know." Sarah's brother was a stringer for *The Oregonian,* the daily newspaper, and the thought of inviting the media to come nosing around his place filled him with a feeling of profound dread. Although the skeletons were perfectly newsworthy subjects, he realized, the publicity they could attract was not the most welcome kind. He did not relish the thought of advertising his personal life, or the life of the commune in general, to the entire Northwest, nor did he want trespassers coming around, tromping across his property to look at the hand-holding remains. Also, he simply did not like the idea of becoming a passive object of media scrutiny, without any control or power over his image at all. There was something degrading about that, to receive the attention of the camera for something that had involved no real work or invention. It was not the sort of attention he valued. But on the other hand, Neil was never good at keeping secrets. It would be hard to resist.

"I'll think about it," he said.

The next morning was hot. Neil woke up to the sound of a distant airplane engine dragging across the sky, and something in the flat-tened quality of its sound told him the air was already filling with humid particles of heat and exhaust. Outside, the sky had a bleached-out look. The earth and the plants and the insects, all of them were waiting in the shadows to get scorched. Neil moved slowly about the cabin, savoring the coolness indoors before starting in on the day's chores.

Sarah's brother and his photographer arrived late in the morning, right on time, and Neil led them down to the marsh, where the cameraman snapped some pictures, and Neil told Sarah's brother what he knew about the skeletons' origins.

"See the worn-down teeth? The narrow pelvises?" he said. "The tall one is probably a white guy. The small one could be either Indian or Oriental. Their bone structure is quite similar I'm told."

Sarah's brother nodded and scribbled in his pad. He was a quiet guy, almost the opposite of his sister, who could be pretty lively when she felt like it. He took many notes, but he did not ask many questions, and Neil worked to fill up the conversational space on his own. He could sympathize with the young man's passivity in a way. He had a special affection for the siblings of people with big personalities. But he was annoyed by it as well. The guy was supposed to be a reporter, after all, and it was his job to show some curiosity. Neil just hoped he was getting the information right, and stressed that he himself was only saying what he remembered and no one should hold him to it, because he had no training and no authority in the matter whatsoever. The kid nodded meekly, and finally Neil gave up trying to talk to him at all. He was a professional, accredited by the daily paper, he must know what he was doing. He gave the kid the name of Mr. Grimsrud, the forensic anthropologist, in case he wanted some more quotes from a real expert.

An hour later, just as Neil was beginning to contemplate chopping some wood, Mr. Grimsrud himself showed up, this time with a case full of measuring equipment and a gallon jug of water. He wore a tight pair of khaki shorts and black socks with leather sandals, and a forest green golfing shirt with black spots of sweat already forming under the armpits. Neil stayed in the cabin while Mr. Grimsrud went down to the marsh and measured the distances between joints and vertebrae, and took photographs of each component in isolation. For the time being, Neil decided not to tell him that a newspaper reporter had been there just an hour before, not that he had any reason to hide it, but he just figured it would be better to wait. Mr. Grimsrud would be working for hours, digging and scraping and taking notes, and there would be plenty of time for everything to come out into the open. There was no need to say everything at once. The facts were the facts regardless of when they eventually arrived.

\*    \*    \*

Neil dug out his cigar boxes of rocks and flint and old shattered chopsticks, and took the time to fix some lemonade. Mr. Grimsrud showed up at the door a little later, dusty and wet from his hours in the sun, his forehead and cheeks flushed with red. A patch of freckles had appeared on his sloping nose.

"Great stuff," he said. "I'm beginning to distinguish a curvature to the spine that would seem to indicate some lifelong labor of contortion."

"Really," Neil said, and gave an interested nod, and Mr. Grimsrud continued speaking as he entered the cabin. "I wonder if I could take a pinky bone from the tall one for radiocarbon testing?"

"No problem," Neil said, leading him out onto the back deck, where they sat down on a bench overlooking a shallow canyon of box elders and manzanita trees. Neil handed over the box of arrowheads and rusted nails, an amber ring, spent bullets, shards of pottery and shreds of woven baskets, and Mr. Grimsrud made sounds of enjoyment as he pushed his fingers around, and the objects clacked and rattled against the floor of the box.

"Great stuff, great stuff," he repeated. "This fine sand and silt up here is perfect for preservation."

While they sat there, Neil asked Mr. Grimsrud some questions about forensics, which led to some questions about Mr. Grimsrud himself, which was the real object of Neil's inquiry in the first place. It turned out Mr. Grimsrud had gone to college in Seattle, where he had studied geology and math, and had spent his summers in Alaska. He had never been married, but he was not opposed to the idea. It would be a shame never to have children, he thought. For some reason he told Neil a story about a friend of his up north who had gotten his hand stuck to the frozen fuselage of an airplane once, and how they had to piss on it to get the skin loose. By the time the lemonades were gone, there was something resembling casual good feelings between them, and Neil felt like he could count the strange man as a regular acquaintance of sorts.

The last thing Neil showed Mr. Grimsrud was a calligraphic scroll tacked onto the wall of his living room, a piece of long parchment the color of burnt tapioca, singed on the edges and filled with columns of beautifully inked Chinese characters. Neil said he had found it during his first few weeks on the land, papered inside the wall of one of the old cabins.

"I think some Chinese immigrants used to live here," he said. "Probably worked the farms down at Sauvie Island, and then when the railroads were built, they worked on those."

"It's a beautiful manuscript," Mr. Grimsrud said. He lifted his glasses and rubbed his porcine eyes. "Do you know what it says?"

"Nope," Neil admitted, and paused a moment to gaze at the lovely, indecipherable script. "Never really found out."

"So we'll see you tomorrow?" Neil said through the open window of Mr. Grimsrud's driver-side door, and Mr. Grimsrud nodded his head yes. Neil had considered inviting him to stay for dinner but decided against it. The process of his dinner was such a delicate routine that any imposition on it was sort of a burden. And besides, he and Mr. Grimsrud had arrived at a solid place, and by departing on good terms they still had some places left to go. There was no need to push it farther than necessary.

All that was left to do was to say good-bye. Neil was a great believer in the power of a warm and well-timed good-bye, the way it set the stage for the next meeting and wrapped up the whole encounter in a tidy bow. As long as two people could part on decent terms, he believed, everything was cool in the world. If he could just glide this good-bye into port, they would have the groundwork for a perfectly functioning relationship.

"Very good," Mr. Grimsrud replied, pumping the gas once and turning the key. The engine turned over and began to purr. Neil thought briefly about the visit from the newspaperman, but decided to keep it to himself. There was no need to complicate things.

"See ya tomorrow," Neil said, and thumped his palm on the roof as the car began to move.

Neil visited the bones again before nightfall. They were getting cleaner now, their outlines more defined, as the earth around them fell away in a smooth and sculpted surface, softened by Mr. Grimsrud's busy hands.

The next morning, to Neil's dismay, the newspaper carried a full-color photograph of the skeletons on the front page, above the fold, accompanied by the fourteen-point headline, "Ancient Couple Found In Bog." The photograph was edged in a pica-sized outline cordoning it off from the hard news, and accompanied by a short human-interest story on the serendipity of their discovery. It was strange. A picture taken just yesterday, down the hill, reproduced on the front page of the newspaper and dispersed all throughout the region. It was like a little part of his memory had been taken out and multiplied a million times.

Neil brought the paper inside and tossed the mass of it onto the kitchen table, carrying the front section along with him as he got his coffee brewing. Although the article was brief, Sarah's brother had managed to get almost everything wrong. The article said the skeletons were likely an ancient man and wife, dating back to the time of the migration of the Indians over the Bering Sea, and had been interred in some ritual involving shards of glass and forks, and that the pelvis bone was the seat of human evolution, whatever that meant. The only thing it got right was that they had been excavated on the property of Neil Rust, who it described as a former popular musician and aspiring organic farmer.

"Fuck!" Neil said. Mr. Grimsrud was going to kill him. The misrepresentation of basic facts was probably anathema to a man of science like that. He was going to have to work very hard to get him back on his friend list.

Neil talked himself down, though. No one really read the newspaper, did they? It was just a formality of civilization, the tissue of lies that a society told itself to convince itself it was an actual coherent thing. It was no big deal at all, if you looked at it like that. Nothing was.

He was just settling back down and starting in on his coffee when the phone rang. Hoping it was a wrong number, he picked it up.

"Howdy, Neil," the sheriff said. "Seen the paper today?"

"Yep." Neil said. "Sure did." He anticipated some kind of reprimand from the sheriff for allowing the press such immediate access to the remains, but the sheriff did not seem to care about that at all. He just moved briskly on to business.

"Well, I just got a call from Jay Feather," the sheriff said, "member of the Chinook Indian tribe? And they have some things they'd like to talk to you about. They saw the picture and, well, their tribal council would like to come out to your spread and examine the remains themselves as soon as possible. They think the bones might be Indian." The sheriff sounded a little drowsy, as if this kind of thing happened all the time, but Neil could tell it was the kind of drowsiness designed to muffle someone else's panic, to lead them into a false sense of comfort. He used the same tactic himself sometimes, and it made him wary.

"Indians?"

"Yeah, Jay Feather is a member of the Confederated Tribal Council, big into repatriation issues." The sheriff continued, "He wants to reclaim any human remains that can be traced back to Indian ancestors. And he thinks the ones you found might apply. There's no solid laws on the books governing this stuff, so ultimately you can do what you want, but some of the other confederated tribe members are getting pretty aggressive about it. They have a real P.R. machine."

"Okay," Neil said. That seemed fine. If that was the extent of the sheriff's bad news, then everything was all right. He had nothing to worry about. Let them examine the bones if they wanted to. He welcomed it. If the bones were theirs, they could have them.

"Oh, and another thing," the sheriff added. "And this is where it gets a little sticky. It seems Mr. Grimsrud is holding a press conference in a few minutes himself. He has a statement to make. He saw the article too and got a little angry about it. Apparently he wants to block the Indians from looking at the remains at all. He says it's out of their jurisdiction and they have no right. He claims he's already established the skeletons were not indigenous people at all."

A moment later Neil placed the receiver back in its cradle and headed out onto the porch. Two more calls had arrived in rapid succession, from the newspaper and from a radio station, and after politely refusing to be interviewed by either one of them, he had unplugged the phone.

The sheriff had been kind enough to fill him in a little bit on the real story of the situation, the trap that Neil had wandered into. A few years ago, it seemed, Mr. Grimsrud had encountered the Chinook tribe in a professional capacity, and they had come to some fairly serious divisions. Mr. Grimsrud had unearthed a burial site on public land in Washington that included burnt remains of some kind. The Confederated Tribes had sued him in federal court to keep him from investigating further, and things had gotten a little ugly. There had been lawsuits, and counter lawsuits, and a court case that eventually took four years to conclude, during which time the remains were lost numerous times, by various governmental agencies, and in the end only handed over piecemeal to the Indians, who buried them again on their own reservation. In the end, neither party was wholly satisfied, and many bones remained in government possession even today, though no one knew quite where.

It appeared to the sheriff that the bones in Neil's possession were shaping up into a rematch between old enemies. Neil owned them for now, but he might want to start thinking about who to give them away to.

Neil sat down on his steps and sipped his coffee, which was already cold. The pile of unchopped wood mocked him from the garden, fastening to the land in a shape of frozen permanence. Up on the ridge the poplar trees shimmered like razor blades in the sunlight, but Neil was not fooled by their beauty. Somewhere in the distance great forces were aligning against him, major powers converging to bum him out. Slowly but surely he was being placed in an awkward position and eventually, whether he liked it or not, some decision was going to have to be made. Someone was going to lose.

# 8

"**D**ON'T GET RAPED," Tina's mom said as Tina left the house, and Tina managed to roll her eyes just as the door slammed shut behind her. She stepped down the stairs and held her hand out to feel for rain. It was a drizzly day outside, but not too cold, and a high, thick layer of clouds made a pearlescent plane where the sky should be.

Trixie was waiting for her at the garden gate, wearing her nurse hat and orthopedic shoes. "The General is in the Bolus," she said, which meant Neil was in the dining hall.

"Roger," Tina said. "Stinky Sessions is with him. But we're clear."

The girls set off toward the intersection of Upper Drive and Highway 30 to catch their bus, which arrived there every couple hours to park on the shoulder for a few minutes, and then turn around, having touched the furthest extremity of the tri-county metropolitan boundary. Beyond the shoulder of the dirt road the earth smelled of spores and mildew, and old leaves rotting in the dark shadows below the trees.

"Did you tell your mom anything?" Trixie asked.

"No. Not really," Tina said. "What do you mean?"

"Like where we're going. What we're doing. You know."

"No way," Tina said. "I don't tell her stuff like that. Why? Did you tell Beth?"

"No way!" Trixie said. "That would not be good."

When they got to the bus stop Trixie pulled a wad of aluminum foil from her pocket, which she unwrapped to reveal a smaller envelope of Saran Wrap, inside which nested two scraps of paper, each one a perfect square. "Shall we?" she said. She picked one up by the edges and put it on her tongue, and Tina did the same. They smiled at each other knowingly, and stood around the plastic bus depot, throwing pine cones at a mailbox across the street and sometimes burning wet leaves in the hissing butane flame of their lighter. Occasionally a car zoomed by, its rubber zipping on the road, and blew their coats around their waists, and then the street would be quiet and empty for a long time again.

There was nothing more exciting than a new best friend. And one of the best things to do with a new best friend was drugs.

By the time the bus arrived, the acid was coming on. Tina's mouth was watering and her jaw was clenching up, and she was trying to remain calm about the racing palpitations of her heart. Taking a whole hit went somewhat against her more cautious nature, but with Trixie there was never a sense of moderation. It was everything all the time, and anything less than that was not worth the effort.

As the bus approached, gasping and squealing to a halt, Tina stepped back from the edge of the road. Cars are real, she reminded herself. That was a good rule on acid. The bus's folding doors flopped open before her.

"After you," Tina said.

"Why thank you," said Trixie.

Tina took the fat steps of the bus with a series of hollow-sounding thumps, and dropped her coins into the slit with a clangorous tinkle that stayed in her mind long after it was gone. She followed Trixie down the aisle to find their seats, brushing her fingers on the vivid surfaces as they passed. Everything seemed outlined in a fine edge, like it had been cut from the world and then set gently back in place, a little off its drop. The strip of scored rubber leading down the center clutched tiny nuggets of dirt and hair in its corrugated grip and the plastic shells of the seats were scuffed and dinged, some of them with whitened initials scraped into their surfaces like shaved ice. When they sat down, it began to rain, and the sound of raindrops snapping on the windshield was like a newspaper burning up, just as the ashes were about to float away.

"Are you feeling it?" Trixie asked as they settled in.

Tina curled her mouth into a smile. "Uh huh."

Soon the bus lurched into gear and the landscape outside the window began to move, changing quickly from one thing to another, meadows and forests and rivers all scrambled together. They drove past stacked railroad cars like colored soaps, and old quonset huts in gravel lots, and the warehouse for Jacob's Heating and Air Conditioning. They drove by a field of sheep that looked like Ireland, a meadow of alpine wildflowers that looked like Switzerland, and an uprooted stump like a huge, white heart, its pale roots rising into the air like ripped arteries. Tina raised her camera and snapped a picture of it just as the bus turned off Highway 30 and up into the hills toward Beaverton.

"Good one," Trixie said, and wrote something down on a pad of paper.

"Thanks," Tina said back, and returned her camera to her bag.

Tina and Trixie had work to do. For the past month they had been writing movies nonstop, almost one every day, and they had a whole repertoire in various states of completion. There was "Shitface," the story of a hippie couple who moved to the woods, and who named their baby Shitface to demonstrate their contempt for the strictures of society's language; "The Babies," a horror movie about a swarm of human babies crawling all over and devouring everything in their path; and "The Rocker," the story of an aging rock star whose teenage groupie, it turns out, is his own daughter. Their ideas arose mostly from the things they saw in life, cut out and placed in a frame, or from the television set, dictated by the vacuous material of the networks and advertising agencies as it passed through the distorting lens of their own tastes and politics. What they wanted was movies about forgotten things, unseen things, things that boys would never think about.

Their favorite movie so far was "The Lobotomist," the tale of a nineteenth-century Philadelphia doctor struggling to invent the full frontal lobotomy. They both saw it clearly. Working at night, the surgeon hoped to wipe out the scourge of melancholy in the world by removing small portions of people's brains. At first the doctor used clay busts and animals, but soon he decided to test his procedure on a woman from the local women's prison, where inmates were often used as medical experiments, as they had no family or friends to prevent it. He selected a woman with a rich history of mental disorder, and a beautiful, haunted face. After interviewing her a number of times in preparation for the surgery, a kind of intimacy developed between them. She came to love him in a way, even though he planned to hurt her, and he grew to love her as well, believing that he was hurting her for her own good.

Then, at the end of the movie, he lobotomized her.

Today they were on a mission to scout for locations, and carried with them a whole list of imaginary country roads and turrets and buttressed asylums to nail down to specific places. They were looking for a woman's prison, and a cobbled street with wrought-iron railings and Gothic-y architecture, and a forest with properly stunted trees to represent the Pennsylvania countryside as they imagined it. They were also looking for places like an antique pharmacy and a Victorian sitting chamber and perhaps a bedroom with a four-poster bed and a dusty candelabra. While they traveled, Tina would take pictures of the locations, and Trixie would write them down in order on a pad of paper. Their bus transfers were good for at least three hours at a time, if anyone even checked.

At Germantown Road the bus wheezed to a stop, and two more passengers got on board, a woman with almost no lips and a man with a long overbite. They took the seats directly ahead of the girls and immediately struck up a conversation. The woman waved her hand around in circles, fingernails speckled with eroded red polish, while the man nodded up and down in powerful jerks. Gradually, Tina fell into their conversation for what felt like forever.

"That Popsicle I ate yesterday, it hurt real bad," the woman said.

"You need to get a cotton swab with medicine on it and stick it in the cavity," the man said, his voice like a cartoon. "It tastes bad and it smells bad, but it works."

"Huh?"

"It tastes bad and it smells bad, but it works! Or you could pull it out yourself," he said. "My old lady'd borrow my pliers and go out to the garage and come back with this bloody tooth."

Tina's window had begun vibrating and the specks of water made jagged streaks along the surface. The nuts and bolts and plastic ribbings of the bus were vibrating as well, and all the seams between the different parts of the interior were fluttering in her vision.

"Oh, I wish I had the guts to do that," the woman said, "but I'd be afraid I'd break it off without getting the roots."

"Oh, her roots were real small," the man said, holding his fingers about half an inch apart. "Mine are a lot bigger." He opened his fingers to an inch. Then he mimed a yanking motion, pulling up and out of his mouth, which made Tina wince with sympathizing pain. Beside her Trixie winced as well, and it was good to know that their perceptions were so well calibrated.

Tina turned her head slightly to catch Trixie's eye, but found her face adjusted toward the aisle. Her inner ear was crusted with a yellowish wax, and the fuzz of her round cheek had collected tiny flakes of foundation. Her blond hair looked brittle with product.

Suddenly, without trying, Tina recognized something ugly in Trixie's face that she had never seen before. Something in the way Trixie's pores dotted her nose that seemed to shape the very contours of her personality on the most unconscious but obvious level. Tina looked away, and stared out the window to get a grip on things. Today was not a day for hidden feelings, she told herself. Today was a day for perfect honesty, a trick unto itself.

Tina watched a single electrical line dipping and rising between poles for a while, as her mind skipped from thought to thought, and spun out into elaborate helices of association. The acid was coming on harder now, and each thought extended to its outermost extreme, then inverted, and became a box within a box.

Tina scrolled through their friendship in a quick montage—their first bike ride into the city together, their long evening playing

Monopoly, their midnight swim. In the movie of her and Trixie's young friendship, she thought, there were many roles to play. Dumb and smart, and funny and straight, even pretty and homely, which they managed to share somehow, although Trixie was definitively the more attractive one. Sometimes Tina would be fast, and Trixie would be slow, or Tina would be spastic and Trixie would be mellow. Sometimes they would swap roles midway through. In the end, though, no role was better than another. It was just that two of them needed to be filled in order for the system to work.

In this way Tina's thoughts about Trixie became thoughts about thoughts about Trixie, and her worries became more abstract and diffuse. When she glanced at Trixie, she found that she looked perfectly normal again, staring quietly at the rings on her fingers.

Tina relaxed. The acid was a struggle they were enduring together. They had poisoned themselves, and they were seeing how their bodies processed the toxin.

Tina rummaged through her backpack and pulled out a honey jar filled with water. She unscrewed the top and drank some, and it tasted so clean it was almost sweet. She pressed the jar toward Trixie and asked if she wanted some, and her voice came out surprisingly serious and alert, like she was in good control. Trixie nodded and took the jar and when she was done, Tina screwed the lid back on and put it back in her backpack, feeling somehow accomplished for having completed the operation so efficiently.

Suddenly Trixie laughed out loud.

"What?" Tina asked.

"I just thought of a good name for a baby."

"Yeah?"

"My first baby is going to be named 'Danger.'"

Tina laughed.

"Or 'Vice,'" Trixie added.

"Mine's 'BeBop,'" Tina said.

"My first daughter is named 'The Bobaloo Bird.'"

"My son is named 'Bundar.'"

The girls were still going on their list when the bus finally opened up and the moist valley dipped toward Beaverton. The sun came out, and the wet ribbons of highway spreading across the farmland turned bright silver. They zoomed past thin braces of trees hiding scalped earth, and huge piles of shattered wood. A pulp mill pumped out ruffles of sulfurous smoke and steam rose from sogging piles of lumber and stumps. Aluminum shacks echoed with sunlight. The sound of the bus rumbled around the girls and they passed a dirt trail leading into a scrubby forest of pines, where Trixie hit Tina on the shoulder and she raised the camera automatically to shoot it. The sky above them was a sheet of blue silk and the clouds were made of plastic. The world was an architectural model of the world.

"What?" Trixie asked.

"I didn't say anything."

The bus stopped more often as it reached the outskirts of town, and soon they were traveling along a horizontal plane of strip malls and car dealerships, all ablaze with snapping pennants and shimmering tinsel. A generation ago this had all been farmland, but new buildings were appearing in every empty space, wedged into lots like ginger-bread houses. There were condos and subdivisions and sprawling mansions crammed onto postage-stamp lots, many of them without dormers, or lintels, or even windowsills. All the buildings looked just like buildings from somewhere else, flimsy and deceptive.

"It's such a façade," Tina said.

"Dollhouses," Trixie concurred. "I can't believe they build this shit."

When they passed Fred Meyer, they got off the bus to investigate a photo shop they had never seen before. They often went behind one-hour photo booths to pillage the Dumpsters for discarded misprints and doubles, and whatever other photographic ephemera they could find, negatives and contact sheets and slides. They had amassed a whole library of stolen snapshots that way, which they kept in a file cabinet in an old schoolhouse in the woods. They had pictures of handicapped men in rubber body suits, girls giving their boyfriends blowjobs on mountain trails, badly framed pictures of bored children in suburban homes, sitting on flame retardant bedspreads. They had a whole piece of binder paper devoted to cut-out red eyes, and a special file on people they knew, or people who looked like people they knew. It was like gazing straight into the deepest recesses of other peoples' lives, they agreed, and using those peoples' very eyes to do it with. It was like taking control of their bodies through demonic possession.

They found a roll of pictures of a family vacation in Mexico, and got back on the next bus. It was not the best find, but not too bad either. The picture of the flushed father in a giant sombrero was a keeper.

Now the bus turned east and rose over the hill toward Portland, past the zoo and the science museum, where Tina had the passing insight that her own cynicism was a poisonous substance of some sort, released by glands directly into her muscles and organs.

And then, around a curve, the whole city appeared, a cluster of skyscrapers visible in a single eyeful, bordered by green-black masses of land. In the distance, the Willamette River peeked into view, or at least the empty air above it, and farther on, the white cap of Mount Hood, though it was half-erased by cloud cover. The bus rolled into the city streets, dotted with people on the sidewalks, bobbing past each other in streams, where Tina began experiencing a strobing effect in her vision, like tiny frames had been cut from the flow of time. The bus overtook one person after another, and the flashing continued, and Tina had an insight about how time worked, and also something about the nature of film. She could see now that time consisted of tiny, immeasurably brief moments, which when linked together gave the illusion of continuity, just as the frames of film scrolling past the lamp blended together into the illusion of forward motion. Tiny fragments of time interlocking to give the impression of a rushing stream.

She tried to explain this to Trixie, but it came out as something else. She ended up describing how movies took time and cut it up into little pieces and rearranged it into different order like a deck of cards. How yesterday and the week before could suddenly chafe together in a movie without any of the soft padding of sleep and boredom between them that normally quarantined one important moment from the next. All the dead time could be scraped away, she said, and only the significant parts left in place. The amnesia of duration could be disappeared.

Somehow Trixie seemed to understand what Tina was talking about, even though her knotted tangle of words and gestures barely made sense, and she nodded gravely the whole time in utter agreement. She demonstrated her understanding by saying that the jarring juxtaposition of different moments was how we learned about justice, by seeing two things unequal side by side, which to Tina seemed immeasurably deep.

They crossed the river over the Morrison Bridge, where their transfers ran out, and got off the bus and smoked some pot. Tina's skin felt leathery and the cigarette they had was the greatest thing in the world. She rubbed her face and stared as hard as she could at the pebbles on the ground, the cars on the overpass nearby, the paint peeling on the wall of the B&O building.

"Keep going?" Trixie asked.

"Yeah. Keep going," Tina said.

They turned around and got back on the next bus, this one going north, rolling past the Coliseum and along Albina, then out to the airport. As they passed near some radio towers, Tina felt on the verge of some massive revelation that never came. The world seemed to crouch in waiting, ready to pounce, or rip open in some dramatic display of meaning, but always just beyond her field of perception. Trixie felt it too and for a long while the girls clutched the air in front of them and whispered the word to each other over and over again, "Almost . . . almost . . ."

On Eighty-second Avenue, past the Unicorn Inn and B.B.'s Gun Rack, the bus wheezed to a stop and a stocky young Mexican man climbed on board, wearing a cowboy hat and a denim jacket with the sleeves rolled up as far as they would go, tucked into a bulging utility belt covered in key chains and padlocks and pouches, clasped with a huge silver belt buckle of molded curlicues. His tight black jeans appeared brand new, and their cuffs were spattered in mud. As soon as he sat down across the aisle from Tina, he pulled out a can of chewing tobacco, which he limply attempted to pack. He flopped his hand back and forth, but could not get his finger to thump against the tin properly, and eventually he just scooped out a dip and put it in. He sat back in his seat for a second but immediately began to jerk and twitch and look around the bus like he needed someplace to put something. He leaned over and spit out the window; he stood up; he walked to the front of the bus for a schedule; he sat back down; he stood up. Finally he pulled off his jacket, which he folded carefully and set down on the seat beside him. Underneath it he was wearing a brand-new T-shirt, black with red lettering, that read, I'M THE COWBOY THAT YOUR MOTHER WARNED YOU ABOUT.

Trixie and Tina laughed so hard they almost peed in their pants. They laughed until their cheeks hurt and their ribs ached. The laughing went on for so long, in fact, that they nearly missed an abandoned hospital passing by on the side of the road, hidden by some fir trees, with an empty flag pole standing guard. The building was a long, three-story structure, with peeling paint and broken windows, and a pretty impressive massing of parts. The roof sloped to a dramatic peak, and the windowsills were all molded and fine. The brickwork looked complex, and the eaves were imposing, if somewhat dilapidated. It was not precisely Victorian, but neither was it too modern. It looked definitely institutional, but also vaguely residential, which was just right for their purposes in a way. For night exteriors, it might do just fine as a Philadelphia women's prison.

"That could be it," Trixie said excitedly, tapping on the glass. "That could totally be it."

"Maybe," Tina said. "I guess."

"No," Trixie maintained, "that could totally be it."

"So," Tina paused, "you want to check it out?"

"Yeah," Trixie said. "Do you?"

"If you want to," Tina said. "Is that what you want?"

"Well," Trixie said, "yeah. I guess so. I mean, yeah, let's do it."

The bus stopped at the next intersection and the girls got out and walked back toward the building's long driveway. Tina found the absence of the engine sound disconcerting. The air seemed dead, the chirping of birds was shrill and abrasive, but slowly she grew accustomed to the new environment. The grounds of the building were weedy and unkempt, and the driveway was filled with potholes and cracked concrete.

Trixie skipped on ahead to the front door, and as she moved farther away Tina began to dread the coming exploration. Now that she was out in the air, she realized that she had been enjoying the comfort of the bus, the lack of options it imposed on them, the strapped-in sameness of the whole thing. Confronted with an enormous, condemned building to roam around in, full of dirty, broken things and skittering noises, she started to get nervous. She hoped, on some level, that the hospital was locked and shuttered, that some giant padlock would turn them away, but Trixie seemed intent on getting inside no matter what. She was already peeking in windows and pulling on door handles and eyeballing rickety drainage pipes as if they might hold her weight.

Tina stepped over a plaque in the ground that Trixie had raced past without seeing. The building, it said, had been a Shriner's hospital a few decades before. Something about finding the plaque made her feel superior to Trixie, like she was more observant than her more adventurous friend.

The girls reunited at the front door and peered inside. A chrome-plated reception desk curved from one wall around to the next, its frontispiece embossed with the Shriner's insignia. "This used to be a Shriner's hospital," Tina said, and Trixie said, "Looks like it."

It seemed the interior had been redecorated at some point, in a more modern, art deco style, and Tina made a disapproving sound, but Trixie's enthusiasm did not diminish. They stalked around the perimeter of the building, framing possible shots and trying to excise power lines and modern appliances from the imaginary frame. The windows stared blankly, striped with bars, which Tina had to admit was pretty perfect, and some of them even had lacy drapes, yellowing and dusty, from some long-forgotten era. From different vantage points, the building looked properly angular and pitched. By moonlight, surely it would read as intimidatingly authoritarian.

"Look here," Trixie said, holding her hands in the air. "A bounce light with a blue filter, rumbling storm clouds. Movie magic, Colonial women's asylum."

Tina closed one eye and peered up at the eaves. "Yeah. It'd be pretty great. No doubt. If we can only find out who to talk to."

"Oh, we can find that out," Trixie said.

Around the back, the girls found a window without any bars, and Trixie started looking around for something to break it with. Tina paced back a few steps, and kept her eye on the corner of the building, where she figured any security guards might come from, and from where she might escape quickly if they did. Trixie finally settled on a crumbling brick and smashed the glass, using a branch to clear away the shards left sticking to the frame. She looked back at Tina as she slipped inside and for a second everything seemed to narrow down and become hypersignificant. The image of Trixie moving through the broken window into the darkened room sent off alarms in Tina's head. "No one does that, no one does that," she heard squawking in her ear like seagulls, and felt a black swarm of fear tighten around her skin. But she climbed in the window nonetheless. Anything else would be embarrassingly lame.

The light inside the hospital was gray and feeble, filtered through dirty, streaked windows. The floor was covered in rubble, and the walls were water stained. It smelled clammy, with a slight hint of ammonia. Metal cabinets lined the walls, and the blue stripping on the counter-tops peeled back to reveal black rubber pocked with dried glue. Tina saw light from the window fall through Trixie's ear, and blood infusing the tender skin, and could not help but intuit that the quiet air was heavy with some evil vibration.

"Yeah," Trixie said, with a leering grin. "This is it."

"I bet there's more," Tina said, mastering her fear. "Let's look around."

"Okay," Trixie whispered. "But be careful."

For the next hour the girls moved from room to room, rolling old wheelchairs around and listening to their footsteps echo through the hallways. They found rusted beds with rubber mattresses, and old washbasins filled with strange, putrid fluid. They found cabinets with mouse-eaten towels and closets crowded with straw brooms and cracked buckets. Finally, they wandered into a cavernous room with a wall made of cloudy glass bricks and a huge indoor swimming pool gaping at its center like a mouth. The ceiling of the room arched high above them, chapped with water stains and crumbling plaster, and the battered walls were covered in harsh streaks of red and black graffiti. Broken bottles and old candy wrappers littered the edges of the concrete floor.

"Let's rest," Tina said.

Trixie nodded, grinding her teeth.

"How about here?" Tina said, brushing some dust from the lip of the pool.

"Good," Trixie said tersely.

The girls sat down side by side, and stared at the pool's cracked tiles, as the walls ballooned in and out almost imperceptibly, and the floor coursed with glowing arabesques. Time passed slowly, and the sounds of the building came to them in distant pops and bangs.

At some point, after the light had changed a little, and the space of the room had become more familiar, Tina let her mind wander. She let go of the current moment long enough to reflect a little, and think about herself in a somewhat objective way.

Tina was overcome with a feeling of profound sorrow, like some phantom organ was throbbing inside her chest. All the missing parts in her life assumed mass and shape. The people she had left behind and places she would never see again flowed into her consciousness like apparitions. She felt like an empty vessel filling with water, volumes rounding out with pressure, and more than anything else, among all the things she had lost or forgotten, she recognized an inexhaustible guilt feeling toward her mother, who she realized responded to everything with fear. She saw her mother's face wrinkled with pain, and sensed the incredible amount of time that she spent alone. And then, when Tina stepped back from these thoughts, she glimpsed a gaping maw behind all the colors and shapes of things, sucking oxygen like a flame, and then the gaping maw became pinwheeling, photo-negative flowers.

Beside her, Trixie made a gasping sound and it seemed like they had both been traveling on the same plane of reflection, as strange and convoluted as that might seem.

Tina had no idea how long they sat there next to the shattered pool, but finally they concentrated hard enough to get themselves out. They stretched their legs and made a final circuit through the empty hall-ways, where they located a small, closet-sized room they had missed before, with a huge lock that had rusted open. Inside the room, the walls were covered in scratches and gouges, and marks that looked like they had come from fingernails clutching into the wood, and they realized after awhile that it had been a detention chamber, where violent patients had been interred. They got a terrible chill, and hurried away. It was time to go.

When they finally emerged from the hospital the sunlight was blinding, and the air smelled so clean it seemed to scrub their lungs. The sun was like a tremendous klieg light pouring color onto the world, and the invisible stars were some kind of elaborate gaffing from heaven. Tina looked toward the strip of buildings visible through the fir trees, where cars were driving, stopping at lights, and people could be seen moving around on the sidewalks, going into grocery stores and opening bank accounts, all the many things that people do, like some enormous plot in progress.

"Tina," Trixie said. "Look at that cloud."

Across a patch of grass, Trixie was leaning against a lamppost in her nurse hat and shoes, staring into the sky. Her arms were wrapped loosely around the metal pole and she craned her neck upward, glancing at Tina to reveal the life of her glittering blue eyes. For a lovely moment Tina felt as if she had been split neatly in two. She had two bodies now, roaming the earth and communicating by a kind of telekinesis, a probe, to report back to her all the things it saw and felt, and to whom she would report back as well. One life was not enough she could see. One life was only half of the story.

"Yeah," Tina said, spotting the hard, sculpted cloud in the sky. "It's great."

Tina was glad now that they had made the exploration, and gravely agreed with Trixie that it was the perfect place to shoot their movie. They stood around and gnawed on the same thoughts for a while and sometimes nodded and said out loud, yes, it will work. It makes sense. They must find a way to do it. They smoked some more pot and walked down the road to a Safeway nearby, where they could get some orange juice and catch another bus. They walked beside a cyclone fence, which wavered a little in Tina's vision, and it occurred to her that the entire thing was made out of holes.

At the supermarket the plate glass windows were covered in hand-painted signs on butcher paper that said Super and Cool and Save. They wandered down the aisles of food and soap, all packaged in colorful bags and boxes. Saccharine musical arrangements floated overhead and the fluorescent lights made everything pop. Light seemed to emanate from the cereal boxes, the bread, the cylindrical barrels of orange juice frosted with crystals, and off the speckled linoleum floor. There was a whole wall of chips, the same bags repeating over and over again, in orange and blue and white. There were bricks of gum and chocolate bars and laundry detergent, a rack of mascara dangling from narrow pins. A pale square of sunlight fell from the window and mixed with the fluorescent light from over-head, and the overlapping effect of light on light made Tina shiver with pleasure.

The block of sunlight coursed with sparkling, calligraphic halluci-nations, and Tina raised her camera to capture it on film. She took a picture, and then another. She kept taking them until Trixie finally touched her on the shoulder and asked her what she was doing.

"Taking pictures," Tina said, clicking a few more shots, "of all the shapes and colors," and after a beat the girls both laughed so hard they practically died.

"No way," Tina said, when they finally made it outside again.

"What?" Trixie asked.

"Look."

Walking through the Safeway parking lot between the hard, metal cars was Bob Grossberger, wearing a long yellow muscle shirt and knee-high moccasins, carrying a huge bag of raw potatoes in his arms. He stopped at an old station wagon, where he unlocked the door and threw the potatoes inside, then swung himself in behind them. The girls watched him from behind a tan Eldorado, delighted to find him so far from his natural habitat. As he pulled out into traffic and disappeared from view, his back window flashing white in the sun, they nodded at each other approvingly. They did not have to say a word. They had been keeping a list of Bob Grossberger sightings, and this one was going right on top.

# Part Two

# 1

T HE SHIP LEFT before daybreak on a glass of morning river. The prow
slid through the water parting cobwebs of mist, and the stars blinked
out one by one. The grain of darkness thinned, and the color that had
drained from the fir trees and bulrushes returned to their surface, like
blood returning to a sleeping limb, in needles and pins. Distances
became measurable, masses discernable. The birds began to dot the air
with their encoded songs.

Cookie stood at the prow of the *Astor* and felt the ship's lean strength
moving beneath him, the wide wake expanding toward the shore. The
*Astor* was a young ship, sharp-bowed for speed and hard-driving, with
a graceful sheer curving from fore to aft like a sleek, hard-skinned cigar.
High above the main deck loomed sturdy teak spreaders, crossing the
masts on axes of iron, and beneath the deck of yellow pine lay a
skeleton of molded steel. The hull was fitted with a tight sheet of green
copper.

The passage of the *Astor* from the docks of Fort Vancouver down-
river to the open sea was slow going at first, rife with hidden shoals
and sandbars. The men kept themselves busy shaping cleats and towing
line, with their breath glowing around their mouths like strange halos.
Cookie watched them from the prow, lulled by the lapping sound of
the waves against the nearby shore, the clink of metal and the groan
of bending wooden joints.

Down the main deck were the rangy Nebraskans, Brian Apelt and
Andy Cotton, lashing a rope to a barrel of coal; high on the upper
rigging stood Tillamook the Clatsop Indian, born just a days' journey
from the docks, keeping lookout for jutting rocks; Wing and Chin,

black-eyed brothers from China, were heaving a metal pole near the fife rail.

On the main deck, the captain, Monsieur Boucher, a melancholy Frenchman with sagging cheeks, stood silently in place. He was a mild fellow, and rarely spoke, but his reputation ran counter to his demeanor. Rumor had it he had once sailed from Honolulu to New York in just a hundred and fifteen days, including a week of rerigging after rounding Cape Horn, and carrying two thousand tons of sperm oil the whole way to boot.

Soon enough the peak of Mount Hood brightened in the east, glowing orange against the indigo sky, and the last of the distant stars throbbed and went out. The predawn light lasted just a few heartbeats, during which time Cookie imagined cutting along the mountain's luminous edges with a pair of enormous scissors, and slipping the rosy shape into his breast pocket for safekeeping. He closed one eye and held the mountain between his fingers like a tooth. On the cusp of leaving the territory, Cookie had begun to feel like Oregon was home, and he reminded himself that soon enough he would be finding his way back.

When the sun appeared, and the mountain dimmed to a light pinkish hue, Cookie quit his reverie and dropped down a ladder in the middle of the deck to begin his workday. He landed in a long, narrow hallway lit with a few oil-burning lanterns bolted to the damp walls, and crept cautiously into the briny darkness. He turned a corner, passing a small door, and was just starting down a short flight of stairs when a shambling, wide-hipped sailor came bustling toward him from the shadows, his cotton trousers flaring and his wooden clogs beating on the floor. Cookie flattened himself against the wall and let him pass.

"Pardon," the sailor growled, as his belt buckle scuffed against Cookie's with a dull chime, and gave Cookie a blast of sour, garlicky breath in the face. Then the man was gone, ascending the ladder into the open air, and Cookie was brushing himself off and continuing on to the galley.

\*    \*    \*

Two doors down, Cookie arrived at the room where he would be spending the vast majority of his time at sea. The galley was a small room, about four paces in any direction, sporting a low countertop lit by a single porthole, topped with a thick cutting board commandeered from some decommissioned galley in the company's fleet, softened by long years of use. The shelves of the pantry were crammed with cartons of dried fruit and vegetables, bags of rice and flour, and jars of sauerkraut and bottles of lemon and orange syrup to fight whatever scurvy might break out among the men. In the corner squatted a hulking, four-burner wood stove, with a removeable griddle and segmented chimney pipe leading crookedly into the ceiling.

They were tight quarters, Cookie thought, but he had seen worse. The knives were sharp and the cupboards were well stocked, which were the important things. He closed the door gently behind him.

After stoking the fire with a pair of iron tongs, Cookie took down a tin pot and placed it on the stove, where he mixed in a few buckets of fresh water and fistfuls of dried oats. He covered the pot and returned the oats to the shelf, planning out his next few moves in his mind. Sugar? Dried currants? He was reaching for a container of golden raisins when his eyes grazed over twelve small jars labeled "honey" wedged between the molasses and the salt box.

Cookie stopped and stared at the jars for a moment, keeping his eyes as blank as possible. The jars did not contain honey at all. The substance was too thin, too yellowish, and it frothed too much with the swaying of the ship. Cookie smiled imperceptibly. The jars contained castoreum oil. Five pints in all. Enough to cure an entire army of gout or a medium-sized city of chronic hiccoughs, assuming it was used sparingly and combined with proper exercise and salty sea air.

Cookie's gaze lingered on the cloudy amber fluid, the fruit of his and Henry's time together, the promise of their great future, until he caught sight of his own reflection in the glass and hurriedly returned to his work.

Extracting the castoreum from the anal glands of the dead beavers had not been a pleasure. Cookie and Henry had spent five days collecting skinned corpses from outside the walls of Fort Vancouver, and piling them into a wooden wheelbarrow to cart back to their cabin. Without their skins the animals were small, rat-like creatures, with greasy, marbled bodies and exposed, protuberant teeth. For the next week they had plunged knives into their soft, rotting flesh and drilled out cones of meat from their hindquarters, then peeled back the cored sections and collected the raisin-like glands they found there, placing them in canning jars half filled with briny water to keep them from drying out in the air. Finally they had spread the tough nuggets on sheets of tin, and pressed them in a vise between heavy logs, with grooves indented to catch the oil and funnel it into thick glass jars. They had worn cheesecloth on their faces, and leather smocks over their clothes, but the smell had been something terrible, and by the time they were done, just hours before the ship set sail, they were promising themselves never to visit their cabin on that plot of land again, a nightmare of mangled tissue, pulled apart sinews and strands of fat. Cookie blanched at the mere thought of it. He would hang himself before going back.

But if the substance they had collected was indeed worth three times its weight in Chinese silver, as Henry maintained, it would all be worth the effort. Cookie and Henry would return to America wealthy men, at least enough so to claim some acreage and build something on it, and furnish it with some decent things, and certainly to plant an arbor of hazelnut trees or erect a brick-oven bakery, as the plan now stood.

Cookie chopped some walnuts and stared through the round portal above his cutting board at Indian villages where dogs and children played near cedar lodges, and old women hunched over piles of kindling. A young woman carried two bulbous water baskets on a stick across her shoulders, and placed them delicately beside a splintered stump.

Gradually the banks of the river became more sparsely inhabited, rising in damp, jagged cliffs with wispy waterfalls spouting from the trees. Just as Cookie finished with the walnuts, a huge, brown bear emerged on the river's edge and began swiping at the water with his tremendous paw. Silver chandeliers crashed around him and his wet fur seemed to shake over his meaty frame. Cookie watched the bear raise a flopping steelhead on his talon and throw it onto the land, craning his white teeth and pink mouth toward the sun, as the joists and braces of the ship squeaked and sighed pleasantly, hugging each other tightly for support.

Within a day the ship had passed from the mouth of the Columbia into the Pacific Ocean, and soon the shoreline disappeared from view, thinning and snapping like a tightening string. A plane of blank ocean extended in every direction as far as the eye could see. Seagulls drifted around the ship in a shared air current.

Early in the morning Cookie emerged from the galley to feed the chickens and collect a few logs for the breakfast griddle. The smell of the ocean surprised him, the cold wind needling his cheek. He padded from the hatch to the starboard railing, trying to avoid the sailors as they moved along in their elaborate pathways of labor.

"Excuse me. Pardon," he said, as the thick bodies milled around him, choreographed in some dance he could not comprehend.

When he reached the chicken coops, he took a moment to watch the crew going about their work, tying their intricate knots and moving their heavy crates from one place to another. Already, it seemed, the men were coming together in a spirit of teamwork, pairing up to lift things, and warning each other when booms were lowering their way. They treated each other like sons and fathers. "Well done," "good job," they said, patting each other on the rear ends. Standing on deck, a handful of chickenfeed draining through his fingers, Cookie watched the men chasing each other up and down the rigging, hollering into the wind, and for a moment got to wishing that he was a regular crewman himself, and not just the cook, sequestered in his dingy little room all day so far from the action. The men were itching for the high seas now, he could see, getting ready to put the ship through its paces.

At the center of the crew's boisterous collective life was Henry, who from their first crew meetings and dock-loading work had established himself as the fulcrum of all things sociable. He took a hand in every task, had the last word of every argument. He moved from joke to joke and game to game, sometimes straddling as many as three con-versations at once. Cookie watched him now, hauling a rope, his bagging, cotton pants held up with a length of cord, his hair covered by a piece of red cloth. Sweat gleamed on his back like wet metal and his spine curved under the strain, his muscles tensing with each tug on the line. He straightened and smiled at someone, flashing his teeth. There was something in Henry that belonged to everyone it seemed, and Cookie watched him like a proud mother, until their eyes met and he looked quickly away. Cookie and Henry had an agreement between them now. In order to hold their partnership in strict confidence, they would be keeping their contact in public to a minimum.

"Tillamook!" Henry called out. "Help me with this line over here!"

Cookie took one more glance and scurried back down to the galley.

Belowdecks, Cookie polished the forks and knives, and set beans in water for the evening meal, while tracing Henry's movements around the ship by the quarter hour. At eight he knew Henry was tending the chickens; at eight forty he was polishing the brass; at nine he could probably be found rolling dice behind the chimney stack, where the men with gambling streaks turned their luck.

Cookie laid out the silverware and bowls on an oaken table, and placed shoots of lemongrass in a ceramic vase to brighten the room, then finished off the setting with a huge bowl of bananas and oranges, which he took care to arrange with their bruises and soft spots turned toward the middle. A minute before breakfast, the table was a perfect arrangement of steaming bowls, glinting spoons, and clean napkins folded into crisp triangles.

Then the morning whistle blew and the first shift of men came stomping in, grumbling and laughing and elbowing each other through the door. Cookie recognized some of them from the main deck, Hammerhead and Four Fingers and Nick Stacy, but after a day at sea together they all seemed to be calling each other "Bastard."

"You're next to the bastard."

"Oh no I ain't. You are, bastard."

"Cookie," Nick Stacy nodded. "Smells fine in here, little man."

"I hope you like it," Cookie said.

After wrestling for places around the table, the men set on the food like a pack of starving dogs. They squeezed the bananas into their mouths and ate the oranges straight from the rinds, slurped down their oatmeal in rapid spoonfuls. Within a minute the bowls were empty and limp banana peels were hanging from the rafters, and the men were already kicking up their feet on the table to digest. Cookie moved nimbly around them, scooping up butter knives and washing bowls and refilling glasses of water and coffee, until eventually he returned to the galley and sat down on a stool to wait them out.

He was doubting that his little flourishes would last long.

Henry arrived in the third shift, and took his place at the table without a glance in either direction. Cookie played his part and treated Henry just like the others, calling him sir and keeping his bowl filled, giving him more coffee when he tapped the table with his index finger. When Henry's meal was done he left behind a mess of crumbs and squashed fruit just like the others, and exited like them without a word of thanks.

Cookie swept up the remains into the trash, and piled the dirty plates and silverware into a soapy bucket, muttering to himself under his breath. He could not understand how their mutual disregard was putting him on the bottom somehow.

At the end of their third day at open sea Cookie came up onto the deck to find the full moon surrounded by a vague aureole, and the stars spilled across the jet-black sky. Down by the poop, Henry was holding court in the firelight, recounting old adventures to a ring of young men arranged around him in a variety of attentive poses, elbows on their knees, half-smiles plastered over their bleary, sunburned faces.

"Never seen one like it!" someone yelled.

"Just you wait!" someone else bleated.

"What happened next, Henry?"

Orange flames flashed in Henry's eyes and danced over his arms as he launched into the story about the time he lost his virginity to an eighty-year-old whore in Bengal, one that Cookie had heard at least four times by now. Cookie rolled his eyes when the men exclaimed at some perilous part, which Henry phrased, as always, in perfectly self-deprecating tones, but which also managed to express his ultimate control over everything he ever touched or saw. Someone else piped up, but Henry turned the conversation back onto himself, and the men sat there waiting, rapt.

"Henry!" one sailor exclaimed. "You are a mindless idiot!" which was a high compliment among this crew.

Cookie drifted toward the starboard railing, where moonlight hit the water in a long, sparkling streak, casting about for some place to spend his off-hours. By now, he knew all the ship's ladders and platforms, the handful of secret hiding places it held. The fortress of freshwater barrels, for instance, or the backside of the chicken pens. His favorite place, though, was the crow's nest, a wooden cup on top of the central mast, like a thimble stuck on a long toothpick.

Cookie climbed up the rigging, one square of rope at a time, the wind snapping his hair, and heaved himself into the crow's nest's wooden bowl. He rested his chin on the lip and stared out over the huge volume of water. The sounds of laughter wafted up to him sometimes, little phrases and half-formed exclamations. Against his will, Cookie strained to catch the details, like a child wiggling a tooth or picking a scab.

"Did not! I don't believe it."

"I'm afraid so, fellas. And that ain't all . . ."

Cookie watched the curve of the ocean bending away from him toward the horizon. The sphere of water nested inside a sphere of sky, turning in a void of space. From a single point the world moved in every direction, farther and farther apart, getting thinner and thinner as it went, until finally it made no sense at all. With a friend you could mark the blank surface of time, though. You could pin it down together, triangulate. Without a friend, however, you were lost.

Cookie gripped the edge of the crow's nest until his fingers started to go numb, and the wood dug into his chin with a bite. He stared at the ocean from one end to another until he settled on a particular patch of gleaming wavelets and named the empty quadrant as his own property.

Suddenly Cookie's teeth clacked together with a shock. The crow's nest jiggled and shook. Someone was climbing up toward him, he realized, a shadowy figure hitching his way up the ropes, loose-limbed and slow. Cookie tried to collect himself, falling back down in the cylinder to wait.

A moment later a hand appeared on the rim of the cup, with strong knuckles and a weatherbeaten map of creases and calluses. It was Henry's hand, and sure enough Henry's face presently popped over the rim of the crow's nest like a jack-in-the-box.

"Howdy," he whispered. "So this is where you're at." He carried with him a bottle of port and a pouch of tobacco, which he handed to Cookie before hoisting himself over the lip. Cookie squeezed against the wall to make room and Henry dropped heavily to the floor.

Henry's skin was browner than before, with dark freckles spread over his forearms and nose, and his body held a sharp, salty tang. He offered Cookie a drink from his bottle, and set his tobacco pouch out for both of them to roll from.

"Haven't seen you in a while," Henry said, grinning. "Where have you been keeping yourself? You stick down in that galley all day long."

Cookie smiled wanly and said, yes, he'd been busy. He knew Henry had been busy as well.

"Well, you better make some time for me, pal," Henry said, "or else I won't remember what you look like." He smiled broadly and squeezed Cookie's arm in a quick, vise-like grasp, and in one moment all Cookie's worries were gone.

For the next few hours they watched the stars billow in the sky together, and conferred about the character of the other men. They agreed that Trent was not the worst of them, and that Tillamook saw things deeply, and that Jethro was fine but not to be trusted. They whiled away the time second-guessing the captain's orders and discussing the day's events, smoking cigarettes with the dome of the sky curving above their heads.

They talked about the ship for a while, and Henry got Cookie to appreciate the scientific advances that had been incorporated into her sleek design.

"Look at her, Cookie," Henry said. "She's a beauty, ain't she? Never seen anything like her in my life. Them timber galleons I shipped on as a boy, they're always rotted and falling apart. But this one, boy, she's different. Iron laced right into her skeleton, and none of them figureheads or fancy woodwork. She's a work of science, Cookie, I'm tellin ya. Gonna tighten the net of commerce around the whole globe. The laws of evolution are on our side, buddy. The next generation of clipper ship'll make our business even easier than this one."

Cookie nodded along with Henry's excitement, and could not help feeling a little bit of it himself, now that his fate was intertwined with Henry's somewhat. He had never been on the side of the future before.

Next Henry explained to Cookie all about the partnerships and contractual agreements that made the international fur trade possible, how the sea otter and beaver pelts in the hull were owned by the British Northwest Fur Company, although the ship itself was owned by the Boston-based company of Rhubarb and Lix; how due to an exclusive Chinese franchise granted to the East India Company by the royal crown the British firm had been forced to enter into an arrangement with the American firm to do trade in Cathay. For carrying the cargo, he explained, the American firm received a quarter of the gross profits and 5 percent commission on sales, while its British partner, for amassing and packing it, got the rest. As for the return load, tea and spices purchased in Canton and bound for San Francisco, that was split down the middle, having been purchased and traded using the profits of the pelts.

Cookie listened closely to all of it, though his mind wandered, mostly fascinated by Henry's fascination itself. He was like a child watching an anthill or the migration of birds. Together they gloated over the infallibility of their plan. Castoreum oil was surely the trick. It was the logical next thing.

A flock of seagulls passed over the disk of the moon, and beneath them the ocean heaved and raced like mercury. Their cigarettes cast reddish accents on their faces and their knees sometimes bumped together with the swell of a wave or the rattle of the breeze. Down on deck the men had begun singing slurred verses about maidens and demigods, who loved each other and were pulled apart, only to meet again in different guises. Cookie finished off the port and corked up the bottle, then reached for a last twist of tobacco to smoke before bed.

Henry stubbed his own cigarette out on the wooden wall, his face a mask of shadow, almost skeletal in the moonlight. His lips were polished in silver and his teeth flashed between them like bits of candy. He looked evenly at Cookie through the gloom.

"Good night, partner," Henry whispered, and then he was gone, lowering himself back down the rigging toward the fire.

That night in his hammock Cookie slept peacefully for the first time in days, rocked in the cradle of waves. The rules of the sea were different than those on land, it seemed, but in many ways they were the same; he was becoming resigned to the sweet, excruciating simplicity of their limits.

As the *Astor* drifted south toward the Sandwich Islands, the crew settled into a steady pattern of work, hoisting sails, swabbing decks, mending whatever leaks appeared in the hull. The winds were strong and the ship made good time, crossing the thirty-fifth parallel in near record time. At dawn every morning the captain unfolded his ivory ruler, and at noon he operated his friction divider. Sometimes he unsheathed his compass from its shagreen case to inscribe the ship's location in a thick, leatherbound log of yellowed paper.

Cookie observed the workings of the *Astor* with a kind of detachment, and gradually came to view the ship as a world composed of three distinct bands of space. There was the galley, the deck, and the crow's nest, and each had its own, unique logic and rhythm. The galley, in Cookie's mind, was all heat and noise, and constant busy work, the smell of scorching lard and billowing clouds of steam, while the deck was a place for quiet contemplation, where the bland spectacle of other men's labor played out before the repeating patterns of the ocean's breath, like a painting or stage play produced for his own dry amusement. And the crow's nest was a dream world of nocturnal pleasure, which he sometimes could not believe existed at all. As callously as Henry might treat him in the light of the day, he was always pleasant under the moon and stars, and they continued to meet there whenever they could to report back to each other and express their devotion to the plan.

As the days progressed, the self-enclosed system of the crew found endless ways of recombination. Loyalties shifted, cliques formed. The mechanics of the crew tightened and loosened as the situation allowed, producing with the same parts under different circumstances the conditions for both joy and abject boredom. There were tensions, but the men remained largely well-behaved, never ganging up on one person more than a few times in a row, and sometimes displaying surprising degrees of generosity. The weather always changed the men's mood, causing them to sweeten or sour on each other, and liquor affected them even more profoundly, for better or worse depending on how much and how long they drank. They were always looking for reasons to break the monotony, and so birthdays and longitudinal crossings became major events on the calendar.

The captain was partly responsible for the harmonious state of affairs. He kept to himself, and made the men find their own pecking order, which in a way brought out the best in them. He made suggestions here and there, and seemed sorry when things did not work out, but trusted his men to do their jobs efficiently, and to think critically about the how and why of their daily chores. He wielded his authority, when he did, with a kind of regret, and the men came to feel almost sorry for him, and worked harder just to keep his spirits up. They worried about him the way a boy might worry for his older brother, and their pity was made sweeter for its hidden quality.

A month into the voyage the *Astor* arrived at their first portage since Fort Vancouver, the Sandwich Islands, famous for its sweet hogs prepared with pineapples and mangoes, and rubbed with wild garlic. Over the weeks the men had developed almost indecent fantasies about the meat, describing the juicy wedges to each other in the lurid tones of a sexual encounter. They imagined meat so soft it melted on their tongues, and left a buttery rime on their lips and teeth.

The beach of Whittity-Bay was made of fine white powder, and beyond it coconut trees bent under the weight of their hard fruit, and rainbows curved over the palm fronds. By the time the thatched huts of the natives appeared, the ship was already surrounded by catamarans, propelled by half-naked men with short, black hair cut into bangs, wearing only small strips of cloth to cover themselves, and sporting welted tattoos along their bellies and arms. The ship dropped anchor in a turquoise inlet and lowered the skiff.

When the hunting crew reached the land, the men were greeted by a loosely organized gang of natives, bearing official permits to stalk the islands' game, which came as something of a surprise to everyone who had ever landed on the Sandwich Islands before, because in the past the ownership of the islands' wild boar had devolved to whoever caught one. Now the wildlife belonged to the chieftain of the nearest village, however, and hunting it demanded a piece of parchment signed and stamped by his office. This permit, it turned out, could be purchased only with guns.

The captain hung his head. It seemed the islanders had become seasoned merchants in the short time since the European ships had arrived.

"Very good," he said, and agreed regretfully to the terms of their bargain. He turned around and ordered up a box of flintlock pistols from the hull, which although rusted and salt-encrusted he convinced the natives were perfectly good, and threw in some wet gunpowder as well, so that everyone came away happy for the time being.

The ship set sail the next morning, full of pork and mangoes, breadfruit and tuna, and although no one was proud of their dealings, they were not particularly remorseful about them either. In some ways the cheating of the natives even brought the men closer together. They shared a small sin between them now, and by not discussing it they sealed with each other a clear, unmentionable bond.

From there they sailed on toward the Philippines and the barren Lema Islands, and then toward Macao, as the ocean elapsed in a slow-changing kaleidoscope of gray and green and blue. The colors shifted, the waves rose and sank, and at night the constellations slowly revolved in the sky, like a huge, ticking clock. During this leg of travel the men's spirits began to waver. Their initial politeness wore off and they began to resent one another. Their stories had all been told, the jokes had run their course. The diet had become routine and the labor redundant. Everything had been done many times before. It was the long afternoon of their journey, and a different form of camaraderie grew, a complaining, cynical kind. The gentle captain appeared simply weak, and the teasing sometimes became cruel. Some of the men went for days without talking.

Cookie and Henry continued to meet in the crow's nest, though the topics of conversation were getting harder to find, and they had to dig deeper for good material to discuss. They talked about old memories they had, and failed ambitions, and the crazy personalities of some of the people they knew. They talked about the political situations of the day, the accomplishments of Thomas Jefferson. They even got around to talking about Cookie sometimes, which came as a surprise to both of them, as usually Henry held center stage. But on some nights Henry was too exhausted to play his role and needed a break.

One night, after spending an hour sitting there quietly, Henry suddenly turned his head and stared directly into Cookie's eyes.

"Where were you born, Cookie?" he asked.

"I told you that," Cookie said. "You know already."

"I do not know," Henry said. "You've been holding out on me."

"No, I haven't," Cookie said, looking away and smiling a little under the attention.

"I think you've been holding out on me," Henry said again.

"I haven't."

"You have. I think it's time you told me a little something about yourself, Cookie. Only fair. If we're partners, I got a right to know."

"You don't care," Cookie said, teasing.

"Yeah I do."

Cookie looked at the sea. The moon glared a hard, white light, its face bunched in pain, and silver clouds bundled on the horizon, dimpled with cauliflower folds. "Well," he said, pinching some tobacco from Henry's pouch and lifting his eyebrows for permission.

But Henry was already fast asleep, snoring evenly in the moonlight. Cookie touched his hair, and then rolled himself a cigarette. He did not question Henry. He did not want too much. He recognized that their whole arrangement, including the nighttime talking, was only temporary, and that once they arrived in China it would be something else again entirely. He knew enough simply to relish what he got, and in the meantime to wait. Their plan was getting done, and there was nothing much to do beyond that.

When Cookie's cigarette was finished he climbed heavily down the rigging and found his hammock, where he slept soundly until daybreak, swaying gently in the eastern breeze.

The next day the spell of sluggishness was finally broken when Tillamook spotted a Chinese village on the horizon, which was strange, as there was still no land in sight.

An hour later, however, his warning became clear, as the *Astor* passed through an offshore fishing fleet of some two hundred small junks. They worked in pairs, with nets trailing between them, carrying whole families on board, with cooking fires, and paper lanterns, and chickens in cages. It was like a floating township transposed whole cloth from the countryside. The ship sailed right through them, without a word of greeting or recognition. None of the fishermen looked up from their work or raised their voices. They simply parted to make room. Some of the children watched blankly from the decks, but overall it was a quiet, ominous interaction, and seemed to mark the entrance into a world of odd and unknowable rules.

Soon after that the Lema Islands appeared, where the ship fired its gun and hoisted its colors to signal a Chinese pilot aboard, an old fisherman who would guide them through the dangerous waters ahead. The old man carried testimonials from other ships he had taken up river, and for thirty-six dollars he navigated the maze of islets and rocks guarding the mouth of Canton Bay, leading them finally to anchorage off Portuguese Macao, where Cookie could see rows of pastel, European-style houses facing the sea along Praya Grande, and behind them the spires of thirteen churches.

Here the ship backed her topsails and hove to while pigtailed, silken-robed officials examined her hull and barracks. Eventually the Chinese emissaries issued a chop, permitting the vessel to take on yet another pilot and proceed up the shoal-beset Pearl River to Canton.

As they passed Lintin Island, the wind died down, and a crowd of sampans towed the ship toward its final anchorage at Whampoon, swirling about the vessel like ducklings around their mother. The river traffic became a dizzying concourse of native vessels: Chinese fast boats, more sampans, lighters, supply boats, customs boats, six-hundred-ton seagoing junks, and salt junks with eyes painted on their bows. Gangs of near-naked men walked on paddle wheels or manned sweeps, and rowboats with families and tiny cooking fires clustered together. There were barber's boats, fortune tellers, clothing merchants, bunion removers, and entire theater troupes. The sounds of gongs and music and yelling and laughter circled around the ship like a crazy dream.

Lining the banks of the river were ramshackle piers and floating buildings, leading up to cobbled streets and low, shingled rooftops. A hill rose over the city, topped with an elegant pagoda, nine gauzy, scalloped stories surrounded by clouds of blossoming cherry trees.

Cookie took in the scene with a strange sense of resolve and self-confidence. He was used to sneaking into a town and expecting the worst, but this time was different than normal. He had a partner to watch. He had a product to sell. China's antiquity seemed full of great promise and opportunity. Every taste and color imaginable was here, like America's newness in reverse. Cookie gazed out over the piers of

Canton with guarded optimism, and allowed himself the Henry-like intuition that anything might be possible here.

Moments later the *Astor* swung into a space near the head of a column of vessels anchored at the edge of the city, crowned by a spider web of masts and netting. There were American ships and Dutch ships, and a French one as well, and all the rest were British, sent from Bombay and Madras, Bengal and the Malabar Coast, carrying spices from Batavia in the Dutch Indies. Cookie heard voices calling out in every tongue imaginable, from one boat to the next. He watched Henry watching the scene seriously, leaning low on the railing counting the ships, doing a census in his mind, gauging the market.

Soon the anchor clattered into the water and the captain emerged from his cabin in his best outfit, a ruffled shirt and fancy maroon waistcoat beneath a dark, calf-length jacket. His trousers were buckled at the knees above stockinged shins, and on his head was a flat, wide-brimmed hat. Off the port side, a barge propelled by ten rowers was approaching, flying the dragon flag of China and a medley of silken pennants. A band of two brass conchs and three or four pipes was playing, growing louder and louder until the whole thing formed a honking racket like a flock of geese.

A moment later the chief customs officer boarded the ship. There was much bowing and gesturing, and drinking from small bejeweled cups. Finally the Chinese official produced a silken ribbon from a black teak box, and ran it from the forward part of the rudder to the after-part of the foremast, and from gunwhale to gunwhale. He multiplied these two measurements together, and then added a 100 percent bribe, along with a 50 percent opening barrier fee, and a 10 percent surcharge for the superintendent of the Imperial Treasury. The total came to seven thousand dollars for the Permit to Open Hatches, payable to the Chinese treasury.

Cookie and Henry nodded at each other. It was nice to have the company paying their tolls for them.

The captain handed the customs officer a sack of silver, which the officer weighed and deposited in another teak box carried by a young man with a cylindrical hat. Finally the officer bowed deeply, his palms pressed together, and turned on his heel to return to his boat.

As the barge departed into the teeming water, the *Astor*'s crewmen were dismissed for shore leave and began milling around the deck to make plans. The unloading of the cargo would not begin until the following morning, and an evening of strange entertainments stretched out before them. They assembled quickly into small clusters and pairs, whispering and pointedly evading one anothers' gazes, as the question of who would accompany whom began in earnest. It was a treacherous time, but there was no getting around it.

Cookie avoided the scene and crept down to the galley to finish his chores, listening to the men above him pacing around and hashing out their plans. If Tom the Blade came, he could imagine them saying, then likely Dashiell would come as well, which might cause a problem for Long Bones, who owed Dashiell money from a game of blackjack the night before. Trent would most likely go where Tillamook went, as Tillamook was the only one who could tolerate him for more than ten minutes, which made Tillamook a kind of pariah by association. Cookie smiled to himself. None of it concerned him.

Cookie picked up the honey jars filled with castoreum and loaded them one at a time into a sturdy wooden box, then surrounded them with golden straw. Before closing the box, he pried open a jar and took out a dropperful of amber liquid, which he spilled into a small glass vial and sealed with a plug of wax. He repeated this until he had a dozen sample vials for potential buyers and then nailed the box shut.

He and Henry had errands to do. They needed to move as quickly as possible. The ship's portage lasted only three days and the clock was now ticking. Cookie heard the planks above him creaking, the men moving back and forth along the deck. He heard a low grumbling and then a shrill dipthong of complaint. He already had a partner for going ashore, he told himself. He had no reason to worry. For once, he did not need to stand around waiting to be picked.

# 2

TINA STEPPED OUT into the blinding stage lights as the audience roared and a big band blared a snippet of a reorchestated popular song, which seemed to catch on the chorus and repeat over and over again in a shimmering, brassy refrain. The smiling host, orange with makeup and smelling of breath mints, who had just narrated her meteoric rise to success, greeted her warmly against a backdrop of a city skyline at dusk, and after shaking hands twice he led her to her seat.

Thank you, she said, rolling her eyes and sipping on a glass of water. No, she said shaking her head, she was not the voice of her generation. She spoke only for herself.

Tina took another modest sip of water and laughed, then explained something offhandedly poetic, which caused the host to shake his head in disbelief, while she tucked a stray lock of hair behind her ear and ducked her head demurely. She spoke brashly, and then stared sadly into the middle distance, sullenly quiet. The host nodded and the audience clapped.

Through the heat of the stage lights, Tina could feel the obscure, adoring gaze of the audience, and the mild fear that she instilled in the host. She could sense the approval of the camera operators and the electricians, who knew the real thing when they saw it, and the nervous labor of the many unknown publicists and agents behind the scenes.

Now it was time to show a clip, from the movie all agreed was the most brilliant debut of the past ten years. Cinema would probably never be the same. The lights dimmed. The screen flickered to life.

Tina roused to the sound of gentle tapping on her windowpane and opened her eyes to find Trixie waiting for her as always, her petite face and shoulders squared by the sill like an oil painting, and the streaks of scum creating a soft focus over her cheeks and mouth. As usual, she was dressed like a nurse, with her boxy hat and white smock, and this time her honey-colored cat-eye glasses. "Hey," she said, and pressed her nose to the windowpane, where her lips went flat and white. She exhaled a silver cloud of breath while banging the upper pane with her fist.

"Come on," she said, with her mouth still pressed on the window. "Get up." It was a game they played most mornings, Trixie trying her best to wake Tina, and Tina lying in bed and making her wait.

Tina sank back into her pillows in a flagrant display of delighted exhaustion. Her pillow puffed around her head and her arms flopped over her eyes. "Ughhh," she moaned loudly. "I'm so tired."

"Come on," Trixie said, and banged on the glass again as the silver of her breath shrank and disappeared. Tina glimpsed her through the crook of her elbow, knowing that however annoyed her friend might look, on some level Trixie actually enjoyed her ridiculous sloth.

"Relax," Tina finally said, and slowly turned and put her feet on the floor. She rubbed her eyes and sat still for a long count, until she heard a vexed groan from the window and Trixie's head sank from view. Only then did Tina begin moving about the room, smiling to herself, and getting her things in order, knowing she could linger as long as she wanted to, for Trixie needed her audience too badly ever to go somewhere by herself.

Tina brushed her teeth and washed her face with a wet towel and a finger of Noxema, then stared at her floor looking for an outfit. She pulled on jeans and a black T-shirt, the usual, and sat down on her bed holding her canvas tennis shoe limply in her left hand, spacing out on a tiny blemish in the wall where a thumbtack had once been. She tried on four pairs of sunglasses and two pairs of sweatbands, until she sensed that her prep time had reached its limit, and she scrambled to find a hat and sunscreen before rushing out the door.

She found Trixie waiting for her at the edge of the garden, sitting beside her bicycle with her peppermint-striped stockings folded beneath her skirt, just finishing a poem in a book by Anne Sexton. She posed there quietly while coming to the end of her page, and made a pensive display of pausing as the last words sank in. Her finger scratched idly on the worn edges of the jacket, her lips pursed ever so slightly. Tina watched her pink cheek obstructing the hot rectangle of the printed page, as nearby the pillars of corn rustled in the breeze.

"Okay," Trixie finally said, slamming the book. "Let's go."

The girls rode down the hill at top speed, wildflowers blurring beside them and the sound of spokes whizzing against the gravel shoulder, and spent the remainder of the morning picking blackberries near Sauvie Island. After that, they loitered at the farmer's market, where women from the city came to buy peaches and plums and carrots coated in dirt, and often left their car doors unlocked with spare change laid in the ashtrays.

"You keep watch," Trixie said, leaning into the open window of a Lincoln Town Car.

"All right," Tina said, stepping onto the bumper of a Volvo to scan the parking lot. She could see all the way to the battered stand of fruit bins across the street. "Clear," she said. And a minute later, "Still clear."

When Trixie had collected a few dollars, they continued on toward the city, past the ruined railroad house, its charred beams and broken windows, and the propane plant with its white domes of molded cement, until they reached the 7-Eleven near Montgomery Park, where they intended to shoulder tap for beer.

The girls locked their bikes to a Dumpster and slipped inside the store's refrigerated environment, grateful for some refuge from the heat. They poured themselves cherry Slurpees, and sidled up to the magazine rack, its deep pages of shiny, perfumed paper, like a flowerbed of pictures and words.

"Well, well, well," Trixie said, and picked up a copy of *Interview* with Malcolm McClaren on the cover. Tina started grazing the new issue of *Rolling Stone,* where she found out that Eric Clapton was touring Europe with George Harrison, and Bob Dylan was a great artist indeed. Trixie stood there flipping through pages without so much as glancing at the text, sometimes making a sound of curious, partial surprise. Against Tina's will she wondered what the other magazine might hold.

"Check this out," Tina said, pushing her magazine toward Trixie. A spread of Mick Fleetwood unfurled—a photo of him bugging his eyes out for the camera, with a grizzly beard covering his sallow chin and cheeks.

"Mick Fleetwood's no beard," Tina said, and waited with some satisfaction for confirmation of the fact.

Beards, the girls found, were a fascinating and repulsive phenomenon, and a topic worthy of great contemplation and discussion. They were not interested in the well-groomed professorial beard or the mere five o'clock shadow, nor the goatee or the ring of facial hair around the mouth they called "the assassin," but only in the full, flowing, frizzing beard, smashing against a man's face like a wave against a rock. A beard like Allen Ginsberg had, or Harry Smith, and which implied some gnomic knowledge apart from that of ordinary men. They were interested only in the beardedness of saints.

Trixie looked at the picture of Mick Fleetwood in the magazine, grinning like a naughty child in his blousy shirt and a black vest. He stood in a white room with white furniture. His beard was scraggly and unkempt, and he seemed to be shoving his nose right into the camera's lens.

"What?" Trixie asked, distractedly.

"He's not a beard," Tina said again.

The word "beard" had many meanings—both the object and the wearer, the hair and the man. Spoken tersely and almost uptight, it could often send the girls into near hysterics. The words "big beard," uttered at the entrance of a man with a big beard into a room, were almost a form of punishment, capable of debilitating the other for long minutes at a time.

Trixie returned her copy of *Interview* to the shelf with bored distaste. She shook her head slowly and kinked her mouth.

"I don't think so," she said. "He's a beard. Totally. Why not?"

Tina frowned. She could not see the controversy. Beards. What? Mick Fleetwood was not a beard. He did not deserve the high honor.

"You think?" she asked.

The soft-serve machine hummed loudly in the background and the freezer door opened with a slurping smack.

Trixie stared at the magazines. "Totally. He's totally a beard."

The sound of the magazine page turning was like a huge match igniting. The sheet of glossy paper folded and fell over on its back. The next page was an ad for rum.

"I don't know," Tina said, and flipped slowly through the remaining pages. Trixie fingered the stacks for something new.

They stood there, defending themselves in their own minds, and letting the tension between them grow. Normally this was an argument that would resolve itself very quickly. No, no, they would say, you're totally right. I totally see what you're saying, and they would come to realize that in some way they had meant the same thing from the start. They only had different ways of saying it. It always came out the same, with both of them on the same side. But this time there was no apologizing and redefining of terms, no going back and finding a core consensus. They just stood there, looking at their magazines, Trixie appearing stern and unapologetic and Tina feeling somehow chastened for her opinion on Mick Fleetwood's identity as a false beard.

"I need a cigarette," Trixie finally said, and Tina followed her sullenly through the glass doors. Outside, the heat clapped her on the face and shoulders, and the smell of the hot asphalt rose up in a thick cloud. The parking lot was dotted with oil stains and flattened Big Gulp containers, shredded straws and Popsicle wrappers. Tina stared at the cars on the road glinting harshly in the sunlight. Some boys rode by on dirt bikes and a second later another one jogged along behind them, trying to keep up. A pickup truck filled with gardening gear rolled into a parking spot, its radio blasting something full of fretwork and wailing falsetto. The emergency brake squealed and the radio suddenly clicked off.

"You want one?" Trixie asked, and Tina reached two fingers into the air.

"Thanks," she said blandly.

Tina turned her face toward the sun and watched the blood trapped in her eyelids swirl on her pupils. When she opened her eyes Trixie was lighting her cigarette in the shade of the awning.

Trixie had a particular style of lighting her cigarette. It began by setting the filter casually into the corner of her mouth and striking the match with a practiced nonchalance, looking elsewhere, then cupping the flame quickly in her palm and tilting the matchstick to feed the small fire with its cardboard. When the flame was large enough, she lifted it to the tip of the cigarette in the cup of her hand, and took a long, confident drag. The leaf would kindle and the paper would crackle, and then, eventually, she would blow out the fire with her first pull of smoke, as if some crowd of admirers were gathered around her to watch. It was just one of the many performances she executed each day, for the benefit of Tina alone, and which somehow suggested a relationship between them of audience and performer, and all the unequal adoration that implied.

"Did you find out about that tripod?" Trixie asked, when the match had been extinguished. She was talking about a tripod in the *Nickel Ads* that Tina was supposed to have called about.

"Nope," Tina said, lighting her own cigarette hastily and sucking in a lungful of smoke. Nor had she written the dialogue she was supposed to write, or asked any of the adults if they owned an antique stethoscope.

Trixie sighed. "We're going to make this movie, Tina, you know that, right?"

"Oh yeah?" Tina said, and blew some smoke out her nose.

"I have the money," Trixie said.

"Sure you do," Tina said, and walked a few steps away. She kicked a bottle cap skidding across the asphalt.

Tina knew for a fact that Trixie did not have the money. She did not have any money, in fact, as evidenced every day in their budgeting for food and cigarettes, and their happy recourse to shoplifting. She did not have any money and Tina found it strange that she kept insisting that she did, though normally she just let the suggestion slide by without remarking on it.

"I do," Trixie said prophetically. "No problem. I'm getting tons at the end of the month." Tina took a step into the shade. There was always an extra secret in Trixie's pocket, it seemed, always one more corner to turn with her. Tina was getting tired of chasing after Trixie and her little whims.

"Uh-huh?" Tina said with a subtle note of challenge in her voice. "How's that?" but Trixie was already wandering around the convenience store toward the Dumpster, looking for something to distract them with.

"I don't want to answer any more questions," she said over her shoulder.

"Any more questions?" Tina tagged behind her. "You haven't answered any yet."

"I don't want to answer any."

"Great, what does that mean?"

"What do you mean what do I mean? You don't believe me?"

Trixie turned and stared at Tina and flicked her cigarette against the metal of the Dumpster, where it blossomed into sparks. The sun was hitting the wall behind her, beating against it, and her eyes had turned liquid with reflected light. For a moment a million things passed between them, all their time together siphoned down into a thin tube. It took Tina somewhat by surprise. She found herself suddenly trapped in a game she had not realized was happening, a tricky game of domination and submission. On the one hand she wanted to press Trixie for a good answer, wanted to get to the bottom of her cryptic promises, but on the other hand she found herself afraid to pursue the argument any further. She was afraid because she knew Trixie would never tell her what she wanted to hear. She knew that ultimately she would lose the battle and Trixie would beat her.

"Fine," Tina said and let the subject drop. Her only recourse in a situation like this was blank indifference.

Just then, as if on cue, a beat-up Volkswagon van pulled into the parking lot, blaring the exhausted freak-out of a Grateful Dead bootleg, and some shirtless guys with long hair and mustaches got out and loped their way toward the store. They looked young and seedy enough for the purposes of buying the girls beer, and so Tina hurried away to intercept them. Normally she dreaded the act of shoulder tapping, always a gamble and a vague embarrassment, but in this case she actually welcomed the prospect. Anything to get away from Trixie for a few seconds.

Tina caught up to the hippies in a few steps, and whispered to the smallest one, a rodent-like guy with soiled wide-wale corduroys and a thinning T-shirt.

"Hey. If I give you some money, could you pick up a shortie of Hamm's for me and my friend?"

The guy stared at her breasts. "All right," he finally shrugged. "Meet me around back."

A few minutes later he arrived with a twelve-pack of Coors, which, although politically objectionable to Tina due to the labor practices of the brewery's owner, Adolph Coors, she took. At first the hippie wanted four beers for himself, as payment, but Tina got him to take the change from the transaction instead, and then she and Trixie pedaled off as fast as they could to a spot they knew under the Fremont Bridge, where they proceeded to drink until their lips became numb.

"You don't believe me that I'm getting money, do you?" Trixie said after a few beers, holding a rock she planned to throw at the cement pylons stacked nearby.

Tina sat on a boulder, making a neat pile of empties for whatever homeless guy might want them. The sound of cars whizzing overhead ebbed and flowed, vibrating in her chest.

"No. I believe you," Tina said, liltingly, so that it was clear she did not.

"No, you totally don't," Trixie said. "But that's cool. You'll see. We're going to be shooting by November."

"Whatever you say, boss."

When the girls finished their beer they rode back toward town. Tina's feet slipped from her pedals a few times, and she wobbled when she went over the railroad tracks, but mostly she kept her balance and rode fine. Off in the rail yard she could hear a train reverse, and the shock of its coupling ran through the chain of empty cars, a succession of hollow explosions receding down the line. They rolled passed the lot where the old Rose Parade floats sat decaying into faded and shabby piles of mush. A huge bumblebee pressed its googly eyes against the cyclone fence, its armature of chicken wire showing through rags of bleached crepe paper and dead posies. It was okay, this burial ground of parade festivities, but there was nothing they could really use there.

They ended up at a party on Thurman Street, crowded with teenagers wearing beer cartons on their heads and butting each other in the chest, where a band with two drummers played Grateful Dead covers, and covers of covers, in the basement. In one of the bedrooms they found a notebook filled with crimped handwriting, which they put in Trixie's pocket for later examination, and in the bathroom they found a girl who was crying. After stealing some beer from the refrigerator, they went out in the backyard to watch the flux of teenagers through the sliding-glass door, until the cops came and they escaped through the laurel hedge.

After that, they ate at Quality Pie, a diner nearby, and played a game of "find and replace," in which one of them stole an item, and the other one had to put it back without being caught. Tina stole a pack of menthols from a drunken housewife at the counter, and Trixie stole a set of car keys from the purse of a dire looking goth. Both items were returned successfully.

By two o'clock they were walking their bikes up the hill toward the cabins, and then quietly pushing them along the pathways, their gears clicking softly between them.

"Night," Trixie said.

"See you in a few hours," Tina replied, and they drifted to their respective beds to get some sleep before the first day of school.

Tina woke up with a revolting taste in her mouth, and a hot headache ringing in her skull. Her chest felt mealy and dried out from too many cigarettes and her skin smelled like alcohol mixed with onions. For ten minutes she physically could not move, her arms and legs were so dead, until finally her alarm went off a fourth time and she realized she had to get up or she would never catch her ride with Peter Sessions.

She took a quick shower and put on her black slip and a pair of black-and-white-striped leggings and black elbow gloves and a black bandanna, and went out to meet Trixie at the garden gate, where she was waiting for her, entirely dressed in white. Trixie wore a white trench coat and white pancake makeup, with white nail polish and frosted, teased-out hair with white barrettes and white-frame plastic sunglasses. They were like salt and pepper, one boy said, as they walked down the hallway to their new lockers, but they ignored him without even trying, they were too hungover to care.

After school they met on the edge of the football field, where the empty bleachers yawned at them and the pock of a tennis ball could be heard knocking back and forth. Trixie was irritable after sitting through classes all day, and already full of hatred for most of her new teachers.

"Mr. Bowman is a fascist," she said, rifling through her purse for cigarettes. "He made us watch a fucking Amway tape, I'm serious."

"What a prick," Tina agreed. She had seen Mr. Bowman pulling on a kid's ear in the hallway, and taken an immediate dislike to him.

Trixie could not find her cigarettes so they decided to walk to the 7-Eleven to get some more.

"I got a book in the library today," Trixie said as they slid through the fence. "It's on early medicine and stuff. The chapter on lobotomies is excellent. I'll show you."

"Cool," Tina said.

Briefly, Tina considered asking Trixie about the budget again, but she decided against it. Sometime during the night she had made up her mind to go ahead and believe in Trixie's secret, although she refused to acknowledge it out loud just yet. She would play along and see what happened, pretend Trixie was right until the bills came due. Tina did not mind biding her time for a while. It was fine, so long as Trixie was never granted the opportunity to deny her again.

# 3

**W**HEN THE INDIANS arrived to inspect the bones, Neil was a little surprised to find they were just regular guys, three men in faded jeans, workboots or tennis shoes, with lazy, monotonous speaking voices much like his own. No headdresses or buckskin moccasins at all, no deep, noble-sounding intonations. Jay Feather seemed to be the one in charge. He was a meaty fellow, with big, thick fingers and a barrel chest, wearing a flannel shirt and a single braid down his back. He seemed relaxed in the manner of an old athlete, graceful and self-confident in his movements even beneath a few layers of fat. His friends were more taciturn, and declined to speak directly to Neil, but they were decent enough guys as well. Bill was older, with a pockmarked face, a sheen of grease on his forehead, and jagged gray wires in his ebony hair. His eyes were a little misty, either born sluggish or softened from a long life of drinking and drugs. Joe was the youngest of the three, and stern in a youthful way, at moments almost hostile, but he was alert and intelligent to the world around him, and made up for his arrogance with a sharp wit. Or so Neil imagined, if he were anything like the guys who he reminded him of.

Neil took them down to the marsh where the skeletons remained half-excavated in the dried earth. He tried talking to them about the weather, but they did not have much to say on the topic, so he asked them about their drive, and the scourge of new buildings in town, but they kept their responses brief. "Yup," Jay Feather said, regarding the construction of a condominium complex on the waterfront.

When they arrived at the pit, they stood around the skeletons silently. Neil stood off to the side, waiting patiently for their investigation to end, entertaining himself by thinking about the things in his pockets, the house keys and car keys and tin of breath mints holding his half-smoked roach. It was a little frightening, he found, the banal order of a man's life, the secrets he shares only with himself. He did not like it. The total privacy of his pockets was like a tiny, nagging horror.

The men stood at the lip of the pit staring at the two skeletons in the dirt. The bones were clean now, almost polished to a shine, just as Mr. Grimsrud had left them. There had been no rain since their discovery, and the walls of the pit were dusty and dry, the floor worked smooth with the oils of Mr. Grimsrud's hands. There were some chalk markings here and there, some strands of string gridding the basin.

"The forensics guy did all that," Neil said, "he's been real careful."

"Yeah. We know Mr. Grimsrud," Jay said, and left it at that.

The Indians mumbled among themselves, and threw some powdered chalk the color of a fresh persimmon down into the pit, where it settled in a clump near the elbow of the smaller skeleton.

"I think they're ours," Jay said, turning to Neil. "No doubt about it. The worn-down teeth, the burial arrangement. We used to do things like that all the time. We improvised a lot, but the basic burial rites were always the same. A couple together like that. It makes sense."

"You know they're both guys, right?" Neil asked.

"Yeah, that's okay. We had couples that were men. Still do."

"Huh," Neil said.

"Have the remains been touched?" Jay asked.

"Well, yeah," Neil said.

"I mean has anything been removed," Jay Feather clarified.

"Oh. Well, the finger on the big one was taken for radiocarbon dating, but that's all."

The silence that followed was frightening and complete. The three men scowled at each other and shook their heads, and for a moment Neil worried that they might turn on him and begin pummeling away. They huddled close together and talked in low tones, their bodies perfectly still and their arms hanging at their sides.

Finally Jay Feather broke away from the other two and looked at Neil with sorrowful eyes.

"That's real bad, Neil. The remains need to stay whole. Otherwise the soul will be incomplete in the afterworld. You need to get that pinky bone back."

Neil walked the Indians back up to the parking lot, as he had done with the sheriff and the forensic anthropologist before, and then with the journalist, and then with the forensic anthropologist again. He felt like the pathway was becoming rutted with traffic to and from the bones. They walked in silence and Neil cast about the cabins and garden for something to distract him. Beside the garden the pile of firewood was still clumped in place, where it had been sitting for a week now. The four-by-fours for a retaining wall were stacked near the shed, and the post digger was visible inside the open door. Everywhere Neil looked he saw unfinished work to be done.

"So you guys are going to make an announcement about this, I guess?" Neil asked as they reentered the parking lot. Mr. Grimsrud had had his press conference, and the Confederated Tribes had already had one as well. Theirs had struck a more patient tone, a measured message of waiting and seeing. But now the conciliatory tone could be dropped.

"Yeah, I guess we better," Jay replied. "People should know."

"And then what? You guys come and take the skeletons away? You can do that?"

"Well, not quite, Neil. It's not that simple. In fact, it's pretty much up to you. You could keep the bones if you wanted to. They showed up on your property, after all. But assuming you don't want to keep them, and you want get yourself out of the equation, you'll give them to some state agency, and it will decide where to place them. We'll petition for them, and Grimsrud will, too. And then Grimsrud will probably sue us. And then it'll probably go to court. It might take a long time, actually. We're trying to set some precedents here." By now they had reached their truck, a beat-up blue Chevy with a coating of fine dust on its hood and top. "But what's a few years in the big picture of things, right?"

Neil nodded wanly.

"Hey, thanks for having us, Neil," Jay said, climbing into the cab. The cab shifted with his weight, and he squeezed against Bill beside him. "You're all right. But don't forget that pinky bone. That's a big deal."

Neil watched them leave, as he had watched all the others leave, and wondered why was he the one who always had to deal with this bullshit.

Mr. Grimsrud's laboratory was located on the ground floor of a Victorian house in North Portland, a "painted lady," they called it, tricked out with frills and fans, rounded banisters and leggy columns. The dormer had a diamond-pattern shingle scheme on the sides, and a balustrade, and a rooster-shaped weather vane salvaged from the early times of pioneer settlement. Mr. Grimsrud lived on the upper floors, and ran his business from below, which ramped up in the summertime, and slowed down during the school year when he taught classes at the junior high school down the street.

Inside, the house was filled with old photographs, dusty cactii, shelves of books on anthropology and histories of the region's tectonics and plant life. There were old filing cabinets and writing desks covered in reams of paper and canisters of pens, boxes blocking the hallways and collecting cobwebs in the living room. While Mr. Grimsrud finished categorizing a handful of pottery shards, Neil waited in the salon and browsed through the new issue of *Scientific American*. He read an interesting article on fulgurites, glass formations created by lightning bolts striking the desert floor.

A coffeemaker wheezed. The smell of formaldehyde stood in the air like sour wine. Neil flipped through the pages absentmindedly until finally Mr. Grimsrud emerged from his lab in a smock and gloves. He blinked a few times as if startled by the light, and lifted his glasses to massage the oily pouches of his eyelids.

"What can I do you for?" he said. "How was the meeting with the Injuns?"

"Well," Neil said, getting up from the couch. "Pretty good. Nice enough guys."

"Mm-hmm." Grimsrud sounded a neutral tone.

"Actually that's what I came to talk to you about," Neil said. "I understand it's an inconvenience and all, but I'm thinking I should get that pinky bone back for a while. The one you were going to do the test on? I'm hoping we can hold off for a little bit. I think it might be better. Just until we have a better idea of who those bones really are."

Mr. Grimsrud looked surprised. "Why's that, Neil? Why wait? The radiocarbon dating could actually help us determine the identity of the remains. I don't think I'm following your reasoning."

Neil looked at his shoes. "Well, the Confederated Tribe guys seemed upset about the idea of losing that pinky bone before we knew whose it was, and I thought that seemed pretty reasonable. Don't want things to escalate if they don't have to, you know."

Mr. Grimsrud gritted his teeth and shook his head.

"Look Neil," he said, "the radiocarbon test is one of the basic fundaments of forensic anthropology. I cannot do my job without running a test on some portion of these remains. And the tribal council will have to deal with that fact. It is part of the protocol of a situation like this."

"I don't doubt how important it is," Neil said, "I'm just asking if we could wait. I don't want to get anyone upset here."

"Look, Neil. Tell them how many tests I'm abstaining from doing," Mr. Grimsrud said, and proceeded to delineate a battery of tests he wanted to run but would not. X-rays, electron microscope scans, isotope analysis. He would like to study the specimens' teeth, make casts, find out what they ate, which would involve the removal of the dental calculus. He wanted to take a thin slice from an arm or leg, and remove four grams of well-preserved bone for DNA analysis. All these tests he would refrain from doing until the initial radiocarbon test was finished.

"You are a reasonable man, Neil. Make them listen to you. They have no cause to block this test from happening."

Neil went back to the Indians with that, visiting Jay Feather in his office in the storefront of a brick colonial in Old Town. Jay's desk was also piled with paper and pens, affidavits and half-used memo pads. The walls were covered in posters for the American Indian Movement and a single frayed dream-catcher with a drooping feather attached.

"No, Neil, it's all or nothing," he said. "An incomplete soul is incomplete. You don't want that. It's not worth the risk. This is a problem. If Grimsrud doesn't turn over the pinky, there will be some big trouble."

"He says the radiocarbon test is important for the identification, though."

"Neil, there are plenty of ways to make an identification on these bones. We only need to compare them with bones of other native peoples in the area. The bone structure of the small one is obviously similar. And the burial itself tells us a lot. The radiocarbon test will tell us how old the remains are, which is basically beside the point. If they are old, then they are obviously ours. And if they're not so old, then who cares about them anyway, right?"

"I guess that's true." Neil crossed his knee and rested his chin glumly on his palm.

Jay Feather sized up Neil for a second.

"Let me tell you a little story, Neil," he said. "Back in the 1700s, this land was all wild. Out on the coast, along the river, all the way to the desert, it was a beautiful, unspoiled place. My ancestors lived here, and fished in the streams, and hunted in the forest. You know this story. You learned it in grade school, I bet.

"Then, about two hundred years ago, some trappers arrived. They were looking for beaver pelts, and they set up a fort near the river. We made room for them, traded with them a little, and we believed them when they said they wanted to share the land. We got along for a while, but then more of them came, and then armies came. Pretty soon we were fighting for our lives, Neil, and then we were living in shacks out

156

in the desert. They came in friendship and they betrayed us.

"Do you know where most of the remains and artifacts of my ancestors are stored now? They are stored in natural history museums, with all the animal bones and plant specimens. My ancestors have been treated like shit, Neil. It's no good.

"So for the last few years we've been trying to get some of our ancestors back. We want to establish some kind of standard for the repatriation of their remains. This case means more than just a few bones in the ground. It is one piece of a much larger campaign."

Neil shifted in his chair, and tugged on the hem of his pants. "Yeah, well," he said. "I see what you're saying."

"You're a good guy, Neil. You're in a tough spot. I think you'll do the right thing."

Neil returned to Mr. Grimsrud's office just as the sun was going down. They sat on the porch together and drank some soda, while the crickets rubbed out their nighttime song.

"Goddammit," Grimsrud said. "They are so fucking unreasonable. You realize this has nothing to do with this fellow's pinky at all. You know that, right? This is a much larger issue than that. This is purely retribution from them for things in the past."

"Maybe so," Neil said.

"It is," Grimsrud said. "Believe me. We think of the Native Americans as these pure-hearted people. We have all kinds of romantic ideas about them. But they are political creatures just like the rest of us."

Neil listened as Grimsrud recounted a story he had been waiting to tell. The scientist stared into the darkened street while he talked, the flesh beneath his chin vibrating with each breath.

"When I was just starting out in this business, a few years ago," he said, "I was digging at a site out at the end of the gorge, near The Dalles. It was a good site, lots of stuff. About two weeks in we made a big find, a whole room in the side of a cliff. We unearthed a doorway, which was basically a small hole in the rock, and found a cremation hearth almost ten feet wide, with the remains of six bodies in it. Three adults, an adolescent, and two younger children. The bones were badly burned but the left side of one of the children's faces was reasonably intact. We also found two halves of a huge stemmed spear and a lump of red ocher the size of a child's fist. It was incredible, Neil, a window straight into the ancient past.

"Now let me tell you something else, Neil. When bones are burned with the flesh still on them, the fire burns much hotter than when the bones are defleshed and dry. The fire burns from both the inside of the bone and the outside, because the fat inside the bone, the marrow, fuels the flame. The bones not only char but they almost melt. They become severely misshapen. Wavy cracks appear in the surface, and eventually the bones warp and shatter along those cracks." Mr. Grimsrud was growing excited, his voice flowing out into the street.

"Neil, the bones in this hearth were severely warped and broken. It's entirely possible that those bodies were burned alive. I could have discovered that given the time. I could have run tests that would have proven it.

"Well let me tell you something. The Indians were not happy to find this out about their ancestors. They blocked any further study. Put up this big smoke screen about indigenous rights. They were just pissed as hell that anyone could tell them something they didn't already know." Mr. Grimsrud's face was balled up in a mixture of enthusiasm and anger, shifting uncontrollably.

"That's an amazing story," Neil said. He sipped his drink and looked away.

Mr. Grimsrud went on, "Yes! It is. And these bones could be an amazing story as well. These have all the hallmarks of a fascinating, rich story. Think about it, Neil. Two men, one of them with his skull broken and one of them with a smashed chest plate. Aren't you curious about them, Neil? Don't you want to know everything you can?"

"Neil," Jay Feather said. On the phone his voice was sweet and slow, right in the cradle of Neil's ear. Neil sat in his cabin petting one of the neighbor's long-haired cats.

158

"Grimsrud is making a big mistake. It's the same mistake that all the scientists make, over and over again. He thinks that he can discover something about a time that is already long gone. He thinks he has a window into some long lost world. And what does that window show? Almost nothing, Neil. As if it matters what people ate and drank and died from back then. As if no one remembers. We do remember, Neil. We already know all those things. What did we eat? We ate fish. Where did we live? We lived here, all along the Columbia Basin, and other tribes, they lived out the gorge, and on the coast. Our stories tell us that. How did the Indians die? The white man came and murdered everyone, and started tearing down trees, and building railroads and cities. The mystery Grimsrud's trying to solve is not a mystery at all. Our people have been living the same way for centuries. Up until the last one, anyway.

"There is no reason why he should study the bones of our people. They are our bones, and they should stay with us. We are a living people, Neil, with living beliefs. Our traditions are still alive. Did he tell you about the last site he found? How he tried to invent these things?"

"He mentioned something," Neil said. The cat yawned and leapt onto the floor, stepping with stiff legs to the middle of the room where it began gripping the rug with its claws.

"I bet he did. He found a crematorium. He found a crematorium with some old charred bones in it. He wanted to convince people that we burned our people alive. He figured that because some bones were burned with the fat still on them that we were cannibals of some kind. We were not cannibals. We would know these things. We cremated, sure. The Clatsop, the Klickitat. All of them did. But there is nothing in our stories that talk about live sacrifices or anything like that. We wouldn't lie to ourselves, you see what I'm saying?"

"I think so." The cat continued to knead the floor, popping its claws on the rug's fibers.

"I hope so, Neil. There are real mysteries in life. But the history of our people is not one of them. We know everything about ourselves that we need to know. We have passed it down for many, many years. And no DNA testing or radiocarbon testing is going to change that. We already own our past. And we intend to keep owning it. Because that's how we will continue into the future. This is a matter of life and death for us, Neil. You understand that, I think."

Neil called Mr. Grimsrud: "Let's just wait," he said. "I need some time to think this through. I don't want to rush into anything I'll regret."

"That's fine, Neil," Mr. Grimsrud said. "That's fine. Take your time. But let me tell you something. Don't take too long. Because the pressure is only going to get worse. The longer you wait, the harder your decision is going to be to make. But take your time. Take your time. I don't want to rush you yet."

# 4

O N THE NORTHERN edge of Canton, stretched along a quarter mile of
waterfront, lay the Respondentia Walk, a series of wharves and
warehouses where every day a riot of global trade held forth, a giant
shell game of commodities and currencies moving back and forth and
magically multiplying into wealth. The piers were filled with boxes in
the process of being unloaded from chop boats to the wharves or from
the wharves into the boats. There were crates of tea and spices,
cylindrical barrels holding bolts of silk, and casks of plum wine. There
were oak boxes, teak boxes, and wicker baskets. There were boxes
inside boxes, and baskets covered in baskets. At the center of the wharf,
lording over the proceedings, stood a massive tripod of wooden planks,
suspending an industrial-size scale attached to calipers, that weighed
every container for shipment in and out of the port.

In the entire Empire of China, from the arid deserts of Mongolia
to the mystical mountains of Tibet, the quarter mile enclosure of
Respondentia Walk, along with a few short alleyways behind it where
alcohol and knickknacks were available to touring sailors, was the
only patch of ground where foreigners were allowed to set foot.
Everywhere else was forbidden. No foreigners allowed on the
streets of Canton, or in its gardens, or in its ancient, bustling public
squares. No sailors were permitted to speak to the citizenry, barring
those employed on the docks. No contact was acceptable between
foreign men and Chinese women.

Before allowing his sailors off the boat, the captain had gathered them
together and read loudly from a Chinese proclamation, issued only four
years before, that was somewhat astonishing in its presumptions: "Our

Empire produces all that we ourselves need. But since tea, rhubarb, and silk seem necessary to the very existence of the barbarous Western peoples, we will, imitating the clemency of Heaven, who tolerates all sorts of fools on this globe, condescend to allow a limited amount of trading through the port of Canton." The penalty for entering the closed city, the captain warned them, was very severe. The Chinese were not to be trifled with. Don't test them.

"Official chest-thumping," Henry said. "Just to make us walk the line. This market's beyond any government's control. They know it and so do we." The real China, he declared, was open for trade, and the wharves of Canton were proof of that. The wharves were all they would need, anyway.

And indeed, all around them the wharves teemed with economic life, men swarming and hustling for pay. There were Chinese men in high cork-soled shoes and wide pants billowing above the knee; Indians in turbans, muslin shirts, and sashed cotton pants; Muslims in robes with cashmere shawls and morocco slippers embroidered with golden thread. They carried satins and crepe, preserves, lacquerware, screens, snuff boxes, chessboards, and ivory carvings. Their pockets bulged with dollars and yen, crowns and lire, pounds and ducats. The men and their money flowed together, buying and selling and moving on in a rush to liquidate their holdings for something better and more portable than before. The pier was like a giant funnel, filled with brightly colored oils swirling in whorls, fed by the entire world.

Henry and Cookie stood at the center of this throng, dressed in their finest clothes. Cookie wore a pair of thinning chinos and suspenders over a denim shirt buttoned all the way to his neck, and on his feet old, scuffed boots he had spent the evening before painting with hot tar. Henry wore a white, featherweight suit, white canvas shoes, and a light cork hat covered with white cotton, along with a silk tie and golden brooch for good measure. They had stored their clothing beneath heavy boxes for the duration of the trip, in order to keep the lines pressed, and for Henry the plan had worked just fine. He looked presentable, even dapper, with his face clean and his hair combed back in a shell. Cookie's jacket, on the other hand, looked like it had passed through a cotton gin, and his pants were a topographical map of hard-edged wrinkles and lines. Not that anyone noticed in the bustle of the wharf. No one seemed to notice them at all. The crowd jostled and flowed, bottlenecked and corrected itself, until finally Cookie and Henry broke its skin and slipped into the traffic, carrying their samples of castoreum oil and hoping for the best.

The mechanics of their plan, it turned out, were a little vague. Although Henry was still full of confidence in their product and the price it might get, he did not seem to know precisely how to set the gears in motion. There were undeniably men who had accomplished this sort of thing before, men who had made fortunes in ambergris or hemp textiles, but Henry did not himself have any hard contacts or connections to draw on. He did not have a single letter of introduction, or, for that matter, a license to do trade. This did not worry him, however, or if it did he did not show it.

"Business," Henry said, "is a God-given right. A universal language like mathematics or music. Men everywhere are itching to trade what they got for what they don't got, and if one of them doesn't want to trade with you, then another one will. It's human nature, Cookie, whether it's wrapped in the skin of a sultan or an Eskimo. You hear that? You hear what they're sayin? These Chinese hongs talk the same pidgin as the docks of the northwest coast of America, or the bazaars of Oman for that matter."

Henry was full of optimism about their mission, because optimism, he explained, was also part of the international language of business.

"Merchants can smell the confidence," he said, "and they welcome it like a breath of fresh air. Just like they can smell the fear, and want to get away from it."

Cookie did not necessarily agree with all of Henry's axioms, but he kept his thoughts to himself. If anyone could trade drops of oil from a beaver's anal gland for silver good in any tavern in the known world, it was this man, Henry.

The first place the two approached was a warehouse filled with crates of porcelain. There was porcelain in the shape of elephants and swans, porcelain bowls and plates and soup ladles, porcelain temples the size of small houses guarded by porcelain lions, all of it being packed in dry straw by children the age of eight or below. Henry bowed to the first grown man he saw, who bowed in return and then blew his nose on the ground in a powerful splat. But Henry had already launched into an upbeat speech regarding the curative powers of castoreum oil and the fresh, purifying diet of the Northwestern beaver, truly the greatest producer of castoreum in the world.

"The beavers of the Northwest are raised on the finest fungi and mosses of America, made vigorous from the region's arctic air. The beaver of the Northwest coast of America secrets the sweetest and most potent oil in the world."

He rattled off his pitch and pulled from his coat pocket the vial of liquid, which he offered to the man for a look. The foreman, a froggish-looking fellow with heavy eyelids and a downturned mouth, wiped his hands on his pants and accepted the vial, which he held up to the sunlight and shook back and forth. Bubbles formed and he smiled politely before handing the vial back. Henry kept talking and uncorked the vial, which he waved under the man's nose, who smelled it, and who nodded his head in appreciation.

No, he communicated by flapping his hands in the air, he could not help them today.

Cookie and Henry cut their losses and gave up fairly quickly. The man they had chosen to speak to likely held little power in his organization, they realized, and besides, he seemed to deal in porcelain anyway. The conversation had not been an entire loss, however, Henry claimed, for it had provided them with valuable practice in the presentation of the goods. He now realized that his speech could probably use some polishing.

"I oughta state the bargain right away," he said. "Less talk about origins and purity." All that information would arise in the negotiation, he told Cookie, and it was probably best saved for later in the conversation. At the outset, the primary question was simply whether or not a particular merchant was interested in trading, and if so, where and when. Obviously this process would demand multiple steps, and they needed to weed out the serious customers from the mere looky-loos. Likely they would have a bidding war before long.

The next attempt took them to a tea factory, where they made more of an effort to locate the man in charge. The workers were busy packing tea into wooden crates by jumping up and down on the leaves with their bare feet, and ignored Cookie and Henry for a long time before pointing them toward an adjacent office building where potted plants swayed on a veranda, and men in white linen suits lounged about on wicker chairs. They were executives for the East Asia Tea Company, one of the greatest international conglomerates in the world.

Cookie and Henry were met at the office by a smiling houseboy, who made some gestures with his hands, and nodded vigorously when Cookie and Henry gesticulated in return. But it was clear he had no idea what they were trying to say, and in the end the conversation only moved forward with a grease pencil and a piece of rice paper, and Henry drawing pictures of beaver tails and money signs connected with a bristling cloud of arrows. The houseboy seemed quite interested in their castoreum until he realized they were trying to sell it, at which point he stopped smiling and guided them out the door. "Howqua, Howqua," he said, brushing the air with his hand, and sent them on their way.

Similar scenes repeated themselves over and over again throughout the wharves and shops that day. Merchants would inspect their castoreum, signify some appreciation, and then regretfully decline to entertain the notion of buying it. By sunset Cookie and Henry had tried every establishment on the wharf. They had presented their vial of castoreum to tailors and food vendors, masseuses and moneylenders, merchant after merchant, all of whom had expressed disinterest on a spectrum from lukewarm to violent. Henry's pitch became abbreviated, and eventually despondent, until finally he simply held the vial aloft and replaced it in his pocket without even speaking.

After hours of fruitless labor they found themselves standing before a tavern called Chow Chow, down the alley from the British East India

Company between two hongs, named Peace and Quiet and Collective Justice. They stepped down the stairs through the door, well ready for a drink.

The bar was dark, with low tables and dingy rice paper lamps, occupied mostly by Parsis, Armenians, Arabs, and Jews, all playing cards together and drinking tall glasses of rum. Cookie and Henry ordered a round of "fire liquor," the house specialty, which turned out to be a combination of alcohol, tobacco juice, sugar, and a touch of arsenic. The putrid drink took some getting used to, but its strange, curdled taste more or less matched their mood.

Henry sat at the table with his head in his hands, staring into his drink. His fingers slowly scratched his head until his hair had formed into a landscape of brambles and thorns.

"There must be a way to do this," he said, "a door or a key. Some combination of words that'll set the tumblers in place." Here they were, he said, in possession of a substance of great value, which they had carried all the way across the Pacific Ocean to sell, and yet which they could not find the most tepid interest in. He could not comprehend why that was the case. It was such a simple and straightforward equation—supply, demand. He felt oppressed by a whole world of invisible rules.

Henry went over the events of the day again and again, as if they would change in the process of thinking about them, or as if someone in the last five hours might have meant yes when if fact they had clearly said no.

"We don't have much time, Cookie," he said, and in this he was undeniably right. The *Astor* sailed in just three days, and they needed to broker their deal as quickly as they possibly could.

Cookie watched his friend across the table while pressing his hands between his knees to keep them from fidgeting. The smoke and shadows of the tavern obscured a smattering of men near the bar, all with their own dreams of fortune and good luck. Henry continued moaning about the stupidity of everyone in the world. "It shouldn't be so hard," he said. "They just don't listen."

166

Cookie sipped his drink and rolled his eyes apologetically. Although he and Henry had never discussed this contingency before, the prospect of failure was suddenly looming above them, and he could see there were plenty of reasons for it. For one thing, they lacked any real knowledge of the protocols of business in Canton. They did not know Chinese and they did not know the market price for their product, nor did they know where to find the representatives of the industry they sought, or, for that matter, precisely what that industry would be. The fact that Chinese merchants would hesitate to trust them outright, or throw silver at them, did not come to Cookie as any great surprise. Why should the rules be different for them? They were no more blessed. Henry believed the world should beg him for his happiness, but Cookie did not harbor that illusion. Nations had rules. Cultures worked within traditions. In retrospect, it was all too clear how delusional they had been. It was clear how their failure was almost preordained.

Cookie greeted their failure like an old friend. He found a certain comfort in it. There was something liberating in failure's deep absolution of control.

Cookie sat there nursing his drink, and wondering if perhaps Henry deserved this lesson a little. He should know by now that defeat was a prospect for any man, that sometimes life threw you down and beat you up badly. He should know by now that even Americans could fail.

As Cookie sipped his drink, a Chinese bird seller wandered into the tavern, carrying a long wooden stick over his shoulder dangling with variously shaped birdcages. Some were cubical, others lozenge-shaped or cylindrical, all made of bamboo. Each cage contained a single colorful bird—red and green birds and birds the color of a papaya. They warbled and croaked and shook their combs as the man holding them approached the bar and ordered a drink. He stood there with the bridcages balanced on his shoulder, and somehow managed to pay for his drink and gulp it down without once lowering his cargo to the ground. There was something instructive in this gesture, Cookie felt, something that spoke of patience and finesse, and the careful weighing of limits and burdens. Something the barging, blustering Henry might do well to observe.

They sat this way for an hour, Cookie brooding and turning doleful and Henry writhing like a man in a straitjacket, until finally a young boy entered the tavern and walked across the room right to their table. He was young, perhaps ten years old, and wore robes embroidered with fish and octopi. His skin was almost translucent, and his hair pulled back in a black ponytail. He stood beside them with his hands folded and his eyes staring at the ground, waiting for an invitation to speak.

Cookie recognized the boy from the wharves, from the entourage of a green tea merchant who had shown some initial interest in their castoreum, but who had quickly terminated negotiations. This boy had listened intently to Henry's pitch while sorting through tea leaves for stems and burrs, obviously unable to participate due to his lowly status but curious in a disinterested sort of way. Cookie kicked a chair toward him and he sat down.

"Jim Lee," the boy said, bowing his head and pointing at his own chest.

"Henry," Henry said, "and Cookie," pointing at Cookie. The two men eyed the boy as if he might pull a snake from his shirt, but also with a desperate sense of hope.

Jim Lee spoke in perfectly turned English, like a London schoolboy twice his age. His speech was sober and well reasoned, and he explained to Cookie and Henry the source of their problems.

"Sirs," he said, "as I am sure you know, the importation of foreign-produced medicines through the port of Respondentia Walk is strictly prohibited by Chinese trade law." He spoke in a light, lilting voice, blinking his eyes rapidly. "And any merchant caught doing so is subject to severe punishment. Beheading or public caning, depending upon the substance and social standing of the merchant in question. The merchants are sanctioned only to trade in fur and tea and durable goods. The Emperor is quite strict on this matter. The profit margin must be very high for a merchant to risk trading in anything else."

He lowered his voice to a girlish whisper, "There are ports devoted to such products as your own, but only pirates and soldiers go there, of which you are neither. And besides it is much too late for that."

He leaned back and spoke loudly again, "There is one man, however, who might be willing to buy from you. Howqua is his name. The Timid Young Lady."

Cookie and Henry exchanged a glance. The name Howqua had come up numerous times that day, quickly uttered and then forgotten, always on their way out the door. They had assumed the word meant "no," in some especially virulent form. It never occurred to them it was a proper name.

Howqua, Jim Lee told them, was a very successful man, a powerful merchant and pillar of the trading community. He had been known to trade in many substances before, and he owned pharmacies throughout the province in a position to distribute their goods. He had many, many friends and he was above the reproach of the law. If anyone would do business with them, it was surely he.

For a small sum, Jim Lee offered, he would be willing to deliver a vial of castoreum to Howqua, who lived on the hill in Canton, and return immediately with a letter of interest or not.

Cookie and Henry looked at each other. Although they hated to part with even a drop of their commodity, the whole interchange had surprised them to the point of taking a chance. They shrugged and gave the vial to the boy, who bowed and ran off, and then they were once again sitting alone.

They ordered another round of fire liquor and settled into the rising smoke and chatter of the bar, its waves of mellow talk and laughter. They lazily discussed the new turn of events. Henry doubted seriously whether anything would come of it. Jim Lee's promise seemed far-fetched at best, but the very fact of something happening had shaken him out of his torpor. Soon Cookie was chortling a little. He joked with Henry and let Henry tease him in return. Although some small part of Cookie had relished the failure of Henry's plan, and hated to let go of that, he began talking excitedly with him about all the times they had ever been cheated.

169

"I once traded some pigs for a bag of Dutch crowns in Delaware, Ohio," Henry said, "and got burned pretty good. I never even counted the coins until I was home, and it turned out to be nothing but copper pennies. When I went back the bastard had already pulled up stakes and moved on to the next town."

"I once bought a milk cow in Memphis," Cookie recounted, "but the teats were chapped and the milk shot out sideways in a fine spray."

"I think we've been had," Henry laughed, "by a boy in silk pajamas."

Soon they were laughing uncontrollably. Most likely they had just lost a valuable beaker of castoreum to an enterprising young boy, perhaps in the employ of some criminal mastermind, and they would go home to the ship that night with a little less product to sell. But they would sell their castoreum, they assured each other of that, and even if they did not sell it, they would certainly survive.

To the partners' surprise, however, Jim Lee returned within the hour, just as he said he would, his face flushed and beaming. He plowed through the door and did not slow down until he was halfway across the room, at which point he stopped, tugged on his skirts and composed himself, and continued on in measured steps before arriving at their table to speak.

"My friends!" he said. "I have very good news." He pulled a paper scroll from his gowns filled with calligraphic lettering, and stamps in every corner. He presented it to Henry and translated the script: "Howqua is interested in seeing your product. He would be honored to meet with you tomorrow afternoon. You should bring your goods to the address listed below, and ring the bell. Howqua will be expecting you."

Cookie and Henry looked at each other. Jim Lee explained to them what an honor they had received, and thanked them for allowing him a small part in its coming to fruition. Cookie gave Jim Lee a few dollars and put the scroll in his knapsack. They paid their bill and parted with Jim Lee on the cobbled street, where he ran off into the night, his robes flailing behind him, and his wooden sandals clattering on the ground, a happy boy.

The wharves were quiet now. All the boxes and netting and barnacle-covered ironworks stood frozen in place, glowing in the moonlight as if dusted with powdered sugar. Cookie and Henry walked through the empty wharf, pondering the same cycle of thoughts. They had been warned about the strict policies governing their movements, the restrictions on tourism and trade in Canton. They had been told to keep their movements limited to the wharves and to the boat. But their appointment tomorrow demanded a trip outside the stated boundaries.

What was the worst that could happen? What could they lose? They were not Chinese, after all, and thus the laws of the Chinese Empire did not precisely apply to them. The code they followed was more abstract and universal than that. The law they obeyed was the law of freedom and opportunity, apart from any nation or tribe.

Some rats scurried in the dark, and the men's footsteps made a simple tattoo on the wooden planks. The waves sloshed against the pilings, and released a ripe, rotting fume. The masts of the *Astor* rose ahead of them, among a forest of other ships and sails. Somewhere in the night a sailor called out "Ahoy!" to a distant companion. As they walked slowly toward the ship, the men sensed the walls around them gently falling away, like cotton sheets slipping from the drying line. They felt as if they were walking into a different realm, a realm where anything might be possible. They granted each other permission. It was as easy as that.

Cookie glanced at Henry and shook his head, as both of them began to laugh. His friend was right after all. There was a global merchant class.

# 5

*O*NCE UPON A *time there was a doctor who lived in colonial Philadelphia. He was a kindly man, with bifocals and a slightly rumpled demeanor, and he kept a clean, well-respected medical practice in the ground floor of his brownstone apartment. He lived on a quiet street, near Liberty Square, with elegant gas lamps along the sidewalk that glowed in the evenings, and small yards framed by black wrought-iron fences. His office was tidy and compact, with all the tools of his trade carefully placed in their various corners and shelves. He had a ceramic washbasin, and a metal examination table, and walls full of medical diagrams showing the inner workings of pink muscles and purple organs and bundles of multicolored nerves. His surgical implements were neatly arrayed in a linen-lined drawer, a spectrum of crooked picks and gracefully curving scalpels polished to a bright silver gleam.*

*During the day the doctor saw patients from throughout the city. He treated men for gout and rheumatism, backaches and bruised muscles, women for fainting spells and troubles related to pregnancy. He pulled children's teeth and lanced old people's boils, all according to the most recent medical advances of his time, which he learned about in prestigious journals from Europe and New York. His patients admired his combination of gentleness and forward thinking, and rewarded him for it by returning to him year after year.*

*At night, however, the doctor was full of dreams. He sat at his desk smoking a chestnut pipe, watching the wisps of tobacco fold in the air, and imagined grand, ambitious accomplishments he might achieve if he could only find the time and inspiration. He imagined curing diseases and reversing the effects of old age, knitting wounds and healing commonplace ailments like pneumonia or the grippe. He saw himself conducting experiments that lay the groundwork for entire new fields of medicine, and publishing his findings in the most respected scholarly magazines of his day. He longed for the kind of acclaim that arrived from a life of important, uncompromised labor.*

*There was one dream the doctor returned to in particular, night after night, and which over time grew from the smallest glimmer of an idea into the sturdy outline of something that might in fact work. He burnished this dream until the facets sparkled in his mind whenever he summoned it to view. Every night he came to believe it was possible, and then every night he admitted it could never be done.*

*The doctor's dream was to wipe the scourge of melancholy from the world using a technique called the "full frontal lobotomy."*

*The frontal lobotomy, in the doctor's mind, would be a simple procedure, demanding a minimum of tools and training—just a long, pointed, metallic prong, with a gentle hook on the end, and a very steady pair of hands. The process was quite straightforward. First of all, the metal prong would be inserted into a patient's eye socket, above the eyeball and below the eyelid, and then, incrementally, pushed upward into the brain. Once it had penetrated the cerebral tissues, the soft, bundled nerves and jelly, the surgeon would aggressively stir the prong to destroy the malfunctioning circuitry, and with it the dark passions that clouded the healthy mind. There would be no incision involved, no heavy bleeding, just a precise penetration of the architecture of the face.*

*It was a simple yet radical procedure, with a kind of elegance to it that the doctor considered almost artful. To single out and destroy the cluster of nerves that resulted in depressive states seemed almost too simple a process to invent. He felt as if he had discovered something. In flights of optimism he imagined the procedure sweeping the world, ushering in a new era of personal happiness and mental clarity. At night, in his office, poring over medical journals and pamphlets, he imagined the world's hospitals and private practices cleansed of their* brooding shadows and awash in musical light, and the feeling of this prophecy pleased him immensely.

The doctor's wife was a stern and masculine woman. Every day she wore a bonnet and a Shaker dress with a bib, and spent her time nagging the doctor about the progress of his research. She was a selfish woman, who craved nothing more than a place in the social register, which she imagined as a huge and beautifully bound book. She believed strongly in her husband's research, but not for the same reasons that drove him. She did not imagine a better world, for example, or the abolition of mental sickness. She did not dream of healing the world's anguish. Rather, she recognized in the lobotomy the potential for great financial gain, and she urged her husband to publish his theories as quickly as possible so they might begin to profit from them immediately.

The doctor and his wife ate dinner together in the evenings, by candlelight, and rarely spoke.

The doctor's wife had a wooden leg, which made a clumping sound as she walked about the rooms above her husband's clinic. He could hear her pacing from place to place as she cleaned the house, slowly moving around the furniture, grunting and dragging her wooden appendage, sometimes losing herself in the velvet shadows of the piano room or the den. She cleaned the windows and polished the floors and dusted the paintings each day, although she paid a servant to do the same tasks, because she was ultimately a frightened person, and she felt the judgment of others like a lash.

The doctor's wife pressured him constantly. She goaded him about the progress of his career and chided him for his laziness and stupidity. In many ways, she simply told him the truth. The kindly doctor was in fact distracted in some ways, prone more to dreaming than to action. Left to his own devices, he would be perfectly happy running a modest family practice in his home and never pioneering a thing. But through his wife he became more ambitious, ashamed of his merely moderate success. His dreams of greatness took deeper root. To progress entirely as a doctor and a man he came to believe that he must pursue the idea of the lobotomy to its final conclusion.

One night the doctor was called to the women's prison of Philadelphia, an imposing estate on a hill near the Schuylkill River, where an inmate had attempted to take her own life. He tethered his carriage to the front gate and strode toward the asylum's imposing, iron-laced door, through air that was cold and damp with coming rain. In the sky, the moon illuminated the ragged clouds like torn paper.

When the door creaked open, the doctor was greeted by the mole-like warden, who led him hurriedly down a long hallway of barred windows, each one framing a stricken, snaggletoothed face. The women of the prison watched the doctor using the fragments of mirrors, whispering and cackling sometimes, and grasping at his sleeves.

At the end of the hallway the warden guided the doctor into a dismal cell. In the corner huddled a pale, haunted-looking woman, with damp, uncombed hair and black bags beneath her eyes. Her brow was beaded with sweat and her teeth were gray and widely spaced. She wore what looked like old potato sacks that chafed against her white, grimy skin. Her slender arms, he realized, were covered in blood.

The doctor stitched up the woman's wrists and bandaged them with clean gauze, as she moaned and rocked slightly in place. He gave her a sedative and by dawn the danger had passed. She slept peacefully on her thin mattress, as the pink glow of morning brightened her caged window.

At the door of the asylum, the warden thanked the doctor profusely for his efforts. The woman he had saved was one of his favorites, he said, and losing her would have surely broken his heart. She was prone to bouts of severe melancholia, he added, but harbored a deeply poetic soul.

The doctor bowed modestly and returned home for breakfast, which was shortbread and black tea with milk.

Throughout the day, the doctor thought about the woman he had saved, idly pondering whether she might benefit from a full frontal *lobotomy. Her mind had obviously turned on her, he recognized. Her faculties were actively attacking her from within. In many ways, he ruminated, she presented a perfect test case for his progressive medical techniques.*

*His wife encouraged him. "You saved her life," she reasoned. "And thus you have some claim to it." He did not see things quite that way, but he wanted to do well by his wife, and to live up to her expectations of him. And the dream of taming melancholy was powerful within him. He imagined his name in the table of contents of the nation's leading journal of advanced medicine,* Doctor and Patient. *He saw himself regarded as a wise and honored physician. The next morning he contacted the prison officials and set the wheels in motion.*

*The woman came to his office the next week for a variety of tests, mostly in the form of extensive interviews. They sat together in the garden and talked at length. She was much different in the light of the day. Outdoors, properly dressed and made up, she did not seem so morbid or tormented at all. In fact, she proved to be a nimble conversationalist, often curt and sarcastic, and sometimes genuinely kind. She knew things about the herbs and flowers of the garden and gave the doctor good advice on making them grow. She had an affinity for cats.*

*Slowly, over the course of the interviews, the woman grew to trust the doctor, and disclosed to him the general outline of her life story. She was born to a poor family in York, Pennsylvania, and raised in a Baptist household, among didactic, pious people, who beat her as a child and forced her to do hard labor. She cleaned chimneys and tended swine, and every night attended religious services in a country church, where the pastor sermonized on the evils of music and adulterous sex.*

*She did not learn her religious lessons well, however, for when she turned fourteen she took up with a local farmer's son and became pregnant out of wedlock. Her family disowned her, and her child arrived stillborn, and soon after that she fled to Philadelphia, where she wandered the streets as a charwoman and descended into a black gloom of depression and self-hate. She mutilated herself in alleyways and beneath bridges, and came to know the precinct policemen on an intimate basis. Many nights she spent alone in the parks and gutters of their fair city, shivering and despising the world, accosting the well-heeled pedestrians of Rittenhouse Square. Eventually she was transported to the women's prison, more of a poor house than a real correctional facility, she claimed, where she became more desperate, and more chronically unquiet in her mind.*

*The doctor felt great sympathy for her, and she expressed sympathy for him as well, although she had no particular cause to. He found that her own self-diagnoses, and the objective manner in which she discussed the symptoms of her illness, provided him with rich material for his notebooks. He transcribed the conversations verbatim in the pages of his medical log. In general, he considered her ability to place herself in the social context of family and church an advanced sign of higher functioning, and he found her opinions on matters of religion and law well wrought. At moments he even doubted the need for surgery at all. But his wife continued to goad him. She pressed him daily to publish his findings. And there was no doubt that something in his patient's psyche was damaged beyond her own ability to repair.*

*After some persuasion, the woman consented to be lobotomized. The doctor promised her a relatively painless procedure, and a footnote in the annals of medicine, and the undying gratitude of women like her everywhere, and those yet to be born, all of whom would benefit greatly from her courage. He also promised her that she would never be sad again, which was a prospect that seemed to appeal to her very much. She was ready for a change, she said, or perhaps something more like an escape.*

*Ultimately, however, her own permission was merely a formality. The asylum retained the power of attorney over its inmates, and the warden had signed the papers the day before.*

*The day of the operation was unseasonably warm. The surgical room was darkened with shutters to keep floating contagions from polluting the air, which made the room hot by midafternoon, and stifling once the lanterns were lit. The doctor sweated as he paced back and forth.*

He had practiced his technique on cadavers before, but the flesh of a living human face posed a much greater challenge. There were nerve endings and veins and ridges of bone that would be difficult to navigate. There was the potential for a terrible mistake. The doctor realized, if the operation was to succeed, that he would need to strike a perfect balance between confidence and delicacy, assertive gesture and responsive reaction.

Meanwhile, the nurses prepared the patient for surgery, disrobing her and washing her hair. They sedated her with a potion of ether and strapped her to a metal gurney, which they wheeled into the operating chamber beneath the eyes of watchful students and colleagues, who were gathered on the dais surrounding the well of the room.

The doctor arrived and spoke briefly to the head nurse, who rolled his tray of surgical implements beside him and stepped away. He selected a cruel silver pick and raised it to the light to ascertain its cleanliness. The pick gleamed coldly beneath the flaring lights.

Then the doctor slowly lowered the pick toward the woman's face. With a caliper he lifted her eyelid, bright, wet red inside, and placed the sharpened point into the gap between her eyeball and skin. The metal indented the soft surface of the eyeball, and he pushed the long, custom-made prong carefully toward her brain. Step by step the point made its way over the iris and beneath the bone of the brow, up into the mass of the frontal lobe. The doctor pushed the pick back and forth a few times, snagging it on the fleshy tissues, as blood dripped steadily into a shallow surgical pan.

The woman lay stiffly on the operating table, clenching her teeth on a folded towel. The doctor was sweating profusely. He rinsed his bloody fingers in the washbasin as the crowd of doctors and students looked on. The woman's face was tense and constricted, the spike emerging straight from her eye. One more time the doctor wiggled it back and forth, causing her eyelid to writhe as if a thin worm was caught underneath. He could feel the pick scraping on the bone of her forehead, beneath the plate, and catching in the coils of her sad brain.

*     *     *

179

The operation was deemed a success. The woman emerged from the hospital less tempestuous than before. She no longer expressed the same desires to hurt herself, or exact revenge on those who had wronged her. In fact, she expressed almost nothing at all. She did not harangue people, or curse to the air, or speak at length about plants and animals when no one was listening. Her eyes were cloudy and blank, and her face seemed half-dead. But the pain that had driven her to self-destruction was gone as well. She was no longer a threat to herself or others.

A reporter from the city newspaper came to interview the doctor, and write a feature on his great accomplishment. He congratulated the doctor on his success, and then interviewed the patient. She was confused by his questions, however, and failed to answer them very clearly, but the doctor's wife helped her along, explaining to the reporter how much happier the woman had become since undergoing the surgery, and how much simpler her life now promised to be.

"Sorrow Cured," the headline read. Below it ran two photographs of the lobotomized woman. The first was a portrait from before the operation, which showed her frenzied and unkempt, her eyes flashing with anger. The second had been taken soon afterward, and showed her clean and demure, with massive black rings around her eyes, as if she had been beaten and kept in a closet for two weeks. Her skin was sallow and her eyes were as dull as fog.

The doctor published a scholarly paper in a prestigious journal, where it received much acclaim, and he accepted a commendation from the medical society of Philadelphia. The Board of Medical Examiners hosted a lavish banquet in his honor, attended by the great surgeons of his age. The night of the ceremony, the doctor's one-legged wife tied his bow tie and walked with him grandly through the dining hall, more openly affectionate with him than she had been in years.

A month or so after the surgery the lobotomized woman returned to the prison. Not as an inmate this time, but as a paid member of the custodial staff. The warden felt she served as a fine example to the *other women, as someone who had overcome her antisocial behaviors through the advancements of modern technology. Her duties included cleaning the kitchen, sweeping the hallways, and washing the linens on the second Saturday of every month. Her room was no longer barred. Her door was no longer locked. She could come and go as she pleased.*

*Every day she wore a corset and a lacy collar. She replied to questions in a breathy whisper, rarely saying more than "yes" or "no" or "perhaps."*

*The lobotomized woman took many solitary walks along the pathways of the asylum grounds, where there were topiary trees and bushes to look at, and a fountain that sent up a spout of water that crumbled in the wind. Her color returned, and the black rings around her eyes began to fade. On her walks she gathered baby's breath and wild sage, which she arranged into simple bouquets. When she touched the petals she seemed to appreciate the flowers' beauty, but it was impossible for those around her to tell. She might be glum and she might be euphoric. Her face was a dead, inscrutable text.*

*One day the lobotomized woman found herself walking alone on the outskirts of the garden, where the manicured lawns and shrubbery gave way to snaking underbrush and wild thicket. She veered from the flagstone path and entered the shadows of the woods, and soon was shuffling through rugged landscapes of birch and pine, elm and poplar, past a glinting creek bridged by a fallen log. She came to a meadow of lupen and daisies that looked strangely artificial in the late autumn light.*

*Back at the prison, a search party was assembled, but the lobotomized woman had walked so erratically that her path was impossible to reconstruct. The dogs led their masters to the creek, where the scent was lost, and when the project became difficult, the searchers grew impatient. They went home before nightfall, hoping for the best.*

*Meanwhile, the lobotomized woman wandered through winding forest pathways and along ledges carved in the granite canyons until she descended into a glade of birch trees sheltering a simple stone hut.*

The hut had a thatched roof and a sturdy chimney made of rounded gray rocks. Behind it the sun was setting in a molten bath of orange light, stippled with the elegant black skeletons of naked branches. The hut, resting on a carpet of fallen leaves, seemed to shimmer softly in the gloaming. The lobotomized woman approached the yellow window and peered through its thick layer of milky scum.

Inside, she could see a potbellied old man smoking a pipe, reclining in an overstuffed chair with a mangy dog at his feet. A massive, gray beard spread over his chest, and his feet were covered in a purple and orange patchwork quilt. He muttered to himself and fingers of smoke curled from his mouth, blending with a stream from his nose. All around him were cozy, colorful things—melted candles and statuettes, old books and collections of rocks. The hearth was lined with peacock feathers bundled in clay pots. Somehow the bearded man sensed her presence and came to the door.

He greeted her with a strange look in his eyes, a sort of gleaming puzzlement and delight. His pupils spun like pinwheels behind his thick eyebrows, but something about him put her at ease. He spoke to her in a low, monotone warble, a dialect of some kind, from Scotland or Wales, but perhaps from Amish country as well. She answered him in halting, sluggish syllables, which were equally indecipherable as his own.

The house was warm inside. The smell of simmering stew flowed from the pot on the stove. He opened the door wider and invited her in.

They shared a meal that night of black bread and onion soup, eating in awkward yet tender silence. When they were finished, the bearded man heated water on the wood stove, which he poured one bucket at a time into a large, tin barrel in the corner. The lobotomized woman disrobed and bathed herself, her body smooth and lovely in the dim light, starkly in contrast to her haggard, slackened face. The bearded man was a gentleman and kept his back turned until she was clean.

She stayed with him, and in the morning they ate again, this time porridge with raisins and toasted walnuts.

*Quickly, they fell into a routine. The lobotomized woman gathered wood in the forest and the bearded man hunted for pheasant and wild boar. She stitched his clothing and he maintained the roof and the fire. She fed the chickens and he lifted the stew pot when it was full, and rubbed her shoulders while she chopped the scallions or carrots.*

*At night they sat by the fire and stared in the same direction, or lounged naked on the soft, feather bed, his wrinkled, leathern pouches of flesh beside her alabaster curves, both of them tufted with dark patches of hair.*

*The lobotomized woman remained null of expression or apparent thought, but performed the duties of a wife with slow efficiency. She cleaned the laundry, mended the sheets, knitted oblong hats and gloves from scraps of colored yarn. She bottled salves and elixers with twigs selected from the forest plants, and sold them at the farmer's market on the weekends. Sometimes she traveled to Philadelphia with the bearded man to sell the game he caught, wild turkeys and pheasants, or smoked venison, wearing a large bonnet to hide her face from view.*

*The doctor was informed of the patient's escape, and under the strong advice of his wife, he made a large donation to the women's prison, where the issue was promptly forgotten.*

*Over time, the frontal lobotomy became an accepted technique, practiced regularly throughout the country. The doctor delivered lectures on his neurological theories, which were attended with great interest and enthusiasm. Sometimes students or colleagues would inquire as to the fate of his first patient, curious about the life she lived and the changes that had manifested in her condition over time, and the doctor answered them by saying she was happy, living somewhere on her own, until gradually he began to forget her.*

*One day, years after the surgery, the lobotomized woman was sweeping the hearth when there was a loud, thudding noise outside, a great stomping and crashing about. She continued with her sweeping, but more hesitantly than before, as if some distant thought was sparking in her ruined brain. A moment later the door slammed open, and her husband appeared, holding himself up on the wooden cross beam. Beneath his long beard his skin appeared blanched of all color. His eyes winced with pain and then he promptly collapsed, moaning softly into the frayed carpet.*

*The lobotomized woman gazed at him uncomprehendingly, as if staring at a pile of ragged clothes. Her husband rolled onto his back clutching his leg, tiny bubbles of spit collecting in the gaps of his yellowed teeth. He gasped and wheezed. His pant leg was covered in blood.*

*The lobotomized woman lifted the bearded man's trouser to find a terrible gash running alongside his calf and over his knee, deep enough to expose the white bone. The bearded man groaned in the back of his throat. She pulled the tablecloth from the table nearby, scattering candlesticks and plates onto the floor, and wrapped it around the wound four times, then tied it off in an ungainly knot. She hooked her hands under his arms and dragged him to the bed, where she lifted him up and tucked him under the sheets.*

*There had been an accident while chopping wood, he communicated. He had fallen down and cut himself and his artery had sprayed blood against the bark of a tree.*

*That night the lobotomized woman swabbed her husband's forehead and fed him broth from a ceramic cup. At some point he developed a terrible fever. She checked his wound again to find it had become badly infected. Black shingles covered his skin like a fungus and the gash itself was weeping jewels of white pus.*

*The lobotomized woman went into the other room and swept the floor. She dusted the tops of the windowsills. Then she walked onto the porch and stared into the darkness.*

*When she stepped back inside, she went to her bureau and put on a bonnet and cloak. She doused the candles one by one throughout the house and walked out to the stable, where she harnessed their horse to the wagon. Then she went back inside and wrapped her husband in a flannel sheet. With much scuffling and prying and* clomping of boots, she dragged him outside, and managed to bundle him into the passenger seat, and then climbed into the driver's chair herself.

She was just about to flick the reins when suddenly she stopped, and got down, and returned to the house once more to check the candles, which were already extinguished, and finally came back and took her seat again.

The lobotomized woman guided the wagon along the mud road as swiftly as she could. Meadows and fences raced by in the night, and gradually the homes became more frequent. The mottled path became paved with wide flagstones. Beside her, the bearded man grew paler and a tinge of green came into his cheeks and lips. They crossed the Schuylkill River and the lobotomized woman whipped the horses again. The wagon sped through the narrow streets of Philadelphia, shaking past wooden signs for tailors and blacksmiths and taverns, down Market Street and on to Liberty Square. She lay her hand across her husband's burning cheek as the wooden wheels clattered over the stones.

Meanwhile, although it was late in the evening, the doctor was wide awake, examining a wealthy patient too busy to see him in the daytime. The man had a digestive problem, he claimed, and a swollen gland in his neck, which he had acquired on a recent trip to Spain. He spoke dismissively of that nation's cuisine and ethnic character, while the doctor felt the lump in his neck and bowed his graying head toward his chest.

Suddenly there was a loud clap in the room, and the office door opened violently on its hinges. Wind swept through the office and blew the papers from the desk, snuffing the glowing candles in the hanging candelabra. A shadow entered the room and strode over to the doctor in a flowing, dirty gown.

At first the doctor stammered and backed toward the wall, raising his hands over his face, convinced that the ragged figure was an avenging angel of some sort. His conscience had become tortured over

185

*the years, having seen the results of the lobotomy in many failed cases. The patients who survived suffered a terrible cost, he now saw. He realized that his invention was a source of pain in the world rather than salvation.*

*The ragged figure stepped into a bar of moonlight and the doctor gasped out loud. He recognized the face of his first patient. Her hair was gray now, and her skin was etched with deep, graven lines, but there was no mistaking her features. The doctor was positive that his time of judgment had come.*

*But the lobotomized woman had no time for that. She grabbed him by the sleeve and dragged him outdoors until he began walking on his own. She guided him to the carriage, which was hitched to the wrought-iron fence, and where her husband lay unconscious in the passenger seat, shivering in the cold. His bandage was leaking with blood. His lips were pale and drawn. The doctor approached the bearded man and touched his leg in the grimy, lamplit night.*

And then? What?

Tina stood on the porch of Patty Sandoval's cabin and waited for someone to answer the door. She had knocked once already and she was ready to go, but she decided she should probably wait another few seconds before turning around. She thought about knocking again when suddenly the door creaked open and Patty stuck her head out and squinted into the afternoon light. She had graying, frizzy hair, and a pair of round spectacles pinched the bridge of her nose. She wore a faded denim jeans and an oversized oxford shirt, with a vest made of some natural fiber on top. In the background Tina could see a grand piano gleaming in the shadows, beside a lumpy couch covered in Southwestern blankets and a palm tree in a plastic pot.

"Tina?" Patty said.

"Hi Patty. I, um . . ."

"Come on in."

Patty opened the door wider and Tina walked inside. Patty's cabin was similar to the other cabins on Neil's property, decorated with vintage rock posters and dangling ferns, wicker furniture and rice paper lampshades. The floor was covered with a worn Persian carpet, and the air smelled of a certain combination of spices—garlic and coriander and cinnamon or something—that seemed to infuse everyone's kitchen and living room.

"You want some coffee?" Patty asked. "I was just making some."

"No thanks," Tina said, keeping near the door. "I just wanted to ask you a quick question."

Patty wandered into the kitchen, "Okay. Yeah?"

Tina called after her, "Well, me and Trixie are working on this project together. This movie? It's about this doctor who does lobotomies and a lady who lives in a mental hospital." She went on to explain the basic outline of the film, with special attention to how the doctor's drawing room was dominated by a silent grand piano beside velveteen burgundy drapes.

"We were wondering if we could use your piano for a few weeks," she asked. "Starting later on this month. Would that be okay?"

Patty stood in the kitchen doorway smiling. "I hear the script is really wonderful, Tina. Everyone's talking about it."

Tina gave a little stutter of false modesty, a trick from Trixie's repertoire. "Oh, um, yeah, thanks," she said, and Patty's face warmed with approval.

"Of course you can use it, dear. As long as you're careful."

"All right! Thanks a lot, Patty! We'll be extra careful."

"I'd love to see the script sometime, Tina. I'm dying to read it."

"Okay, yeah. I'll bring you a copy. We're still working on the last few scenes, though."

Tina left the cabin and pulled a wrinkled piece of paper out of her back pocket. She uncapped a pen in her teeth and crossed out the third line on the list, "grand piano or harpsichord," then found the bottom of the list and wrote, "Script to Patty." Then she capped the pen. "Cool," she said quietly to herself.

Tina walked down the pathway toward the geodesic dome above the garden, where acting rehearsals had begun, and where she could find Trixie and tell her about the day's score. For the past two weeks Tina had been going door to door, telling the adults about the movie and scouring their cabins for usable stuff, leading each of them to believe that the things they had, the extension cords or Second Empire chairs, were desperately needed, much more so than anything else.

She passed Bob Grossberger's cabin, where she now knew the arrangement of throw pillows suggested something smarmy and sexual, and Gwyneth's cabin, where huge lampshades illuminated walls covered in old maps, and Margaret's, where the smell of cats was unbearable, and Larry's, where the only chairs to sit in were the backless, ergonomic kind. Each cabin was like a museum of itself, a reliquary of weird collections and memorabilia, similar in ways, but always full of surprises—photos of dead people, or hoarded baubles of some kind, or a cleanliness that bespoke some hidden neurosis. Having a reason to go into someone's home was a kind of gift, she thought.

Tina had developed a little rap she would do during her visits, saying all the things adults crave to hear from children, all the things they impose onto their ideas of their own younger selves. She sparked old notions of dreams and imagination, and the power of creativity to solve any problem it faced. She admitted how helpless they were, she and Trixie, how unprepared, and confessed to every amateur impulse and ambition they had, which was a trick she had also learned from Trixie, the disarming effect of total honesty. She told them that they planned to begin shooting by the middle of November, in order to capture the autumn sunlight from its most feeble yet pellucid angle, which meant they had approximately a month to get everything in order. One month to cast the film, rehearse the actors, acquire the sets and costumes, and generally prepare for every contingency that might arise. Please help us, she said. We need you.

Overall, the response had been overwhelmingly positive. Susan had immediately pulled out a whole trunk of Victorian dresses, and agreed to do makeup if they needed it. Barry had located a tripod they might want, and a set of gels that he had picked up at a garage sale long ago. Robert knew of an old pharmacy filled with rubber stoppers and old vials of medicinal curatives, and John had expressed some interest in doing pyrotechnics, if they needed anything like that, even offered to set himself on fire. It seemed absurd in a way, but it turned out that everyone, on some level, wanted to be in the movies. Talk of the movie spilled over the property like a warm flood. As the Indian summer dragged into October, an energy came over the place that no one remembered seeing before, a thrum of excitement that passed easily from one person to the next. And the drama of the skeletons only confirmed their sense that something special was happening.

Tina crossed the garden and started up the hill, where the geodesic dome emerged, its green and purple hexagons like a big blackberry stuck in the trees. Every day after lunch the cast congregated there, as none of them had regular employment at the moment.

Tina walked up the brittle steps and into the weak light of the dome, bluish green over a mildewed shag carpet, to find Trixie standing in the center of a circle of folding chairs. Beside her was Peter Sessions, their Philadelphia doctor, and Margaret McDonald, the stout, stern-looking lesbian who would play his wife. Sitting in two chairs side by side were Beth Bowler, their crazy woman, and David Sterner, one of the more excellent bearded men they knew, her gnome-like love interest.

Tina slid against the wall and listened in as Trixie moved Margaret closer to Peter, and offered some instructions.

"Okay Margaret, I want you to look like you're eating aluminum here," she said. "Think of the taste of the metal on your tongue." And to Peter, "I want you to play this like you're on the bottom of the ocean."

Trixie backed up and leaned against a chair, watching the actors with a look of intense concentration.

The actors went to their marks and began pacing around. It seemed Peter had invented a stooped posture and a hurt gaze to express the doctor's passive aggression, while Margaret limped gamely on what would be her wooden leg. They moved around the circle of chairs and

Trixie held her fingers up like a camera frame. Margaret pretended to look out a window while Peter stood quietly aloof.

Margaret stumbled over her lines at first: "Dr. Eldridge is, uhh, already recognized in New York for his practice . . . What about you, husband?" Tina imagined her dressed in a woolen frock, with starched frills around the neck. She saw her hair molded into a librarian's bun, emanating Puritan hypocrisy and rectitude. She had been a good choice.

Peter wandered a few steps and answered slowly, "I . . . I can only do what I am able." His bony body and craggy features, ravaged by a long history of methamphetamine abuse, would bring a mature, masculine presence to the part, hopefully marred by an occasional hand tremble. With a waistcoat and cuff links, his hair in a ponytail, he would be pretty much perfect.

"Okay, hold on," Trixie said, cutting them off. She took Peter off to the side and whispered to him, then whispered something else to Margaret, and they returned to deliver their lines again.

"Dr. Eldridge is already well known for his practice in New York," Margaret said, more dolefully this time. "What about you, husband?"

"I . . . I can only do what I am able," Peter said. His damaged-looking eyes expressed a thousand disappointments.

"Great," Trixie said. "That's perfect."

"Thanks, Trixie, thanks," they both mumbled, and moved off to the side.

Now Beth and David stood up. Beth had been cast as the crazy woman because of her high cheekbones and her dark, haunted eyes, not to mention her perfect skin, which was like white dough dusted with cinnamon. She was a natural movie actress, Tina thought, fascinating to watch for no particular reason at all, which was important in a role that was mostly just staring blankly into space. Post-surgery they planned to use some spirit gum on her face to deaden it a little, and give her jowls some sag.

Choosing David as the bearded woodsman had been a tougher decision. He was physically appropriate—squat and hirsute, and gnarled to a leathery texture—but then there were many men who fit the same approximate description. Few of them could act, however, or even take direction in the least, due to hazy mental situations and their reflexive distrust of anything aspiring to popular culture. After pinning the names of all the bearded men they knew to a cork board in Tina's room, a pleasure unto itself, the girls had finally decided upon David simply because he would do pretty much exactly what they asked him to do with a minimum of talking back. He might be sluggish sometimes, but at least he would not misbehave.

Trixie moved them into position, with Beth facing out the window and David, after some aggressive prodding, hunched over beside an imaginary fire. The scene they rehearsed had no dialogue, but a fair amount of moving around. David pretended to stoke the fire with a hand broom, and Beth flowed from one section of the floor to another with a dead look in her eyes. Trixie followed her with her hands forming a square. At one point she came up behind Beth and guided her somewhere else.

Trixie paid special attention to Beth, for the lobotomized woman was clearly the role she coveted for herself. If she had been only a few years older, she would have demanded to play it. She clamped Beth by the wrists and moved her arms like a puppet, stood behind her and breathed instructions into her ear. They took walks together sometimes, and discussed the character's grim history at length. Tina would watch them, their heads bent toward each other in intimate conversation, and detect the roles of authority almost seem to reverse. Beth, the godmother, looking to Trixie for guidance, and Trixie patiently looking after her.

Tina sat on the edge of the room quietly, watching the scene elapse. The actors' gestures and intonations were becoming more refined, expressive, conforming to the strict standards that Trixie was setting. She had a natural talent for filmmaking, there was no doubt.

Tina was proud of her friend on one level, but also slightly upset. Trixie knew how to do things that no one had taught her, had abilities that made Tina wonder about her own creative powers. Tina reassured herself that she was not any less talented than Trixie, only different, and that her talents lay in other arenas. She was more sensitive to life's quiet side, she told herself, and her contemplative manner opened a window onto perceptions that Trixie would never understand.

But it was not true. The fact was that Trixie saw and heard the small things better as well. She simply responded to people more subtly than Tina did, felt things more powerfully. Her intuition was stronger in almost every way. Tina balled her sweatshirt in her hands. Somehow their friendship was becoming a constant game of judging and comparison. A long scrutiny of limitations.

When the scene was over, having drifted off gradually into reality, and the actors had begun to talk among themselves, Trixie looked up at Tina with an inquiring gaze. Tina pretended to clap, then mimed that she was playing the piano.

Trixie ran over and hugged her. "Fucking way to go!" she said, "You rock!" and Tina's worries were momentarily swept away in the good burden of Trixie's dependence.

Tina left the rehearsal to make some more phone calls at her desk, where she stared at the ceiling awhile, then picked up a copy of the script and flipped through the pages to scan for general blocking. She shuffled the pages with her thumb, feeling the bulk of the paper as it tickled her skin. The script was eighty-four pages long now, and the ending still maddeningly unclear. Tina read the final pages over again hoping for some new direction to emerge. She liked to sneak up on it sometimes, when it was least expecting her.

The girls had debated the themes and plotlines of the screenplay at length, searching for precisely the proper image to close the film with, but they could not seem to figure it out. They had considered many different options. A tragic death for the bearded man. A full recovery. Or perhaps a scene of some reckoning between the lobotomized woman and the doctor's wife. But none of their ideas quite satisfied their desire for ambiguity and dread, or achieved the strange, cryptic power of their most favorite movie endings, like *All About Eve,* in front of the mirrors, or *McCabe and Mrs. Miller,* with Warren Beatty in the snow.

Tina put the script aside and procrastinated awhile by calling a few prop shops and returning a call from the owner of a bed-and-breakfast they hoped to use as the doctor's office. Then she went through some advertisements in the paper, circling the weekend flea markets where she hoped to find some kitchenware and bedding. In the past two weeks she had managed to pull together a decent lighting kit and a good number of costumes, and had moved on to more expensive stuff. Although she could not buy anything outright—they still had no money—she could place things on hold. She already had a shotgun mic waiting at Radio Shack and an examination table at a medical supply warehouse, along with a wheelchair for dolly shots. She figured they would have plenty of time to gather the items before the first day of shooting began. Trixie was fine with the plan, just so long as they did not talk about issues of money with the adults.

Tina took a break and went outside for a walk, passing Neil at the woodpile, staring at its many pieces.

"What's up?" he asked, and she said, "Not too much."

She stepped into the garden, where the smell of rotting apples hovered like a faint, sweet perfume. At the edge of the empty cornrows the geodesic dome became partly visible behind the trees. The light inside was trapped in the hexagons, which looked dirty around their edges, and slightly bulged. Above the ridge, the sky had shifted from sallow gold toward purple, the color of a dark, deep-tissue bruise.

Tina sat down on a cedar bench and hugged herself, scowling at the fading details of the ground. She rocked back and forth, wondering how Trixie had ended up as the director of their movie, and how she had become something like a glorified P.A. The division of labor seemed unfair when she thought about it too much, and she considered going up to the dome and taking control of the rehearsals herself. But the time had obviously already come and gone for that. The chemistry had been established and it did not involve her at this point.

Tina fingered the rough fiber of the gnarled bench. There would be more phases in the movie ahead, she told herself, more opportunities to assert her opinions. The shooting of the film would be a place to reestablish her voice, for instance. She would be in charge of the camera, the look of each shot down to the smallest detail. This thought reassured her in a way, gave her something to look forward to.

At some point, Tina believed, she would be undergoing a great metamorphosis of some kind. She would become more like Trixie, and, moreover, she would discover that she always had been. She just needed to hold on until that time of recognition arrived.

At about nine o'clock Trixie returned from the rehearsal and stomped into Tina's room, where Tina was busy drawing storyboards at her desk.

"Wow," Trixie said. "Beth is so good. Did you see her today?"

"Yeah," Tina said. "She looked really great." She kept her eyes on the storyboards, where she was sketching out a picture of a woman cleaning the surface of a black piano, her reflection visible in the grain of wood.

Trixie walked over to the rows of index cards they had tacked up on the wall, alongside a long chart tracing the arc of each character in a differently colored pen. The diagram of intersecting lines was an inscrutable map to anyone but themselves. She fingered the edge of one of the cards and swapped it with the one below. Every day the cards changed order depending on their most recent revisions of the script.

"God, what are we going to do about the end?" Trixie asked.

"I don't know," Tina said. "I'm trying to figure it out."

Trixie flopped down on the bed and rested her shoes on the head-board. "I'm not worried. We'll think of something."

"Yep," Tina said eventually.

"What are you doing?" Trixie asked. She rolled onto her stomach and propped her chin on her palms.

"Storyboards," Tina said. "Colors, angles. You know. What the shots are going to look like."

"Huh." Trixie said. She seemed hesitant to endorse the project, but she refrained from outright objection.

After a few minutes she got up and put on her coat.

"Well, I'm going out," Trixie said, and paused for a moment at the door, as if to let Tina ask her some question.

"Right," Tina said, and continued staring at the page beneath her hand. Every few nights Trixie snuck away to attend to some unknown chore in the woods, and every few nights Tina relished the small stabbing pain that she imagined her disinterest to cause.

Trixie disappeared from the house, and Tina watched from the window as she marched into the mouth of the trees. For a moment she considered following, but then decided against it. That would be undignified, she thought, and returned to the work at her desk. Tina filled in the cross-hatching of a receding shadow, and redrew the slant of the doctor's mouth, listening to music and tapping her foot on the rung of her chair. Somehow she managed to beat down the fascination she had, she beat down the anger and frustration and the amorphous jealousy.

When Trixie returned hours later with dirt under her nails and scratches on her arms, Tina continued working on her drawings as if nothing had occurred.

The next morning, Tina climbed onto the school bus for the first time in almost a week, locating a cold, empty, vinyl seat and settling in beside the window. She did not have a regular place on the bus, like most of the kids did, because she had been missing classes so often to work on the film. Her mother, who prided herself on her unconditional support for any creative endeavor her daughter engaged in, had written Tina a note excusing her from anything she needed to be excused from, and had even petitioned the administration to give the girls credit for their work outside the classroom, a prospect looking doubtful but not entirely out of the question. Tina still tried to attend classes at least a few days a week, though, in order to keep from falling too far behind, and Trixie attended most of the days that she missed.

Tina always enjoyed her time on the bus. A few minutes where nothing could possibly be done. She leaned into her cold seat, watching the now familiar landscape pass beside her. The corrugated rooftops of the railroad yards, the black wall of fir trees heaving like a wave.

The bus arrived at the school and she walked through the breezeway to her locker, keeping her eyes fixed on the ground. She passed by the heaters and the trophy case, the janitor's closet and the science lab, counting the brown squares on the floor as she made her way. Morning light slid on the floor's beige tiles, and Tina noted the feet that sometimes encroached on her line of vision. Top-Siders, Stan Smiths, Converse, penny loafers.

Suddenly, as Tina approached her locker, she found herself surrounded by a crowd of monsters. There was a coven of witches in her way, and some goblins and devils, kids in werewolf masks and mummy bandages. There were boys wearing dresses and girls wearing insectoid fairy wings, laughing and pushing each other in small groups. Batman raced through the crowd, shouting at someone far away, and another Batman leaned on the banister, waiting to be approached.

"Boo!" a ghost said as Tina passed by. "What the hell are you?"

Tina walked through the crowd in a daze, wondering how she had completely forgotten Halloween this year. The pumpkins on the porches, the piles of little candy at the grocery store, all of it had failed to register. Which was strange, because normally it was her favorite holiday of the year.

# 6

**C**OOKIE AND HENRY emerged from the tailor wearing conical hats, ankle-length robes of combed silk, and wooden shoes. Over the robes they put on collarless jackets, and under them knee-high breeches, and around their shoulders they strung jade necklaces, which was something they had noticed the merchants of Canton seemed to do. They squinted their eyes at each other and stuck out their teeth and Henry did a funny, shuffling jig, which Cookie found mildly amusing from inside his layers of finery.

They loaded their jars of castoreum into a wooden wheelbarrow and made their way toward the gateway into Canton. On the far end of the wharf, there was a single portal that allowed workers in and out of the city, marked by an elaborate arch covered in carved dragons and colorful shingles and guarded day and night by armored guards. Cookie and Henry had no real plan for how to get through it. Foreigners, as they had been told innumerable times, were prohibited from the city's streets. And yet they avoided thinking about that. They believed that in convincing each other they were invisible, they would also convince the world.

They had directions, written on a scrap of rice paper, to the home of Howqua, whom, they had learned since their meeting with Jim Lee, was a very famous hong merchant indeed, renowned throughout Canton as the shrewdest and most versatile entrepreneur of his generation. He had amassed a large fortune in his brief career by acting as middleman for many of the products sold in the region. He owned land, buildings, and factories used by Chinese and foreign merchants alike, speculated in commodities, even cornered the market in pepper as a young man. He loaned money. And perhaps more than anyone else, he understood the increasingly interconnected nature of the emerging trade networks that had lately stenciled themselves onto the globe. He sold artworks at auction in London and Paris, underwrote expeditions to Greenland and Argentina for fur and exotic goods, and invested his capital in American railroads.

Cookie and Henry jostled among a large crowd of Chinese men streaming in and out of the wharves and the city. They hulked over the diminutive citizens and hunched down to blend in better. The crowd moved at a steady pace, weaving and clotting, trudging toward its destination of the gate. Up ahead, the entrance loomed, colorful tiles encrusting the shapes of lions and pillars and spheres. On either side of the passage stood men in wooden armor, holding long, pointed spears that glinted in the light. Their faces were covered in woven masks, like turtle shells. Behind the mesh their eyes could be anywhere.

Henry pushed the wheelbarrow ahead of him and kept his own eyes on the cobbled road. Cookie walked beside him and did the same. All around them murmured babbling, incomprehensible voices. The clipped, singsong cadences of the spoken Chinese rose and fell, tripped and trilled. A baby swaddled in thick blankets smiled at Cookie, which he took as a good sign.

They held their breath and simply kept walking, right past the soldiers, right into the streets of Canton, and no one noticed, it was as easy as that.

They emerged into a dirty avenue, paved with granite slabs and scored with thick gouges and cross-hatchings, so narrow in parts that Cookie could touch both walls with his outstretched fingers. The crowd trundled along without pausing. Where the streets of the tourist area had been clean and well-groomed, these were covered in grime and filth. Gnarled fingers of ginseng hung from rafters, alongside baskets of lizards and bugs. Butchers displayed kittens, puppies, and skinned rats, grocers strange fruits and vegetables with spikes and spiny ridges. Druggists offered deer antler, dried tiger flesh, snake gall. On the sidewalk men lay facedown in strange chairs, receiving aggressive massages, or being stabbed with long pins into their necks and backs. Cookie and Henry hunched farther down.

They passed from the narrow canyon of the streets and into a wide plaza, where the ground became a mosaic of interlocking red stones, and a troupe of performers was busily entertaining a crowd, accompanied by crashing cymbals and rolling drums. There were strong men, and tumblers, and bird trainers, and a performer who allowed an adder to bite his tongue, which sent him into convulsions, which he then cured by applying a substance to his gums, which was for sale.

Cookie and Henry continued on without stopping. The crowd carried them farther into the plaza, where the flagstones ended and turned into a wide expanse of yellow dirt, baking in the sun. Dotting the hard earth were the heads of men buried up to their necks, flies buzzing around their faces, crawling on their chapped, whitened lips. Their eyes were glassy and blank. A tired soldier stood guard beside them, beneath written signs covered in official-looking insignia and stamps. The citizens of Canton walked past the buried men briskly, averting their eyes, or sometimes spitting on them. Cookie and Henry looked at each other cooly.

"Keep moving," Henry said.

Their map led them up a cobbled road toward the pagoda on the hill, and onto a wider avenue lined with fig trees, where they matched the symbol on their paper to one painted on a massive red door. The building was four stories tall, with arching, shingled awnings on each level. They pulled a rope that connected to a chime somewhere, and soon a ponytailed servant appeared. They handed him the scrap of paper that Jim Lee had given them, and the servant ushered them inside.

The air inside smelled of incense and spices. The walls were made of fitted pine panels. The servant led them down a lacquered hallway to a sitting room filled with burly armchairs and couches from Europe, where they were seated in high-backed chairs with matching suede ottomans, beside an end table laden with a bursting bouquet of wildflowers. The servant instructed them to wait. He offered each of them

199

a crumpet and a cup of tea, along with a silver chalice filled with white, granular sugar.

"From Cuba," he said.

They sat down, each resting a decent-sized box of castoreum in their laps. When Cookie shifted his weight, the jars rattled and clanked like glass chains.

"It's all gonna be just fine," Henry said, and then audibly gulped.

"Of course it is," Cookie said, and straightened his robes.

Cookie and Henry waited a long time in the room, sipping tea and pressing wrinkles from the folds of their gowns. Henry glanced around while rubbing his hands on the arm of his chair. He smiled at Cookie reassuringly, and Cookie gamely smiled back. Henry made some strange sounds in his throat, some long sighs, and then a grumble. On the far wall an Austrian cuckoo clock tapped its metronomic beat, the pendulum dipping back and forth. Cookie tugged on his earlobe and straightened his sleeves.

Eventually the servant returned and led them down another hallway, shuffling and swishing his feet on the floor. This hallway was lined with oil paintings of European landscapes and a vitrine filled with enamels and carved ivory. They passed an empty suit of armor and the bust of a Roman senator, a rusted trident and threadbare tapestry of unicorns. The jars of castoreum rattled in the boxes, and their feet echoed on the polished wood floor. They walked up stairs carpeted in a fine weave the color of a bright tangerine.

At the end of the hallway was a set of double doors rising all the way to the ceiling, engraved with scenes of equestrian battle in two columns of panels. The servant grasped the knobs, each as large as a sunflower, and swung the doors open.

The light from the hallway fell into the room like a knife, cutting through the murky shadows to reveal the surface of an imposing oaken desk, barren but for a jar of ink and an array of golden nibs arranged in a neat semicircle.

Behind the desk stood a leather chair, turned away from them like a gravestone, and behind that a massive picture window spread across the entire wall, cloaked in thick curtains. Around the edges of the drapery glowed the soft, graded light of the outdoors, and along one side a crease of white-hot sunlight.

As Cookie and Henry entered the chamber the chair rotated to reveal a corpulent man, perfectly bald, with a long mustache hanging over his mouth. He wore a white linen suit, cut in a Western style, and a long necklace of jade spheres strung over his ox-like shoulders.

"I am Howqua," the man said, and smiled to show a row of perfect teeth the size of corn kernels. "Please. Sit." He gestured toward two chairs on the other side of his desk.

The door closed gently behind them and the room went dark. The outline of Howqua's bald head shone in the near total blackness, and the sound of his rustling jacket filled the room. His chair creaked. Cookie and Henry arranged their bottles of castoreum oil on the floor.

"Set your goods anywhere," Howqua said from the shadows. "Make yourself comfortable. When two cultures meet, certain formalities are better left behind, don't you agree?"

The two men mumbled that yes, they agreed, formalities were unhelpful.

"Thank you for seeing us, sir," Henry said, and immediately began prattling on about their good luck in passing through the city gate unmolested, how they had simply averted their eyes and gone through without a hitch. "Very good," Howqua said politely, though he seemed slightly bored.

While Henry talked, Cookie's eyes slowly became accustomed to the gloom. Howqua's face was round and nearly ageless in a way, no wrinkles or marks, no blemishes or protrusions. His nose was a small button, and his eyes were narrow, his mouth was thin and partly pursed. Cookie scrutinized Howqua's face for clear signs of honesty or deception. He knew a trustworthy face in New York, in Oregon, but what did an honest Chinaman look like?

"I admire your resolve," Howqua said when Henry was finished. "My home is always open to young entrepreneurs. One never knows, after all. You Americans are so ingenious. You come to sell me so many things:

amomum, aniseed stars, benzoin, bezoar. Cudear, gamboge, olibanum. Asafoetida. Terra japonica, damar, gambie. Smalts. Whangees." He relished the list, pronouncing each item with a precise diction. "You bring whole sandalwood forests from the South Pacific, and seal fur from Antarctica. You wish to please us so badly." Howqua smiled, a leering, awkward contortion of his face.

"It is regrettable that the Empire makes it so difficult for us to do business with the world. Nonetheless, much of my business is done with Englishmen. I have tried to make my home comfortable for them." While Howqua spoke a side door opened and a shuffling servant entered with a document of some sort, which he placed before Howqua, who stamped it in the corner, and the servant shuffled out.

"Please, please show me what you have to sell," Howqua said. "I am very curious what my nephew considers so pressing."

Henry lifted the box of castoreum to Howqua's desk and unscrewed the top of the nearest jar.

"Castoreum oil," Henry said. "Fresh from the Oregon Territory. Extracted from the healthiest beavers in the known world. Pure juices in these fellers."

"Yes, yes, I understand," Howqua interrupted him, and rose to his feet.

Howqua turned toward the curtains behind him and parted them in a powerful jerk, sending a flood of sunlight through the room. The light was shocking at first, but once Cookie's pupils contracted, he found himself faced with a tranquil scene—a wide picture window filled with a commanding view of the harbor. The waters were dotted with white sails, like smudges of paint, and the rooftops met in a series of ragged planes, overlapping like the scales of a fish. A whole city behind a pane of glass, like a beautiful painting whose light shifted with the gradual movement of the sun.

Howqua's lap was covered in crumbs, which he halfheartedly brushed away. He held the jar to the light and nodded his head.

"Very pure," he said, "no clouds."

Henry sat stock still, watching Howqua inspect the castoreum, while Cookie took the chance to glance around the room. It was larger than he had realized. Down a single stair, in a slight depression, stood a billiard table, a long bar, a dartboard. The ceiling was crossed with long beams of black teak wood.

Cookie looked at Howqua looking at the castoreum, but found he could not bear to watch. He felt a pit in his stomach, as if Howqua might discover some new substance in the jars, as if they were lying.

Howqua opened the lid and smelled the castoreum. Again he nodded. "Clean. Where is it from did you say?"

"From Oregon," Henry replied.

Howqua pondered this.

"Inland?" he asked.

"Yes. Just in from the Pacific."

"Loaded at a coastal port? Or are there rivers that allow ships to travel upstream?"

"The rivers are good," Henry said. "There's good access to the interior."

"Interesting," Howqua said, and shook the jar of castoreum to see bubbles explode from inside and race to the top. He turned toward them again, smiling broadly.

"I believe we can do business, my friends," he said. "This is a very impressive product you have brought."

Cookie exhaled, realizing he had been holding his breath the whole time.

"I must admit," Howqua said, pulling pieces of a large scale from behind his desk. "I did not anticipate my nephew's deal to prove so lucrative. This is a pleasant surprise indeed. Jim Lee has shown very good judgment in bringing you to me. He will be well rewarded for his efforts."

Howqua rang a bell and began assembling the weights and levers of his scale on the desktop.

"Ahhh," he said, as the scale slowly took form. "It is a beautiful thing, the way objects grow value as they move around the earth. The markets of America are the markets of China are the markets of Europe these days; there is money to be made in sending items from place to place. That is how it should be, my friends. There are no borders in nature, no nations.

"One day," Howqua went on, "the whole world will be partners in trade. A web of commerce will be woven in every direction. Tell me, my friends," he said, as the scale fell into place. "What would you consider a fair price for your castoreum today? How much did you come to sell your oil for?"

Henry spoke assuredly: "Five ounces of silver for every ounce of castoreum," he said. "Five to one, money for oil." Cookie felt his stomach seize up.

Howqua raised an eyebrow. "Five to one, eh? Is that what they buy it for these days? That is a very high price. I can only sell it myself for six."

"That's still a profit of one ounce on every sale. A good day's work considering we brought it all the way from America."

"True enough. But I must package it and distribute it as well. The profit margin is eaten quickly that way. I can only buy it for two ounces to one."

"Four."

"Three."

"It's a deal."

The two men shook over the plane of Howqua's desk.

Henry focused intently on the weighing of the materials. First Howqua poured one of the jars of castoreum into a ceramic basin and placed the empty glass on a platform of his scale. He tapped a weight along the opposite arm until the two heads balanced, and proceeded to weigh the jars one by one, against the corrected measure. Each jar came out to an almost equal amount, within a few milligrams of fluid, and Howqua notated the figures in a neat column. When he was finished, he added the weights of the castoreum into a single figure and came up with the total volume.

"Sixty-three ounces," he said.

"Just a minute," Henry said, and pointed at the loose castoreum in the ceramic bowl. "Don't forget that jar."

"Oh my goodness. Please excuse me," Howqua said, and poured the bowl of fluid back into the empty jar, which he then weighed, and added to the ledger. "How embarrassing. Please forgive me."

"Seventy-one ounces," he corrected, "and times three is two hundred thirteen."

Just as the negotiation was coming to an end, Howqua's servant returned with a coffer made of red cherrywood, with inlaid mother of pearl in the pattern of a repeating cube. The coffer was the size of a small trunk, and rolled on squeaking wheels. He opened it to reveal an assortment of silver coins, embossed with Spanish designs or perforated with triangular holes. Each coin was chopped with tiny hieroglyphs, figure eights and starbursts, hammered by assayers who had attested to the purity of the metal. There were milled Spanish old heads, bearing the profile of Charles III or Charles IV, and new heads bearing the profile of Ferdinand VII. There were republican coins minted in Latin America and a basin of sycee, shoe-shaped Chinese silver ingots.

"Three times the weight in Spanish silver, or twice the weight in Chinese, which is purer. And in addition I am willing to exchange the silver at a fair rate into dollars for your convenience."

"No thank you. We'll stick with the silver," Henry said.

Howqua grew a little bit cross. "What good is silver to you? So heavy and burdensome. You will have to exchange it soon regardless. Or carry it all the way across the sea."

"Thank you," Henry said firmly, "but silver is fine." They chose the Spanish silver, at three to one, and watched Howqua measure it out one coin at a time.

"Thank you so much," Cookie muttered, his voice creaking like a rusted gate.

"My pleasure," Howqua said, bowing slightly, and he shook their hands again with a limp grasp. "Now let us drink."

He pulled a bottle of scotch from his drawer, and three crystal glasses. He poured them each two fingers of golden liquid and raised his glass for a toast.

"We have both made good money today," he said. "To our good luck."

When the drink was over, Howqua returned the glasses to his drawer and got up to walk the men to the door.

"Many Chinese," he said as they exited his office, "they fail to understand the Americans. They don't see how young you are. Like an old man and a puppy dog. The old man should be kind. The old man should show affection. We have many things to learn from each other. We should be friends. Money makes all men friends. Money brings us together. Surplus value is the stuff of friendship."

"Couldn't agree more," Henry said.

On the way out the hallways were different, filled now with Hindu mosaics and reliefs, showing bodies in contorted poses of a sometimes sexual nature. In the vitrine where the enamels and ivory had been there was now an illuminated manuscript showing a garden with a beautiful bird in an orange tree. In the sitting room, the European furniture had been replaced by scattered pillows and a low table with a teapot and hydrangia blossoms. The floor was covered in Persian carpets.

It was still light outside, the late afternoon sun slanting low over the rooftops. Howqua stood on the doorstep and watched them go. His large hand gripped the jamb and his rings flashed in the air. A silver cat rubbed against his calf. Howqua squinted into the sunlight.

"Do be careful on your way back," he said. "And next time you bring more."

# 7

B Y EARLY NOVEMBER Tina's list of things to do was full of scabrous cross-outs. The abandoned hospital was rigged for power; a Victorian bed-and-breakfast in north Portland, complete with a gabled rooftop, sinister eaves, and a rickety widow's walk on a shingled belfry, surrounded by unimproved roadways and black ironwork, was reserved as their doctor's residence and clinic. They had racks of costumes, lighting equipment stored in plastic milk crates, and donations from local restaurants and catering companies promised for each day of the shoot.

There was one big thing, however, that remained undone. One thing that Tina had yet to find and which would demolish their carefully laid plans if it went neglected much longer. They did not have a camera yet. And without one they were fairly screwed.

Tina had searched for a decent camera almost every day in every manner she could think of, given the resources she had to work with, which were slight to say the least. She had placed ads in the paper, trawled the thrift stores, garage-saled and pawn-shopped from one end of town to the other, but for some reason none of her regular methods for finding things had seemed to work out. The population of used cameras in Portland had apparently all disappeared, and although Tina could almost sense them languishing in every attic and basement she walked past, hiding in back rooms and broom closets, they refused to be coaxed out into the open. She had found plenty of other things—C-stands, megaphones, walkie-talkies—but none that performed the all-important task of capturing light onto spinning reels of blank cellu-loid, the profound, incomprehensible act of catching time's motion.

The camera had become something of a holy grail in Tina's mind, an object of near magical properties.

Although Tina did not understand the precise mechanics of the camera—far from it, in fact—over time she had begun to discern the basic profile of what she was looking for. After talking to a few semi-experts on the matter, she had come to the conclusion that she needed a used, but not too used, 16 mm camera, preferably constructed in Germany or Switzerland, with synch sound and a variety of detachable lenses, at the very least a zoom and wide-angle. She wanted a body svelte enough to execute the proper pans and dollies and a functioning light meter. No matter what else, she knew she must avoid anything made in the last ten years, and anything where the microphone's sound quality was in any doubt whatsoever.

According to Trixie they had about four hundred dollars to spend, once the money came in, which seemed about right, given the prices Tina had browsed in the consumer guides at the library, so long as they got a deal on something that was practically unheard of.

Now Tina just needed some fantastic coincidence to occur, some fortuitous event to drop the thing in her lap, which was a tough thing to plan for, she realized, but also part of the logic of filmmaking, as far as she could tell, the dumb luck that pushed some people ahead and kept others trapped on the sidelines. Sometimes you just had to believe in something and proceed toward it blindly, hoping whatever it was materialized in your tracks, because otherwise there was almost no reason to go forward at all.

So, two weeks before filming was to begin, Tina found herself standing on the corner of Eighty-second and Division, hoping for a miracle.

Eighty-second Avenue was a flat strip of asphalt running from the airport to the Clackamas River along the general boundary where the city ended and the foothills of Mount Hood began. The street was lined with all manner of failing businesses—second-tier food franchises, shabby motels, ramshackle garages and windowless gun shops—interspersed with weed-ridden vacant lots where weekend carpet sellers decamped, and transient dealerships hawked molded plastic Jacuzzis. Half-primed cars chugged on the blacktop, phlegmy coughs rattling deep in their engines, past faded signs and billboards that were nearly always missing a few blocky letters, FRESH BA T & T CKLE, NO VA AN Y, OLD SODA. And Tina's favorite, GOO EAR TIRES.

More than anything else, however, Eighty-second Avenue was known for its thrift stores, which sprouted among the shacks and warehouses like wild mushrooms. From large department stores filled with all but new merchandise to strange, religiously affiliated junk shops to thinly disguised halfway houses for the mentally disabled, Eighty-second Avenue was the place in Portland where old things came to die. It was part gold mine and part graveyard, a sprawling, horizontal boutique of lost promise.

Today, Trixie had come along with Tina to hunt for the camera, and the two girls stood on the broken sidewalk as their bus groaned into the distance in a blue haze of exhaust. The asphalt receded in either direction, its yellow dividing line faded to a dim, jaundiced stripe, blotted with oil stains and gasoline puddles. A confused woman in a hot-pink sweatsuit swept by on the sidewalk, pushing a baby carriage filled with old beer cans, followed by a man mumbling to himself angrily, on the verge of some terrible bankruptcy or divorce.

"Well," Tina said.

"Well?" Trixie said.

"How about over there," Tina said, and pointed them toward a nearby strip mall fronted by a gravel parking lot and a sunbleached sign for big savings.

"Sounds all right."

They started walking. The air was chilly and the sky looked like a slab of concrete, which added to their sense of remote desolation, and stoked in them a low-burning hope that some treasure was nearby. Only someplace this underpicked might hold the prize.

The first store Tina and Trixie went into was Valu Village, a massive second-hand department store located in a building that had once been a Safeway. Huge, plate glass windows rose to a sine-wave roof covered in tar and pebbles, and the electronic doors opened with a gentle shush. Inside, tinny speakers cooed Simon and Garfunkel, and particles of aerosol air freshener seemed to settle in a film over the landscape of discarded sweatshirts and pants. Long racks of coffee cups and silverware stood near the window, leading to dense rows of crotchless jeans and pilly flannel shirts, depleted down jackets and machinist's uniforms. Toward the back of the room rose piles of acrylic quilts with hardened cigarette burns, beside stacks of mildewed romance novels and softened copies of L. Ron Hubbard's *Dianetics*. Throughout the cavernous space, men and women quietly milled about, touching things and putting them down, lit by a bank of naked fluorescent lights high overhead.

Tina and Trixie joined the search, immediately losing a good half an hour in the T-shirt section, reading the slogans out loud over a barrier of cookie jars and glass ashtrays. The Four Stages of Tequila; Ignore the Turkey; Zero to Bitch in 60 Seconds; Where's Your Aspen? They found T-shirts for Christian summer camps and high school leadership conventions, basketball teams and the Special Olympics.

"Come on," Tina reminded. "We can't get distracted now."

"Shit," Trixie said. "You're right."

The girls located the camera section deep in the back, between a shelf of VCRs and larger kitchen appliances, on a long, folding tabletop. The table was loaded down with old Polaroids and Super 8 cameras, mixed with battered Nikons and Leicas, and a wide assortment of dinged lens caps and dirty rainbow shoulder straps. The girls sifted through the broken stuff with careful attention, making sure to touch everything in order to measure its worth. They knew how easy it was to pass something up by merely glancing.

At the edge of the table, near a stack of used flashbulbs, Tina came across a potential score, a Kodak Brownie with built-in exposure setting. "For Professionals," the box said. The body was squarish, with a flattened capsule on the side for the magazine of film, and came with a dog-eared instructional pamphlet rubber-banded to the lens.

"Check it out," Tina said, raising the camera in the air. The casing was a little scuffed, and the lens barrel scraped when she twisted it back and forth, as if there was sand in the grooves, but the pieces all seemed to be in place.

"Oh my God," Trixie said. "Is this the thing? Could it be that easy?"

"I don't know. Maybe."

Tina briefly compared the instruction manual to the camera itself, and figured out how to load the film. She flicked the heavy switches and levers a few times, and peered through the viewfinder, then flipped it over to find a thick scar gouged in the lens, a white fingernail carved deep into the glass.

"Goddammit," she said, "I don't think this'll work," and the girls decided they had to pass it up.

They tried Bargain Station next, and then St. Vincent de Paul, and even the Mormon-run Deseret, where they found more buckled shoes and a shawl, a stethoscope, but nothing like what they were looking for. Trixie flirted with the cashiers and got them a senior discount, four dollars for everything in the bag, and they left with a sense of some partial accomplishment.

When the girls had exhausted the thrift stores, they switched to pawnshops, where the selection was smaller and the prices much worse. They rifled through boxes of eight-track tapes and Betamax machines and reel-to-reel audio tapes bearing mysterious labels, peered over glass cases filled with pistols and corkboard walls loaded with rifles hanging on metal pins. All of the pawnshops were more or less the same. As for movie gear, the supplies were minimal: busted Super 8 cameras, taped together PixelVisions, empty film tins. Or strange Russian equipment, like the Kragsnogov or the AKS-1r, with their thick, industrial skin and rounded edges, their heavy, war-like sense of purpose.

The girls ate a quiet lunch in a diner called Jo Jo's, overlooking the Fred Meyer parking lot, where a roving carnival had been installed for the weekend. Arcades and shooting galleries and hot dog stands lined the asphalt, surrounding an inflatable castle that jiggled with the bouncing weight of a dozen children, its spire bending and rising with each assault.

Tina poured a packet of saccharine into a spoon and examined the granules in the cloudy light, noting the clean outline of each particle beside the new hugeness of the spoon's silver lip.

"So." She paused and squinted her eyes while moving the spoon slowly back and forth. "What if we don't find it?" she said casually. "I don't know if we're going to."

"We'll find it," Trixie assured her, a little irritably. "We still have two weeks."

"But what if we don't?" Tina said. "We might not. I've been looking for weeks."

"We will."

Outside, the flashing lights of the Tilt-A-Whirl looked exhausted. Off and on, on and off, it was like work.

When their food arrived, Tina watched the way Trixie ate her hamburger, how she pulled it apart and then took out the pickles, which she placed on the tabletop beside her in a neat stack. Something about the action was infuriating. It made Tina want to slap Trixie's face.

By the time Tina and Trixie stumbled into Erwin's Pawn Shop on Eighty-second and Stark, they were both dead tired. They had visited eight more thrift stores and five pawnshops that afternoon, as well as an outlet mall, an antique shop, and a discount electronics store. They had accumulated four more bags of costume material and an ancient-looking pitchfork, but nothing close to that first, damaged Brownie had appeared. Although they had seen this particular shop numerous times from the street, they had never deigned to peer inside. Tucked between a veterinarian and a check-cashing store, backed with twisted fir trees, it was among the least promising storefronts on the strip. They decided it would be their last attempt for the day.

The door jingled and opened into a room of musty, still air. Long metal racks lined the walls, filled with disorganized crap. Dusty packets of air filters and old cans of motor oil, ancient garden tools and a shrink-wrapped potty chair. The drop ceiling was splotched with yellow water stains. The girls wandered down the aisles listlessly. It was all the same garbage as the last place, and the place before that. Eight-track tapes and Betamaxes and Ampex audio reels, everything covered in a layer of rich grime.

At the counter toward the back of the room sat an old man bent over something in the spill of light from a reading lamp. He had red-rimmed eyes, with jagged hairs sticking from his nostrils, and gnarled, liver-spotted hands. His nose was like a fleshy water faucet, covered in burst capillaries, and his gray eyebrows poked from a colorful ski cap, striped with orange and green and yellow, with a puffball of purple on the crown.

The girls approached him quietly and waited for him to acknowledge their existence. On the desktop beneath him lay an old circuit board covered in tiny wires and inlaid chips. He sat bent over the green wafer, intently picking at the wires with a pair of shaking tweezers. His clothes rustled with each gusty exhalation of air. He placed the wires that he extracted in a little pile, like a stack of miniature, multicolored firewood. The girls stood there a moment, but he did not look up from his job.

He had a beautiful beard.

"Excuse me," Tina murmured, but the man did not appear to hear her. He continued pulling on a green wire sutured onto the wafer with a blob of silver.

"Minute," he managed to get out, and after peeling the wire from its mooring he put the board aside and looked up at them with a rheumy-eyed stare.

"May I help you?" he asked. His voice was wobbly, and a little indistinct, but he finally seemed more or less present to the situation.

"We're looking for movie cameras, sixteen millimeter," Tina explained, wanting to hurry the process along. She doubted that he had anything to show them and they still had a long trip home before dinner—two bus rides and a grueling walk up the hill.

"What?" he called out. She could see his ears were crammed with yellow wax.

"Movie cameras!" Trixie yelled back, miming the old-time crank, as in charades.

He grunted and slid off his stool, swiping the pile of wires into his hand, then shuffled into the back without a word. The girls stood there a moment, listening to boxes scraping over the floor and metal poles clattering about, when finally a voice called out, "Back here!"

The girls slipped behind the counter and through a mangy sheet hanging in a doorway into the back room. They were surprised to find a large, dank-smelling warehouse cluttered with bulky lumps and piles hidden under an assortment of old tarps and blankets. Naked lightbulbs dangled from the ceiling, and thick cobwebs coated the rafters like a gauze. There were no windows and the narrow aisles receded in murky shadows. The floor near the doorway was covered in a mess of high school chemistry sets, broken computer monitors, and oscilloscopes. Trixie put her bag on a rusted barrel.

"Don't touch that," the man said, and walked over and pushed the lid tight, even though it was already perfectly sealed. Then he wandered over to a mysterious mound covered by a drop cloth and peered underneath, grumbling under his breath.

"Nope," he said, among other things that Tina could not understand.

He glared into the shadows and walked to another drop cloth and lifted it hesitantly. He shook his head and tried another.

While he rummaged through his inventory, Tina wandered deeper into the warehouse, picking her way through an aisle of metal brackets and old buckets of paint. She found a rack of books crammed into a wooden case and grazed her hand over the spines: *Biological Transmutation, Alchemical Properties of the Elements, Cities of Gold and Lead*.

She could hear the man grunting and puttering about as he searched for whatever he had tucked away somewhere. She was not hopeful, but was happy enough to wait out the search. She pulled a book from the shelf. The pages were almost transparently thin, covered in woodblock diagrams and Latin text. She recognized a carrot and a crystal, a droplet of water bisected by geometrical lines.

"So, you're an alchemist?" Tina called out, to make conversation.

"Oh yes," he said without stopping. "We all are! We are all transmuting materials all the time. How does an acorn become a tree? How does the tomato live in the seed?"

The man grunted to himself as he lifted another tarp. "There is in fact something being hidden," he said, though it was unclear whether he was referring to his own search or something more general than that.

"Your new boyfriend is hot," Trixie said, sidling up beside the bookshelf.

"Shut up," Tina said, and replaced the book in its cavity.

"A-ha!" he said from across the room. He had pulled a sheet off of something in the corner. They walked over and glided into place on either side of him.

Lying at the man's feet were three green cardboard boxes, probably twenty years old but as yet unopened, featuring colorful labels of crew-cutted men fiddling with hefty-looking film cameras. The largest of the boxes said "1957 16 mm Paillard Bolex" on the side, next to the cursive signature of some celebrity endorser.

Tina reached down and lifted the lid. Inside was a camera lying gracefully in a form-fitting bed, every piece in mint condition. She lifted the camera and felt its heavy weight in her hand, clicked its various levers and switches. The barrel twisted like smooth oil. "Made in Switzerland," she read on the side. Other boxes revealed a leather carrying case, a pistol grip, eye cups, and three film spools. There were also color filters, little disks of yellow and orange, and an array of lenses, a tripod specifically made for the retractable zoom.

"Oh my God," Trixie said. "This is exactly it."

The man kicked the sheet to reveal an editing deck to go along with it.

"Just came in," he said, suddenly lucid. "All of it, five hundred bucks."

When the girls exited the pawn shop the world seemed violently white, the overcast day like a fireburst on their tender pupils. Gradually the shadows came back into view, and the colors sharpened. They had a 16 mm Bolex and an editing suite on hold now, covered in strips of masking tape with their names written many times in black Sharpie. They would return in a week to pay for it, they had said, and the gnomish man, named Erwin, had said fine, its all yours. For the past half hour he had been trying to convince them to make yet another movie, this one about the grand story of his life.

"It could be a great film," he said, winking broadly at Tina. "A classic boy-girl type thing."

"Okay, Erwin, sure," Tina said, laughing. "Just show us the script, man. We'd love to see it."

# 8

NEIL STOOD BEFORE the cord of wood and contemplated its many pieces, broken down from its once-unified thing. After putting off the chore for weeks now, he had finally wandered into it without thinking. He had been walking near the pile of logs and before he knew it, he had the ax in his hand. The only way to get something like this done sometimes, he realized, was by sneaking up on it from behind.

Neil surveyed the pile and tried to figure out where to begin. There were hundreds of logs before him, one on top of the other, scattered at angles, full of interlocking nubs and branches and knobs. The pieces were all sturdy and cylindrical, covered in lichenous bark, and they exuded a clean smell of sap and sawdust, which was invigorating.

Neil fitted his worn leather gloves to his hands and gripped the handle of his ax. The wood had to be split before the rain arrived, and no one was going to do it but him.

Neil set up a log and swung the ax, which slid easily through the grain of wood. Then he set up each half and swung again, and tossed the quarters off to the side in a limber, snapping motion. Soon enough his body started to find its rhythm and his brain began to think.

Over the course of the past two weeks, Mr. Grimsrud and the Confederated Tribal Council had come to agree on only one thing. Neither of them wanted to go to court over the ownership of the bones. They had been down that path before. This time they wanted Neil to decide. They both trusted him in some way, and believed their odds were better with him than with the elaborate bureaucracies of the state, where they knew from experience that clean moral judgments were often subverted in a maze of political expediency.

"Okay," Neil said. "Jay Feather gets the small one and Mr. Grimsrud gets the big one. How about that?" But that idea had been summarily dismissed. Jay Feather and Mr. Grimsrud both wanted both of the skeletons. Anything less would be considered a defeat.

Neil selected another log and pulled it from the pile. He placed it upright on the ground, with its round flat face pointing toward the sky. He planted his feet and swung his ax and split the log, then picked up one half of the log and split it again. He was happy to be splitting the wood. The ax felt fluid in his hands, the grain smooth and unknotted. He could not understand why he had waited so long. It was exactly what he wanted to do.

Carbon, Neil understood, was the fundamental building block of life. Entering the world through the window of photosynthesis, it spread itself evenly throughout the cellular foundations of organic matter. It flowed from the leafy green plants to the tissue of the animals who ate the leafy green plants to the tissue of the animals that ate the animals that ate the leafy green plants. Life, Neil had found, was life, bound in its many forms by carbon's single denominator. The same carbon that had once animated Neil's ancestors now lived inside of him.

Pure carbon was the material of diamonds, locked into pristine, crystalline bonds.

Once an organism died, however, its tissue stopped absorbing carbon, and the equilibrium it shared with the rest of creation began to fade. The carbon leaked away in a slow exodus of particles, as life reclaimed the material of life for itself.

Neil split another log, his ax gliding through the hard flesh in a smooth, cracking motion. He grunted and swung again, feeling the grain part beneath the razor weight. His back was beginning to ache. His armpits were growing damp. He took off his down vest and tossed it onto the roof of the woodshed. Slowly he was getting through the stack. On one side he had a pile of gnarled, cylindrical logs, on the other side a pile of sleek, blond wedges. The second pile was gradually approaching the size of the first. His arms and shoulders stretched tautly with each stroke.

Crack. Two more.

The newspapers had fallen in love with the story of the skeletons. They fed on Neil's slow deliberation like flies on shit. Every day new letters to the editor appeared, and the responses to the letters, all of which Neil read avidly for some clue as to how he might behave.

For Mr. Grimsrud and the coalition of scientists that had arisen to support him, the skeletons represented a grand puzzle, a window into the past, a referendum on their professional practice itself. The muscle ridges, the furrows where the ligaments and tendons had been, the fractures on the head and chest—these things could describe events of a long-forgotten epoch, Grimsrud said, details from a world that was otherwise gone. Scientists could decipher the effects of disease and injury through patterns of bone dissoluton, entropy, and regrowth. To Mr. Grimsrud the skeletons were a secret language, a hidden code of cranial plates, dental calculus, forensic placement. Neil liked secret languages.

The Indians, on the other hand, argued that the process of learning the skeletons' secrets would in effect destroy them, that to study them would whittle them away to nothing. And what would ultimately be learned, they asked? They did not care about the language of the bones. They did not care about how old the remains were or what these men had eaten or how they had died. There was a great mystery at the center of life, Jay Feather agreed, a well of lost time that could never be filled, and to destroy something in an attempt to retrieve that time was in vain. What did it matter how men hunted then? Or where exactly they came from?

"Indians don't care about old," Jay Feather said. "Someday everything will be old. Everything is already old.

"I'll tell you what a real mystery is," he said. "What an animal is thinking, that's a mystery. If someone could tell me what a horse thinks when it's looking at you, or how a dog sees, that would be some mystery to solve. But you know what? No matter how many mazes you run a rat through, or how many times you dissect a frog, you're never gonna know. It's one of those things that you just have to live with."

What was it about life that desired carbon, Neil wondered? Why did life divide itself into so many parts?

By now the blond pile was growing larger than the brown pile. The small pieces were stacking up into a considerable bulk.

In addition to the newspaper reporters, other media-type people had begun lurking around the property as well. Every few days Neil received calls from radio stations, television morning shows, and a stringer for *The New York Times,* all of them asking for interviews. They sensed a battle, a trickle of blood from the earth. They were like dogs smelling fresh meat.

Neil looked down at his sweating arms. There was carbon burning inside him, flaring in every twitch of his muscles. He held out his hand and watched the sunlight pooling in his palm.

Why did life long for itself, Neil wondered? Why had man and plant and animal grown apart? Sometimes Neil imagined the whole world as diamonds and ghosts.

The wood was split now. One pile had become a different pile, of equal mass but quadruple parts. The wood had moved from one patch of ground to another.

Neil replaced his ax in the woodshed and tossed his gloves onto a shelf. He stood beside the pile of wood admiring the work he had done, the energy he had expended. He felt the heat of his body coming off of him, the surface of his skin under the falling sunlight. Next the stacking would begin. And then, later on, the burning.

# 9

T HE COLOR OF the chilies hanging from the rafters of the street-side grocer's stall was the purest and most undiluted red that Cookie had ever seen before, blindingly red, hovering above the bins of green onion and ginger and gooseberry in a thunderhead of soft and feathery branches. Beneath the peppers, crouching in the shadow of the awning, was an old woman rolling a pestle up and down the crevice of a canoe-shaped rock, grinding the peppers into a fine crimson dust. Her dry skin hung off her bones like flags of laundry, her mouth was toothless and pruned, and beside her was a short-haired dog, shaded with golden spots. In a doorway nearby stood a young boy with chopsticks darting between his mouth and bowl, the sun hitting him across the face. In Canton, Cookie observed, the old people seemed older, the dogs more doggish. Only the clouds in the sky were the same as everywhere else.

"Goddamn," Henry said, still reminiscing on their meeting with Howqua. "He is one tough customer. He's makin it on every angle."

"Yes," Cookie said, as a huge futon and cherrywood cabinet lumbered by, strapped to a rickshaw and pulled by a shoeless old man. A flock of pigeons congregated on the eaves of a nearby building, and shot into the sky like a spreading net.

"Exchangin the silver for dollar bills? You saw that? That's a profit right there. Hoo-ee. Fantastic. He'll get you coming and going. Terrific. But we made out pretty good, I'd say, didn't we partner?"

"I think so."

Slowly Cookie and Henry were making their way toward the docks and the safe shelter of the *Astor,* where the bags of silver would go into a lockbox that Cookie had stowed at the bottom of an oat barrel. The silver was currently strapped to Henry's body, two big bags slung over his shoulders, hidden beneath his silken robes like pendulous breasts. They were getting plenty of stares from the citizens of Canton, but if they kept moving they figured they would get to the ship in less than an hour.

A procession of men with painted faces and false beards rode past them on high-stepping horses, banging drums and cymbals. Cookie and Henry laughed.

The city's central pagoda bobbed over the tops of the buildings like the moon over the trees. The rooftops parted to reveal its scalloped pillar from a variety of angles, its curling eaves and intricate carvings gleaming in the hard sunlight.

"This way?" Cookie asked, as they wandered into a cobblestone alleyway where both the pagoda and the river became hidden from view.

"Pretty sure," Henry said.

They passed under a string of pennants and Cookie began losing his bearings in the slog of human traffic.

"You're sure about this?" he asked, and Henry nodded irritably. Then Henry began to whistle, which did not reassure Cookie at all.

Cookie tried to remain calm, but the longer they scurried through the streets, the more corkscrewed his sense of direction became. They passed the same stall of fish at least three times, then followed a hunch-backed man whom they recognized from the wharves, but when they caught up to him he was not the man they thought he was at all, rather a woman with a pile of laundry beneath her cloak.

"I don't know about this," Cookie said.

"We're fine," Henry said tersely.

Eventually they began to rise higher, and the walls of the alleyways seemed to tack them back and forth. The walls got taller, and pressed in closer, and finally slid apart to deposit Cookie and Henry in a broad public square, draped on every side with crimson bunting and shining golden tassels. At the center of the square rose the white pagoda, pasted against the glittering blue sky like a crisp piece of paper, alongside a pale fingernail of daylight moon.

"Well I'll be," Henry said.

"Beautiful," Cookie whispered.

The tower was made of smooth, fitted stone, flaring at each story with a skirt of cobalt tiles on top of elegantly carved pinions, and the base was surrounded by an arbor of misty pink cherry blossoms. The pagoda and its surrounding garden were encircled by a richly decorated wall, fronted by a wide set of stone stairs leading to a brightly colored wooden gate.

Cookie and Henry exchanged a glance. The pagoda stood calmly in the sunlight. The cherry petals shifted in the breeze. Cookie lifted his eyebrows hopefully and Henry shook his head. "No."

"Henry," Cookie said. He hoped to celebrate their good fortune in at least some mild fashion.

Henry rubbed his hands over his eyes and forehead. "All right, fine. But goddammit let's make it quick."

Cookie and Henry crossed the square and crept up the stairs, following a group of robed men through the gate. As they entered the garden the sounds and smells of Canton faded away, and they passed into another world.

The garden was quiet and beautifully maintained, full of shiny bamboo and gnarled stones, trees sculpted into the shapes of clouds, pebbles raked into placid, grooved patterns. Manicured pathways curved between miniature temples and topiary bushes, leading to a small fish pond, where aged goldfish glided underwater, losing themselves in the tea-like silt. The garden beckoned the men in different directions, and they parted ways to explore it.

Cookie took a pathway bending between moss and ponds. A thicket of bamboo cut him off from the gate and he lost sight of Henry. The boughs of a willow tree framed a rock garden, which in turn framed a wooden bridge.

He arrived at a cherry tree whose bark looked like polished copper. The wind moved easily through the twisted branches. Cookie imagined the living roots beneath the earth, growing downward in rough symmetry to the sun-drenched branches above. He compared the blossoms to one another, the tiny variations, each unique and yet utterly the same. He rubbed the petals between his soft fingertips, noting the whorls of his fingerprints beside their rich pink fabric.

He touched the hard wood and a fluff of petals fell to the ground, whispering in the air. They came to a rest but the whispering continued. The whispering of silk.

"Henry," Cookie said as he turned around, but standing in the pathway was not Henry at all. Instead, three Chinese soldiers were waiting there, dressed in armor made of quilted rope and ribs of wood, each with a long bamboo stick. They stepped toward him menacingly. The soldier on the right spoke to the others in low, brutal tones, and they lowered their sticks in unison. The middle soldier stepped forward and expertly jabbed Cookie in the stomach.

Cookie grunted and doubled over in shock. He tried to catch his breath. "Henry!" he called out, but the soldiers had already grabbed him by the hair and started dragging him back through the garden.

Cookie's footsteps scuffed through the pathways, throwing gravel into the moss and water to each side. He reached out for a passing bench but his fingers were pried loose, and when he grabbed the edge of the gate on the way outdoors, they were pried loose again. The soldiers held him tightly at the armpits, digging their fingers into the soft muscle of his underarms, and yanked him down the stairs toward the square.

Cookie looked around wildly as the speeding ground clattered beneath his feet, spotting the distant wharf, the alleyway that had brought him there. Through the narrow streets he could see a sliver of the bay, the masts of the *Astor* surrounded by coins of sparkling water. At the bottom of the stairs he caught a brief glimpse of Henry, standing among a crowd of onlookers, a head taller than anyone else. Their eyes met briefly before Cookie was pulled roughly away.

The next thing Cookie knew, the colors of Canton had smeared like wet paint, and the sound of squawking roosters was screaming in his ears. He was rushed through the streets of Canton at the center of a jostling crowd, with his robes fluttering at his sides, watching the progress of himself from a slight remove. He saw himself fending off a blow from one of the soldiers, saw himself bursting into tears. He saw himself stumble and lose his sandal and turn to grab it before being kicked in the stomach and pulled forward by a man in a fencing mask. He saw the citizens of Canton spitting on him, cursing, and shaking their fists, although possibly they were just going about their business as usual.

In time, the soldiers had dragged him to an imposing public building, an enormous garrison of gray brick and mortar, with stone lions straddling the steps, and windows the size of postage stamps. The walls were streaked with grime and the gutters in front were full of discarded paper and rotting trash. Cookie passed through a cold archway, and stumbled across a courtyard dotted with straw men bristling with arrows and bayonets, over hard earth scuffed from sparring. On the far edge of the courtyard he entered a room filled with lounging soldiers and sullen bureaucrats in moth-eaten clothes, where he was rushed past a desk into a bleak room with a table and a cot.

In this room they took off his robe and his sandals, his jade necklace and pillbox hat, and presented him with a pair of thin pajamas, which clung to his legs and shoulders when he tried to squeeze into them. The buttons did not fasten and the slippers were too small for his suddenly large feet, so he held them in his hand limply. Because this was not happening, it did not matter that his hands were so cold.

From there they led him through another stone archway and down a flight of stone stairs where the air turned dank and chilly and the footsteps of the soldiers echoed flatly against the walls. They proceeded down a long corridor lined with barred doorways, where men's faces peered from the shadows, their eyes glistening with clouded, feverish thoughts.

The soldiers slowed down for a moment and Cookie got a good look into one of the cells, where a young man with a moony face sat cross-legged at a low table, writing on a piece of parchment with a brush.

The prisoner looked up from his writing table just as Cookie lurched past, and for a brief moment they caught each other's eyes. Gray light fell on the man's smooth skin, a birthmark near the corner of his mouth, and his dark pupils flashed like onyx. He held his hand aloft, perfectly still over his rice paper, and a single droplet of black ink fell from its flame-like curl, spattering on the column of shapes. Then the wall moved between them and the man disappeared from view.

At the next door the guards stopped and pushed Cookie roughly against the wall. One of them reached inside his pocket and withdrew a clattering ring of keys, which he sorted through and finally raised to the lock. The door opened with a creak and the guards shoved Cookie inside. The door slammed behind him and the footsteps receded down the corridor. He heard a distant door slam, and then another more distant door, and then silence all around.

When Cookie's eyes adjusted to the light, he found himself in a stone cell about the size of the ship's galley. A small window above his head let in a single, tepid shaft of light, which made a small, golden square on the opposite wall. Outside the window, Cookie could see a sliver of blue sky, and occasionally a passing knee or a shin. In the corner of the cell was a pallet of straw. He stood in the middle of the room for a while, trying not to touch anything, wringing his hands together and cracking his knuckles. He raised his hand to his mouth and spit out his amber ring, which he placed back onto his finger. He had at least had the presence of mind to slide it into his mouth before the guards could take it away. He turned it on his finger, and fondled it with his thumb, spinning it on the cylinder of his skin. His finger had ached without the familiar pressure.

The walls were built from enormous blocks of limestone, sealed together with a smooth, white mortar. The straw on the floor, he found, was teeming with mites. A ceramic bowl sat near the door, encrusted with dried grit and eggy fluid. There was a washbasin with a spoonful of water. As his eyes continued to adjust to the darkness, Cookie noticed other details. The walls were covered in scratches, arranged in a simple pattern, and when he examined them more carefully, he realized that they marked some passage of time, days or weeks or some unknown unit of another calendar, and they had all derived from the same hand. It appeared that someone had once languished in this cell for a very long time.

As Cookie squinted at the walls, he eventually came across a small hole low to the ground. One of the blocks of limestone had a shaved-off corner, which created a triangular passageway about the size of a large coin all the way through to the adjoining cell. He pressed his eye to the hole. On the other side, through a foot of brick, he could see a tiny fragment of his neighbor's room. He saw the desktop, the man's hand moving over a scroll of parchment. He saw the tip of his brush touching the paper, and then moving away, only to return again coated in black ink. Cookie watched this miniature scene repeat itself until finally the hand put down the brush and the body rose, and the unattended desktop remained frozen in place.

Cookie got up and stood in the middle of his room again. His hands were shaking. They flopped around like gasping fish. He realized he needed to keep them busy somehow, so he sat down beside the infested straw and began to clean it. He extracted one filament at a time, which he wiped down with his thumb and forefinger, crushing whatever insects he found.

The task calmed him somewhat, and he began to think about the day's events with some clarity. He recognized that he was in a bad situation, but not a hopeless one. Diplomacy would take its course, he was sure of it. He returned to this thought over and over again. He had faith in diplomacy. Nations spoke to each other, they maintained relationships. One nation could not simply imprison a member of another nation, that was not allowed. Also, Henry was still free. Cookie could see him even now melding into the crowd. Henry would not allow him to be forgotten here, left behind. Henry would not abandon him, nor would the ship's crew. He had too many friends to simply fester in prison. He lived in too many people's minds and hearts. He could not simply disappear.

He continued cleaning the straw, his hands moving quickly from one length to the next. Having started, he realized, he needed to finish the job entirely, because to disinfect a portion of the straw would only invite reinfestation. He took breaks to pace back and forth sometimes, or stretch his arms above his head, but he kept working. The cellblock was utterly silent. He could hear the smallest rustlings and clinkings from the adjoining cells. Sometimes a groan or a mutter would emerge, but largely quiet held through the prison like a thick fog. He rewarded himself for long runs of cleaning by checking on the hole in the wall. Sometimes the hand was there, at work, other times the desk was empty. Sometimes a robe would flit past the opening.

Cookie continued cleaning the straw for hours, thinking about what had happened. The crime he had committed was not a felony, he believed. It was merely trespassing. No violence had been done, no exploitation of children or natives. No state secrets had been carried away. As he compared his actions to all the terrible things that people could do in the world, he became more calm. He had merely trespassed in a formal garden. He was an American citizen. He had no enemies to speak of. He was certainly deep in trouble, and he reminded himself to appear always contrite, but he convinced himself that his life was not immediately in danger. Likely the soldiers had no idea that he and Henry had imported illegal goods.

Soon enough, Cookie had amassed a fairly large pile of clean straw. His fingers were blackened with squashed bugs and his tendons were beginning to ache. He figured he could finish the job in another marathon run, so he granted himself a final break and rose to his feet. He pressed his hands against the wall and stretched his calf muscles behind him. He rolled his head around in circles to ease the cramps in his shoulders. He leaned over and dangled his weight between the wishbone of his legs. Finally he decided to check the hole.

He lowered himself onto the ground and pressed his eye up against the stone wall. This time, however, the cell beside him was pitch black, which was a little puzzling, as the daylight falling onto the floor in a hard shaft still illuminated his own cell clearly. He looked back into the hole and stared harder, until the darkness on the other side blinked. It was an eye, staring back at him.

Cookie jumped away from the hole, embarrassed, until he realized his neighbor was as guilty of spying as he was. They were both guilty of peeking in on each other. He crept back to the hole and looked again, but by this time the eye was gone. He could see the surface of the calligrapher's table, bathed in a ray of sunlight swirling with dust.

Cookie returned to his piles of straw, realizing that his own positioning gave the man next door a clear line of sight. He did not move, though. Cookie did not mind being watched. In a way he found some comfort in the idea.

No word came that day, and the beam of sunlight eventually thinned and disappeared. The sky darkened and soon enough Cookie lay down on his greasy straw and curled into a ball, trying to sleep. The longer he could sleep, he figured, the more time would pass by unnoticed.

The night air washed into his cell. The cold earth seeped through the bricks and filled the room with a clammy, mildewed smell. He awakened midway through the night, covered in goosebumps, shivering. His teeth clattered like dice. He curled tighter and tried to remain as still as possible. Whenever he moved, the air would move on his skin, and what small warmth he had generated would go away. He moved his leg and a cold patch spread along his body. His cotton clothing did almost nothing against the night air. He slept in small fits, never far from waking. He did not escape a moment of time. Sometimes he opened his eyes to glimpse a glow from the hole in his wall. He peered inside to see his neighbor bent over his desk, touching his brush to the paper in delicate strokes. A pile of paper was slowly growing beside him.

By morning his thin clothing was damp with dew, and the straw was limp, pressed hard against the floor. He felt every crevice and lump of the stony ground on his spine. As the pale light of morning brightened the corners of his cell, Cookie heard clanking sounds emanating from down the hall. They came in a pattern. First, the echoey sound of a lock tumbling into place, then a door creaking open, finally a scraping sound of something sliding on stone. Then the door slamming shut and being locked again. The sounds got louder and louder as the footsteps progressed down the hall. The turn of a key and scrape of an object, until finally Cookie's own lock rattled, and his own door creaked open, and a hand shoved a ceramic bowl inside, steaming with something to eat. Cookie crawled toward the gleaming bowl, bone white against the dirty rock floor. His stomach was tightened and raw. The bowl contained a dollop of white rice and a single anchovy.

The rice gave Cookie a burst of strength, though, and he felt the humid atmosphere of his mind clear a little. He did some pushups and deep knee bends to warm himself up, and paced around the room. He stretched his muscles and pedaled the air while lying on his back. He worked up a thin sweat, and lay down on the floor and breathed heavily. The ceiling was obscured by thick spiderwebs. He sat on his straw and stared at a wall. Soon enough, his burst of energy had faded, and the empty room closed in around him.

The cell became more familiar that day. Cookie found a crack in the rock wall, and a weed growing near the window. His eyes moved from place to place, and moved on. A pebble in the corner, a patch of moisture on the wall. The walls receded when he imagined something, and returned when his concentration flagged. He began to hear voices speaking in his head, resigned voices, amused voices. He staged long conversations between different parts of himself, and followed the passage of the sunbeam from one wall to the next. The man next door sometimes watched him, but he never spoke. Cookie collected a pile of dust, which he brushed onto his palm and blew toward the window. He looked at the crack again.

The cellblock was silent. Cookie knew there must be other men imprisoned there—he could hear their doors open and food being delivered—but no one made a sound. Cookie hummed to himself, and coughed loudly to see if it elicited any response, but none came. He called out hello, timidly at first and then more confidently. Nothing.

He heard the man next door walk to the hole and stare at him, but then he paced back to his desk and continued to write.

Cookie began muttering to himself. He said Henry's name into the air, coaxingly at first, as if he might come out of hiding at any moment. *Henry,* he said, like a child urging a cat from under a bed. *Henry.* He tried to remain amused by it all. He tried to find the comedy in the situation. *Henry,* he said, exasperated. Then, after a long stretch of silence, he cursed.

That night was cold again. He tried sleeping on the hard floor, with the straw on top of him, but this only made him colder. He had not eaten since morning, and his stomach growled. He developed a low fever. He heard noises out in the yard, sawing and scampering and bells. By the time morning came, and the food bowls were distributed again, he was aching deep inside his bones. His head hurt when he moved, like some weight was being dislodged and resettling with every motion. His ribs pressed against his skin. He scrambled to the bowl. This time the rice was fatter, swimming in broth, with seaweed and shredded carrots. It was warm, steaming even. Cookie took a brief moment to admire the patterns of the soup's breath, the life-like designs it made, then he drank it down in sloppy gulps.

His fever cleared and he did his morning exercises again. He began to get angry. He kicked the walls, yelled out the window. But no one stopped. The boots simply strode past.

Cookie succumbed to a wave of fear, like some high-pitched sound rising in his brain. What if Henry had betrayed him somehow? What if Henry and Howqua had somehow conspired to imprison him? For hours he lay curled in the corner of his cell, his insides writhing, and convinced himself that he had been the victim of some elaborate plot. That was insanity, though, he could recognize that. He sturdied himself, cast the thoughts from his mind. He reassured himself that diplomacy sometimes took a circuitous route. Surely Henry was shepherding his case through the Chinese bureaucracy as quickly as he could. But then other morbid thoughts arrived: What if Henry had been captured as well? Simply because he was not captured at the same time as Cookie did not mean he had made it all the way to the *Astor*. This was a disturbing consideration. For all Cookie knew, Henry could be sitting in the cell above him, or in another wing of the prison. He could have been beaten or worse. No one else on the ship knew where they were. The captain would have no evidence to go on. Cookie tried picturing the brig of the ship, the galley, the barracks where his belongings sat in a canvas bag beneath a tightly made bunk. Nothing there would give anyone a clue. He and Henry had been scrupulous in keeping their mission a secret.

The men would investigate, though, and they would find things out. Jim Lee, the young boy, he knew their plan. He might be able to help. Cookie imagined a scenario in which Jim Lee was contacted on the wharves. The men would describe him and Henry, and Jim Lee would nod that yes, in fact he had seen them. He might lead the captain to Howqua, who might lead the captain to the prison.

It was all too speculative. Cookie built scenario after scenario, based on slightly altered contingencies. Henry was free; Henry was caught. The captain had connections among the Chinese government; the captain did not. The history of the fur company was one of good will and benevolence toward the Chinese; the company was known for its ungentlemanly conduct. All these considerations factored into his situation, and none of them could be resolved.

Cookie rested his head on the wall.

In the cell next door the calligrapher continued painting. He stayed up all night with a candle burning, producing page after page. In the middle of the night, the soldiers came and took the pile away. Cookie watched as they bundled the rice paper into a neat stack and placed a satchel of tobacco on the writer's desk. The door slammed shut and the cell became quiet.

Through the small hole Cookie saw his neighbor's hands examining the tobacco. They disappeared and returned with a packet of rolling papers. Working together the fingers calmly tamped the paper to distribute the leaf, then curled the paper around the tobacco and raised it to the calligrapher's mouth.

Cookie's neighbor lit the cigarette and stood up, idly approaching the hole between their cells, where he kneeled down and placed his mouth against the stone wall. He blew a puff of smoke into Cookie's cell. At first Cookie was taken aback. He worried that some insult had been made, or perhaps a challenge posed. He imagined the action symbolized some kind of coded threat. But when the second puff of smoke appeared he understood. Cookie put his own mouth to the hole and on the next drag he inhaled. A sweet, hot sensation filled his lungs, and he blew the smoke out slowly through pursed lips. Together, in this fashion, he and his neighbor smoked the cigarette down to its nub.

# 10

TINA PLODDED DOWN the pathway holding a battered newspaper over her head, after a long day of fruitless errands. It was almost twilight, the hour when the sky cleared for a moment and a clear sterling light came gleaming over the landscape, sparkling in the leaves and branches and electrical lines like melting ice. Just before the horizon lifted up and plunged the land into darkness again.

Tina walked quickly toward her cabin, past the hot springs' bamboo gate and the fallow beds of the communal garden, and alongside the creek's brown, turgid flow. High above, the tops of the fir trees burned golden in the twilight, but Tina kept her eyes pressed hard on the ground. She climbed the stairs of her cabin and scraped her soles on the doormat, hung her coat on the rack near the refrigerator, and kicked off her shoes into the pile of duck boots and muddy canvas sneakers.

Tina's list was multiplying beyond her control. She had more work to do than she could possibly keep in her mind. Before eating dinner she still needed to break down the script's scenes into a comprehensible shot list, read over a new final scene she had written the night before, and which she was now convinced was another false lead, reschedule the third week of shooting around Beth's trip to Arizona to see her mother, and find a boom operator who knew anything about anything. With shooting set to begin in a week, her whole body was beginning to sour with anxiety.

Tina heard a clanking sound and looked up to find her mother awkwardly feeding a log into the open mouth of the wood stove. Orange light powdered her arm as she dropped the piece of wood into the fire. A burst of sparks flared up and she pulled her hand away quickly. The log settled into place on the crumbling cinders. Something in Tina's mother's thin wrists, pulling away from the fire, and the clank of the metal door made Tina a little bit sad. She hated the thought of someone tending a fire alone.

"Hey," Tina said, and continued toward her bedroom.

"Tina," her mother said. "Come sit down here a second. I have something I want to talk to you about." Tina's mother wiped black charcoal onto her apron, leaving smudges on the thin pink fabric, and hung her quilted glove near the woodbin. She hovered at the edge of the room waiting for Tina to comply.

Tina stood in the doorway of her room politely, as if the conversation might take less than a minute, but her mother asked her to sit down again, this was kind of a serious thing.

Tina scowled and let her backpack drop to the floor with a thunk. She slid herself onto the futon and put her feet on the table, waiting for her mother to do all the work.

Peggy Plank sat down across from her, in a plush chair the color of milk chocolate, and with some effort tried to smile. She glanced over the coffee table, cluttered with old newspapers and mugs holding dried tea bags, and took a moment to collect her thoughts. After few false starts she found her line of reasoning.

"First of all," she said, "I just want you to know how proud of you I am for doing this movie project. I'm so impressed by the work you and Trixie are putting into it, all the creativity you guys are expressing. You have such an incredible gift, so much talent. It's just inspiring. It really is."

Tina felt her stomach tightening. She could not tell quite where her mother was going, but it was obvious the words of praise were not the endpoint of the conversation. She was building up to something, and Tina braced herself. The wet wood sputtered and hissed in the fire, a staccato of airy explosions inside the metal chest.

Her mother paused and tightened her lips. The preface had been easy for her, Tina could tell, all supportive, pro-creativity talk. She could do that all day. Now she began to search for the real words. She looked up at the ceiling and kneaded her apron. She twisted a strand of fabric around her finger.

"I heard that you hired a horse and carriage for next weekend. That's what Peter told me. Is that true?"

"Uh-huh."

Tina's mother paused again.

"Look, Tina," she finally said. "I don't want to make any accusations here. I just want to get clear on some things. I know that film-making isn't cheap. The film stock, the costumes. I'm just curious how you guys are paying for everything."

"How are we paying for it?" Tina asked.

"Yeah. How are you paying for it? I'm curious." An edge had come into her voice.

"I don't know," Tina said. "Different ways." She pushed on a page of the newspaper drooping off the table. "We saved up for it, for one. And we're doing it real cheap."

"Uh-huh." Tina's mother was not going to be put off so easily. "There is a reason I'm asking you this," she clarified. "I think you know why."

"I don't, actually," Tina said.

Tina's mother looked at her and did a calculation of some kind and decided to proceed calmly.

"Well. You know that Trixie has gotten into some trouble in the past."

"Yeah." Tina knew of a few things, but nothing precisely relevant to the conversation at hand. Trixie had stolen a car, for instance, and crashed it when she was ten; she had gone to rehab for huffing paint when she was twelve; she had been handcuffed after shoplifting from a Safeway and taken away in a police car when she was thirteen. There were any number of blots on Trixie's record, but Tina did not want to reveal any of them that her mother might not yet know about.

Tina's mom continued. "You know for instance that she got caught growing dope at her father's house last year? Down in L.A.? I know

237

what a quick way that is to make some scratch." Her mother was trying to sound worldly or something.

"No she didn't," Tina said hotly. She had never heard of this episode before, and found it inconceivable that it could have gone unmentioned.

"Well, yes, she did," her mother said, in her most patronizing tone, which drove Tina insane, but which also generally meant she was absolutely positive of something. Tina stared angrily at the floor, hoping for a little more information.

Tina's mother wanted Tina to know that it was not cool to grow dope on Neil's property.

"What?" Tina said.

"Tina," she said, "I don't care about you doing drugs. You can smoke as much dope as you want to, you know that. Smoke it here at home, right at the dinner table. That's fine. It's safer than riding those bikes. But just don't jeopardize other people's lives by growing it on their property. It's not fair to our friends." She stared at Tina sternly to make sure she understood. Her normally placid eyes had gone hard. The number of times Tina could remember hearing such a steeliness in her voice were so scant as to not exist.

Tina looked at her gray socks, the toes limp and blackened with rainwater. Obviously her mother and the other adults had been talking to each other, and they had started putting some things together. They saw the script, the list of locations, the intention to shoot on 16 mm film. They were not stupid. Many of them had made movies before, little documentaries and experimental montages, which they had shown in art galleries and warehouses in rundown neighborhoods up and down the coast. They understood the basics of filmmaking, and the massive costs of building one's own images in light. In fact, this line of questioning was something she and Trixie had foreseen.

"God!" Tina said, "I can't believe you would think I'd do something like that. Me and Trixie have worked really fucking hard to get our locations and equipment donated for this thing, and we saved up our money all summer to cover the rest. Plus we won a prize for the film stock. It's being donated by Kodak."

Tina's mother smiled broadly. "You won a prize?" she asked. "Really? What prize?"

"A young screenwriter's prize," Tina said casually. "Just something they give to kids at school, to film their scripts with. It's no big deal."

"Why didn't you tell me that?" her mother said. Her voice squeaked and she grabbed Tina's leg over the table. "When did this happen?"

"I don't know. Last month."

Immediately Tina's mother was overcome with forgetful pride, and she apologized for everything she had said. She was sorry she worried so much, she said, sorry that once a thought took hold in her mind, it was so hard to see past it. She claimed that she had known there was a good explanation for the budget, and that everyone involved in the project would be so happy.

Eventually Tina extricated herself and made it into her room, where she put down her backpack and sat on the bed, and immediately decided she needed to get out of the house. All around her, the story-boards she had been drawing hung on the walls, the angles and compositions for each shot, scolding her. She waited long enough to make it appear that her departure was unrelated to their conversation, and then left, telling her mom that she had something to do with Trixie for a while.

Her mom practically sang the words, "Okay, honey, see you later."

Tina walked up through the trees and hurried along a narrow path. The forest was dusky and wet, and drops of water fell into her collar, chilling her all the way down her spine. She tried to tell herself the lie she had told was simply a lie she had been living for months now, but somehow the new, direct nature of her deception felt different than before.

Soon Tina arrived at an abandoned schoolhouse in the woods, a one-room, barn-like structure likely dating back to the turn of the century. The windows were all broken and the rafters looked like tinder, and gaping holes in the roof let in whatever came out of the sky that day. A month earlier she and Trixie had cleared away the old mattresses and toilets and beer cans inside, and had begun using the old schoolhouse as a production office of sorts. They had organized the space into props and costumes and construction supplies, and in the corner set up a table and a moldy old couch, which had somewhat repulsed them at first but had become less dirty-seeming the longer they used it.

Tina felt her way inside, through the rickety door, and made her way to the pillar where the kerosene lamp was hung. She lit the wick, and the flame buffed everything in a golden light. Thick drapes appeared, stacked over an empty spool of industrial wire, racks of dresses and gowns, and candelabras in a row, everything neatly sorted and labeled. The damp couch emerged, and the thin wisps of her own breath.

She went directly to the filing cabinet and rummaged through the drawers until she found what she was looking for, a clean piece of paper in a hanging folder. She held it up to the light so the cotton weave was visible, and the shadows of her fingers made crisp oblongs on the paper's skin. It said, "Congratulations, you have won the Young Screenwriter's Contest. Please find enclosed a gift certificate for five thousand feet of 16 mm film from Northwest Kodak, and a voucher for processing charges at the developing house of your choice."

Tina and Trixie had designed the letter themselves, and printed it on nice paper, using the masthead of the local film center. Tina would casually show it to her mother next week, as if it had slipped her mind until then. It was a trick they had hoped to avoid.

Eventually Trixie arrived, wearing a tan trench coat with a stencil of a lightning bolt spray-painted on the back, and on her wrist a bracelet made of bicycle chain.

"Hey," she said, stomping into the office. "Did your mom talk to you?"

"Yeah. Did Beth talk to you?"

"Yeah." She had not caved in either.

The girls stood there, listening to the drip of water on the roof, and sometimes a wet pinecone thumping and rolling down the rotten shingles, and let the new situation soak in. They were stepping into tougher places now, and gambling in a way that might have to be paid for. It was time for Tina to know where the money came from.

"Okay," Trixie said. "Let's go. Follow me."

Trixie and Tina walked through the forest toward the northeast quadrant of Neil's property, which was a place people rarely visited because it was so far away and there was nothing to see. While they walked, Trixie asked Tina questions, trying to lighten the mood. Mostly they came in the form of choices: The Clash or Sex Pistols? Clash. Jewish guilt or Catholic guilt? Jewish. John Ritter or Chevy Chase? John Ritter. Fantasy or sci-fi? Fantasy. Vampires or Frankensteins? Frankensteins. On many of the questions Tina had no preference one way or another, but that was part of the point in a way. The point was simply to make a choice. That was how boys did it. They would say something and pretend like it made sense and let the truth of it come out in retrospect. She did not want to give Trixie the satisfaction of showing any indecision.

After a while Trixie stopped at the edge of a sunken meadow surrounded by rough fir trees. Up above, the clouded sky was framed by the treetops, the moon a hazy spot diffusing into gray darkness. Tina followed its light down to the earth, where her eyes settled on a patch of lumpy, indistinct forms. She peered more deeply into the gloom, until a clump of leafy plants became visible, surrounded by a low fence of chicken wire. Her eyes widened.

Sure enough, there in the basin spread a small plot of marijuana plants, each stalk almost waist-high. The leaves were thin and curled, and the sweet, pungent smell hung in the air. She had seen plants like this before, in her mother's friends' houses, or tucked into the corners of community gardens. Her own grandparents had even grown dope for a while, used it to pay for their hot tub. Growing marijuana was not a weird idea, but the sight came as a shock all the same. It was like arriving at a surprise party moments after the secret had slipped,

241

a confirmation of some dim suspicion. Tina silently thanked her mother for clueing her in.

"Yep," Tina said, as if she had known about it all along.

"You knew?" Trixie asked. She was astonished, or else she was acting astonished—it was impossible to tell.

"Of course," Tina said. "Everyone knows you grew pot."

For a second Trixie looked frightened. Her mouth froze in its smile, and slowly worked its way back down to something more neutral, the muscles in her cheeks awkwardly loosening, her lips catching on her dry teeth.

"Do they know about this?" she asked hastily, and Tina paused before answering.

"No," she said. "They only know about before. In L.A. At your dad's house."

"Thank God," Trixie said. She shook her head and started down toward the plants. "Come on then. I'll show you around."

The girls walked through the rows of plants, brushing their hands against the trembling leaves. They were actually a little bedraggled, wilting in spots, and missing some of their branches. Trixie explained that they were sensimilla, grown from seeds she had been saving for a long time, and that their harvest would probably net a total of five thousand dollars. Many of the plants were hung with red Christmas balls clustered at random intervals, which appeared grayish in the dim moonlight, their color sparking from inside a cocoon of shadow. Tina batted one with her fingers.

"So the narcs think they're tomato plants," Trixie explained, pruning a dead leaf from a stalk. "They patrol around here in helicopters sometimes."

"Yeah, I've heard about that."

Trixie sat down at the edge of the garden and pulled out her cigarettes, which she left out for Tina to take from as well. Tina sat down beside her and listened as Trixie told her all about her secret history of drugs.

Trixie first started growing pot, she claimed, when she was only seven years old, down in L.A., where two brothers in her neighborhood named Ronnie and Tony used to take her out into the woods and get her stoned each day after school. They would go to some hidden place, a grove of trees or a reservoir nearby, and pass a joint around, and then congratulate her whenever she held a drag down properly. Over time they taught her to inhale without using her lips, and to hold the smoke in her lungs as long as she could, and although she did not remember ever actually feeling stoned, the whole etiquette of the process became interesting to her.

Eventually, for her birthday, these older kids gave her a plant, and vague instructions on how to care for it. They said to water it every day, and keep it in the sun, and so every day she did just that. She would come home from school and ask her mother for a glass of water, which every day she would take outside and pour onto her plant, which grew and filled out with its skeletal leaves until eventually she got bored of the endeavor and let it wither in the sun.

She did, however, keep some of the seeds from the plant, and when she and her friends got old enough to begin smoking for real, around seventh grade, she broke them out and planted them again. She cared for her plants more assiduously this time, and raised a few bushy, pungent specimens covered in wide spreading leaves, which she smoked off for a while, until she got tired of it, and sold the rest. She used the money to buy herself a few records, and it was then that she learned about the simple economy of selling drugs and getting things with the money she made.

Throughout junior high school she dealt fairly regularly, selling weed to all the young hippies and athletes of her class, the poor kids and the kids who wished they were poor, the comic book collectors and the total illiterates. Everyone wanted some, she found, it was one thing they all could agree on. She enjoyed the work, and not just for the money she made, but for the access it gave her to everyone she met. Dealing placed her at the center of the school's darkest, most secretive heart, in the sanctum of her peers' most jealously guarded wants. She was everyone's best friend in a way, and a participant in all their greatest stories and private jokes.

"I had no idea what I was doing," she said. "I'd let the plants grow to full leaf and then dry them into shake on my mom's roof. It was like smoking old newspapers, but the kids didn't know any better. They thought it was real primo shit."

By ninth grade, Trixie claimed, she had a private lock on her bedroom door, and a million records bought with her ill-gotten earnings. She received phone calls at all hours of the night, and had her own line installed. Her mom and dad were too concerned with their own problems to notice her much, and on some level they appreciated her strange independence. Besides, she never smoked much of it herself. She considered it almost beneath her.

It was that year she bought a Super 8 camera, and began making short films. She did a sci-fi picture, with a computer console constructed from cardboard and Christmas lights, and a live-action rendition of the comic strip *Nancy*, starring a boy in her neighborhood with premature-aging syndrome as Henry. She found that she liked to make movies, and there was no shortage of people wanting to help. With a little money it seemed like anything was possible.

That year, however, she also got caught. She was expelled from her high school, and then from a couple more schools after that. It was after a few of these episodes that she was shipped up to Oregon, California's soft, northern neighbor. Neil was her father's best friend, the closest thing to a good influence her parents could think of, and Beth had an extra room in her cabin to spare. Trixie had arrived with the full intention of walking the straight and narrow, but the surrounding woods had proven too inviting to resist. The earth was so fertile and there was so much of it. The dry dirt and cruddy vacant lots of L.A. were nothing in comparison. Oregon could be huge, she realized, and once the idea hatched, it was impossible to stop feeding it. Just as the money she had earned from growing tiny batches of pot in L.A. had funded her short films, the money from a larger batch could fund the production of an entire feature. It was a pretty simple equation when you thought about it.

"We have such good ideas," she said suddenly, bringing Tina in. "It would be worse to not make them than just to grow a few pot plants. We'll be famous soon."

"Uh-huh," Tina said, though she was not yet certain of her new role in this scenario, and found herself recoiling unconsciously from Trixie's warmth.

Trixie went on to explain that the plants had now entered their time of peak THC production. The male flowers had become visible but they had not yet opened, and all the cutting and bundling must be done in the next few days. They had about a week, she figured, before the THC began to degrade, and the street value plummeted. It was coming to fruition just as she had planned it. All the streams were converging at once.

Trixie continued talking for at least half an hour, with Tina beside her, staring at the bleached spot of the moon, smoking one cigarette after another. Trixie was electric, glowing like a lamp, her story bursting to get out of her. She said she had customers lined up, some of Neil's old friends from the music business, who would buy the product off her, hold some for themselves, and sell the rest to street dealers in Portland and Seattle. They were decent guys, and generally reliable. They lived in a house covered in kudzu, and called themselves the Goons. She described how she dug a trench from the edge of a beaver pond, and then laid in irrigation pipes over a month of weekends. She explained the perforated rubber hoses of the water system, and circling everything with chicken wire to keep the deer out. She seemed to surprise herself at times with the elaborate stages of her confession.

Trixie's eyes glistened. She had built an entire world for herself, Tina could see—a world where thoughts were never wasted, and energy was never misspent. A world devoted solely her own burning idea of freedom. A world where the best someone else could be was her servant.

"I am so glad I met you," Trixie said in a lavish half-whisper. "I could never have done this alone, Tina. I really need you."

"Yeah," Tina said, "right," gnawing on the inside of her mouth. Her feelings of isolation and betrayal included an element of stunned

245

sympathy as well. What a strenuous and lonely place Trixie had made.

"Are you okay?" Trixie asked. "You look kind of sick."

Tina shook her head. "I'm fine," she said, although everything inside her had gone heavy and still. There was a room within the room of their friendship, she now realized, where Trixie had been hiding herself all along. Tina wanted her own room to retreat to.

"Are you sure you're okay?" Trixie asked.

"Yeah," Tina said. "I'm just tired is all. It's been a really long day."

"I thought you'd be more excited," Trixie said, as the girls got up to go. Tina brushed herself off and said something about how she was excited, she was just incredibly tired, and how she still had a lot of work to do tonight.

"It's totally amazing what you've done," she added. "I'm, like, blown away."

Tina took the lead back toward the cabins, hoping to hide the weird look on her face, the envy and self-pity and confusion etched in her slack mouth and frozen cheeks. She made an effort to stumble over an exposed rock to demonstrate her genuine exhaustion.

They came out on a ridge, where moonlight tippled the trees and ground, and where Tina became dimly aware that the landscape was beautiful. The night was clear and the sky was enormous, but she could not bring herself to enjoy it, as all her thoughts led back to the same dark inner gravity. Who was she? What was her problem? How could she feel whole in this life? She had become so bound up with Trixie that she no longer knew what she wanted anymore, if she had ever truly known in the first place.

"Listen," Trixie said eagerly. The forest was making settling noises of pops and snaps, branches cracked and animals skittered about. "You hear how the forest sounds? We should remember how the trees sound at night."

"Oh yeah?" Tina said.

"Yeah!" Trixie said. "For the ambient sound track. You know. We'll need that."

"Oh," Tina said, "right." The movie had burrowed so deeply into Trixie's mind that it seemed to lurk in all her perceptions now. Everything implied film. Everything fed her huge vision. It struck Tina as an elaborate repression of some kind, a neurotic symptom of some harsh, hidden pain; the sick thing was she even envied Trixie's pain.

"Yeah," Tina said dully, in response to nothing, and continued plodding into the forest, a pale, transparent ghost in the world of the living.

# 11

THREE WEEKS AFTER the bones were uncovered, the first television crew to bear witness to the dramatic events brought on by Neil's epic indecision arrived on the edge of his property, sent by NBC. The van bounced and tilted its way up the rutted road and parked at the edge of the dirt lot where the county-owned line ended and the border of Neil's land began. The back doors opened and a metal ladder extended to the ground, and soon after that a man emerged carrying a portable satellite dish, which he set up on a boulder between two manzanita trees, then retraced his steps while rolling out a white cord one loop at a time.

Neil came across the setup on his way to do errands. He was bearing down on the driver's side door of his truck when a man came running toward him from behind a bush, zipping his pants and bobbling a microphone under his arm. He called out Neil's name and waved to a burly man with a portable video camera between his legs, who was peeling an orange on a stump at the edge of the parking lot, and who promptly got up and lifted the camera to his shoulder.

"Neil! Neil!" the man called, and Neil stopped in his tracks.

"What are you thinking? Where do the skeletons go?" he asked, as a red light flashed on near the camera's lens.

"Hey, fuck you, man," Neil said, and raised his middle finger by instinct.

Then Neil thought better of that approach, and answered a few questions while getting in the cab of his truck. He was forthright and direct, telling the man that he had many considerations to weigh, and he did not see much use in hurrying. The bones had been lying in the ground for at least fifty years, if not five thousand, and anyone who wanted to rush him along had a very short-range idea of how good decisions got made.

"Great!" the reporter said and the red light shut off.

Neil drove out to Canby for a load of fertilizer and some four-by-fours he needed for the retaining wall, catching glimpses of aisles of hops and lettuce scrolling by like shuffling cards. For a moment everything seemed bright and vivid, and Neil felt as if his mind were a prism. He imagined the earth packed dense with hidden bones, gleaming underground like scattered slivers of quartz.

On the way back from Canby the scenery returned from farmland to buildings and cars, and soon the truck was surrounded by the glinting of sunlight on chrome and glass. Neil stopped in for a late lunch at a coffee shop where he met Beth Bowler. They talked for a while about how things were going, and mostly about her role in the girls' movie. Neil was a deferential conversationalist; he talked gamely about whatever anyone wanted to, even if it only mildly affected him.

"I'm loving it," she said. "Just loving it. I think acting is a good thing for me. Those girls are really something."

"Seems pretty fun," Neil said. The depressed Beth had been getting on his nerves of late and he was glad to see her coming out of it finally. There had been a time, long ago, when he had wondered if they might someday have something together, and on occasion the thought still came back to him. Whenever the happy Beth appeared he could almost see it.

Their food arrived—tofu scrambles and biscuits with almond gravy—which gave them a chance to switch topics. Now it was Beth's turn to ask questions. They had known each other a long time, and she still loved to give Neil the tough interrogations about his life.

"This whole skeleton thing, Neil. Seems like a real hassle." She shook Tabasco sauce onto her potatoes.

"I know. It's pretty crazy, right?"

"Yeah," she said. "So what way are you leaning?"

"I don't know," he said. "I can see both sides. Which I guess is why it's so hard to decide."

"But you have to decide something soon, right? People are waiting for you."

"Right. But I don't really care about that."

Beth liked to push Neil sometimes, just to get under his skin. "So what do you care about, Neil?" She pointed at him mock accusingly with a potato wedge stuck on the tines of her fork. "I've always wondered about that."

"What do I care about? That's a good question." Neil stared at his plate. The puddle of ketchup he had quarantined to the far edge was bleeding toward the garnish. It was a question he asked himself sometimes. "I don't know. Not too much, I guess."

"Well then what don't you care about? Maybe we can narrow things down."

He groaned. "Shit. Almost everything."

"Come on, Neil. You're not helping. Let's get specific here. Money? Do you care about money, Neil?"

"No. I worry about money. I don't care about it, though."

"Sex?"

"I could go a long time without it. No, I don't care that much about sex. Judging from my life." He laughed.

"Fame?"

Neil knew there were people who considered ambition a virtue, people in New York perhaps, but he had always found it more of an embarrassment than anything else. He was certainly not proud of his fading ambition toward fame. He thought of it more as a fault he would someday overcome.

"No, don't care about fame."

"That took you a while."

"Well, I don't. I wish I cared even less, but I don't care that much as it is either."

"Okay, how about your friends?"

"Do I care about my friends? Sure. As long as they don't bother me too much," he laughed. "In fact I care about them most of all when they aren't even around."

"That's funny," Beth said. "I think I understand you, though. Okay. Your family?"

"I care about them in a certain way, but it's more like worry or fear. But that counts, doesn't it?"

"Sure, I guess so. You sort of care about your family. How about the environment?"

"Shit, I barely recycle."

"So what does that leave? What do you care about all the way, Neil?"

Neil crunched on his toast. "I don't know. Maybe I don't 'care' so much at all. I'm interested in certain things, but I don't really care about them."

"Like what? What are you interested in?"

"Whatever. Space and time."

"So give the skeletons to the forensics guy. He cares about history."

"I guess I care about my reputation a little bit, too, though. I don't want to be the guy who stole shit from the Indians."

"Jesus, Neil. You're impossible. The glass is always half empty for you isn't it?"

"Yep. Always. Always half empty." He was liking the attention.

"Okay, I've got one more for you. What about yourself? And I don't mean your personality or soul or anything. I mean your body. Actual flesh and bone. Do you care about that? Let's say your fingers. You care about those?"

"My fingers." Neil made a show of looking at his hands. "I guess so. I mean, losing them would certainly cause me pain. But I don't know. Having them doesn't exactly bring me joy."

"So the absence of the fingers is the opposite of joy, but the having of the fingers is not joy."

"Right."

"So maybe if they were taken away and then given back."

"I bet I'd be pretty joyful then. If I lost my fingers and then they reappeared."

"That would be a miracle."

"Yeah. I could probably work up some joy if a miracle happened."

Neil drove home over the Fremont Bridge, with the tall buildings of downtown Portland gleaming in the sunlight off to the side. He felt his senses polarize a little, vision and sound and touch. The wide expanse of the Fremont Bridge made him feel like Napoleon sometimes.

When he got back to his property, he found some more vans parked nearby, and more people hanging around on the field next to the parking lot. The pasture that sloped up to the ridge belonged to John Vaughn, a developer.

"Vaughn knows you guys are camped here?" Neil asked.

A man in khaki pants and a baseball hat answered back: "He's renting us the space. You have any new ideas where the bones go, Neil? Are you feeling a decision coming on?"

Neil shook his head. "No comment." John Vaughn was a dick.

The footage of his interview appeared that night on a national television show, including the bleeped, angry flip-off, along with an interview with Mr. Grimsrud and a news conference with Jay Feather. Both of them had wonderful things to say about Neil, and they supported his slow deliberation on a complex topic. It was good television, one could not deny it. Neil found himself wanting to know how all the stories might end.

The next morning two more vans had arrived, and the hum of their generators could be heard all the way to the bulrushes near the creek. Neil got a call from a friend in San Francisco, who had seen a segment about the standoff on his local affiliate.

"Slow news day up there, eh?"

"Every day," Neil said. "Last month they spent two and a half weeks waiting for a boulder to roll onto the highway. We jump on what we can."

After lunch, Neil made some rounds through the cabins, talking to everyone and trying to figure out whether they cared about the reporters camped out near the parking lot. Which was also a way of asking them if they minded his own indecision too much. Which they did not. But of course not, he was the landlord.

Near the garden, he ran into Peter Sessions puzzling over a two-by-four that was too long for what he needed to do with it. "They can wait," Peter said, as if he knew something no one else knew. On the banks of the creek he found Margaret blowing soap bubbles with the kids, the glassy spheres wobbling in the sunlight until their skin thinned and burst. "Fuck 'em," she said, "take your time."

Neil stepped over the wooden footbridge and felt the hollow, echoey sound come up through his boots, which always gave him a certain satisfaction. He could hear a yoga class in session in the geodesic dome; Bob Grossberger was leading a group through the long sequence of poses. In the dining hall a group of people were brewing some beer. Last year it had been canning, and the year before that smoking jerky. Neil heard a shrill outburst of laughter and a breaking glass. He saw a colorful ball rise into the air near the creek and left it there as he looked away.

He came upon Beth Bowler and Trixie Volterra sitting near an oak tree, practicing their lines for the movie. Trixie stammered something about the melancholic mind and Beth stared at her blankly. Both of them held pieces of paper in their hands.

"Hey," Neil said, but he could tell he was interrupting and turned away.

Finally he walked back up to his cabin for dinner, which was Greek salad. He always had Greek salad on Thursday nights.

The next day there were camera crews from two networks on the perimeter of Neil's property, one radio station, and a reporter from the Associated Press. The story would have died out immediately if not for the impromptu secondary shell that had grown around the media after the first few stories had aired. Within hours, a group of regional Indians had come to stake out the television crews, and local newspaper reporters to stake out the Indians, and soon enough there were teenagers and college professors watching the watchers. A pair of gay rights activists had shown up, wanting the two dead men for themselves, and a handful of ancestors of Vikings, who believed they might prove an entirely new theory of ancient mass migration. The observers came from all over the city, wearing ski hats and down coats and pouring coffee from aluminum canteens, and once a critical mass had been achieved, the logic of the event took on a life of its own. The spectacle had built its own rationale somehow, and everyone needed a witness.

Whenever Neil stepped outside, or tried to get something from his truck, he was accosted by a collage of voices yelling his name and fighting each other for attention.

"Neil? What do you want to do?"

"Neil? When will you know?"

He avoided them by staying inside, where he fiddled with his recording equipment and waited patiently for the day's hunger to come over him. He sat on the sofa and listened to the sound of his own breath in his ears, or the hum of the refrigerator clanking on again, or the fabric of his pants scraping on the upholstery. Half-empty beer bottles dotted the floor, and plates with dried ketchup and hummus peeked from the sink. Along the floorboard stretched a row of apple cores, desiccated in varying degrees.

Every few hours he checked the answering machine, where new messages from Mr. Grimsrud or Jay Feather were waiting. Mr. Grimsrud was losing his patience, it seemed, judging from his increasingly terse tone: "Neil, give me a call," he said. "Looking forward to catching up on where you're at." Jay Feather was more resigned to the process, though he was not above a sarcastic barb now and again: "Okay, Neil, you're a pretty big guy. You can make everyone wait with the best of them. We're all really impressed. Call me."

After listening to his messages, Neil would go to his refrigerator and stare at the contents for a moment, some cheese and tortillas and beer, and then return to his living room. He would look out the window to make sure that everything was just as he had left it one minute before, or sit down on the rug and read the liner notes to *Sketches of Spain,* or slide the disk of *Ummagumma* from its sleeve and inspect it for scratches.

Mr. Grimsrud called: "Neil, I know you're there. I'm not trying to pressure you, but I would love to talk. There are things that I want to explain about the way calcium registers the climactic changes of a given time period. Could be very interesting to you. We could learn a lot. Call me."

Neil felt a measure of affection for Mr. Grimsrud and Jay Feather both. He wished they could get along better. When he talked to them one after another on the telephone, sometimes he forgot which one was which.

Neil walked from one end of his cabin to the other, muttering to himself as he touched the walls and corners and tabletops. His body was growing clammy and moist in its creases, his hair lank and unwashed. He had been wearing the same T-shirt for going on three days now. He parted his curtains for a brief look at the tent city on the edge of his land, glowing with its shells and bounces. It was still there, surging with electrical power, exactly as he had left it.

Sitting in his cabin, waiting and making the world wait with him, Neil felt the impatience of public opinion hardening around him. His situation did not leave many options anymore. He could watch television, or he could listen to music, or he could read a book, but the loop between these activities was getting tighter and tighter. He was going around in circles, he realized, waiting for some finish line to appear, or for some coil finally to snap. In a way, he took some perverse pleasure in the situation.

Neil had gone beyond mere deliberation, he recognized. He was working on something else now, an experiment in social control. Beneath his languid exterior lay a hard principle at work, a resilient passive aggression that guided him through subtle, negative clues. His indecision was not merely a weakness, he told himself, but a form of pointed resistence to a powerful and normally ineffable foe. He relished the control he exerted through his adamant failure to act. This was the part that the television could not understand.

At night, Neil walked out onto the porch, keeping to the shadows as he drank a cup of tea and smoked a cigarette. The encampment was quiet now, largely depopulated until morning. A few propane lamps glowing inside tents.

He crept to the corner of the porch and rested his shoulder against a wooden brace, letting his mind flow out over the landscape. The moon was a dark shadow edged in silver, the curve of the ridge was the spine of some huge, long-sleeping creature. Low over the horizon Neil could see a helicopter wheeling into view, a glinting jewel sparkling in the air, a brooch pinned to the fabric of the sky. He watched it coldly while he finished his cigarette and stubbed out the butt on the railing. The helicopter hovered near the trees for a while before making a pass over the murky waters of the marshland and raking the ground with its spotlight. Neil held some power over the helicopter he believed. He had placed it there by his waiting.

# 12

A MILE FROM Cookie's cell, over the shingled rooftops of Canton, past streets dotted with blooming apricot trees and crossed by lines of drying laundry, beyond the wharves of the Respondentia Walk, the *Astor* floated quietly in Canton Bay, anchored at the center of a sprawling gridlock of ships. The entire marina was clotted with boats, side by side, tip to tail. Sailors simply walked from one deck to the next, visiting friends from foreign ports, catching up on the news from abroad. More than one hundred ships sat waiting, their hulls loaded with goods, their crews confined and growing more unruly by the day. All the boats were spotlessly clean, as captains up and down the marina kept their sailors busy polishing and repolishing the brass, scouring and rescouring the pine. The air was thick with boredom and resentment and pent-up aggression.

And all of it was Cookie's fault.

It was public knowledge now that the Chinese had captured a *fan kwae*, or foreign devil, in the sanctum of their Imperial Garden, the most sacred site in the city of Canton, if not the entire province of Kwangtun, and since then a series of actions had transpired with brisk, bureaucratic efficiency. The police had immediately reported the arrest to the local marshal, who in turn had reported it to the chief of police. The chief of police had sent an embossed scroll to the governor's office, and the governor's aides had read the notice right away. The governor, upon hearing the news, had issued a decree to shut down the entire port until further investigation, an order which sped back through the strata of bureaucrats to the hong merchants, who dutifully closed their warehouses and waited for the soldiers to arrive, which they did, the following day.

Cookie's arrest had become a major diplomatic event. All trade had been suspended through the port of Canton for two weeks, and by now every sailor on every ship, from the most elevated British officer down to the cabin boy of the junk from Ceylon, knew that an American sailor was being held in Cantonese prison. An American sailor who had been arrested in the most sacred of Canton's traditional gardens, a shrine unsullied by foreign hands for likely a millennium. A stupid, naïve American sailor too incompetent to recognize the repercussions of his own childish curiosity.

Among other things, the incident had offered the Chinese an opportunity to reassert their authority over the foreign merchants, and to reissue their Eight Regulations of Limited Trade. No teaching of foreign languages to the Chinese. No learning of the Celestial tongue by foreign sailors. No investment by foreign parties in the development of Chinese industries. And on from there. Although the regulations caused an initial uproar, the captains had quickly realized that any protest would only lengthen the moratorium. They found it inconceivable that the economic life of a port should halt while the political sphere deliberated, but in the end it was just another example of the inscrutable and strangely inefficient ways of the Chinese.

Henry spent his nights pacing the deck of the *Astor*. Aft and fore, fore and aft, he brooded his way over every inch, as the smells of frying dumplings and basting chickens came to him from the neighboring ships. Far away he could hear the sizzle of a wok, the groan of bending masts. A few ships down, a large group of men had gathered around an open fire, where they were joking and drinking in the warm light. The lamps of Canton spread across the opposite bank, illuminating the low clouds that tore apart overhead. On the central hillock the pagoda taunted him, like a finger wagging under his nose.

Henry went over Cookie's capture again and again in his mind. He had been surrounded that day as well. Three soldiers in wooden armor had encircled him with their lances drawn, and he had stood there frozen, his feet planted. Slowly he had reached beneath his robes to produce a sack of silver, which he had extended toward the nearest, and strongest, of the men. The soldier had accepted the bag hesitantly, and weighed it in his palm. He then undid the purse strings and looked inside. He had conferred with the other two soldiers for a moment, and a moment later they were gone, their backs disappearing into the labyrinth of the garden.

The other sack was sitting beneath Henry's bed.

Since that day, Henry had been working feverishly to get Cookie free, only to be confronted with the most Byzantine bureaucracy he had ever encountered. It was as if the entire system, at once rigidly hierarchical and strangely diffuse, was designed specifically to frustrate open communication. He had learned that the highest local official was the governor of Kwangtun Province, who supervised three regular commissioners and several special commissioners, who in turn supervised two more levels of geographic administrators, who in turn supervised the magistrates of districts or departments, who were responsible for everything that transpired in their given quadrant from crime prevention to sewage. To further complicate this system, many offices were split among ethnic lines, Chinese and Manchu, with parallel offices assuming overlapping jurisdictions and duties. Below these officials were the hong merchants, to whom Henry had access, but whose association with mercantile pursuits, not to mention with foreigners themselves, placed them on a tier incapable of asserting any real effect. In other words, the only people who would talk to him were by nature powerless to help.

Henry paced along the starboard bow until he came upon Tillamook staring out at the red and gold lights of the city. The distant sounds of drums and bells came over the water. Tillamook made room on the railing, and Henry leaned in beside him, appreciative of the gesture. Most of the men, having lost all sympathy for Cookie's plight, had begun to avoid him.

"How was the meeting?" Tillamook asked.

"Don't ask, buddy," Henry said.

Two days earlier, Henry had petitioned the customs office for a hearing on the matter of Cookie's imprisonment, and that afternoon the meeting had taken place. He had met with two customs officers at the Consoo House, the center of the hong merchants' operations, where he had been tersely informed of the official state position. Cookie was being held for trespassing and would remain so until the Chinese magistrate decided to free him. A typical opening gambit, he thought.

Henry had then produced various forms of identification—Cookie's birth certificate, his travel papers, his contract with the sponsor company—which the agent had pushed back toward him without even inspecting. Also typical.

Then the real negotiations had begun. Through a series of small gestures, the more retiring of the agents had managed to imply a possible resolution to the case. Answering certain of Henry's questions with more questions, hesitating to dismiss the idea of a certain, unspecified fine, he had allowed for the slightest possibility of a bribe to come forth. But Henry could not quite tell. The hints were too subtle, and he did not know how to ask the agent for clarification without tipping his hand. He was prepared to use the remaining silver for Cookie's freedom, but he hesitated to hand it over without some assurance that it was in fact going to work. What were the probabilities of Cookie's release, he wanted to know? How much did he need to give?

When the meeting was over, Henry had spoken to Jim Lee, who had sent a message to Howqua, who had sent a message back saying that he was unable to help. He expressed his deepest regrets, however, and advised Henry to be patient.

This was the problem Henry now faced. To bribe the customs official or not.

"How are you, Tillamook?" he asked, ready to hear someone else's troubles for a change.

"Tired," Tillamook said, in his deep voice. "Ready to go home."

The two men slouched beside each other and watched the city's reflection on the water.

"Had a terrible dream last night," Tillamook finally said. "Dreamt

I was trapped in the white man's heaven. Way up in the clouds."

"Huh," Henry said glumly. "And what was that like?"

"Funny. I could see almost everything from up there," Tillamook said. "The birds flying, the rivers bending, the tops of the mountains covered in snow." He stared out at the water. "The white man's God was there, too. And the ghosts of all the white men I've ever known. They all seemed happy to see me, and the gates opened up to let me in. Big iron gates with golden spikes on the bars. I walked into a garden full of flowers and palm trees, with a waterfall tumbling over some rocks. Some children were playing with hoops and balls, and their mothers were watching them from the shade."

Tillamook paused and raised his thick arms above his head, hanging his weight on the netting between the masts.

"But I saw a terrible thing up there, Henry."

"Oh yeah? What was that?" Henry asked. Tillamook furrowed his brow and pursed his lips.

"Thousands of beavers, locked outside the gates, crowding all around the fence. They were trying to get in and when they couldn't, they started falling off the cloud back down to the earth. Hundreds of beavers, like buffaloes over a cliff. They were barred from the white man's heaven for some reason, and there I was trapped inside. Forever. It was a terrible dream, Henry. I can't wait to go home. I never should have come."

"That's a bad dream all right," Henry said, and shook his head. Then he squeezed Tillamook's big shoulder and left him to his own thoughts.

Henry climbed to the crow's nest and stared at the circle of sky coursing above his head, changing in the wind and the moonlight. The smell of the river blew over him, rotten with sewage and old fish.

He closed his eyes and pressed his arms and legs against the cylindrical wall, imagining confrontations with Cookie at his prison door. He imagined grabbing Cookie by the lapels and shaking him back and forth. If only he had stayed within sight, he would tell him, if only he had not wandered off into a blind corridor. If only they had never entered the garden in the first place, everything would be just fine. He wondered what Cookie would do in the same situation. He tried to figure out how much happiness he was meant to sacrifice. The longer Henry argued with Cookie in his mind, the more he realized that he was letting go.

The next morning, the *Astor* set sail for the Pacific, and eventually to Oregon via San Francisco. Having been loaded with tea and spices just before the wharf's suspension, she had no good reason for staying in port anymore. The ship pushed off into the current at sunrise, guided by barnacle-covered junks. A string of firecrackers exploded on her bow to awaken the gods and give her good wind and good water on the long voyage home. Henry and his silver were safely on board.

# Part Three

# 1

THE TV COMMERCIAL opened with a wide, high shot of a gallows in a clearing of cottonwood trees, surrounded by a crowd of garishly clothed cowboys and pioneer women waving their fists in the air and shaking pitchforks and rakes. Standing on the platform was a black man with a noose looped loosely around his neck, his head bowed, his shirt strangely clean and modern-looking. The murmuring of the angry crowd increased as the camera punched in to reveal the condemned man in closer detail, his bugging eyes and chattering teeth. Tina thought she recognized him from some National Lampoon movie or a deodorant commercial, but she could easily be guessing. It was a sunny day, and the man gulped visibly in the momentary intimacy of his close-up. Then the camera reversed to show the crowds' faces roaring in approval, women in bonnets and men with ten-gallon hats, all of them partly obstructed by the foundation of the gallows.

At the sound of a trapdoor and the squeak of a tightening rope, the condemned man's shoes dropped into the frame, an off-brand running shoe scuffed and dinged in the scramble of some chase. The camera lingered on them a moment, their flat insoles and soiled nylon siding, until they jerked a final time and went slack and the crowd cheered wildly in celebration of the victim's death.

Now the commercial cut to a remote location, booming up on a creek alongside strawberry fields and a few stately oaks, where another black man was jogging on an empty country road. His eyes were also bugged with fear, and his breath was panting in his ears, and when he stopped, a cloud of his own dust swirled around him.

"Jackson? Jackson?" he asked, looking over his shoulder, but no

267

one was there. He squinted into the distance to see if anyone was following him but they were not. Finally he shrugged and continued jogging down the country road at a leisurely pace. The camera cut to his shoes, the good kind, the kind that made you go faster. The company's logo appeared and Trixie made a sound of blood gargling in her throat.

"Can you fucking believe it? They're using a fucking lynching to sell some fucking track shoes. Look at this fucking bullshit," she said.

Tina and Trixie had been watching television for three days straight, and the commercial they considered the worst commercial in the history of advertising had burned itself into their memories forever, reappearing every forty minutes during the arid plains of weekend sports programming, and almost as often as that in the lusher realm of prime time. It dropped out during late-night TV, and during the morning talk shows, but inevitably reappeared the next day, like a satellite circling the heat of some supernovic demographic to which Tina and Trixie embarrassingly belonged. Tina knew every cut by heart now, including the shortened version, though at this point she had much bigger things to worry about.

Outside, a quiet bedlam was taking place, a days-long pandemonium of waiting. On the edges of the property an impatient crowd of news reporters had assembled to stake their claim on the slow-moving spectacle of Neil's indecision. With no elections in the offing or flamboyant murders to report, no wars in the hemisphere or treaties being signed, the news industry had decided to turn the battle for the unearthed bones into a full-dress scandal, and once the decision had been made, there was no turning back.

With the TV reporters had come the battalions of gaffers and grips and makeup crews and production assistants needed to support them, and it had become almost impossible to walk outside without encountering someone with a fat microphone in hand, or a cameraman sucking every visual nugget of information he could from the trees and the dirt. They had shot the garden and the creek, the street sign out near the turnoff from Highway 30. They had shot the skyline of Portland from various angles, and numerous waterfalls and public artworks. Their interns had scoured the historical society library, and secondary teams had interviewed local congressmen and city commissioners. Their researchers had ransacked the local affiliate's archive for old stories about anything relating to the main players at all, turning up only some degraded concert footage of Neil's defunct band, the Dopplers.

Sometimes, after rush hour, helicopters from the local channels would fly overhead and beam their spotlights like white bars over the rooftops of the cabins. They would hover above the half-buried skeletons with their stabilized camera riggings and collect an image, and then send it off to the city to be spliced in an editing suite and dispersed in all directions, only to wheel abruptly and roar away, like the flying monkeys in the *Wizard of Oz*.

Regardless of their efforts, however, the situation remained balanced precariously in place, teetering on the fulcrum of Neil's mental scales, inert.

The crowd had begun talking to itself, arriving at all kinds of judgments and suppositions, turning Neil's property into a much more exciting place than it really was. The activists argued with the journalists who argued with the police, and the police hassled the onlookers for no discernable reason at all. People with no real stake in the matter imagined strange things happening inside the cabins, and envisioned Neil as a colorful, indignant figure. Most of all the crowd hoped for some terrible event to occur.

Outside Tina's window, across the garden and up the hump of the parking lot, the cube vans and satellite dishes of the network news teams formed a shifting frieze surrounded in a nimbus of artificial light. The boom operators marched like squires with their lances, and someone with a sun gun flashed it on and off at random intervals. Tina could see shadowy figures bending and coiling cords, a wall of moving silhouettes, and deeper in the distance some red lights flashing.

Trixie sat on the bed, watching the coverage while bouncing her knee on the mattress and eating Pringles four at a time. The bed was a twisted landscape of rumpled quilts and sheets, and the boneless torsos of Tina's pillows, lit by a single reading lamp clamped to the lip of her desktop. The air was close with the smell of stale cigarettes and dirty socks, Doritos and cold jo-jos sodden with ranch dressing. The floor was covered in a film of candy wrappers and old magazines, cassette tapes and wadded clothes, and the spilled contents of an ashtray that had been perched on the windowsill, where the girls took turns blowing their smoke outside into the wet air.

Since the media had arrived, the girls' film had come to a complete halt. The rehearsals had been suspended, the shooting date pushed back, and all of their carefully laid plans had been swept into the distance. Nothing was possible while the siege continued. All they could do was sit and wait. They rarely talked anymore. They rarely communicated. All they did was watch TV in the hopes that some break would come, and also, though they never uttered this thought, that the marijuana plants would remain hidden from sight.

"So we wait," Tina said. "Big deal." She turned from the window and scooped the ashes and butts into the ceramic bowl and placed it back on the sill. The thought of postponing the shoot did not seem so catastrophic to her, and she doubted that the plants would be recognized in the general hubbub of activity. They were too well hidden and the story was too focused on other things. In the meantime she figured they could hash out the ending of the script, finish some costume work, get a step ahead. She saw plenty of work they could do, if Trixie would only peel herself away from the TV screen.

Trixie stared at her from the bed. Her head was pushed back, her mouth curled. She snorted contemptuously out of her nose.

"Tina," Trixie said, using the tone of oracular authority she reserved for her most patronizing statements. "No, actually. We can't wait." She paused for a moment to allow Tina the chance to agree with her, and when Tina did not say anything, the lesson continued. "Those plants are mature now. The resin is losing its potency. If we don't cut the stalks, like, in the next few days, their street value is going to be almost nothing. We'll have shake. And then we'll have to wait another whole year to grow again and longer than that to start shooting. It's actually a very big deal what's going on right now."

Tina remained silent and Trixie reiterated the dilemma:

"You see what I mean, don't you? Every hour we're stuck in here is an hour closer to losing the harvest. And that means losing the film. I can't buy that camera without that money. It's like the crystallization of the resin on one side against the bone stuff on the other. You see? Unless Neil decides something soon, and tells everyone who owns those bones, we're like fucked. Our money's wilting on the vine."

"Well let's go do it. Tonight. After the news is over."

Trixie rolled her eyes again.

"Look. See that van out there?" She pointed to a van bristling with antennae and disks. "The generator for that thing is parked about ten yards from the beds, on an access road that cuts right nearby, with a guy sitting there twenty-four hours a day. Plus, those fucking helicopters keep flying around. We can't do it with that going on, all right? All we can do is hope things blow over."

"Yeah, yeah, I get it." Tina scowled at her desk. A sickening lump was growing in her stomach, and her chest was packed with hot ashes. She and Trixie had come to take pleasure in arguing with each other, and correcting each other whenever the opportunity allowed. The actual positions they took were secondary to the power their positions allowed them to wield, but a good point on the end of the argument always made the sting even worse.

Tina stared out the window, glowering with the humiliation of being proven wrong again, wishing that she could jump-cut ahead somehow and arrive safely on the other side.

Trixie switched channels to a live feed from Channel 8 coming in from the ridge overlooking the commune. A reporter dressed in casual clothing—new hiking boots, new flannel button-down—addressed the audience in a tone of casual command. "Quiet night on the perimeter of Neil Rust's property. The world is waiting . . . ," he said. Behind him the cabins and garden were spread out, and Tina could see her own window, glowing in the still darkness.

She waved her arm once to see her shadow appear in the background of the shot, momentarily delayed. Then Trixie moved on the bed and blocked her view.

"Hey," Tina said, and Trixie shifted back to where she had been before.

Tina stared at the back of Trixie's head for a while. Her hair was a nest of oily curls falling around the nape of her neck. The slope of her shoulders ran into the wide mouth of her T-shirt, and her vertebrae were like rivets beneath the flesh. The shape of her thin arm disappeared inside the shirt's cotton sleeve, and her jaws flexed as she ate another potato chip.

Tina imagined squashing Trixie's head in her hands.

The tape on the boom box stopped and Trixie reached over to switch it. The choice was hers this time—they had tacitly agreed to rotate selections—and for the third time in a row she put in *Blood on the Tracks*, an album that neither of them particularly liked. As she corrected herself on the mattress, some chips spilled out onto Tina's bed and got crushed under her knee. She brushed off her leg and let the crumbs sink into the folds of the bedding.

"Jesus," Tina said, but Trixie ignored her and kept eating.

"Where is Channel 2's camera right now?" Trixie asked, staring at the screen. "Can you see it?"

"Huh?" Tina said.

"Nothing," Trixie said, and stomped to the window herself. Then she returned to the bed and switched the channel and the screen filled with a picture of Bob Lampher, a local car dealer, speaking into a salami-shaped microphone, branded with the logo for Channel 2. He had an opinion like everyone else.

In the past day or so, Tina had noticed, the reporters had begun filing stories that showed signs of real desperation. They had begun to massage the story, turn it over in their hands, and look at it from odd points of view. Channel 6 had done a segment on the parking problems in the vicinity of Neil's property line, Channel 8 a human-interest story on the challenges endured by a nearby neighbor. Channel 2 had sponsored a town hall meeting debating the fairness of the media's own ongoing attention to the drama. They had begun inventing controversies that bore no effect on the real substance of the situation. They elevated sidebars to full headlines. Eventually their opinions had become lopsided simply to differentiate themselves from the other, more obvious opinions, and the whole story had begun to lose its shape. The reporters were looking for some twist now, some hidden doorway that would lead them to someplace new and unexpected. A place where some kind of suspect could be unmasked, or some hidden truth flamboyantly revealed. There was life there, they seemed to think, if they could just find the proper avenue of attack.

Tina was fascinated by it all, she had to admit. In the pressure of the boredom she sensed that something was shifting, something new coming into sight. The newscasters felt it as well, and they coaxed it along. They threw words and images into the maw of public attention, to watch them plummet downward toward the invisible bottom. They tossed in uninformed speculation and inexpert witnesses, opinions about opinions and all manner of armchair strategizing. They dropped pieces of totally irrelevant data, and personal recollections that bore only the slightest relation to the news at hand.

Tina stared through her reflection. In the garden, Bob Grossberger was laughing with Peter Sessions near a barren fig tree, and Gwyneth Sandstrom was walking up to join them. They laughed again, and Bob touched Peter's sleeve.

"Get me the script," Trixie commanded. "I want to see something."

This was one way she inflicted her torture, by giving orders that were too small to argue with.

Tina waited a long minute before moving to do her friend's bidding. Pointless delay was her own way of fighting back. She went to her desk and pulled her copy from the top drawer, tossed it to Trixie, and returned to the window without speaking.

They battled each other for time. Every tiny scrap.

A few minutes later Tina left the room for a breath of fresh air, taking a walk down to the skeletons, rehearsing in her mind various things she wanted to say to Trixie given the chance. She thought of arguments she might make, rejoinders to old arguments, new accusations she could level. She had trouble controlling the conversation in her head, however, and she lost track of her points before they even began. The problem between them was too vague to confront head on, and Tina could not think of a way to wring the apologies she wanted from Trixie without confessing something herself.

Tina worried sometimes that Trixie had overcome her, had taken over her eyes and hands, burrowed underneath her skin. She could feel Trixie's taste working inside her, Trixie's past playing out in her own life. Trixie's ambitions coursed in her veins. She imagined a thing they did together, and it was Trixie's story, not her own. Tina did not want to be Trixie anymore. That was not the problem. On the contrary, she felt like she already was.

After glancing at the skeletons, Tina walked slowly back up to the cabins, taking time to skirt the garden and pluck at the fence, listening to the creek move on its perpetual journey to the Columbia's depths. The mounds of dead weeds and leaf litter looked silvery in the reflected light of the scattered TV lamps, which poured down from the field above the parking lot. The cylinders of chicken wire caught the light and turned into fine netting.

Tina slipped in the garden gate, crouching to avoid the eyes of the reporters and cameramen camped overhead, and crept her way toward the tool shed beyond the dried cornstalks. She heard low voices break out in subdued laughter and then mellow down again, as her footsteps made crackling noises on the beds of fallow dirt, which were growing cold and brittle in the autumn frost. To her right the geodesic dome, a favorite backdrop for the live feeds and cutaways, hung shrouded in the trees.

Midway to the shed Tina stepped through a patch of bright light

274

bouncing off a distant umbrella and watched her shadow grow to the size of an oak tree. She paused briefly to admire it. She had a special thing for shadows—her first movie, her first friend. She had played with them for as long as she could remember.

A moment later Tina was undoing the shed's latch and stepping inside the musty holding space. She flicked her lighter and took a quick inventory of the contents: some old coffee cans filled with nails, a circular saw, cans of paint and lighter fluid. Beneath a plastic tarp sat the five gallon container of gasoline that she and Trixie had hidden there in the event of a truly worst-case scenario. Should the helicopters discover their beds, or seem about to, they had agreed, they would destroy the evidence before the authorities could seize it.

Tina lifted the rounded metal cannister and felt its weight. It was practically full. The gas sloshed and pinged inside the walls, releasing its faint smell through the rusted cap. She imagined the lovely shape the charred spot might have, the strange burned forms that would be left behind. What would people make of it? she wondered. How would they interpret the design? The reporters would sift through the ashes for nothing, she thought. They would find only the mystery of some great fiery event. A part of her almost welcomed the opportunity to commit such insane arson. She wanted to be someone who had lit a fire as a young girl.

Tina heard a growling sound outside and she hurriedly placed the cannister back in its hiding place. She opened the door to find the nearby trees kicking back and forth, and bits of dirt and wood darting wildly in the air, speckling over her bare arms and face. The grumbling noise continued to grow, a throbbing roar with a high-pitched whine underneath. Tina craned her neck as the night air began ripping to pieces.

Tina turned her face skyward just in time to watch Channel 8's helicopter come floating over the roof like a giant shark. Its wide belly was full of rivets and seams, illuminated by the hard, artificial bursts of its own blinkers. The sled-like runners vibrated angrily, and the tail slid impatiently from side to side. Tina stared up at its metal skin, and

275

for a brief moment, caught up in the whipping downdraft, she felt a surging respite from herself, a crazy loss into the massive disturbance of light and air. She glimpsed a new future ahead, glowing with bright colors and promise. The sound of the spinning rotors engulfed her.

The helicopter hovered for a moment and then began edging its way toward the perimeter of trees. The shapely body revolved to reveal sleek side panels painted with bright stripes and designs, the crisp logo for NewsCenter 8. The lamps attached to the rudders poured light onto the garden, and Tina caught sight of a TV camera attached to the fusilage. Behind the glaze of the Plexiglas window a reporter and a pilot appeared, obscured by white flashes of reflection. The pilot spoke commandingly into the mouth piece of his headset, while beside him the reporter leaned backward to confer with the cameraman in the back seat.

Tina pressed herself against the wall of the toolshed, watching the spotlight roam over the berms directly before her. She was Steve McQueen in *Bullitt,* she thought. Jane Fonda in *Klute.* The cone of the helicopter's vision was a terrible, incinerating laser beam. A tractor beam trying to abduct her. She had slipped into another story, she imagined, traded one in for another. In this story she was all alone. This story demanded fire and flight. It was full of wind and heat, and the sound of flames eating air. It was about a girl who controlled the eyes of the world, and who turned the world's tools against it. Tina watched the dim oval of light pass greedily over the earth until finally it reached her, a spike of pale halogen, and flaring coronas and sunspots filled her eyes. Then, in a single loud rush, the helicopter was gone.

As the sound drifted off into the distance Tina felt the promise of new things fading inside of her. Her new story, her new character, disappearing. She turned and headed back to the cabin, and by the time she reached the porch, the feeling of freedom that she had been touched by was extinguished entirely, replaced by a paranoid intuition that Trixie was using her for some dark ulterior purpose. By the time Tina got back to her room, she felt exactly as she had when she left it.

Trixie was sitting on the bed, scribbling something in the margin of the screenplay and crossing out a line of dialogue. She held the script in her lap and wrote furiously.

"What are you doing?" Tina asked.

"I decided she should say something to the doctor at the end. I'm writing it down so I won't forget."

Tina looked out the window again. Outside, she could see the P.A.s talking among themselves under an alder tree, one of the reporters talking to Jay Feather. The light caught in his moussed hair and gleamed on his nose. She decided not to inquire as to the details of Trixie's edit. They had always used the pronoun "we" before.

Cold rain tapped the window. A branch scraped the roof like a rat skittering on its claws. The distant sound of the burbling creek droned like static.

The ticking of the clock stuttered slowly, ". . . it's . . . it's . . . it's . . ."

Tina listened to the pages of the magazine whisper as they turned, filled with morose-looking people staring into space. Every image and every word was cobbled together from other, earlier images and words. All the leaves on the maple tree were replicas of each other. Everything seemed very old and repetitious. Even this was an old thought.

Time barely moved. The television flickered against the wall. Every commercial was like a week, every sitcom a year.

Tina put the magazine aside and returned to the window and watched the people talking outside. A government guy talking to an Indian guy, a producer talking to a cameraman. Someone looked into the crowd, and someone else turned away.

"NewsHour," Trixie said and turned up the volume on the TV, as zooming letters and spinning globes appeared, intercut with portraits of anchormen and helicopters and accompanied by martial-sounding music somehow distantly related to the tapping of a typewriter keyboard. The bombastic theme song of television journalism. This evening's broadcast opened just as it always did, with grave greetings from the coiffed anchors, Jim Honor and Tracy Bond, and then Tracy Bond took over the screen with a photograph of the skeletons hovering near her shoulder, each with question marks imprinted on their eye sockets. The studio image cut to a helicopter's shadow racing over the trees and creeks and meadows of the commune, grazing, among other things, a neat grid of marijuana plants hung liberally with red Christmas balls.

Tina glanced at Trixie quickly, her pink cheek and black lashes, but she was too absorbed in the screen to notice. The plants zoomed by undetected.

"They're getting close," Tina said, holding back her alarm. The consequences of the plants' discovery had been discussed at length. The arrest of Neil would probably follow, and then the seizure of his things. The loss of his property. The dissolution of the entire community, most likely. The laws of society were far worse than anything the adults of the community could devise.

"No shit," Trixie said, and reached for a bag of corn chips on the side table. She tapped her fingers through the folds but the plastic rattled emptily at her touch; only a salty rime remained. She wiped her greasy, powdered fingers on her pants.

The helicopter slowed and came to a stop above the marsh, where the water frothed, and the pussy willow shook, and the two skeletons at the dry edges stared upward blankly into the camera's eye. There were sound bites from Jay Feather, from Mr. Grimsrud, and from various activists and scholars arrayed on either side of the controversy. During a sequence of shots showing life at the commune, Tina appeared briefly holding a shovel, bending over as the shot cut to Bob Grossberger playing bocce ball.

Then a reporter appeared, walking through a meadow of grass, speaking into the camera as the wind tousled his hair. "Who owns the past?" the reporter asked. "Who will decide the future? Once again we find ourselves at a crossroads, waiting, waiting . . ."

"Jesus Christ, Neil," Trixie said to the television. "Just give the bones to the Indians and get this shit over with."

Tina agreed, but she kept her thoughts to herself. To agree with Trixie would be like ripping a piece of skin from her own arm, a source of physical pain. Tina wanted her own opinion now, or none at all.

After the segment, Trixie went outside for a walk in the dusk. Tina watched her from the window, a brooding figure in the trees. She went to the bed and pulled the quilt around her and stared at the glass screen. Moments ago, her image had crossed its face briefly. Her image had been imprinted in the minds of the viewers. A moment of her life had been cloned. She imagined the transmission of her image to houses and apartments across the country. She imagined her face appearing on screens in California and Colorado and New York, staggered at one-hour intervals. She imagined her body nested in the airwaves, moving through the clouds and over the hills, to appear in a flash of light and sound somewhere far away.

Tina fell asleep in front of the TV, the quilt wrapped tightly around her body, the blue light shifting on the walls. When she woke up, Trixie was beside her again, her face chalky white in the glow of the screen. Her eyes flickered in the changing hues.

Tina burrowed deeper into her quilt to find its warmth, slowly remembering who she was. The TV was showing an old Western. The sage and cacti of southern California. Old land, old sky. The people in this movie were probably dead by now.

"What'd Margaret say?" Tina asked drowsily. Margaret was throwing the I Ching tonight.

"Nothing," Trixie replied. A daddy longlegs was creeping across the wall, its spindly legs stepping along in slow order.

"Come on."

Trixie kept watching, and spoke without changing her gaze:

"She said 'All day long the superior man is creatively active. At nightfall his mind is still beset with cares.' It was stupid. She said if I change, it means I've been corrupted somehow and you should never forget who you are."

With that, she got up and began buttoning her sweater over her

T-shirt, then rummaged around on the floor for her orthopedic shoes.

"Going?" Tina asked.

"Yeah. Nothing to do here tonight." She slipped her toe into the shoe and pressed her heel over the lip.

"Did anything else happen while I was asleep?" Tina asked. She pulled the blanket around her shoulders more tightly.

"No," Trixie said, yanking on her laces. "They still haven't found anything. But there's some special report coming up tomorrow. Something they won't say what its about."

Tina contemplated a piece of lint on her pillow.

"Do they know something?" she asked gravely.

"No idea," Trixie said. "How would I know?" Then she tied the knot on her shoe without looking and left.

# 2

OOKIE'S BEARD BEGAN as mere bristles covering his cheeks and neck, like a coating of sandpaper, which he rubbed sometimes with the flat of his hand. He liked to hear the scrape of the whiskers against his fingertips. It was a small pleasure that made his restless thoughts seem connected to some physical action for a moment.

Over time, the skin beneath his beard began to itch and burn, and Cookie wished he could shave it all off in a single stroke. But the prison did not provide him with a razor blade, and he did not know how to ask for one. So his beard got longer. Slowly it formed a soft padding around the planes of his face. On afternoons when a storm was coming his whiskers stood on end. Cookie combed them with his fingers, twisting tufts around the knuckle of his index finger and yanking lightly until his skin stung pleasantly. After a while he came to like the beard again. The itching had stopped and now he had something to play with.

Finally, his beard turned downward, flowing over his neck and his chest like a waterfall.

Cookie went through many washbasins, countless pairs of chopsticks, a wardrobe of prison clothing. He maintained his body through daily exercise in the yard, where the prisoners led each other in long sessions of tai chi. He watched the other men and through imitation came to feel the rhythms and tensions of their movements. Slowly, as he moved his cupped hands through the air, and raised his knee, and pulled breath in and out of his lungs, he came to recognize the profound connection between his body and his mind. He stretched the tendons in his finger and felt a whole circuitry of nerves and arteries spreading up his arm and neck. A certain gesture, a certain series of motions, opened a passageway to a thought. He greeted each sunrise with the taut poses.

He wondered idly what had gone wrong sometimes, what had led him to this place, but gradually the pain of his confinement drifted away. He felt little in the way of rancor or animosity. He accepted his imprisonment as a fact of life. His body accepted it, and then his mind. Sometimes he wondered if Henry had made it home to Oregon, and if Howqua had orchestrated his own capture from the start. He wondered if the market for castoreum had ever caught on, and if Henry was a rich man by now, or if Henry was a pauper. He had no way of telling, and eventually stopped thinking about the circumstances of his capture at all.

Cookie thought of Henry often, though. Every day he renewed his memories based on the memories of the day before. And like copies of copies they slowly began to mutate and fade. The appearance of Henry's face, his smell, the texture of his skin, these things became abstract and symbolized. They distorted into codes and glyphs. On occasion visceral memories of Henry came to him in powerful bursts, but mostly they hovered just outside his senses. Cookie's memories never entirely burned away, though. They simply weakened and shrank in a never-ending asymptote of decay.

Sometimes the absence of Henry was unbearable. It came late in the day, when Cookie's mind was tired and he had nothing to look forward to, and he would lie on the floor of his cell, curled up in a ball, feeling huge lobes of emptiness aching inside him. He took solace in sleep, and tried to remain unconscious for at least fifteen hours a day.

In dreams they spoke. They talked on and on, in the crow's nest. In these dreams their words were meaningless, empty ciphers in elaborate scaffoldings of grammar. Their sentences twisted and moved forward as real sentences would, but upon inspection turned in on themselves and collapsed into nonsense.

*　*　*

The man in the cell beside Cookie was named King Lu. King Lu's head was like a huge pumpkin, and his hair stood straight out in spiky tufts. He walked with a slightly bowlegged gait, and he never spoke above a low murmur. He was among the most skillful calligraphers in China, Cookie learned from a guard, but he was also a member of a religious sect at odds with the current Emperor, and thus had been imprisoned for life. His style was known throughout the Empire for its whispering strokes, its watery confidence, its dynamic asymmetry. The soldiers treated him with deference due to his artistic skill, but he was never allowed outside of his cell.

Cookie spent hours watching him at work. Softening his inkstick in a bowl of water, grinding his ink on a rectangular stone, collecting the ink in a marble well. He watched him stretch his rice paper on his table, and take the ink into the fibers of his rabbit hair brush with its hollow bamboo handle. King Lu held his brush loosely, and set his center of gravity low over the table.

Often he began with a vertical line, sweeping downward, lifting his hand straight from the wrist. He crossed it with a horizontal line, darting left, back to the right, lifting left. He applied more pressure at the beginning of a stroke, raising his hand as he moved across the paper, and finally returning the pressure as the stroke ended. No stroke was ever corrected, for to do that would destroy its lifeforce. King Lu's writing was grounded in impulse, momentum, momentary poise.

He wrote poems and love letters and important proclamations for wealthy men and government officials. He wrote public condemnations of his own beliefs. His option was death.

King Lu worked for brief, intensive spurts, and then rose from his low desk to gaze out the small window above his head or pace the cell from one end to the other. Sometimes he laughed to himself, but more often he sighed.

After a certain number of years, Cookie was assigned to work in the kitchen, a crowded room full of inmates and guards, bustling with steam and the cheering hiss of boiling oil. The walls were faded yellow, perpetually sweating, and at the center of the room stretched a long wooden table surrounded by various work stations. All along the table there were men patting rice, folding wontons, peeling squabs and dicing long swaths of seaweed.

Cookie began by cleaning the sinks, the dishes, the toilets nearby. He cleaned anything that needed to be cleaned. He learned the order of the knives in their rack, the sequence of the woks and where they hung. He learned the way to arrange the kindling in the oven and how to add more wood when the temperature began to drop. All around him the other men chattered away in their tonal language. Cookie became attuned to the pitch movements of their voices, the shaded contours of the vocal peaks and valleys, the melodic shifting of tone. He was grateful to be surrounded by voices again—their entrance, and rise, and departure—even if he could not understand them.

After years of cleaning Cookie began to prepare the raw materials of the food for the cooks to combine into meals. He shucked corn, peeled potatoes, and chopped ginger. When he finished one task, they gave him another. All the while he watched the men around him, and learned from their quick combinations of ingredients, their blurring hands and appraising looks.

Cookie surprised the prison officials with his precision and speed, and his responsibilities increased. He learned to cook in the Chinese fashion, with thick sauces and glazes. He learned about bamboo shoots and duck liver and the consistency of gluten. He prepared bird's nest soup, shark fins, pigeons' eggs, sturgeon's lips. He invented various specialties. In one, he picked the veins of fat from thin slices of beef and used them as a netting for pork dumplings, which he deep fried and served with a peanut sauce, infused with rice vinegar. He ground peppercorn and fennel seeds, and rubbed them inside the body of a suckling pig, which he served on banana leaves sprinkled with coarsely chopped scallions. He learned the Chinese characters for fish, and carrot, and mung bean. He learned to count.

Over time, his cooking improved. He learned the proper pacing of a meal, the component courses and how they should interrelate. He built his meals like stories, progressing from one flavor to the next. A narrative of taste and texture and presentation. It was a slow process, and there was always more to learn.

Soon his cooking became too accomplished to waste on the prison staff and midlevel officers of the court, and the warden arranged for his meals to feed rising politicians and ambassadors instead. Cookie spent his days after that, from sunrise until dark, toiling in the clamorous kitchen, among sizzling woks and squawking birds, catfish and flashing butcher knives. Occasionally he baked an American dish, much to the delight of his patrons. It became fashionable in Canton to serve the odd hybrids that Cookie invented, jewel duck in sauerkraut, fish balls and peanut butter with a side dish of bacon, and he received many small gifts from his grateful clientele, such as woolen gloves, and jade rings, and new books.

Every evening he returned to his cell smelling of garlic and spices, and bearing a small dish of food for King Lu, who thanked him profusely with clasped hands and bows. He took the bowl of food, whether it was string beans in oyster sauce or red-cooked chicken, and ate it greedily in the back of his cell.

Often they played games together. They both had chess boards, which they positioned in view of each other through the hole between their cells. When one moved, he knocked on the wall, and the other would arrange his board to match, and move again and knock on the wall.

They never spoke; they never touched. A wall of stone separated them, and yet, over the years, the two men came to own each other in a way. They watched each other. They knew each other's rhythms and moods. King Lu was like an animal to Cookie, a smooth, thinking animal that breathed and hummed and produced beautiful shapes on paper. King Lu paced in his cell. His robes hissed at his feet. His rice paper crinkled in his hands. Cookie watched the columns of characters amass beneath his gaze, and the sheets of paper pile into stacks beside his desk. Eventually a ream of paper would be finished, each leaf covered in characters, and the soldiers would remove them and deliver a fresh ream. Cookie listened to him fill his bedpan.

One winter, many years into their sentence, King Lu became ill. He coughed from deep inside his chest, a gristly, wet rattle, and sweated into his straw bedding. Cookie brought him tea from the kitchen, sweetened with honey and ginger. When the guards would allow it, he swabbed King Lu's forehead through the iron bars with a damp towel. King Lu recovered, but only after a long and arduous struggle. During this time Cookie realized how much he depended on King Lu. He needed him for his basic sanity. Without King Lu's quiet presence beside him, Cookie did not know how he would make it. He wondered if his own presence gave King Lu as much comfort. Their love for each other was a secret they kept even from themselves.

One day a rich man whose daughter's wedding banquet had brought him much honor sent Cookie a gift. Four workers arrived at the prison bearing large tools, rams and saws and chisels. The guards had been advised to let them through, and they proceeded directly to Cookie's cell block, where two of them stood outside his window, and two of them inside, and over the course of the day they enlarged his window to the size of a large hanging scroll. When they finished, sunlight streamed into the cell, and a cherry tree had become visible. Cookie was very pleased.

Before they departed, however, he spoke briefly to the foreman, a humble man with bloodshot eyes. He led the foreman to the wall between his cell and King Lu's, and with a series of gestures described a small project. Finally the foreman nodded and concurred. His men stayed a few more hours, and when they packed up their tools they left behind a small doorway.

That evening Cookie invited King Lu to his cell, and the two men watched the boughs of the cherry tree move in the breeze. Petals floated in the air, and Cookie imagined the pathways they made, like streamers forming complex, elegant designs. He had no idea what King Lu was thinking, but he was glad to share the view with him.

The guards ignored their arrangement and the men spread their things throughout the two cells. Cookie and King Lu both had many benefactors on the outside, and the bribes and gifts they brought to the prison had improved everyone's life. There were blankets, and tapestries, and fine bamboo boxes scattered throughout the homes of the soldiers and guards. The warden had become an important man. Within the confines of the prison, they were practically free.

Over the years Cookie's worries wore away in the daily progress of cooking and cleaning. He swept his cell, and rearranged his possessions sometimes. He brought things from the kitchen, like sage and eucalyptus leaves, that sweetened the air. He became oddly content. His world was small and proscribed, but his kitchen was well stocked and he knew where he stood. The guards treated him respectfully, as long as he did the same. The cherry tree grew.

In the winter, he watched a shelf of snow fall from its branch, the glittering grains sifted through the air to reveal a ray of light.

With the wall removed, Cookie learned a few things from King Lu about the written Chinese language. He learned the seven basic strokes of calligraphy, the turns and pressures used for different angles, curves, widths, points. There was the horizontal stroke, like a cloud formation stretching a thousand miles; the dot, like a stone falling from a high peak; the downward left thrust, like a rhinoceros digging its tusk in the ground; the upward hook, like shooting from a hundred-pound crossbow; the vertical stroke, like a dangling needle; the wave-like ending stroke, like rolling thunder; the left hook, like the sinews and joints of a mighty bow.

One word used all seven strokes. It meant eternity.

Gradually Cookie began to comprehend the structure of Chinese. He learned of full words and empty words, the concrete and abstract. Unlike his own language, a closed set of forms, Chinese was an open system, ever expanding and building on itself. The number of Chinese characters was staggering. King Lu knew between three thousand and four thousand characters; others knew many more than that.

Slowly, Cookie learned to speak better, but never very well, and King Lu never learned more than a word or two of English.

To Cookie the meaning of the Chinese characters always remained semi-opaque. They turned to abstractions before his eyes. A flock of butterflies shadowing a page. A net strung between a nebula of stars. An army of skeletons. In some ways, his incomplete understanding allowed him to see the writing for what it was, mere ink on paper, slashes and spaces for things that in fact were not there. There was something sad at the heart of writing, he thought, some distance that could never be overcome. Something broken that could never be repaired.

Over the years Cookie invented various life stories for Henry. He imagined a life of good fortune, and profitable business endeavors. He envisioned that Henry's hazelnut farm had expanded to many acres, and that he exported his product to every corner of the globe.

Henry was the governor of Oregon. Henry was a wise beggar full of unheard stories. Henry was a father of many children.

In Cookie's mind Henry never forgot him. He imagined Henry raging against the cruelty of the Chinese political system in a futile attempt to save him. What they had done to Cookie was unforgivable, he imagined Henry thought, and moreover they treated the youthful nation of America like a child. It was Cookie's place to forgive, Henry's never to forgive. He let Henry feel the anger that he could no longer feel himself. The Chinese ports remained the most impermeable of any in the world, Henry would complain, even as their people yearned for goods and services from abroad. The Chinese remained aloof from the growing family of nations. Henry attempted many legal maneuvers to get Cookie free, and came to many dead ends in navigating the Chinese diplomatic bureaucracy.

Cookie thought of Henry almost every day. He considered their separation the true tragedy of his life.

One year, there were executions in the prison yard, huge public events that Cookie could see from the kitchen window. Howqua was among the victims, hanged for his transactions with the Americans and British, his import of opium through the gates of Canton. One year a plague came. People died in the streets, and the survivors buried them on the outskirts of town.

Over the years Cookie's beard turned white as milk.

And then, one day, the Emperor died. The kitchen closed and all the prisoners were returned to their cells. They gathered in the yard for a eulogy at noon.

That night the warden called certain prisoners to his office, one by one. It was good fortune to be called. Cookie was called, as was King Lu. The warden told them they had been pardoned, and he suggested they pack their things quickly and leave. The time between emperors was short, and once the throne was occupied again it was doubtful the pardons would hold. He presented Cookie with a sack of gold coins, just a small portion of the profits he had made for the prison officials over the long years of service. It was not much, but enough to start on.

Cookie returned to his cell and began packing his bag. He did not have many items to take. A few robes, an incense holder, a bowl with a matching spoon. He was an old man now. He did not want to carry much.

He wondered if perhaps they should stay where they were. They had their cherry tree, they had a simple, well-contained life. But King Lu was ready. His eyes were shining with the dreams of freedom.

The next morning, Cookie and King Lu stepped out of the prison, into the streets of Canton. The city was silent with mourning. Banners and pennants flapped in the wind. Images of the deceased Emperor lined the streets. The stores were empty. An enormous painting loomed over the central square, surrounded by cones of incense. Throughout the expanse of worn cobblestones, streams of salmon flashed in the sun.

The two old men walked through the streets, passing a few people here and there, having spent their lives together, not so differently from anyone else. They wandered down toward the wharf, where Cookie found an American clipper ship and booked them a passage home, to Oregon. As far as he knew, the plan remained the same.

# 3

**N**EIL'S HEADPHONES WERE awesome, Sennheiser HD 220s from Germany, ordered from the *Whole Earth Catalogue*. They fit like big pillows around his ears, and inside them the sonic landscapes of his musical compositions took on rich three-dimensional mass. The textures became almost tactile to the mind's eye. He could hear his chiming xylophone, like tinkling glass spread across the horizon, and his languid guitar lines humping through the air like floating snakes. The sunburst of a cymbal dilated and dispersed, and the bass throbbed from beneath the earth, vibrating the stalks and blades that grew there. The cosmology of his aural environment was so big and variegated inside the headphones that he could almost get lost, like a snail in a wet garden, moving slowly from one floral amazement to the next, everything vivid and small and shining with fresh rain.

Neil enjoyed listening to his music while watching TV, and found rich visual analogues for his weird sounds and percussions. The orange explosions of a cop show's conclusion matched with a lanky drum track; a chase through old warehouses and rooftops paired with a chiming guitar solo; the long, raucous pauses of *Monday Night Football* filled by some squalling feedback loop. He liked matching the tracks to the most unexpected of pictures, and sometimes spent hours appreciating the new, unimagined combinations he could make.

This evening Neil was flipping between a blooper show and a documentary on lions while listening to a droning synth line, and waiting for the nightly news to come on. All day Channel 8 had been promising a "major development" in the story of the bones and he was highly curious as to what they might have in mind. After all, there had been no "major development" in his own head. He could only imagine what a major development might be. A pimple on Jay Feather's back? A sliver in Mr. Grimsrud's finger? The stories the media had begun to pursue had become almost nonsensical, which filled Neil with an obscure sense of pride. Most likely the major development was nothing, he figured, or some new fabrication of groundless hyperpole, but at this point there was really no telling.

Two policemen were defusing a time bomb to a choogling guitar riff when the television seemed to cough and blink, and without warning switched into a new phase of programming. A hard news flash, evidently more important than the thrilling denouement of *Hardcastle and McCormick*.

At first Neil figured it was just another advertisement for the "major development" the station had been promising—the news graphics appeared, the reporters holding their microphones—but eventually, as the images and titles stacked up, he came to see that it was not an advertisement at all, but rather a whole new story unto itself, something about a blazing fire somewhere on the outskirts of the city. The TV showed an aerial picture choked with smoke and yellow flames and then a square-headed reporter appeared, prattling on a road shoulder as fire trucks zoomed past. By the time Neil became fully interested in the piece, the news break had already been interrupted by a commercial, and he was forced to wait for the next round of programming before finding out the real details.

Neil took the opportunity to click off his reel-to-reel and lift the headphones from his temples and hang them gently on the arm of the sofa. The sounds of his cabin bloomed around him with newly subtle gradations. The hum of the refrigerator, the slough of his socks on the hardwood floor. And in addition to the normal sounds, there were other sounds as well. Faraway sirens swirling, and yelling voices, and the beep of a backward-moving truck.

Neil thought nothing of it—he was accustomed to unwanted annoyances from the tent city by now—and lifted himself up from the couch with a long groan. He paced into the kitchen and opened a bottle of beer, then a bottle of salsa, and returned to the living room to drag the card table toward the seat.

He sat back down and pulled apart a plastic bag of tortilla chips with a whoosh, then picked at the blackened crud caught in the grooves of the salsa jar. Finally he poured the lumpy contents into a shallow bowl and arranged the chips and salsa on the card table in front of him.

The sounds from outside continued to grow and diversify. The squawk of a walkie-talkie, the growl of a hydraulic lift, the chopping whine of a distant helicopter. The sirens reached a certain peak level and then abruptly stopped, but Neil managed to put the commotion out of his mind. He assumed it was just another flare-up among the bored reporters again, and turned his attention to a fresh Mitsubishi commercial.

Neil was digging his first corn chip into the bowl of salsa when the commercials ended and the news report came back on, continuing right where it had left off:

"And we're back," the anchorman said, sitting in a conspicuously busy newsroom with his shirt sleeves rolled up. "We bring you live footage tonight of a late-breaking story in the hills northwest of Portland. A fire raging on the edges of Forest Park."

Neil watched the image of pulsing smoke and flames, violent shadows playing on the thicket of underbrush. The fire seemed to be arranged in parallel rows, he noted, like lines of flaming Braille, and it was separated from the hulking trees that surrounded it by a moat of empty earth.

He heard the sound of people shouting outside, and the gunning of a diesel engine. The sirens started up again briefly, then stopped again. He looked back at the TV screen with a look of some consternation.

"Oh shit," Neil finally said. The fire was here.

Neil got up and crossed to the window, and pulled back the curtains to find the tent city in full attack mode. There were vans and cameras moving around with a renewed sense of purpose, newscasters stirring, lighting rigs going up. P.A.s were running back and forth and the grips were lumbering with their sandbags. The eyes of the cameras were opening again, preparing for a new, coordinated assault on his property.

Neil strode to the porch and scanned the horizon, where he spotted a thick column of smoke rising over the tops of the trees, silver and black in the moonlight.

"What the fuck?" Neil asked.

On the TV, a balding reporter had materialized, stuttering and collecting his thoughts. He pointed at the glowing cloud of smoke on the horizon. "We have no idea yet what is going on," he stammered. "But there is a fire on the property of Neil Rust. There are speculations. That arson is involved." Neil could see his own placid rooftop in the foreground of the shot, sitting dumbly while the sky smoldered behind it.

He stood there in the doorway while his body waited for some useful command, but none were forthcoming.

Soon enough the TV cut back to the aerial view, where the fire blew out the pixels of the screen, breaking the image into writhing blotches and haloes.

Slowly, the camera zoomed in and began tracing the perimeter of the flames.

"There are reports," the airborne reporter said through peals of static, "Reports of a perpetrator at the scene of the fire. A suspect on foot. We are now trying to make visual identification."

Neil crouched down near the monitor. It felt strange watching his own fire on television, but it provided a kind of information he could not possibly gather himself.

Suddenly, from behind a large rock, a small figure appeared. It was Trixie Volterra, staring directly into the camera's hovering lens.

"Oh, Jesus," Neil said, and rolled back onto his palms.

Trixie stood there in her white shoes and nurse's smock, clutching a five-gallon can of gasoline, as rising cinders crossed the frame, and the shadows of the trees behind her went wild. The fire cast orange highlights over her body, and her slight figure warped from the heat. She shielded her face and staggered backward.

Somehow, it seemed, Trixie had shrunken herself down, flattened herself, landed entirely on the other side of the screen. "No fucking way," Neil said. "No fucking way."

"We have a visual," the reporter said. "A girl in the vicinity of the fire. This is live. We are live."

Trixie's mouth opened and closed and her lips scraped on her teeth, as particles of burning material danced around her like fireflies. Her eyes darted around and she batted at a falling spark. Then she turned and ran into the woods.

"Oh great," Neil said. "Really great idea."

The helicopter followed behind her, narrating Trixie's progress from above.

"Up, up over the embankment," the reporter said, "and yes, yes, she seems to be following the pathway. No idea what she has in mind yet."

Trixie's figure blurred through the branches, illuminated in the helicopter's arcing cone of light. She ran through a meadow of moonlit lupen and stopped near a beaver pond, where the helicopter hovered over her, beating the water with its air currents, edging lower and lower until the water shivered and seemed to part like a curtain, revealing more curtains of water underneath.

"No positive identification yet," the reporter said. "No good looks."

As Neil watched, his anger transformed into mute fascination and then into worry and fear. It dawned on him that someone was going to get hurt.

"What the fuck are you doing?" he asked the television.

Neil watched Trixie turn and climb through some ferns and then cross a ravine on a slick, moldering tree trunk. He watched her duck through a patch of maples and splash through a shallow creek. Sometimes the camera lost visual contact, and Trixie would emerge someplace new, stumbling through sharp sticks and pointed rocks, a million things that could cut her apart, as all around her the colorless rocks and plants of the nighttime slid by like smoke.

Trixie hustled into the underbrush, fighting against the slapping branches and twigs. A twining nettle clutched at her skirt and she ripped it away with a powerful jerk, and then she broke through onto a dirt path. She climbed up a hill along a series of switchbacks, cutting corners as she went, until she reached the ridge and rested for a moment, looking down over a long, bumpy run littered with thin birch trees and clumps of poplars, and rotting snags perched on the backs of large boulders.

Outside, the newscasters and Indians and those with televisions in the commune huddled around their screens. The reporters prepared themselves for cutaways, though there would be no cutting from this chase.

Trixie seemed to gauge the ground falling away from her, full of indistinct moguls and crevices, slick lichens, until finally she selected a pathway through the stunted trees and began her way down. She moved quickly, letting her momentum carry her over the divots and rough parts, over the minefield of ankle-twisting traps, until finally reaching the last embankment and sliding on her ass to a deer run.

At various points her identity was confirmed, then denied, then confirmed again.

"Come on, come on," Neil said, coaxing her forward.

The helicopter came and pressed close in, and for a moment the forest became dappled in brilliant, artificial light, a slow flashbulb of platinum. The stumps and ferns went white and their shadows moved quickly over the ground. And then the helicopter rose again and the darkness returned, inky black.

Neil paced around his living room as the chase proceeded in its agonizingly slow movements. He sat down on the couch, got up and walked to the window, then edged toward the bookshelf. Everything in the room seemed electrified. The desk, the television, the walls and floor. A small charge, repelling him into motion. Neil filled up with anger again. The drama of teenage girls annoyed him profoundly. The way they believed the whole world was against them and then had to make sure of it. The way they had to test everything. Neil clasped his fingers behind his head and stretched his knuckles with the pull of his neck.

At a barren plum tree Trixie paused and caught her breath with her hands on her knees, as the helicopter waited patiently above her. Then she began jogging again, along the edges of the marsh, where the water wrinkled and a white circle of light skimmed over the pussy willow, pounding in the rotors' hard wind.

She kept going, through a shaggy rhododendron, over an old stump, gradually curving her way back toward the cabins. For a moment Neil thought perhaps she was returning home, in which case the question of how to receive her should be addressed, but then she cut up into the woods again, toward the developments over the hills, and the long boughs of the fir trees obscured her from clear vision. On the forest floor Trixie became a rough blur of information.

"Come on, come on," Neil said, wringing his shirt into a hard handle. "Where are you going?"

The helicopter lifted up for a better view, widening its angle on the black landscape, and a moment later Trixie emerged near the chestnut tree on the cliff overlooking the bend in the creek. The helicopter's spotlight located her quickly, and followed her as she walked directly to the ledge, where she put her hands on her hips and peered over the lip.

Neil could hear the helicopter outside now, thrashing at the air. A stray beam of light flashed on the windowpane and caught briefly in the weave of his drapes. He heard footsteps padding on the ground, voices calling, the sound of doors slamming and children wondering what to do.

On TV, Trixie squinted into the buffeting wind. The grass flattened on the ground all around her, and her long shadow revolved back and forth. Her face was bleached by the glaring lights, and her eyes were black pools, unreadable. Her hair whipped over her mouth, which opened and closed in a silent monologue.

The bank below her was beginning to fill up with spectators. Neil could see Beth Bowler with her black hair in a tangle, Peter Sessions moving in his low, slouching lope. He saw Bob Grossberger and the children of Paul Winowski gathering around each other in a tight huddle of alarmed speculation.

Again, Trixie stepped to the edge of the cliff, this time shouting something to the crowd, and then seemed to take a moment to think.

"What are you doing?" Neil asked her again. He would not be surprised if she suddenly flew straight up into the air.

The reporters had stopped talking. The helicopter had ceased circling. The people on the bank of the creek were standing stock still. Trixie was staring into the sky, her image coursing with soft pixels, and Neil stared right back at her, the screen's reflection pulsing whitely in his eyes.

# 4

TINA OPENED THE door to find the property lit up like a stadium. White halogen poured from the sky, and from the ridges nearby, and the hanging fern exploded with wet light. Her shoes were only halfway on her feet and her jacket was dangling from her arm, but she was already running toward the creek as fast as she could. Her muscles had become soft and weightless.

Tina leapt from the stairs and the screen door slammed loudly behind her. The rooftops of the cabins glowed pale blue, and every pebble on the pathway was marked by its own tiny shadow. The branches of the trees thrashed violently in the wind. The whole world was shining like the surface of the moon.

Tina hurried down the pathway toward the creek, pulling her clothes on as she went, and keeping her eyes on the helicopter locked over the chestnut tree, pinning Trixie at the base of its spotlight. She ran past the rock wall of the garden, past the doorway of Peter's cabin swinging on its hinges, past the dining hall. The bounce of the wooden footbridge vibrated through her shoes and gave her a small bit of momentum. In the distance she could see a billowing cloud of smoke.

A crowd was already gathering along the pebbly beachhead when she got there, clustering along the narrow shoreline sinking toward the creek's swift current. Beth Bowler, craning her neck as her purple bathrobe flapped around her knees, and Peter Sessions, standing with his arms planted firmly on his hips, wearing only black cowboy boots and boxers. Bob Grossberger was walking back and forth in a lustrous kimono decorated with fire-breathing dragons, and kneading his shoulder in a frenzy of nervous energy. The sound of the rushing water was completely lost in the din of the helicopter's blades.

Across the creek, the cliff rose in a beveled plane, with tufts of grass sprouting from the cracks, gleaming with dampness in the changing light. On top loomed Trixie's silhouhette, shooting out streaks of shadow, leaning over and gauging the distance to the water below. Tina's stomach disappeared from her body and her legs began to tingle with fear.

"Trixie!" Tina yelled. "Get back!" But her voice was swallowed in the commotion. She could feel the pull of gravity on Trixie's body, like a lead anchor on a twine. Then Trixie jerked away from the ledge and her shadow was gone.

"Tina!" Bob Grossberger said, and yelled some incomprehensible words in her ear. Tina nodded and pulled away, scowling at whatever he was trying to say, then grimaced at Margaret, who was also yelling at her.

"Tina, what's going on?" Beth asked into her ear. Tina shook her head. "I don't know!"

The helicopter above Trixie rose and sank in a slow rhythm, like a gentle piston in the air. Its metallic skin was traced with bright flashes. For a brief instant Tina could see the rotors appear crisply in the haze of circling motion, a tiny chopping blink, and she watched further for any more nicks in their blind revolutions. She found the bobbing motion of the helicopter's body almost peaceful in a way, lulling, and convinced herself that the intimidating machine implied some control over the situation, an authority that would keep things from going too far awry.

"Trixie!" Tina yelled, as fear and rage again clawed inside her.

Trixie crept to the edge of the cliff again. She peered over, as if she was looking for something in particular, but there was no way of knowing. She held her hands up in the air and widened her eyes, as if she had just been caught doing something private, but also something not particularly revealing.

"Poor girl," Beth said. "She doesn't know what to do."

"Poor girl, my ass," Bob said. "She loves this shit."

300

Tina blinked and noticed Trixie's position had changed. She was no longer peering over the cliff, but rather leaning out, with her body bent into a strange posture of flapping, or flailing. And then, without warning, Tina watched her friend take two running steps and a ginger, one-footed hop, and leap from the cliff toward the water.

Tina tried to call out but her throat had stopped working and the only sound that emerged was a dry, choking wheeze.

For a long moment Trixie's body just seemed to hang there, floating in the air, waiting patiently for the whole crowd to focus. And then, gradually, when everyone was ready, she began her descent.

To Tina, the fall elapsed in a slow, arduous crawl. The moments swarmed and expanded around Trixie to pillow her in feathery wings, moving her downward in tiny, flickering increments. Her legs kicked and her arms windmilled, stuttering like an old movie, and her shirt rose up to expose the dot of her navel. The cliff face behind her softened, and the motion of everything else in the world seemed to grind to a halt. Every expression on her face registered in fine detail— a look of pain, a look of smug satisfaction, a look of shame, a look of powerful determination, blending together in a seamless, uninter-rupted flow.

Tina gasped as her heart made the same sickening plunge inside her.

Then the skin of the water opened and closed. The white splash zipped from view. And the surface of the creek tumbled onward as if nothing had happened. A silk sheet snapping in the wind. Tina waited for Trixie's head to appear, or her arm, her voice to call out, but the water continued rushing soundlessly ahead.

"Come on!" someone cried out, and suddenly the creek was alive with arms and legs, slapping the water in white frothing bursts. Bob Grossberger was bouncing up and down like an astronaut, Peter Sessions took long, elegant strokes. Others were feeling in the dark waters like blind men.

Tina ran to the creek and threw herself onto its surface as well. Her arms began beating and her legs kicked back and forth. The water filled her clothes and sucked her downward, and she struggled against the sudden, unexpected weight. The water cupped her ears and entered her mouth, so she slapped her arms harder, lengthening her strokes to get some kind of momentum. She felt for the bottom and found the creek was only about four feet deep.

Tina moved ahead slowly, pushing through the water, as Trixie's head splashed in and out of view. Or was it someone else's head? She lost sight before she could tell.

Suddenly Neil was beside her.

"Oh my God," she cried. "Is she okay?"

"Everything's going to be all right," Neil yelled. The cold water streamed around them, breaking apart and molding together again. She saw something white break from the surface, like the moon in the clouds. Then it was gone again.

Tina and Neil followed the white disk and watched it come to the surface once more. They moved closer and then lost it. Then they found it again. Neil reached out and hooked Trixie in his arms.

"I've got her!" Neil called.

Within a few steps they were standing on gravel again, moving away from the silty mud of the creek's middle, then staggering upward toward the shore. Neil floated Trixie's limp body along in the water, dragging her by the armpits, until the water was too shallow and he scooped her up into his arms.

"Trixie!" Tina said. "What happened?" Then she seemed to remember herself and stopped talking, racing ahead of Neil to clear a pathway.

Neil lifted Trixie into the air and water poured off of them. Her face fell against his shoulder. Her legs flopped over his arm. Her hair caught in his mouth. The thin cotton of her blouse bunched up in her armpits.

"Be careful with her, Neil!" Peggy screamed. "Be careful moving her!"

"I'm trying," Neil said. "All right? Just gimme some room."

Neil carried Trixie to a clean place on the bank, where Tina was waiting for him, and set her down gently before asking her if anything was broken.

Trixie did not answer. Her eyes were closed and her skin looked almost greasy with wetness. Neil tapped at her cheek and a dribble of water ran down her chin.

"All right," he said numbly. "It's fine. Just lie here."

Neil cradled Trixie's head and arranged her arms alongside her body. Then he leaned toward her mouth and listened for breathing. Someone brought over a blanket to wrap around his shoulders, but he pushed them away.

Up in the parking lot, an ambulance arrived in a blaze of dust and sirens, alerted to the crisis by the live television reports. Two paramedics leapt from the cab and sprinted toward the water, carrying a stretcher piled with medical equipment. "Here, here!" Bob Grossberger cried out, waving his arms in the air. When the paramedics got to the creek, they squatted beside Neil and began pulling instruments from a huge black duffel bag.

"Tough night," one of them said, and Neil nodded grimly. The crowd had begun breaking into confused groups, whispering to itself, trying to keep calm, forming into a large, vague circle around Trixie's body. One of the paramedics unsheathed a collapsible splint, and the other dragged his finger through Trixie's mouth and began pressing on her chest.

Neil rose and took a few paces back, where Beth and Peggy joined him. Tina crouched on the ground near their feet, staring at Trixie's face through the jerking movements of the paramedics. Trixie was covered in a southwestern blanket now, one of her hands peeking from beneath the folds. Her orthopedic shoes sat nearby, tipped over onto their sides. The coils of her hair were drying, filaments coming unstuck from the dark wetted patches to curve singly into the night air. Tina waited for some sign, some wink or smirk of recognition, but Trixie's face remained still. Her fingers curled slightly toward her palm, as if holding onto an invisible egg-shaped object.

The paramedics breathed into Trixie's mouth and listened for her pulse, and then they started the process all over again. They blew into her mouth and pressed on her chest, and grasped her limp arms for life signs. Tina squeezed some water out of her shirt and moved her toes in her sponge-like socks. The shadows of trees and people shifted in the red light of the siren. Everything seemed unreal, broken apart into separate pieces. The sound of the water, the stab of the light, the cold of the wind. The screaming noise of the helicopter came through muted and distant.

Beth looked over at Neil and Neil looked back at her evenly. Bob Grossberger placed his hand on Tina's shoulder.

"What is it?" Bob whispered to Neil. The white light shook tremulously on the ground.

Neil took a moment before answering. "She's gone," he said finally. "She was already gone when I got her."

With this, the blood seemed to leave Tina's fingers, and she fixed her attention on a small rock near Neil's foot. The shape and the texture of the rock seemed vastly important suddenly.

"Shit," Bob said.

"No," Tina said rationally. "That's not right. She doesn't do that." Perhaps there was still some time, she imagined. Perhaps they could still double back and change something. The moment was so close they could almost catch it.

Tina could see Trixie's feet extending from the scrum of action, the damp fabric of her twisted socks against the earth. Then she felt her face cave in and she began crying. Beth and Peggy were talking in sweet, reassuring tones—"You're okay, honey. It's okay." "Just hold on. Everything's going to be all right." High above her, the shining body of the helicoptor floated on a pillar of air.

# 5

SOMETHING TERRIBLE HAD happened along the banks of the Columbia River. The Chinook and Flatheads had disappeared somewhere, and their cedar lodges had been burned to the ground, reduced to blackened tinder jutting from overgrown clearings in the trees. Their long canoes, carved with hieroglyphs of ravens and elk and salmon, sat beached above the shoreline, filled with rainwater and rotting leaves, while brown bears snuffled around the remnants of their old fire pits and smokehouses, overturning rocks and stumps and licking for grubs.

The ship rounded a bend and a corridor opened between two cliffs, where the white peak of Mount St. Helens appeared, staring out over the serrated plane of trees, its grim, hooded face reflected in the ponds and lakes in every direction. The white surface was marred in places by patches of brown, summer earth, and the edges shivered cleanly against the blue skin of the sky, etched with the fading scratches of whirled cirrus clouds.

Cookie's hands moved from pocket to pocket, tugging briefly on his downy white beard or picking at a piece of lint on his waistcoat, until one of them finally slipped inside his vest pocket and emerged with a pouch of tobacco. He pressed a pinch into the bowl of his pipe and struck a match on the anchor iron, then drew delicately on the mouthpiece until the red ember had spread through the leaf.

The ship steered from the Columbia into the slimmer vein of the Willamette, where the ridges of fir trees moved closer, and the sheer walls of the rocky shore shrank down to tufted embankments. Cookie watched King Lu on the railing, gliding past a painter in a rowboat dabbing at a canvas, a boy sleeping beside a loose fishing line. They passed Sauvie Island, where lettuce and strawberries and summer squash grew, alongside farmhouses and wooden fences, piles of empty corncobs, a crooked windmill.

Soon the city of Portland appeared. It was smaller than Cookie had imagined, but larger than he remembered it from so many years before. The spiked wooden fence of the fur-trading post was still visible in the center of town, surrounded by a handful of new structures where the old stables and gardens had been, and roads that were not paved in sucking mud anymore, but peeled logs laid out in long, washboard rows. The buildings topped out at three or four stories tall, and thinned considerably a few blocks in any direction from the downtown's central core, where vacant lots took over, riddled with short, tough-looking stumps, and occasionally the skeletons of simple, half-finished bungalows. The city resembled a small, partly constructed theatrical set, its modesty and newness and sparse population, backed by the drab, forest green drop of the hills to the west. All this time, and the town was still just getting started.

The hills in back of Portland were covered in the dense canopy of evergreens that Cookie recalled, but they were scarred with huge gashes and bald spots now, and dotted with pillars of black smoke that combined in a smutty haze over the skyline. The drapery of the land was carved with rutted pathways, and wide skids running from the ridge all the way down to the docks on the riverfront, the largest of which knifed directly through the center of town, clotted with mud and branches from the constant traffic of raw trunks being felled and bucked each day on the slope.

The ship groaned and slowed down, easing between small rowboats and tugs and a huge cigar-shaped bundle of tree trunks encircled by mighty chains, bound for a long voyage down the Pacific Coast to Los Angeles. Ferries moved back and forth from one side of the river to the other, carrying people and horses and carriages from the more densely settled township of Portland to the small, nameless village on the opposite bank, where civilization immediately disappeared into the rolling foothills of the Cascades. The ship docked against a pier made of lumber still reeking of sap, and a cheer went up from the passengers on board.

Cookie and King Lu disembarked onto a wooden promenade, where a crowd of Chinese coolies pushed forward to greet their relatives and near relatives from across the sea. They hugged and cried, and then briskly loaded their baskets onto donkeys and shuffled away through the wooden streets, until the promenade was empty again, except for a few polite citizens strolling back and forth and some vagrants snoring noisily on the grass.

Cookie wore a new coat and pants, and King Lu, after a little prodding, had on his best camlet robe embroidered with dragons and autumn leaves. The sun flashed in the golden seams like dabs of paint. They stood beside each other and watched the traffic of men unloading the freight from the hull, taking boxes along the wharves and out into the quiet avenues of the town.

Cookie found himself peeking under the brim of each man's hat, and on the arm of every woman, for signs of Henry, his old friend. He listened closely for his vaguely remembered voice in the air, caught him often out of the corners of his eyes. Every man of a certain age, every body of a certain build, pricked his memory, and the wall of his heart seemed to thin somehow, until it was ready to burst at the smallest quiver of his senses. The sunlight on a young sailor's neck. The turn of a blond head. But Henry was nowhere to be found.

"Look here," King Lu whispered, and gestured to Cookie from the edge of the pier. His voice was tentative, unlike his musical Chinese, and he covered up his self-consciousness with a muffled, clucking laugh.

Cookie took a place at the railing and peered over the boardwalk, where a group of young boys had gathered on a narrow sliver of pounded sand for a rat race. They yelled and clapped as two plump rodents waddled along parallel grooves in the sand, sometimes hopping off course or pausing to sniff in confusion, until one of them finally slipped into the lapping current and swam off in a smooth, thrashing arc.

"Quite a show," Cookie said, and left King Lu watching the water.

\* \* \*

Soon their bags appeared, and Cookie flagged down a wagon, whose driver, a burly Swede, loaded everything into a cart attached to the back axle on a metal strut. When he got to King Lu's trunks, he grunted out loud.

"Heavy," he breathed. "What is it?"

Cookie appraised the box. "Paper," he said. "Lots of paper."

They climbed aboard the carriage, and slowly rolled into the city, where the wooden wheels clattered loudly over the washboard road, bouncing Cookie up and down on the hard seat. He saw a theater sign jostle by, a French bakery, a boutique for women's clothes. Various tailors and bakers and butchers, with scuffed signboards and blond hitching posts just beginning to show some age.

Outside a general store, a group of men talking near a barrel guffawed intimidatingly, while across the street a set of businessmen chatted beneath the eaves of a book shop; a farmer hauled a wheel-barrow of pale, fresh-looking cabbage heads toward the market.

The fort, they found, was no longer a trading post at all, but a public park, with children in the courtyard rolling on the grass, their mothers watching them from paved pathways, and old men sitting on park benches in groups. The old main office had become a museum of the city's brief history, filling two rooms and a handful of filing cabinets.

They wheeled down the wooden streets, bouncing and clacking, past Henderson & Bucks, Hardware; Spencer & Duncan, Tannery; Kitzhaber & Kitzhaber, Law Office.

"&" was an elegant symbol, Cookie thought.

The wooden wheels clattered over the wooden road and they crossed Burnside into the North End, where lumberjacks in thick woolen plaids and wide suspenders swaggered from one beery doorway into the next. They stomped though the streets in their knee-high boots with long rows of silver eyeholes, their shoulders wide and their beards squared off on the ends, bellowing at each other and looking for big trouble.

"Comin to Portland from all over the continent," the driver explained in his lilting Swede voice, "Maine and Wisconsin and Canada, hoping for a piece of the rain forest out there towards the coast. Fast-growing fir and pine and spruce to be had."

With the beavers gone, Cookie thought to himself, the men of Oregon had become beavers themselves.

"Sir," Cookie said, "to the hotel now, please," and the driver snapped the reins, the free tour was over.

The carriage pulled up a moment later at the Governor Hotel, the only stone structure in town, fronted by a canvas awning and green-jacketed valets. Cookie and King Lu climbed down and rearranged their robes, paid the driver with a shiny silver coin, and wandered inside.

The lobby was filled with large couches and divans, lamps with buffalo skin shades, on top of a floor of dark blue carpet. The walls were painted with murals of Indians, prowling through the forest in their feathers and beads, and the emerald drapes appeared chiseled from stone.

"One room, please," Cookie said, as they approached the oak desk. Behind the counter sat a man with red hair and freckles, and an armband around his frilly sleeve.

"Yessir," the man said, and pushed a piece of paper toward him, mumbling something under his breath.

"Pardon me?" Cookie asked.

"Chinamen," the man said, glancing at King Lu. "Not allowed."

Cookie looked at the young man a moment, his chalky skin and thin lips, then at King Lu in the foyer, rubbing the blade of a potted palm tree with his thumb and forefinger. He shook his head sternly.

"No," he said. "I'm afraid not. He stays with me. The rule will have to be broken this time."

Cookie sat on the bed, reading the daily newspaper, while King Lu bathed in the porcelain tub. Browsing the advertisements to see what people were selling these days, he found deals for various elixirs and potions, steam donkeys and percolating coffeepots. One article revealed that a well-known pony express driver from Sacramento was in fact a woman, and another endorsed the merits of the steel-toed boot. The huge pages of the daily paper were full of drawings and political cartoons, large headlines in elaborate, oversized fonts, and the ink came off speedily on Cookie's hands.

King Lu made an inquisitive sound from the other room and Cookie brought him a towel.

They ordered room service and soon some coffee and hard-boiled eggs arrived, along with a large bowl of chili with pork. King Lu examined the beans curiously before dipping his fork in. The gravy slid between the tines and he frowned.

"Try it," Cookie said. "Might be real good."

"Hmm," King Lu growled, and speared a single bean.

Cookie watched him chew the bean and swallow it. "Well?" he asked.

"Fine," King Lu said, "very good," but it was hard to know whether he meant it.

After dinner, King Lu sat down to write. The sun was setting and the drapes filled with soft light. Squares of sunlight fell onto the bed. He opened his box of brushes, mixed a pool of ink, and arranged a sheet of paper on a clear part of the floor, which he held in place with four small rocks he had gathered on the street. Cookie watched the strokes adding up. A vertical line slashed by a horizontal. A set of diagonals touching a square. Not this, not that, the strokes hemming in their meaning like fish traps.

Soon King Lu was tired and he lay down for a nap.

Cookie lay down for a minute as well, but he was not tired, and he quickly got up again to stand near the window. He gazed into the mottled, dusky streets down below. His hands moved from pocket to pocket, to his beard and back again, as he tracked a sturdy young man with a blond ponytail leaping over a brown puddle, his reflection flashing beneath him, then calling out to someone as he turned around the corner.

King Lu lay sleeping on the bed. His mouth was crusted with dry spittle. His chubby fingers twitched with some dream.

Cookie rested his forehead on the glass, watching a girl skip along with two bright sparklers in her hands, spitting sparks to either side, and a boy in knickers toss a bundle of firecrackers, which popped in a furious staccato. Whole families strolled the streets in bunches, carrying collapsible chairs and wicker picnic baskets, streaming toward something festive in the distance.

He tapped the pale reflection of his own fingertip on the grime-flecked window.

A moment later, after pulling his shoes on and patting his beard in the mirror, Cookie slipped out of the room. He descended the stairs and strolled leisurely through the lobby until he reached the front door, where the smell of horse manure and dry wood rose up from the side-walks, and the clamor of the moving crowd filled his ears.

"What's happening?" he asked a young lady in a prairie dress, rushing along the banging slats of the promenade.

"Fireworks," she said brightly. "On the riverfront tonight. Happy Independence Day!"

The entire population of Portland seemed to be spread out over the rocks and grass of the riverbank. Large families on patchwork quilts surrounded by plates of bread and jams and fruit, teenage boys creeping off in groups to fire bombs into the water. Men in thick denim and twilled slacks, herringbone coats, with walking sticks and gold pince-nez. The crowd shifted and a gaggle of wealthy women emerged, in long woolen dresses with high necklines topped by frilled collars, thin leather ankle boots, and gray leggings. A woman with plaited coils of hair and fine beading on her dress laughed from her belly and threw her head back, while placing her hand on a friend's shoulder.

On the boardwalk, a photographer had set up a small studio with a shelf of books and a fake fireplace, where couples lined up for portraits. The photographer's assistant led them to a gilded, high-backed chair, and measured the distance from their noses to the lens.

The photographer said, "Timber!" and the fake room went white with a powder flash.

Cookie picked his way through the narrow alleyways between blankets looking for a place to sit down, while the lights from the boats and the city shone on the river like wobbling jewels. He eventually came to a huge stump carved with blocky initials, and took an empty edge opposite a brooding man with a long chin and a woman with a tight bun of chestnut hair on the nape of her neck, watching over three darling, talkative girls. The husband ignored Cookie, but the wife looked at him kindly, as the children danced and played patty-cake together, and fell down on the mangy sod whenever a rhyme was done.

"Howdy," Cookie said, and the voice in his throat surprised him, the creak of its old age. The couple nodded silently in return.

In the middle of the river floated a brightly painted sternwheeler, purple with pink and powder blue trim, done up with cheerful pennants. It looked like a floating birthday cake, and Cookie could see on the upper deck young women dangling their legs off the railing and calling out toward the rowboats and canoes that passed close by. The jaunty sound of piano music drifted in the air, punctuated sometimes by the faraway pop of a champagne bottle. A rocket sizzled from a window and snapped in the air.

When the sun had gone down, and the sky had turned a dark plum color, the crowd began to fidget, and then, suddenly, the fireworks began. With a quick whistle and a crack, they spread out like fiery blossoms in the sky. A suite of red bursts, spiked with silver and sprinkled with bright yellow sparks, launched from a tugboat anchored a little way upstream. The fireworks flickered on the upraised faces of the crowd, who clapped politely at each thundering crescendo.

Cookie ate a hot dog.

"Excuse me, excuse me," someone said, beneath the oohs and ahhs of the crowd, and Cookie turned around to see what was the matter.

"Hey, watch it there," someone said. "Oh, sorry, officer."

Toward the back of the crowd, six police officers were weaving their way through the tangled spectators, holding a long rowboat on their shoulders like an empty, upturned, tin coffin. They crept through the blankets and wine bottles, over the outstretched hands and feet, with flashes of color sparking on their badges and hats and the hull of their silver-skinned boat. They stumbled a few times, but soon enough approached the water, where they waded in and dropped the vessel with a loud smack.

"Uh-oh," the husband across the stump said, with a tinge of excitement in his voice. He passed Cookie a pair of binoculars, and pointed toward the festive sternwheeler anchored at midriver. "Looky there," he said. Cookie held the lenses to his face and after a jiggle of confusion managed to focus in on a woman snapping her garters on the main deck, beside another woman pulling the straps of her dress down off her shoulders, mugging at a passing sailboat with a practiced leer.

"West side's been trying to shut down Madame Amy's for years," the man said out of the corner of his mouth, and shook his head with a sly grin. "But every time they do, she just pulls anchor and drifts over toward the east side. And when the east side precinct comes calling, she lifts anchor and move toward the west. Never has to close the doors that way. Sits right there in the middle of the river, right on the county line."

"Ah ha," Cookie said, as streamers of honey-colored light sank toward the ground.

By now the policemen had climbed into the rowboat and gripped the oars, rocking it back and forth with their weight. The lead policeman raised a lantern and flashed it three times at the opposite bank, and when three flashes returned, the crew began rowing strenuously toward the middle of the river.

"Looks like a coordinated attack tonight," the husband said gleefully, and made a funny, high-pitched sound while rubbing his palms. "Uh-oh, uh-oh. Looks like a real show."

Cookie squinted at the opposite shore, where sure enough he could see another rowboat filled with more uniformed men launching into the river under dandelions of gold and tangerine, followed by quick pinpricks of crimson.

Some of the men near Cookie stood up and moved casually toward the water, hoping for a better view. The crowd began clapping and shouting, both for the fireworks now, and for the unfolding spectacle of the law.

The husband passed the binoculars to Cookie again and this time a couple of half-dressed men on the brothel's mid deck appeared, trying to pull on the anchor chain without falling down from laughter. Two girls went running past them, dragging their bloomers and hugging each other with delight.

Meanwhile, the two rowboats were moving toward them quickly, leaping forward with each synchronized tug of the oars.

Then, the sternwheeler's chimney chugged out a plume of bright orange sparks, and a black cloud of smoke belched from the coal-burning engine belowdecks. The huge wheel began slowly to turn and, awkwardly, the ship started moving downstream. The paddles circled faster and the ship picked up speed, as paper flowers and bottle rockets sailed off in its wake, and the small figures on board shrieked and raised their arms. The two rowboats of sweating policemen continued chopping at the water, but already they were falling behind. The whore-house was too fast for them.

The crowd on the bank of the river roared happily, as the dry pops and cracks of the explosions collected overhead, and webs of light danced on the water in shimmering strands of pink, and silver, and bright powder blue.

Five days later Cookie found Henry. He was in the graveyard, beneath a modest stone rising from the manicured grass, having died in 1836 of bronchitis resulting from a rafting trip on the Deschutes. According to town records, and a helpful clerk at the county courthouse, he had been a farmer briefly, an innkeeper, and finally a bartender at Erickson's, the largest logger saloon on the West Coast. He had been married once, but his wife had moved away to Idaho.

Cookie set a bouquet of orange poppies on the headstone.

Henry's tombstone was one of many in the graveyard, each with a name and a date, or sometimes a question mark to fill in some blank. Cookie looked over the stones and obelisks, the mausoleum with the broken marble steps. In the corner of the cemetary a group of young people were having a picnic on a hump of grass. Cookie gathered it was a going-away party of some sort. A little girl had stolen an armful of flowers from the nearby graves, and was being reprimanded by her father and mother, while the rest of the party laughed.

Cookie stepped over the dirt where Henry's body lay, and placed his hand on the cold headstone. It was a monument to something he could not understand, an effort to force memory where memory could not go. Images of Henry appeared in his mind like golden shadows, strange pictures from a distant place, too brief and formless to apprehend.

Nothing had changed, really. Cookie's love remained the same, as did Henry's for him. It merely existed in another world now. It existed someplace it could never be seen or touched. The long distance made it seem brighter in a way, or perfect, or invisible, but it never made their love seem unreal.

Cookie turned and walked away. He felt fine in a way, just knowing.

During the first three weeks in Oregon, Cookie and King Lu spent their time searching for a place to live. Every morning they checked the newspaper and every afternoon they wandered the streets hunting for addresses and signs in the windows. They did not have much luck. Portland had passed laws prohibiting Orientals from residing within city limits, and they were being strictly enforced after what they heard was a long stretch of laxity. None of the landlords would allow them to rent. So they widened their search to the townships and villages outside the city, but even there, beyond the urban boundary, the pioneer men and women of Oregon considered the notion of a Chinese lodger somehow distasteful, and found many polite ways of turning them away.

They thought of heading to San Francisco, or Seattle perhaps, or the dry desert heat of El Paso, but they figured any other city would probably be the same, and so they redoubled their efforts.

One day King Lu came to the hotel with a good lead. He walked in the door and sat down on the bed and took off his shoes to rub his aching feet, making noises that told Cookie some statement was coming. Cookie was slicing a pear and arranging it into the shape of a mandala, mixed with wedges of cheese and smoked almonds.

"Kwangtun Province man," King Lu said. "At laundry on Couch Street. He tell me. Shack in hills, over city. Near creek and hot spring. Say we go there. They take us in. Very good place." King Lu chortled to indicate he was more or less finished.

Cookie held the plate of food toward King Lu until he had picked a few items and raised them to his mouth.

"Up in the hills?" Cookie asked. "You're sure?"

"Yes, yes. Up in hill. Chinese. All together. Live in houses." He seemed frustrated by his inability to describe the scene much better than that.

"All right," Cookie finally said. He had no better ideas himself. "Let's give it a try. Why not?"

The next day, Cookie and King Lu set out from the hotel with a basket of sandwiches and a bottle of lemonade, walking slowly through the city streets and into the orchards of apple and pear trees beyond the North End. They followed the curve of the hills, picking honeysuckle as they went, until coming to a pathway into the brush, where they made their way into the forest and began climbing up toward the ridge.

"Careful there," Cookie said, and helped King Lu over a branch.

"Thank you, sir," King Lu said, and laughed softly into his chest.

They came to the edge of a logging site, where the trees turned to charcoal and hunks of bark lay scattered across the ground. The trunks of the trees were as wide as houses, and many of them had been splintered into shreds. They walked along the edge of the clearing, stepping over the abandoned gauges and wedges, the broken ax handles

316

and chew tins, until they found a mud-clogged creek and followed it uphill farther toward the skyline.

They kept going until a single strand of barbed wire appeared, and they turned right to follow it, keeping a straight course all the way. When the wire passed through difficult terrain, over boulders or big ditches, they found an alternate path and rejoined it where they could.

Soon they reached a place where the barbed wire forked, and they did as the man at the laundry had told them, and took the right-hand path. Cookie and King Lu followed this new route farther north and west. They stopped and ate their sandwiches and took sips of their lemonade, and King Lu splashed some creek water on his face, wiping it off with a corner of his sleeve.

Eventually they arrived at the edge of a cliff overlooking the elbow of a babbling creek, beyond which stood a collection of sturdy cabins connected by dirt pathways. Piglets and chickens lurched about, chased by young children, and Chinese in wide, spreading hats attended to their evening chores, sweeping walkways and husking corn. A group of men were fixing the lever of a broken well pump. Cookie smelled frying dumplings and the moist aroma of steaming rice, heard the clatter of cooking ware rattling from its cupboards.

Off in the distance spread a murky pond, where a flock of swifts twisted over the water, blinking in and out of the breaks of pussy willow.

Soon enough, Cookie and King Lu arrived at the edge of the camp, where a group of men were sitting in the firelight, scooping rice into their mouths like efficient, steam-powered machines. One of the men looked up and barked out a startled question.

"Who are you?" he said in Chinese. "What do you want?"

King Lu stepped into the firelight. "We've been walking all after-noon," he said. "We were hoping to rest."

The man eyed them both darkly and came closer. His face was greasy and chapped, with a scrappy mustache bracketing his mouth. Cookie hovered at the far edge of the firelight, ready to turn back when the time came. The man asked a few more questions and King Lu answered them quietly and then, to Cookie's surprise, the man bowed. The other men rose to their feet and made room around the fire for their new guests. Gratefully, Cookie and King Lu sat down to join them.

For the next hour King Lu spoke to the men while they gobbled their food and nodded humbly whenever the conversation required. They scooped out slags of rice from the cooking pot and put them in bowls, which they handed to King Lu, who in turn handed one to Cookie. Cookie gathered that the men worked on farms nearby, and their women took in laundry from the city, that they had begun clearing a portion of woods for a community garden. Lately there was work to be had cutting a pathway through the forest for the coming railroad. They talked too quickly for Cookie to understand everything that was said, however, and their strange dialect did not help matters, so he simply fixed a look of attention on his face and nodded thoughtfully, miming the different postures of comprehension. Eventually he gave that up and passed the time nibbling at the mealy rice, smiling when one of the men slapped himself on the forehead to kill a mosquito.

Finally one of the men stood up and led Cookie and King Lu to a modest cabin at the edge of the firelight.

"No one here," he said, Cookie thought.

The door opened onto an empty room smelling sweetly of new wood. The windows had no glass, but the roof seemed secure, and the man led them from one corner of the room to another, pointing at seams and patches of floor. He opened a door onto an adjoining room, which was smaller, and which looked out onto a thicket of mulberry bushes.

"North," the man said to Cookie in English, shaking his head. "Gold. Build and go north." Soon the man bowed and left Cookie and King Lu alone.

King Lu dropped his satchel to the ground, stretched his arms over his head and groaned.

"Good," he said. "Good and lucky."

He pulled out a woolen blanket and spread it on the wooden floor.

He looked at Cookie, and he nodded at the blanket. "You," he said. "For you."

Cookie lay down on the blanket while King Lu pulled a few other things from his bag. A set of brushes, a piece of paper, an inkstick, and his grinding stone. He laid out his writing materials on a patch of floor and prepared some ink, then crouched over the paper and began to write. Cookie lay there, watching him. Who was this strange man? King Lu made large figures, thick and assured, one on each sheet, and placed them in separate parts of the room to dry. He blew on the paper and when it had dried a bit, he went outside and tacked a few sheets above the door.

King Lu came back a moment later and lay down next to Cookie. He checked his brushes and squeezed the hair to wring out the water. He nodded toward the door.

"Welcome," he said.

Cookie drew a bucket of water from the creek and attached it to a long yoke, then filled another bucket and attached it to the other end of the yoke, and lifted the whole thing onto his neck. He balanced the contraption on his shoulders and made his way back to the cabin, past children playing in the dirt, and women beating laundry with wooden tongs, and men lazing about on the dry earth beneath the boughs of fir trees, his buckets sloshing with every step. He approached the clapboard cabin with its tight black shingles spiked with nails, and went carefully inside.

The front room was now decorated with paper scraps full of inkblots and calligraphic letters and willowy illustrations of ducks and cherry blossoms. A long futon took up the middle of the room; a tall mirror leaned on the far wall. Along the window ledge sat small rocks and ceramic bowls, and a vase holding a single sunflower. The small kitchen area was hung with garlands of garlic cloves and dried red peppers.

Cookie poured the buckets of water into a cast-iron pot on the wood stove and while the water heated, he went outside to pick some fresh flowers. The garden was full of cauliflowers and thick carrots

319

and tightly coiled leeks, arranged near a small cherry tree that Cookie and King Lu had brought from China swaddled in cheesecloth.

Cookie clipped some azaleas and snapdragons and put them in a vase near the window, where he fiddled with the arrangement for a long time, adding a sprig of lemongrass and a shoot of bamboo. He moved the elements around, placing and replacing flowers, cutting stalks, plucking leaves, until finally something crystallized, the hot peach of the azalea chimed with the purple of the snapdragons, and the elegant lines of the stalks came into focus. A serene calm spread out in the room. The spaces in between things assumed pleasing shapes.

A spill of salt on the cutting board became a lightning bolt.

The splinters of light on a glass vase arranged into a tomato-seed pattern.

King Lu belched in the other room, where Cookie could hear him pacing out some idea, padding over the clean floor in his bare feet. A minute later he emerged from his study for the first time that day. His fingers and pants were splotched with black ink, and there was a clear fingerprint on his forehead. He wiped his hands on his smock and sniffed at the soup.

Cookie watched him carefully, preparing to shoo him away when the time came, but King Lu only smiled and patted his stomach. "Good smells," he said.

"Good," Cookie said, and returned to his bouquet. "Good day?"

"Yes. Good work today," King Lu said.


That evening, Cookie and King Lu ate the soup Cookie had made, and talked about small things they were thinking about. They discussed a girl in the village who was having a birthday soon, the ginger candies Cookie might make, and the fall music festival on the waterfront this year, how perhaps they should attend. Cookie told King Lu about a hunchback at a restaurant he had seen, which was about as far as his halting Chinese would carry him in the realm of anecdote.

After supper, the old men changed their clothes, pulling on boots and parkas, and agreed once again on their regular walk. Over the creek and up toward the neighboring valley, where the logging camp could be seen, and the colorful lumberjacks going about their daily work.

The air was sluggish and cool outdoors, waiting for a new episode of rain. They walked into the forest past dark fir trunks and ankle high foliage, until they reached a certain snag in the trees—bone white with a black streak of lightning. King Lu stopped and cocked his ear to the empty woods. He held his mouth in a circle and pushed air from his belly, making a high, falsetto cry.

"Who . . . Who . . ." he called out, two quick cries in a row, then cupped his hand quickly to his ear.

The forest came alive with miniature sounds. The scratch of a beetle through the webbing of fallen needles, the pop of a boil of sap rising to the skin of a cedar, the puff of spores releasing from the cap of a mushroom.

"Who . . . Who . . ." a call finally came back, and the two men chuckled and nodded to each other. The first time the owl had cooed back to them, in King Lu's same double breath, they had been surprised and delighted, but by now they had come to expect it. King Lu called out to the bird almost every evening, and hoped someday that it might show itself.

King Lu nodded his head toward the trees. "Owl-bird," he said.

Cookie nodded in return. "Owl," he said. "Just owl."

Cookie and King Lu continued on, through a brace of marionberry and over a snaking root ball, where the strand of barbed wire that had led them to the camp picked up. They walked beside it for a while until they began to see other strands of barbed wire, gradually moving toward a common endpoint.

Soon they arrived at an enormous boulder, bristling with strings of barbed wire like a fly in a giant spider's web. On the side of the boulder was a plaque proclaiming the coordinates, 1N, 1E, 1S, 1W, and the name of the rock, the Willamette Stone.

The Willamette Stone, the plaque explained, was the point from which the entire Northwestern territory had been gridded and mapped.

Pioneer men had used it as an origin to impose meridians on the waterfalls and basalt drifts in every direction, on the marshlands and snowy peaks, and to establish the coordinates of Oregon City, and Salem, and Olympia. Cookie and King Lu found the site chilling but they went there most every day nonetheless. They were drawn to it for some reason, to the boulder radiating lines of rusted barbed wire, and besides, the view it offered was particularly enjoyable.

They sat near the Willamette Stone and ate plates of apple crisp, which Cookie had brought in a clay bowl covered in wax paper. Down below they could see the mangled expanse of a logging field, full of small men in bright clothing, teams of oxen, and a network of ropes and pulleys moving buckets and heavy instruments over the ground. They ate their food as sharp yells rolled up to their ears, and the exploding sound of a falling tree would sometimes resound through the forest like breaking thunder. They heard the drowsy buzzing of saws, the rumble of a steam engine in the distance, the faraway shout of a chaser or a chokerman.

Cookie and King Lu enjoyed watching the grueling labor immensely.

The last hour of the logger's work day was always a busy time, as some large project came to fruition. A stand of trees going down, a pit filling with water, a creek being redirected to allow access to some ancient block of land.

Today the loggers spent the final stretch packing a massive fir tree with dynamite. The powder monkey drilled holes about fifteen feet up the trunk, where the buckets of sap would not flow so profusely, and laid in brick after brick of gunpowder. Then he rolled a fuse a hundred feet away and made a last call for anyone standing nearby to back down. He lit the fuse and the sparking point wound its way over the tough, weedy ground, stamped hard by all the jackbooted men. When the spark entered the tree, there was a long moment of anticipation, and then a booming crash. The trunk blew out in a bulb of bent wood, and a shudder traveled up to the tree's tip, and slowly the giant tilted and fell. When the trunk hit the ground, Cookie felt the reverberations for a full five seconds. He and King Lu toasted each other with a nip of whiskey.

After that the loggers called it a day. They stripped off their tin pants and covered up the swing donkey, stumbled off the hill toward the taverns below. When the last of the tiny, swaggering men had disappeared, taking their bindles and branding axes with them, Cookie and King Lu collected their own things and left, retracing their steps to their cabin, and cooing again at their invisible owl as they passed the white snag.

When they got back to their cabin that night, the camp was in a flustered state. Babies were crying and women were scurrying from door to door. The men were gathered together near the firepit talking in low voices.

Cookie and King Lu walked slowly toward their door, until the men saw them and called out.

"Cookie!" they said. "Mr. Cookie!" One of them held a rumpled fragment of butcher paper in his hand.

"Come through window," he said. "Tie on brick. What you make?" He held the note out for Cookie to read.

Cookie took the paper and smoothed it on his knee, then held it up to the moonlight and peered at the square-looking letters. The note was written in a scrawling, immature hand with what appeared to be mud or gravy. Or perhaps, smelling it, human excrement.

"Chinks Die," the note said. Just days before, a lumberjack in Old Town had been knifed by a Chinaman, and since then the white community had been making lots of noise. They were afraid of the growing activity of the tongs, they said, and demanded that some grand action be taken. The men waited for Cookie to translate.

Cookie fingered his beard and finally shrugged. "Nothing," he said, but the men pressed him until he made some effort to explain. He pointed at everyone gathered around him, then to the word "Chinks." They nodded and seemed to understand that "Chinks" was them. King Lu watched him evenly, unflappable as always.

Then Cookie pointed at the word "die" and lifted his beard and pulled his finger across his throat. The men did not understand what

323

this gesture meant, however, and he tried a few more. He cocked a gun to his head, he stabbed himself in the belly, he slit his wrists, and finally the men turned away, mumbling to themselves and shaking their heads. They could not understand why someone wanted them to commit suicide. Cookie shrugged and turned to find King Lu already halfway to the shack.

That evening Cookie and King Lu drank a pot of green tea and read by candlelight. Cookie put on his nightclothes while King Lu dozed by the fire. Late at night it began to rain. Cookie listened to the water on the roof, the soft patter of the little drops. The cabin was well constructed, the jambs and moldings were tight. Let it rain, he thought, and smiled to himself.

The rain continued for hours, streaming off the windows and pouring into the barrel from the drain. The creek roared, taking leaves and branches downstream. The puddles shivered with pinging droplets.

Inside the cabin, everything was quiet and warm. Two old men had fallen asleep, holding hands beneath the wrinkled surface of a flannel sheet.

# 6

TINA SAT ON a rock beside the pathway as the paramedics strapped Trixie onto a stretcher and lifted her toward an ambulance parked near the garden. The red lights strobed over the scene, dappling the faces and trees with a quickened heartbeat of color. She watched Trixie's body on the plastic slab, rising up into the air and drifting over the ground. Her lips looked pale and her body somehow shrunken in size. She floated past Margaret and Bob and some reporters who had taken the liberty of crossing the property's boundary line, while up above, the helicopter paced nervously back and forth in the sky. Then Trixie disappeared into the locker of the ambulance.

"Her neck," someone whispered.

"Terrible, terrible," someone replied. "So terrible."

When the ambulance had vanished, and the spectators had begun drifting away, Tina got up and crept toward her room, hoping to avoid any questions or condolences. The reality of the night's events had not yet sunk in, and she wanted to be someplace where she could deal with it in private. But all around her milled the grief-stricken faces of her mothers' friends, pressing in and demanding her attention.

"Tina," Margaret said, touching her shoulder, and burst into tears.

Her mother tried hugging her but Tina pulled away.

"Need to be alone right now," Tina said, and the adults stepped back respectfully to let her pass. She could hear them behind her, coming together, murmuring with concern.

On TV that night the fall played out over and over again, in slow motion, always with the same progression of events. Trixie falling through space in a girl-like pixelated smudge, the water frothing in slow motion. The small faces of the spectators and the slow rising of a pointing hand. Tina watched replays of replays of the rescue operation, consisting mainly of people running into the creek with their clothes on, and eventually Neil carrying Trixie's frail body from the churning waves, exposed in the hard, wobbling spotlight. The jump seemed to last forever. The local television stations worried it, wrung it out, combed the moment until it began to go blank. Through constant repetition it would be drained of all meaning.

Throughout the night the garden was splashed with siren lights, or drenched in the circling helicopter beams, and Trixie's bedroom window would turn reflective and then return quickly to blank black. Finally, Tina drew her blinds and tried to sleep.

Tina woke up the next morning feeling like someone had inserted a sponge into her chest, which had then swollen up and filled in the space between all of her organs, and which was becoming heavier and heavier with each passing breath. She stared at the ceiling, bundled tightly in her blankets, and watched the jump again in her mind, hoping for some last-minute reprieve or intervention. The surprise ending still waiting to happen.

She glanced out the window to find that the reporters were no longer encamped above the parking lot. The meadow was now empty, just beaten down grass and gouges of mud, littered with food wrappers and forgotten blankets.

Eventually, Tina got up and tried to get dressed, but nothing in her closet seemed appropriate for the occasion. All of her clothes had become hateful in the night.

She put on her jeans and a T-shirt, pulled on some socks, then sat on the edge of her bed and kicked her heels against the sturdy boxframe.

Tina cleaned for a while, to avoid leaving her room. She made neat piles of all her papers, swept the ashes and dust balls from beneath the bed. She organized her tapes and books. Finally she collected a handful of dead box elder bugs from along the floorboards, elegant red designs printed on their brittle wings, and swept them onto a sheet of paper, which she used to carry them to the garbage can.

When Tina finally appeared in the front room, she found her mother waiting for her in the rocking chair, drinking coffee from a blue mug with a whale tail for a handle. Despite the magnitude of the night's loss, everything in the cabin appeared oddly the same as it had the day before, the furniture, the wood stove, the futon.

Her mother looked up at her with a pained expression in her eyes.

"How are you, honey?" she finally asked, trying to play it cool.

Tina shrugged and went to the refrigerator. She found a bowl and had some milk and cereal, brown strands of wheat woven into small pillows, sweetened with molasses, then picked at the rind of a pomegranate drying on the table. The dried peppers and garlic still hung from the rafters, and the empty wooden dish rack gaped beside the sink. She could feel her mother watching her from across the room.

"So what's happening?" Tina finally asked.

"Trixie's going down to California," her mother said. "Her parents are there."

"Oh," Tina said. The air in the room seemed dense and metallic, fixing everything in place. The crumbs beneath the toaster appeared heavy as boulders. "So we don't get to see her again?"

"I don't think so," her mother said.

"Oh." Tina said. She could not tell whether to feel relieved or disappointed by the news. The scene of Trixie's funeral had been taking shape in her mind as a moment of great reckoning and personal courage.

"The reporters are gone," her mother went on. "The police made them leave."

"Okay," Tina said. "That's good." She ate another bite of cereal, staring at a throw pillow on the floor, its maze of embroidery in a Hopi pattern. "I'm really sorry. It was her idea, though. The whole thing, almost."

"Jesus, Tina. We'll worry about that later. Believe me, it's the least of anyone's worries right now."

\* \* \*

327

When Tina was done eating, she stepped outside for a little fresh air, to find Peter and Bob sitting on the porch of the cabin next door, staring at her like her hair was on fire, Peter with his cryptic, cavernous eyes, and Bob like his face was about to turn inside out.

"Guys," she said, and turned around and went back inside.

"Is everything all right?" her mother asked.

"Yep," Tina said, and returned to her bedroom, where she checked the messages on the answering machine even though the light was not blinking.

She picked up a copy of the screenplay and flipped through it half-heartedly, finding the dialogue and set descriptions wooden in the light of day, in particular the lines where she recognized her own handi-work. On the wall beside her desk, the index cards and diagrams appeared dusty and sun-bleached with disuse, the storyboards incom-prehensible scribbles of ink.

Tina paced back and forth until she decided that she needed to get off of the property for a while. She needed some room. She poked her head into the front and told her mother she was leaving, then climbed out her window and walked her bike along the narrow alleyway between the cabins and the garden. She hurried toward the parking lot, avoiding anyone's gaze that she passed, and shoved off as soon as the asphalt began.

"Tina!" Margaret called out, appearing from the bushes on the side of the road. "Where are you going?"

"Out. Need to get out for a while," Tina said as she rolled past.

"Are you okay?" Margaret yelled to her back.

"Don't worry. I'm just going out."

Tina rode down the hill as fast as she could, passing near the smoldering pit where the fire had been. She could just see it through the barricade of trees, the sunlight gleaming on the charcoaled ground.

Riding along the shoulder of Highway 30, Tina felt thin and light-weight, prone to some terrible accident, as if a hard wind might blow her into the traffic at any moment. A Peterbilt truck slammed up beside her, buffeting her with violent force, and she nearly pulled off the road and walked.

Eventually she glided into the 7-Eleven parking lot, where she locked the wheel to a pole and went inside to the magazines. She needed pictures in front of her eyes. Pictures of glowing, powerful young people, who were living in a better place than her own. She needed to forget herself in their shallow, manicured frames.

Tina flipped through the new issues of *Vanity Fair, Rolling Stone, Spin,* but none of them held her interest at the moment. The pages seemed to rattle beneath her fingers, and she could not seem to get through them fast enough. The celebrity gossip and band interviews were impossible to parse, the photographs uniformly alienating. The very concept of movie stars, of acting, of trying to be something other than what you were, seemed like a wicked joke played on the audience.

The bell on the glass door tinkled and Tina looked up, worried that someone she knew might come in and catch her doing something so frivolous, but it was only a fisherman in a weather-softened hat. He walked directly to the pile of daily *Oregonian*s near the register, and picked up the top issue, which featured a photo of Trixie's face on the front page. WHY? the headline read.

The sponge in Tina's chest expanded, and pressed against her organs.

"Beautiful girl," the fisherman said to the cashier as he paid for the paper.

"Yup. They should be ashamed of themselves up there," the cashier said. "Cultists."

Tina followed the fisherman out the door and stood in the parking lot, wondering what to do next. She could not stand to be alone, nor could she stand to be by herself. The cars on the road puttered through the chilly air. The handlebars of her bicycle were cold to the touch. She unlocked her wheel and coiled the chain slowly around the neck of the seat.

Eventually she found herself riding toward the river, coming to a remote beachfront bordered by farmland, where motorboats and barges filled with wheat poked by, and tugboats pulling long flats of timber.

329

She sat down on a rock and watched the poplars on the other side shimmering in the breeze, until the sun set in a storm of purples and peach, and a herd of cows wandered silently onto the beach to graze on crabgrass and mustard weed, and low softly at the fading light. Sitting there, not wanting to go home, Tina realized that a part of her was utterly furious at being left alone to clean up.

When Tina got back to the cabins that night, the pathways were empty, the windows shuttered and lit with candles. The dogs were quiet. The creek exhaled its long, sighing breath.

Tina walked her bike toward her room, the spokes clicking softly near her feet. At home she found a note on the kitchen table, held in place with a pair of scissors.

"Tina," her mother's handwriting told her. "Wanted to give you some space. I'm staying at Margaret's tonight. Beth wants to talk to you. She's home if you want to go over. I love you more than anything my sweet sweet wonderful daughter, Mom."

Tina sat in her room, and eventually decided that Beth might not be the worst person to see. She was apparently taking the loss of Trixie pretty hard. She had spent the first night wailing in the dining hall, and had then cut her long hair into a rough bob, patchy and ragged around her jawline. Perhaps she was someone who could be consoled, Tina thought, rather than the other way around.

When Tina arrived at Beth's cabin, she found Trixie's room already in pieces. Her books were lined up in cardboard boxes, her records in milk crates. The walls were barren and dirty under the glare of the overhead light. The floor was covered with grit patterned around the objects that had once been there. The desolation of the half-packed space hit Tina like a slap.

Beth greeted her without stopping her work. She dropped a pile of dirty laundry into the bottom of an orange box.

"Hey," Beth said. Her eyes were tired and dark around the edges, and her new hair was covered in a red bandanna.

"Hey," Tina said. From the window she could see her own window across the garden, the wall of colorful storyboards framed in a square of gold light. Above her roof was a patch of roiling sky, spiked with drab, olive green treetops.

They sat down on Trixie's mattress, and stared at different blank walls.

"She was really special," Beth said. "So fucking talented."

"I know," Tina said. The words were abstract, unconnected to any real person or event. They seemed to evaporate as soon as they exited her mouth. Tina stared at her hands, inspecting the rugged boundary between her nail and the skin.

"I've been thinking about something," Beth finally said. "Something I wanted to talk to you about."

"Yeah?" Tina said. "What's that?"

"I've been thinking . . . I think . . . I think we should finish the movie," Beth said. "I think Trixie would want that."

Tina felt her stomach filling with poison, her arms going weak. Continuing on the movie was something she had specifically avoided thinking about. She knew on a profound level that she did not have the strength to do it.

"I don't know," Tina said. "It sounds hard. No money . . . No camera . . ." She could list many obstacles.

"We could raise the money," Beth said. "I've already talked to people. They want to help us."

"I don't know," Tina said again. "I'm not sure it's a good idea."

"I thought you'd want to," Beth said coolly. "It's your movie, too, you know."

"I know," Tina said. "But I don't know."

They sat there listening to the air vibrate around them.

"Well just think about it," Beth urged. "It might be just the thing we're needing right now." She squeezed Tina's hand and stood up to resume packing.

Tina returned to her room and lay down on her bed, the storyboards fluttering on the walls when she shook out her pillow. She had never even figured out the proper finale. The movie was not hers anymore, contrary to what Beth had said. The movie was Trixie's and it always had been. The work of moving ahead seemed absolutely impossible.

Tina looked down at her own limbs arranged on the quilt, her feet and fingers and hands, and for a moment felt like her entire body was coming apart. Without the ball of secrets inside her that she and Trixie had shared, it seemed that her appendages might actually drift away, her bones and organs float into the air like balloons. She stared at her shin, her kneecap, her palms, from the high vantage point on the top of her neck. Her toes wiggled, her fingers curled, as if by some magic power. And then, gradually, her various parts began to talk to each other, conversations arising between one thing and another.

"Hello, Mr. Thigh."

"How do you do, Mrs. Other Thigh?"

"Fine, thank you, have you met The Slapping Hand?"

She slapped herself on the thigh. It was funny in a way, which helped, and something knit together, if only for an instant.

Cold rain started falling the next day from a slab of cruddy, gray clouds. The hills around the cabins turned dark, and the shadows became wet, and the long warmth of autumn faded back into the ground for good. A bank of briny air moved in from the coast, filled with fog and seagulls, and settled over the trees like a wrath. The leaves flamed to color, then fell, and frost appeared on the garden berms. For all its inevitability, the change of seasons came as a minor shock.

Tina went back to school, where she tried her best to keep to herself. She sat in the back of the bus, the back of the cafeteria, the back of class, and guarded her eyes to ward off any unwanted attention. When she walked through the hallways, every part of her throbbed with vague embarrassment, as if someone was casting her entire body in plaster, and every hot inch of her was on display.

"Why did she do it?" one girl asked.

"I have no idea," Tina said, and hurried off to class.

"What about the movie?" the adults at home inquired.

"I don't know," she said. "Do it if you want to."

Tina watched many movies that winter. One after another, in malls and second-run theaters and art houses around the city. She saw *The Hunger* and *Octopussy*, a new print of *Out of the Past*. Something about being in a darkened theater with a group of strangers calmed her nerves a little bit, even if afterward she felt somehow diminished by the experience.

What is a movie that never gets made, Tina wondered? What is a movie that exists in only one person's mind?

Tina watched talk shows and PBS documentaries, and late-night movies, narcotized in the endless stream of moving, talking, musical pictures. She preferred programming that was slightly boring, that did not require too much attention. Just enough to bar her from thinking about anything else. Even the worst of the movies stabbed at her heart, though. At least they had been completed. At least they had been seen. Hell, Tina came to realize, was made out of unfinished things.

Tina avoided Beth whenever possible, and Peter, and Margaret, and anyone else who wanted to finish the production, or talk to her about the aborted script. They met among themselves in the geodesic dome to practice their lines, but without Trixie their momentum was lost. They ended up hashing out old relationships and big opportunities they had missed. All the bad decisions that Tina never wanted to make.

"We need you," Beth said, but Tina always found an excuse to skip out.

She went to the schoolhouse in the woods, or the charred crater where the plants had been, and smoked cigarettes until she realized that she did not like them so much. She stared at the blackened earth and imagined confronting Trixie in a scene of some tearful finality, but she could never tell why they might be fighting with each other, and she could never figure out what she would say given the chance.

One day, on her way back to the cabins, Tina stopped at the marsh and looked at the two skeletons, which Neil had still not decided what to do with. She inspected the small bones of their hands, the empty sockets of their eyes, the worn-down teeth hanging in their jaws. The wind brushed her cheek, full of rain and wood smoke.

She could hear some voices talking in a bush nearby, dull male voices going back and forth in a lazy seesaw. The name "Trixie" came up and her heart leapt, as if something had been uttered about herself. She strained to hear what the voices would say next.

Tina crept closer to the bush and accidentally stumbled into the middle of Neil and Peter passing a pipe back and forth. They looked up with some surprise.

"Oh. Sorry," she said, and fled back up toward the cabins. Her feet banged on the footbridge and she rushed to her room, where she flung herself onto her bed and buried her face in her pillow.

That night she watched Johnny Carson and David Letterman, a parade of successful people coming to talk about their success, telling stories about other successful people they knew. She compared their different kinds of charisma, the frenetic and the normal and the imperious, as giant earthquakes went off in her chest, and lava poured through her nervous system in scalding waves. The work of forgetting Trixie demanded long periods of immobility, she found, deep concentration. It drained all of her strength. She lay in her room, suffocating the memory in the darkness, obsessively repeating the name, Trixie Volterra, Trixie Volterra, and recoiling from it each time like a hot iron.

She took down the index cards, the diagrams, shelved the script. She buried her storyboards in the bottom of a milk crate, which went into her closet.

She thought of a good ending, though. The injured husband gets a wooden leg.

Late that night an obscure B-movie called *Boggy Creek* came on. Part travelogue and part horror flick, it traced the pursuit of a bigfoot-like creature through the swamps of Arkansas. Normally it was the kind of film Tina relished above all others, almost daringly incompetent, a mistake in the bureaucracy of cinema that showed how good it could be if someone just took a chance. The kind of movie that made it seem impossible to fail. But this time the movie had no effect on her. Its stupid plot shifts and thrillingly weak performances swam over her without registering in the slightest.

Tina lay in bed, aching with the inertia of herself, watching the distant TV transpire in its bright, sickly colors. The noise seemed muffled in a garbage can, the ambient whine shrieking in high, unheard registers. Tina's limbs melted into the bed. Her bones turned heavy and thick. Finally the screen went misty again, and she fell asleep in her tight jeans and high-tops.

# 7

**W**HEN NEIL FINALLY made his decision, there was no clear principle that guided him, no moment of clarity that led him in one direction or the other. There was no sign that appeared, and no sword pulled from a stone. He gave the bones to the Indians because he liked Jay Feather better than he did Mr. Grimsrud.

Neil called Jay and told him the news. There would be no radiocarbon testing, no DNA or X-rays. Everything down to the last pinky would be repatriated, and buried somewhere on the reservation in Umatilla, just as Jay wanted.

"Okay, great," Jay said. "Are you sure you've had enough time?"

Neil called up Mr. Grimsrud next, to apologize, and Mr. Grimsrud tried his best to cover up his disgust, but he could not help getting in a few parting jabs.

"Well, we started with two bodies and ended up with three. I guess I should count my blessings," he said. Neil winced as he hung up the phone.

Neil returned to the life he had been leading before. He built the retaining wall and dug some post holes. He recorded some new tracks, which he put away so he could hear them again freshly at a later date. He spoke to Trixie's parents on the phone, and went through the whole thing with them.

"It wasn't really her, was it?" Trixie's mother asked. "She would never intend to do anything like that?"

"No," Neil said. "Absolutely not. She was a happy girl. I'm sure of it." Although he was not sure at all.

When everything had started to settle down, he agreed to do an interview on the local news show about the night of Trixie's fall, just to have some public closure on the event. Otherwise, he figured, people would be asking him the same questions for the rest of his life. He scheduled the day, and cleared his calendar, what there was of one, and practiced his replies while hiking around Eagle Creek.

"Why did she do it?" they would ask.

"No idea."

"Do you blame yourself?"

"No, not really."

"Do you know why she started the fire?"

"Nope. We never found out."

"Do you blame yourself?"

"I don't think so."

He was all ready to say his piece the morning of the interview when the show's producer called him and told him the taping had been cancelled. No reason, she said. The powers that be had just decided it. The public had moved on to other things.

While they worked to iron out the details of the transfer of the bones, Neil and Jay Feather had a beer together at My Father's Place, a bar on Grand Ave. They sat in a brown vinyl booth at the edge of a brown carpet, facing each other across a brown tabletop with brown placemats. The rafters were strung with bright orange and yellow streamers, left over from some Thanksgiving long ago, and the jukebox played an assortment of anthemic rock songs and Frank Sinatra ballads. Both of them were dressed like cowboys.

Jay bought the first pitcher, and Neil got the second, and the two of them whiled away the night in the smoke and noise of the barroom, talking through the events of the past few months, and admitting their fantastic disbelief.

338

"That was some crazy shit," Jay Feather said. "I bet it got pretty hairy up there."

"Yeah," Neil said, and shrugged beneath the heavy weight of his shoulders.

By midnight, Jay Feather was slurring his words and his elbow was slipping off the table. Neil worried that it was some kind of Indian alcoholism thing, but figured Jay must know what he was doing. He poured another watery beer and pulled on his cigarette.

"We can never know the truth," Jay Feather said, tapping on his chest, looking straight into the space in front of Neil's nose. "But we can know our own hearts." He slapped at his chest again with his thick, limp hand.

Neil raised his glass, though mostly out of good manners. It sounded all right, the sentiment, and he appreciated Jay's implication, but he seriously doubted it was true. Their glasses clinked and they downed another round, then Jay Feather stumbled off to the bathroom.

Neil swung his feet up on the seat, patting his pockets for a fresh pack of cigarettes. His own heart. He should really find himself a new one sometime.

# 8

"**W**HOO . . . WHOO . . ."
Cookie awakened to the sound of an owl calling him. The voice was calm and musical, predatory and reassuring, and somehow seemed to emanate from the nighttime itself. He lay in bed silently, gauging his exhaustion, and realized eventually that he was in fact far from sleep. Beside him, King Lu rolled over with an armful of blankets.

"Who . . . Who . . . ," the owl called again.

Cookie rose from the futon and wrapped a robe over his longjohns, then found his tobacco pouch on the countertop and stepped outdoors into the raw air. He stood under the eaves watching his breath disappear near the railing. The boughs of the trees were heavy with fresh rain. Wisps of white clouds skidded across the sky. Cookie rolled a cigarette and set his pouch on the windowsill. Then he cupped his hands to his mouth and cooed loudly into the forest.

"Who . . . Who . . . ," he called, hoping the owl might answer him, and ease his loneliness in the rough hours going from the nighttime into the morning.

"Who . . . Who," the owl finally called back.

"Who . . . Who," Cookie cried again. He knocked a smudge of ash onto the ground at the base of the steps.

"Who . . . Who . . . ," the owl called again. Cookie had never heard such a talkative owl before. Normally they cooed once and flew away, driven by some odd, nocturnal logic.

"Who . . . Who . . . ," Cookie heard again, this time from somewhere else in the forest.

341

"Who . . . Who . . . ," another bird answered.

Cookie felt his skin turn icy with fear. These were not birds, he realized, but men.

Cookie scanned the forest for any signs of movement, the telltale shake of a low branch, or the flicker of a running body. He stepped from the porch onto the pounded earth between the cabins where the cooking fire smoldered, and craned his head in every direction. Past the creek, toward the garden, beyond the trailhead leading to the marsh.

Cookie turned toward the thicket of brush that led to the canyon between the hills, up where the muddy road began. An orange light flared, illuminating a man's face as he struck a match on his teeth. Cookie watched the man grimace and lower the fire to a torch in his other hand, which kindled in a thick burst of flame.

From there the flame was passed to another man, and then to another beside him, as each one ignited a new torch. The men were on horseback, Cookie could see, and formed a long line, waiting for some signal to cut loose. There were at least twenty or thirty of them. The flame passed from hand to hand, on down the line, whispering and spitting with each new stick of fuel. Soon there was a long strand of fire in the woods, broken into brilliant fists of light.

Cookie looked toward his cabin. The door was ajar, leading to inviting darkness inside, but by now his legs were stuck solidly in place.

When the fire had finally strung itself along the whole gathering, the men raised their torches and a sharp call went up, and then they lurched forward unevenly through the brush. The men's voices began to bark and yell on top of each other—"Outta the way," "Watch it, watch it!"—as the ground shook wildly underfoot, and the branches hissed.

Quickly the horsemen picked up speed as they galloped down the incline, until the final trees parted and they broke into the clearing, fiery halos dancing above their heads. They poured through the camp like a breaking dam, tearing over the ground and smashing everything they touched. Windows and buckets and fenceposts fell beneath them.

One man in a pea coat and galoshes galloped straight through the low-cooking fire, overturning a pot of stew, which beaded on the dirt. The coals scattered in a spray of bright orange sparks. "Whoop, whoop!" the men screamed. The hooves of the horses hammered on the ground around Cookie, and the jumping reins and bridles clattered and chimed.

The Chinamen came running from their shacks, chittering and yelling at the tops of their lungs. There was Mr. Lee, and Mr. Yoo, and Mr. Chin, each one in a state of progressive undress. Mr. Chin swung a hoe at a passing marauder and took a chunk of skin off his bare arm. Mr. Lung threw a handful of mud in the air.

Cookie tried grabbing at a bridle, but the rider waved his torch and brought it down glancingly on his head. "Leggo, Chink," he said, and Cookie stumbled to the edge of the commotion. He watched the man tug a rifle from a leather side holster, then shoot at the treetops, keeping the horse beneath him as he absorbed the hard recoil.

"Yeah-hoo!" someone cried over his shoulder. The sound of the hooves and gunfire was dizzying.

A rider charged past Cookie with a burning kerosene lamp and threw it toward a small shack nearby. The wide wick burned blue in the glass tubing as it spun in the air and the lantern shattered against the cabin wall, spreading fire across the porch and the door. The shack was holding gunpowder, it turned out, for a moment later orange seams appeared on the walls and then the planks burst apart, flying in splinters and charred slats.

From there, everything went crazy. Sizzling comets sailed around Cookie's head, and the noise of all the fighting seemed to escalate in degrees. Men floated around him, their horses rearing and kicking. A crate full of green apples overturned and spilled across the ground. Mr. Lung pitched into a laundry bucket and feathers of blood spread out from his forehead into the clear water.

Cookie tried grabbing a saddle horn, but the horse revolved and threw him onto the ground. The rider continued to the Chin's cabin and tried setting fire to the eaves, but the shingles were too wet, and the fire refused to take. Next door, another horseman was having better luck on the Yoos' place, kindling a flame in the dry underpart of the awning, and then on the flaking mullions of the eastern windows.

Cookie turned toward his own cabin, which was now burning brightly in the pandemonium. Orange sheets raced inside the doorway and thick, acrid smoke billowed from the roof. He felt like a nightmare was unfolding, his arms and legs moving slowly in space. King Lu could not still be sleeping, he told himself. Even he would have roused from bed by now.

Cookie rose and staggered toward his cabin through a veil of flames. Burning sheets of rice paper disintegrated as they climbed in the air, black crescents growing in the squares of whiteness, limned in crackling red. Cookie batted at them and they whispered into shreds. All around him, men and women were running and screaming. Bodies lay twisted on the ground. Cabins were burning. Plants were burning. Clothes were burning. Every fire was the same fire, split into hungry parts.

Cookie approached his cabin and the heat became too great for him, scalding waves rolling from the walls, so he raised his arm over his face and turned away.

Across the commons, near the trailhead, he glimpsed King Lu hurrying into the brush as firelight drummed on his back. Thick smoke blew between them and King Lu disappeared from view.

"King Lu!" Cookie called, but he was too far to hear him.

Cookie crossed the battlefield as quickly as he could, avoiding the falling axes and knifeblades, the kicking hooves and stirrups, and followed King Lu down the pathway. He caught sight of his head bobbing in the shadows, but lost him as he disappeared around a bend. He hobbled as quickly as he could, putting the fiery scene behind him, letting the sound of his own breath rise in his ears.

When Cookie turned the last curve, the marsh came into view, silvery in the moonlight, spreading toward the sturdy backdrop of the ridge. White clouds shone in the fresh, black sky. He could see King Lu in the distance, limping through tall heather and milkweed toward the water's edge, though in the strange, luminous moonlight the figure could be almost anyone.

Suddenly, Cookie was shoved roughly aside, as a muscular horse surged past him on the trail. The sound came next, clattering hoof beats, followed by the sight of flashing horseshoes and the hunched back of the rider. Cookie watched the horse shoot down the pathway, its tail flicking, and begin curving out into the meadow toward King Lu. The rider was frozen on the saddle in a posture of pitiless focus, clenching the neck of his gun in his huge fist. He covered the ground quickly and bore down on King Lu near the shallows.

As the rider galloped past he clubbed King Lu on the back of his head and Cookie watched him crumple to the ground. Almost weightless, like an old rotten tree. The horse continued onward into the water, which splashed up onto the man's boots and pants, until he reined in the horse and it reared up on his hind legs, and he twisted in his saddle and jerked the head back.

Cookie was numb, his breath heaving in his chest, his old hands moving anxiously over his shoulders and hips. The patch of grass where King Lu had fallen was empty now, an obscure shadow of crushed blades and stalks. He watched the horse lunge from the silver bog back onto the land, and turn in circles a few times as the rider calmed it with a few pats on the neck. Then the rider cantered back in the direction he had come from.

When the man arrived at King Lu, he pulled up the horse and stared down at the ground. He seemed satisfied by what he saw there and flicked the reins to continue.

Cookie was standing in the middle of the trail as the horseman approached him. He was a thick and vigorous-looking man, with a brush of brown hair and a bent Roman nose. His hair and beard stuck out from his head, lit by the moon and licked by the orange flames in the distance.

Cookie's robe had fallen open, to reveal his bagging, one-piece long johns, the flannel stretching between his legs. The bones of his shoulders and arms were clearly visible under the thinning fabric.

The horse pawed at the ground, its breath humid and pungent and intense. The saddle squeaked as the man shifted his weight. "You don't look Chink," he said. His voice was gruff and clipped. "Are you a Chink?"

Cookie stared at the man. His small eyes pushed back in his face, his wide gash of a mouth pressed closed. Cookie thought about the question, and all the ways he might answer it.

"Yes . . . ," Cookie said at last. "I am."

With that, the man raised his gun barrel and Cookie saw a soundless yellow burst of light appear. His chest shuddered, and a huge wound emerged beneath the shreds of his clothes. His eyes stared straight ahead as a thick red bubble emerged from his mouth, growing on his lips to the size of a cherry at first, then an apple. The bubble popped and splashed red droplets onto his beard, and then he pitched sideways onto the weedy ground. He heard the sound of the horse cantering off, muffled drumbeats, and then the distant howls of the men spiraling from beyond the trees.

The crackling of the fire, the crackling of running water. The cabins had become husks of charred wood, the stream pink with blood. Smoke blew across the ground, swirling over wrecked barrels and splintered horsecarts.

Cookie rolled onto his back. The sky above him was glistening with stars, pulsing and swimming with each heartbeat. He choked and coughed and began a second cough, but his chest burned too much for coughing, so he swallowed it.

Cookie closed his eyes and then opened them again, wider this time. The sky was not glistening with stars at all, he found, but rather the stars were in his eyes, and the shape of everything behind them had become gauzy and indistinct. He could see vague masses of things that might be fir trees, and above them the swirling nebulae of dancing pinpoints.

Cookie lifted himself onto his knees and checked his legs and his arms. Then he raised his hand to his chest and touched it softly. His fingers came away slippery with blood. He rubbed them together until the blood had soaked into the skin and he could feel the grooves of his fingerprints.

Cookie stood up and looked toward the cabins—orange shapes shifting against the blackness, smothered in thick mist. He turned around and the orange blobs of firelight disappeared.

"King Lu?" he said weakly. He cleared his throat and spoke louder. "King Lu."

Cookie shuffled down the pathway toward the marsh, holding his hands in front of him for balance and feeling along the rocky path with his feet for solid terrain. His head throbbed. His ears rang. He stayed on the trail until the ground softened and the cattails brushed against his legs and only the noise of his feet could be heard, mud sucking up around his ankles as they sank into the earth. He went deeper, lifting his feet from the muck with great effort, until finally he pitched forward onto his knees.

Cookie lay there, listened to his breath rasping in his ears. There was fluid in his lungs, rattling with each intake of air. "King Lu?" he said. "Don't worry. Everything is going to be fine now."

Cookie crawled forward, the long grass bending on his face, lashing his cheek gently. He called again, "King Lu?"

Soon he arrived at a body lying on the ground. He could not see it very well, but he could feel its clothing and contours, the shape of the musculature and fat. He could feel the legs. He could feel the shoulders and arms. The body felt like King Lu more or less. It was definitely a man.

"King Lu?" he said, shaking the shoulders gently. He did not want to feel the man's face, that might tell him too much.

Cookie was tired. This was King Lu, he told himself, and lay down on the ground beside him. The soggy earth seeped into his hair and back, cooling the fever that had begun rising on his skin. The sound of the shifting grass rustled around him. A frog croaked.

Cookie reached over and found King Lu's hand. His fingers slid into the grooves of King Lu's fingers, and his palm touched the pad of King Lu's palm. He whispered to King Lu: "I've got you."

Then Cookie closed his eyes, where he saw the stars pulse and swim, and then flare with bright, speckling colors.

# 9

EVERY YEAR IN the springtime Neil's property became a riot of vegetative growth. The grass grew almost before one's eyes, the camellias unfurled in fans of fuchsia and milk. The cherry tree exploded into pink fluffy piles of sherbet, which crumbled almost as quickly as they formed, and the crocuses shone with dew. The property was rich with worms and snails and centipedes squeezing from the earth. The boughs of the evergreens were tipped in phosphorescent green, the measure of their new year's growth.

It was almost disgusting, Tina thought, the luxuriant feeding and rotting and festering of it all, and the ripe stink of rebirth. She looked out her window at the shining garden, and the moldering cylinders of new compost. Fresh grids of string marked where the new zucchini and corn and tomatoes would grow.

In the middle of the garden, the two skeletons stood embedded in a huge, dark slab of disinterred earth, waiting to be carted away. The tribal council had dug out a whole segment of the marsh and removed it in a single piece, in order to keep the skeletons whole. Their bones jutted out from the dirt, and gleamed like polished enamel. Tina had heard they were having second thoughts about burying them now, and were considering having them installed in a diorama at their interpretive center in Warm Springs instead.

Tina walked outside and joined with a group of people on the edge of the garden, watching four men affix harnesses attached to a metal arm to the skeletons, which were in turn attached to a flatbed trailer parked in the pathway.

"Okay!" one of them yelled.

"Send 'er up!"

The man in the truck threw a switch and the hydraulic arm began to hum and pull against the weight.

The skeletons shook and rose into the air. Roots poked from the mud ball like stripped wires, and clumps of dirt shook from the edges to the ground. The harness squeaked and strained. The mechanical arm groaned. The skeletons rose higher and revolved in the air, the ball of earth dropping nuggets and sand, until soon the skeletons were sitting on the flatbed, strapped safely in place.

The totem pole appeared next. Sixteen Indians carried it from the parking lot down to the garden like pallbearers. They approached a hole that had been dug in the middle berm, and slipped the bottom of the totem pole inside. The pole tilted upward and the base slid to the basin of the hole.

The crowd cheered. It was the same crowd, more or less, that always assembled, Bob Grossberger and Beth Bowler and Margaret and Peter. Tina's mother stood nearby, talking quietly to Neil. There were some new faces as well, but none of them were close to Tina's age.

The men shoveled dirt around the base of the totem pole until it stood up by itself, at which point there were more cheers, and a couple elders nodded their heads and mumbled some incantations. One elder stood over the skeletons and sprinkled them with red powder. The flatbed motored up and rattled its way along the pathway into the parking lot, and finally out onto the road, its pale exhaust fumes settling over the blackberry bushes like a thin, poisonous gilding.

When the ceremony was over, Tina took a walk in the forest, ending up, as she often did, on the cliff overlooking the black rooftops. The geodesic dome stuck in the trees, the far away curve of Mount St. Helens. The sky was perfectly blue.

"Whew," Tina sighed, and clapped her hands together. What to do next?

Walking back toward the marsh, Tina rounded a bend and caught sight of someone up ahead of her on the path. It was Neil, loping along slowly, his hands stuck in his pockets. He stopped to snap a branch from a wild cherry tree and while he scraped the switches from its main shaft, she caught up to him.

"Hey Neil," she said.

"Hey Tina," he replied, and kept cleaning his branch until only a single, smooth rod remained.

"Takin a walk?" he asked.

"Yep."

They continued along together through some blossoming hydrangia, and past a bright yellow golden chain tree dripping with conical flowers. Neil slapped at leaves with his stick, and eventually tossed it into a bush, where it hung in place, suspended over the ground.

"Hey, Neil," Tina said, as they approached a footbridge over the creek. "I just want you to know. I'm really sorry for all the trouble that happened." She worked hard to phrase her apology properly, to avoid both full responsibility for the events, and the cop-out of taking none.

"Oh," Neil seemed surprised. "Don't worry about it, Tina. It wasn't your fault."

"I know," she said. "But still."

"Are you doing okay?" Neil asked. "You must miss her."

"I do, yeah." She looked down at her damp shoes. "I do."

They walked alongside the creek until Neil's cabin appeared, up on its crag of earth. He had a new porch underway, held up with bricks and slats of wood under the crossbeam.

"You want a cup of tea?" he asked. "Good after a hike."

"Sure," Tina said. "That sounds all right."

She had never been inside Neil's cabin before. It smelled like old cigarettes, and it was crammed with all sorts of little things—crystals, Audobon-like etchings, a stuffed deer head. The couch was covered in a worn floral sheet, and the coffee table was arrayed with various pipes and lighters and rolling papers.

"How's the movie going?" Neil asked, while he dropped a needle on a Popol Vuh record.

"It's not. Not doing it anymore."

"Huh. That's too bad. It sounded pretty good." Neil took the opportunity to leave the room and boil some water. Tina heard cups clanking in the other room, and the shushing sound of the water rinsing from the faucet.

Tina looked around the living room, picking up paperweights and snow globes, touching a white rabbit pelt. She rifled through some of Neil's records, scanned his bookshelf. There was something calm, defeated in his place. It exhuded the sweet pleasure of having given up long ago.

She made her way to the stereo, and over to a wall covered in old papers. There were posters, record sleeves, faded photographs, and finally a scroll of Chinese writing, which caught her eye. The edges appeared to be singed, but the paper was otherwise intact, a thick weave of parchment, like linen. The surface was covered in beautiful calligraphic characters, set in columns, full of confident, boldly painted strokes. Overall it was smooth and watery to look at.

"It's beautiful, right?" Neil had returned with two steaming cups of green tea. He handed her a mug, the glaze honey yellow verging into icy blue, with fine cracks beneath, and a tippling of cloudy charcoal gray. "See how the force just races through it?"

"Yeah," she said, and she did. Some binding energy drew the characters together, licking at the edges of the line.

"What does it say?" she asked.

"You know, it's funny. I've had that thing for years and I never knew what it said. But a friend of mine down at U of O does some Chinese translation, and he just checked it out."

Neil rummaged around on a desk and returned with a piece of lined paper. Tina stood beside the couch holding her teacup in her palms, feeling the hotness entering her skin. The strokes of the calligraphy reminded her of bird tracks on wet sand.

Neil skimmed over the page silently, and then cleared his throat. His voice was hesitant at first, but he picked up confidence as he went along. "My friend," he said. He stopped and coughed dryly. "My friend," he started again:

352

*When I put my hands on your body, on your flesh, I feel the history of that body. Not just the beginning of its forming in that distant lake but all the way beyond its ending. I am consumed by the sense of your weight, the way your flesh occupies space, the fullness of your body beneath my palms. I am amazed at how perfectly your body fits to the curves of my hands.*

*If I could attach my flesh to your own so we could become each other, I would. If I could attach our veins in order to anchor you to the earth in the present time, to me, I would. If I could open your body and slip inside your skin and look out your eyes and forever have my lips fused with yours, I would. If I could reduce the world to a single point, a single word, I would.*

*It took a long time for me to recognize you for who you were. It took a long time for me to understand you. To understand that you were in fact a part of me. It took a long time to understand the thing that was happening between us, but I do not regret any of that time.*

*I see you right now, through my bars, with a bowl of steaming soup for me. I see you sweeping. I see your back framed by a window onto a blossoming cherry tree, and the movement of your lips while you speak.*

*It makes me weep to feel the history of your body beneath my hands in a time of so much loss. It makes me weep to feel the movement of your flesh beneath my palms as you reach around my neck to draw me nearer. It makes me weep to love each other in a time of so much sorrow. I want to tell you something. All of these moments will be lost like tears in the rain.*

Tina stood in place while the words faded into the air. "That's nice," she said.

"Yeah," Neil said, and returned the paper to his desk. He seemed puzzled by something, or perhaps just moved, and Tina allowed the room to stay quiet. They shared the silence for a while, not wanting to break it, until the silence had run its course and they smoked a cigarette together.

"I didn't know you smoked," Neil said.

"I don't," Tina said. "So don't tell my mom, all right?"

Tina left soon after with a stack of records from Neil's collection that he wanted her to hear, promising to return them in a week or so.

After dropping off the records at her cabin, Tina walked to the parking lot where her bike was resting against a railroad tie. The air was fragrant with the scent of the jasmine tree, and she pedaled down the hill to Highway 30.

She rode her bike to the city, through the warehouses of deep northwest, and up toward Montgomery Park. The streets were damp from rain that morning, like sweat stains on the pavement, and diamonds of water clung to the electricity lines. She sped down Vaughn and became a bullet, playing a game with herself where she imagined an acrobat running alongside her, jumping over cars and swinging on branches, tumbling over postboxes and flipping in the air. It was the oldest game she remembered.

She rode all the way to Cinema 21, a movie house lodged among thrift stores and old-man bars between Hoyt and Irving, where she locked her bike to a streetlight and went straight to the ticket booth. She did not read the marquee, she did not care what was playing, she simply paid her money and went inside.

The lobby was blissfully deserted, the smell of popcorn and butter in the air, coffee and chai tea, and behind the counter a man with a thick salt-and-pepper beard smiled at her warmly. The carpet was soft beneath her feet, spongy and pliant, and she could hear the final strains of music playing from the previous showing of whatever she was about to see.

The bulletin board was littered with announcements. There were apartments available, rock shows to be played, animals wandering in the world lost, or perhaps escaped.

When the previous audience emerged, eight people in all, she tried to distinguish from their faces whether the movie was any good or not. There was no telling, though. The faces were unreadable, and partly confused, surprised by the daylight still visible beyond the glass doors of the lobby. The audience walked past her and into the late afternoon like newborn children.

Tina entered the theater and looked for a seat. The rows opened to either side of her like tilled crops from the highway. She entered a row near the front, and took a seat toward the middle, in a comfortable chair, soft and squeaky, where she pressed her feet against the back of the chair in front of her and leaned back as far as she could go.

Then she waited. A few more moviegoers came in and took their seats. They spoke in whispers, and sometimes laughed quietly. Their chairs squeaked and sighed. The hush of the theater enveloped her. She stared at the velvet curtains over the hidden screen, the arching ceiling high above her head. She could hear the rest of the audience shifting in their seats, waiting along with her.

Finally the lights dimmed, and the curtain parted, whirring somewhere behind the screen, or in the proscenium below. The curtains stopped partway to the edge, and the preliminary stuff began, shooting from the wall behind her.

First there was a trailer reminding her not to smoke during the film, filled with bursting animated stars, organ grinder music, and a dancing popcorn box. Then a union card appeared, the projectionist union, for which a single person clapped. Next came the previews, for an Indian art film about a child growing up among odd and amusing characters, an animation festival promising lewd cartoons, a rerelease of *L'Atalante* by Jean Vigo.

Finally the lights went black, and the curtains opened all the way to the edges of the screen. The audience hushed and the throw of the projector flooded the frame with light. The reel popped and crackled, filled with scratches and cigarette holes that faded away as the music rose from the speakers, churning chords that promised much heartbreak and redemption. The opening credits began to roll, and Tina sank deeper into her chair. She pulled her knees to her chest. A moving picture was about to begin.

## ACKNOWLEDGMENTS

There are many creative debts to acknowledge:

First of all, enormous gratitude to two artists who came before: Sherwood Anderson, whose short story "The Man Who Became a Woman" inspired much of Part 1, Chapter 6; and David Wojnarowicz, who created the image of two skeletons holding hands, and most of the poem that appears in the final chapter.

Among the living: Michael Brophy, who revealed the strangeness of Northwestern history, not to mention many of its archival sources; Brian Zindel and Jason Robison, who originally thought of the character Cookie; and Miranda July, who inspires through her work in many media. Also, James Yu, whose ideas and friendship have influenced almost everything, and Sean Byrne, who first showed me the real how and why of making art.

This book was also made possible by a number of institutions: New School University, in particular the guidance of Abby Thomas; *Plazm*, in particular the generosity of Josh Berger; and *Tin House*, in particular the confidence of Rob Spillman.

The feedback of early readers was indispensible. Thanks to Camela Raymond, Steve Doughton, Marlene McCarty, Emily Chenoweth, Julia Bryan-Wilson, Michelle Wildgen, Randy Gragg, Storm Tharp, Elizabeth Schambelan, Jeanne McCulloch, Matt Schwartz, Matthew Stadler, and T. M. Raymond. Also to Malia Jensen, Zac Love, Damian Chadwick, Anne Rascon, Gurgi, Amber Straus, Dan Frazier, Betsy Tripi, Domenick Ammirati, Mark Hansen, and many others, who have never gotten copies to read, but in my mind have responded many times.

The early enthusiasm of both Todd Haynes and Oren Moverman was hugely, immensely important. Thank you.

Thank you to Bill Clegg and thank you to Colin Dickerman, enormously. And to everyone at Bloomsbury and Burnes & Clegg.

Thank you to Emily Chenoweth, again.

Also, a number of books were helpful for the gathering of historical detail, in particular *Ancient Encounters,* by James Chatters; *Hail, Columbia,* by John Scofield; *Soft Gold,* by Thomas Vaughan and Bill Holm; and *Holy Old Mackinaw,* by Stuart Holbrook.

Finally, thank you to Portland, Oregon, the most glamorous town in the world.

## A NOTE ON THE AUTHOR

Jonathan Raymond was born in the Bay Area, grew up in Portland, and attended Swarthmore College. He was the editor of *Plazm* magazine, and received his M.F.A. from New School University in New York City. He currently lives in Brooklyn, New York. *The Half-Life* is his first book.

## A NOTE ON THE TYPE

The text of this book is set in Linotype Sabon, named after the type founder, Jacques Sabon. It was designed by Jan Tschichold and jointly developed by Linotype, Monotype, and Stempel, in response to a need for a typeface to be available in identical form for mechanical hot metal composition and hand composition using foundry type. Tschichold based his design for Sabon roman on a font engraved by Garamond, and Sabon italic on a font by Granjon. It was first used in 1966 and has proved an enduring modern classic.